aprons on a clothesline

**Center Point
Large Print**

**This Large Print Book carries the
Seal of Approval of N.A.V.H.**

aprons on a clothesline

Traci DePree

CENTER POINT PUBLISHING
THORNDIKE, MAINE

This Center Point Large Print edition
is published in the year 2005 by arrangement with
WaterBrook Press, a division of Random House, Inc.

The text of this Large Print edition is unabridged. In other
aspects, this book may vary from the original edition. Printed in
Thailand. Set in 16-point Times New Roman type.

ISBN 1-58547-625-0

Library of Congress Cataloging-in-Publication Data

DePree, Traci.
    Aprons on a clothesline / Traci DePree.--Center Point large print ed.
        p. cm.
    ISBN 1-58547-625-0 (lib. bdg. : alk. paper)
        1. Women--Minnesota--Fiction. 2. Female friendship--Fiction. 3. Large type books.
    4. Minnesota--Fiction. I. Title.

PS3604.E67A87 2005b
813'.6--dc22

                                                                      2005008076

To my children,
for whom I gladly wear my apron—
Caitlin, Megan, Haley, Willow, and Jem

acknowledgments

I have a cheerleading squad that is unparalleled. My thanks go out to many. My family does much to inspire and enable me to write. Caitlin, Megan, and Haley, thank you for managing the house and your baby sister, Willow, so I could write. John, for just being you. My librarians and first readers, Dianne Pinney and Jan LaFond—every town should have a library like ours. Sharon Pinney, for your medical know-how. Paul and Mary Braun, for your farming insight. The Busy Lizzies, my real-life extension group—you are an inspiration every time we get together. Dudley Delffs, thanks for your patient understanding. You are a saint. Don Pape, for early morning e-mails. And to the wonderful folks at WaterBrook Press, you are deeply appreciated. Finally to Erin Healy—*thanks* somehow seems a feeble offering for all that you do.

VIRGINIA MORGAN

Virginia Morgan touched the brow of her six-month-old son's head. David was so hot. Too hot. A deep cough rattled in his chest, but he didn't cry. He was too weak to cry.

Virginia slipped into the bathroom and turned on the hot water in the tub until the steamy vapor filled the room in a heavy fog. The mirror above the vanity grew white with the moisture. Then she returned to David's crib and pressed a cool cloth to his head.

"Lord, please bring the fever down." Her prayer rose yet again, along with her fear. She carried David into the steam-filled room and settled on the short stool alongside the tub as she'd done every half hour. The doctor told her the moist air would ease the congestion in his lungs. David nestled in her arms, and his dull eyes closed in rest. Virginia studied his tiny features, so pink in the warm air. The delicate lift of his brow, the curve of his puckered lips. She'd been praying all day since her visit to the doctor's office, praying that David's breathing would clear and that his cough would ease. That his fever would dissipate and his eyes would regain their sparkle. That he wouldn't need to go to the hospital. She glanced toward the open door as the sound of heavy footsteps drew near. Roy. His overalls were dusty from the morning's field work. His pale eyes held the same concern Virginia felt.

"Any change?" he said, lifting his seed cap and raking his fingers through short-cropped hair. Virginia shook her head. Roy came beside her then. He knelt and kissed his son's fevered brow.

"He had his medicine?" he asked.

Virginia nodded.

"How's he eating?"

"Fine, I guess." Her voice was no more than a whisper.

Roy tenderly touched her cheek. "He'll be okay," Roy reassured. "If the doctor were that concerned, he'd have put David in the hospital. We'll keep close tabs on him." He looked her in the eyes. "You're a good mother."

Virginia squeezed his hand. She needed to believe, to trust that God wouldn't forget about them.

"Here." Roy reached for his son. "You've been with him all day. It's my turn."

Reluctantly she placed David into her husband's strong hands.

"I'll make you something to eat," she said. At least she could take her mind off her worries by making Roy some supper.

As she worked, she told herself she'd keep on believing.

one

Virginia Morgan let her embroidery rest and lifted her wrinkled face. Rain plinked against the windows of the white Cape Cod house. Drops rolled down the glass in colorless stripes. The Minnesota weather had been in a sour mood all week. Yet there was something comforting about an all-day rain, especially when she was tucked away indoors with a dear friend.

"Are you sure this is right?" Ten-year-old Jessie Wise fingered the long threads that stuck out from the edge of the apron she was making. Virginia leaned toward Jessie, who sat on the flowered living room couch. Her bent back ached with the movement. Virginia would be seventy-eight in January, and today she felt every day of it. Jessie lifted the apron so Virginia could inspect it. She placed her glasses on her nose and took the apron from the child's hands.

"That's perfect, Jessie." Virginia smiled.

"But it's all scrunched up. It looks messy."

Virginia patted her knee. "It's supposed to. That's the way it looks when you gather. See." She held up the apron they were using as their inspiration. "We gather it and then sew it on the waistband so it looks like this when it's done." Virginia turned it around so Jessie could appreciate the finished piece.

"It'll really look that pretty?" Awe tinged her words.

"Of course it will. Especially with this aqua blue and white gingham you picked out. It'll be lovely."

"But yours has a pocket." Jessie touched the embroidered white-on-white *V* on the front of the original.

"You can always add a pocket later, if you want," Virginia said.

"You think I could do pretty stitching like that?" Jessie's face glowed with excitement.

"I'll show you how."

"This will be my best 4-H project ever!"

Virginia smiled at the girl's enthusiasm. "You like sewing?"

Jessie reached for her apron and evened out the gathering along the top before pinning it to the wrong side of the waistband she'd started earlier.

"It's fun to make things," Jessie said. "I don't know any kids my age who can make their own aprons."

"People nowadays don't even wear aprons."

"Why?" Jessie said.

Virginia loved the precocious child's inquisitiveness—that and her unabashed love of life and her willingness to sit and learn from an old woman. "Oh, I don't know. I imagine people don't need aprons anymore. Young people cook meals from boxes, not from scratch like we used to. They don't get dirty. I knew how to get dirty!"

"Virginia, you're silly!"

"What did I say?" Virginia teased. Her voice grew serious. "There's something about an apron. When I put one on, I just feel like making a pie or two."

"Put one on!"

Virginia laughed. "Now who's being silly?"

Jessie raised her hand in the air.

"Aprons have other uses too, you know." Virginia lifted her own stitchery project, a white tablecloth with a design all in red. "Aprons are great for wiping snotty noses or carrying a load of apples in from the orchard or fanning yourself on a hot summer day."

Jessie finished pinning and handed her apron to Virginia for another inspection.

She eyed it critically. "Looks like you're ready to baste."

"You mean like basting a chicken?"

"No." Virginia patted her shoulder. "I mean sewing it by hand so you know it'll turn out good when you sew it on the machine. Basting helps you make a better seam."

Virginia watched as Jessie carefully threaded a needle and wove it along the seam line. Jessie had amazing patience for one so young. Perhaps the traumas in her young life had given her a deeper appreciation of things. Her mother had died in a tragic car accident; her father battled alcoholism. But the scars Virginia saw when she first met Jessie—the insecurity, the aloofness—had since been taken over by joyfulness. Virginia liked to think she had a little something to do with that, as well as with helping Jessie's father turn away from the bottle.

"Do you like your new house?" Virginia asked. The Wises had lost their home in last year's tornado. Just a week ago they had moved into their new place.

Jessie lifted her face. "I have to get used to it, but I

like it. Dad likes it too. Here." She handed the basted apron to Virginia again.

"You're so good, Jessie. From the looks of this apron, you can do anything you want to do." The pride in Jessie's eyes was all the reward Virginia needed.

Rain spit at the rusty Jeep. Mud coated its abdomen as it splashed through each deep puddle. Mae Morgan dipped her head to see through the wipers' path as she drove toward Lake Emily to pick up her sister, Trudy, Virginia, and Virginia's dear friend Ella Rosenberg. Pea fields that should have been planted by now were instead small lakes with soggy, ever-shifting shores. Mae thought about her husband, Peter, sitting home alone, staring through the living room window, wishing he could dry his precious acres by sheer force of will. Mae was glad for the chance to get away with the ladies from her Extension group—the Suzie Q's—for a little adventure in Austin. Today she would forget about the worries of the farm and enjoy herself.

She had gotten up early to do her chores—feeding the calves in their little white igloos outside the barn, as well as her new chicks that she ordered every spring, and Jessie Wise's 4-H sheep that boarded at the Morgan farm.

Mae's large round stomach shifted left, and the bump of an arm or a leg poked out just under her rib cage. She patted her belly and pushed at the limb. The baby shifted to a more comfortable position. A warmth of joy filled her. A baby. Their baby—hers and Peter's—

grew inside her. In eight short weeks he would be in her arms. She couldn't believe it still. She'd been so nervous, so afraid after Laura had died in her womb, and now they'd been given another chance.

Mae turned the Jeep onto Highway 36 and pressed toward Lake Emily. What would it be like to give birth? Memories of her miscarriage, the loss of their first child, flickered. The knowledge then that her labor pains were for naught had brought so much agony. Would the shadow of that specter descend again? Or would the birth of this child mark a new beginning without the tarnished images of the past? She hoped for the latter. With each passing day she believed with more certainty that they would actually have this child, that their dream of a family would come true.

t w o

Austin, Minnesota, was a thriving little town, built in no small part by the Hormel Foods Corporation. Several local attractions drew visitors, including the Rydjor Bike Museum, the SPAMTown Belle paddlewheel boat, the Mousenik Launch Site, Buffy the Cow—a twenty-foot-long fiberglass Guernsey cow—and the Solafide Observatory. But the attraction that drew the Suzie Q Extension group today was the SPAM Museum, a monumental tribute to spiced ham in a can. The exterior of the SPAM Museum was impressive, a crisp-looking brick building with trim of blue and yellow. Virginia, of course, had visited Austin on many occasions, most frequently during a brief period in the 1970s when Roy considered switching from dairy to hog production. But the SPAM Museum had just been completed in 2002, so this would be a new experience.

Mae pulled past the brick guardhouse and found a parking spot. The rest of the Extension group trickled into other spaces. Virginia touched her left temple where a headache had begun on the ride over. Mae glanced at her, a question in her brown eyes.

"You okay, Virginia?" Mae said.

"I'm fine, dear. A headache is all."

"You need some Tylenol?" Mae reached for her purse.

Virginia waved the offer away. "I'll be fine. I hate taking the stuff."

Mae considered her for a moment, then her shoulders softened. "Still, if you change your mind . . ."

Virginia patted her hand and opened the Jeep's door into the rainy morning. Mae, Trudy, and Ella climbed out and stretched after the ninety-minute ride from Lake Emily. Mae arched her back, emphasizing the growing roundness of her belly.

"Ooh, take my picture with the statue of the hog farmer," Trudy said, her red hair curlier than ever in the damp. She handed her camera to Mae and trotted up to a statue of a rugged-looking farmer with two pigs. Trudy leaned in close to the bronze man's face and gave him a big smooch.

16

Virginia laughed and said, "Oh, me, too." She also handed Mae her camera and joined Trudy.

Ella popped open an umbrella over Mae to protect the cameras and watched, amused. "I didn't know you were such a *ham,* Virginia," Trudy teased.

Virginia gazed pointedly at the two pigs in the sculpture and said, "They'll hear you!" That throbbing at her temple made itself known again.

"Are you two crazy?" Lillian Biddle said as she hustled for the front doors. The heavyset woman's lime green pantsuit made a *zip-zip* sound as she hurried by. "It's still raining out here. Let's get inside."

The Suzie Q's entered the tall foyer, where a wall of 3,390 cans of SPAM reached skyward as a globe turned in its center.

"Welcome to the SPAM Museum," a young man of about twenty-five greeted them. "SPAM-ple?" He held out a tray of cooked SPAM cubes, each skewered by a straight pretzel. The women helped themselves.

"Nothing like a little SPAM," Trudy said to Mae, who shook her head at her sister, warning her to be good.

Virginia laughed and leaned in to whisper, "Is Mae always so bossy?"

"It's sad, isn't it?" Trudy answered. "She really needs to get a life of her own."

"The short movie starts in a couple of minutes," the guide said. "If you'd like to explore the Cyber Diner while you wait . . ."

"Cyber what?" Lillian said to no one in particular.

The women meandered into the fifties-style "diner" just beyond the entry area.

"What kind of diner doesn't have any food?" Minnie Wilkes asked. She was a short, round-faced woman with dark hair and deep dimples.

"It's an Internet place," Mae said, pointing to the computers that lined the Formica counters. The women stood back, arms crossed, bags clutched, while Trudy and Mae explored various items of interest about SPAM on the screens.

After the movie—*SPAM: A Love Story*—the Suzie Q's walked among displays that highlighted the history and uses of SPAM. While this museum was much fancier, it reminded Virginia of the Le Sueur Museum in Le Sueur, Minnesota, with its displays that told of the founding of the Green Giant Company. It was another town transformed by its innovative citizens. How many summers had she worked in the Lake Emily canning factory, her hands soggy from sorting corn, the ever-present, oversweet smell permeating her clothes and hair?

Virginia moved past a small stage where a puppet show was in progress. The ladies moved ahead. Some stopped to chat, while others seemed intent on surveying each bit of SPAM formation. Virginia tried to read one of the message boards, but her eyes hurt. She couldn't seem to concentrate. What was wrong with her? She wasn't usually so distracted.

Next in the procession was an army barracks. A screen in the entrance to a tent bore the image of a soldier. "Hey, you, come here," he said, pointing at Virginia. Virginia jumped. She held a hand to her chest. Mae's laughter sounded behind her.

"He startled you, huh, Virginia?" Mae touched a hand to Virginia's elbow.

Virginia chuckled. "He sure did." The soldier kept on with his spiel. He told about the role of SPAM in World War II and how SPAM was credited with winning the war for the Allies. A cardboard cutout of President Eisenhower stood within the camp.

Mae handed her camera to Virginia and said, "Take my picture?" She leaned far forward to compensate for her volleyball-sized belly and pretended to kiss the thirty-fourth president on the lips.

"That ought to be good," Virginia said, handing the camera back. "I don't know what Mamie Eisenhower would say."

Mae replied. Virginia could see her lips moving, yet she couldn't make out what Mae was saying. A sharp knife of pain penetrated Virginia's skull. She pressed a hand to her head and fumbled to open her purse for that Tylenol she'd refused to take before. The contents spilled out.

"Are you okay, Virginia?" Mae said. The confusion and pain on Virginia's face sent Mae's heart racing.

"My head . . . I . . . da . . ." Virginia tottered. Mae reached for her, but Virginia slumped to the floor in a heap.

"Help!" Mae shouted frantically. "Something's

wrong with Virginia! Come help her!" Mae screamed. Virginia was silent at Mae's feet, and Mae couldn't think of a thing to do. She stood over her, staring in bewilderment.

In an instant, Lillian Biddle was there.

"Virginia?" Lillian said. She knelt and touched Virginia's forehead.

"Ah . . . ," Virginia moaned and then closed her eyes.

"Virginia!" Mae screamed. *Virginia is dead.* Mae began sobbing. "Oh no, Virginia," she repeated over and over again.

Lillian bent next to Virginia's face. "She's still breathing." The other women gathered around. Then Mary Shrupp, the nurse of the group, took over.

"Do you have your cell phone?" Mary said to Mae.

"Phone?" Mae said. Her eyes were glued to Virginia. This couldn't be happening; it just couldn't. Mae leaned back on her heels, then caught herself before she lost her balance.

"Mae," Mary said calmly. Lillian grabbed Mae's purse, which had fallen to the floor, and rummaged until she found the cell phone. She dialed 911 and handed the phone to Mary.

"Hello," Mary said. "We need an ambulance at the SPAM Museum. My friend has collapsed. No . . . no, she isn't conscious, but she is breathing." Mary turned to Mae. "What did she say to you before she passed out?"

"I don't remember. We were talking about President Eisenhower. She had a bad headache before, and then . . ." Mae started to cry again in big gulping sobs.

"She had a bad headache," Mary repeated into the phone. "Yes . . . it could be a stroke." Mary turned back to Virginia and bent to check for a pulse.

"Trudy!" Lillian called to the gathered women. Trudy came around the corner wearing a white hard hat and Hormel lab coat.

"What's up?" Her gaze turned to Virginia and to Mae sobbing beside her.

"It's Virginia. Get Mae out of here. Keep her calm." Lillian's voice was compassionate yet firm. She turned back to Mae while Mary talked to the 911 operator. "I'm not trying to hurt your feelings here," Lillian went on, "but you need to go somewhere else. We'll take care of Virginia."

All Mae could think was that Peter's grandmother had died before her very eyes. She'd never even gotten to see her first great-grandchild. How could Mae tell Peter? Trudy moved beside her and helped her up. "Come with me, honey," Trudy whispered. They walked into the adjoining room, which held a miniature movie theater and a radio station.

"We'll follow the ambulance to the hospital, okay?" Trudy said.

"But she's dead. How can I tell Peter his grandmother is dead?" Mae stared numbly at her sister.

"She isn't dead." Trudy touched Mae's cheek.

Mae wiped her eyes with a sleeve. "She isn't?"

Trudy shook her head. "For all we know, she just passed out. Okay?"

Mae took a deep breath. *Virginia isn't dead,* she told herself. *There's still hope.*

A siren sounded, and emergency personnel flew into the museum and examined Virginia before lifting her onto a stretcher. Mae watched in disbelief as her sister held her around the shoulders. One moment Virginia had been fine—joking, enjoying the sights of the museum. The next she was . . . Mae knew something far worse than a simple fainting spell had hit Virginia. The tears started falling again.

"She's gotta be okay," Mae whispered as a prayer. "Don't let her die. Oh, please don't let her die."

three

When the back doors of the ambulance closed and Virginia was swept away to the hospital, a deep dread settled on Mae. The others must have felt the same way, for the Suzie Q's were silent, staring after Virginia. Mae felt as if she were a spectator watching some horrific stage performance. Yet the ache in her heart told her it was all too real. She thought to call Peter, then decided against it. Maybe Trudy was right. Maybe Virginia had merely fainted.

Lillian handed her phone back. Mae gazed at it absently. "Are you okay?" Lillian said. "You don't look good."

"I'm driving to the hospital," Trudy said to Mae, ignoring her future mother-in-law's question. "Hand over the keys." Mae held her purse out to her sister.

"I'm coming with you," Ella Rosenberg said. She touched Mae's back comfortingly, this woman who had been Virginia's dearest friend for over fifty years. Mae looked into her deep, compassionate eyes and found strength there.

The drive to the Austin Medical Center seemed to take forever, although it was only a few short blocks from the museum to First Drive. The sight of Virginia's collapse ran through Mae's mind like a looping video. It kept replaying—Virginia talking about President Eisenhower, that look of agony on her face as she reached for her purse, the sound of her heavy form crumpling to the floor. Mae should have made Virginia take a Tylenol when she first complained about that headache. Why hadn't Mae done that? Why hadn't she *made* Virginia cooperate? She should have recognized that something wasn't right.

The wipers cleared a path on the Jeep's windshield. The other Suzie Q's followed, the day's activities long forgotten. When they arrived at the hospital, the EMTs were rolling Virginia through the emergency-room doors. Trudy and Mae climbed out of the Jeep as soon as the motor died. Ella was close behind.

"I'm sorry," a nurse said once they passed through the swinging doors. "You'll have to stay in the waiting room until we get her stabilized. I'll bring any news."

Stabilized. The word echoed in her mind. Virginia hadn't simply fainted. Mae sighed in frustration. The nurse was only doing her job, yet Mae needed to know how Virginia was. She needed to know that Virginia would be okay.

Mae, Trudy, and Ella stood in the hall. Medical personnel whirled around the trio in a kaleidoscope of activity. There was nothing they could do but wait. "Come," Ella said, leading them to the waiting room. The rest of the Suzie Q's came in, a somber lot. Even Lillian held her tongue as they waited for word on Virginia.

Weariness swept through Mae. She glanced at her watch; it was only ten thirty in the morning. She sank into one of the padded chairs. Trudy's hand touched her shoulder. "What am I going to tell Peter?" Mae murmured. She dragged her purse onto her lap and pulled out her phone. "What am I going to tell Peter?" she repeated. Tears returned then. This wasn't really happening, was it? If only she could awaken to her happy life. Mae lifted the tiny blue cell phone to dial. Trudy stopped her.

"I'll call Peter for you," Trudy said.

Mae shook her head. "No, it needs to be me." As she said it, she realized that her belly hurt. She pressed a hand to the hard shell around her baby.

"What's wrong?" Trudy asked.

"Nothing. The baby's pushing out really hard."

Trudy gave her the worried-older-sister look as she moved in front of her. "Let me feel." Trudy placed a hand on Mae's stomach. The baby kicked, and Trudy smiled. "Well, the squirt seems okay—" Then Mae's midsection turned rock hard again, and the pain Mae tried to deny returned. "You're in labor, aren't you?"

"I . . . ," Mae began. "I can't be! I just can't." Echoes of her miscarriage collided with worries over Virginia. *No, God. You can't be this cruel.*

Trudy gazed around. When she saw Mary Shrupp, she said, "Mary, can you come over here?" Mae gave Trudy a pleading look, but Trudy shook her head.

"What's wrong?" Mary glanced between Mae and Trudy.

"Mae's having contractions."

"Are you?" Mary squatted in front of her. Her face took on the same grave expression as Trudy's.

Mae nodded. She hated the tears that kept betraying her.

"Let's find you a doctor," Mary said. "Stay here." Mary disappeared down the hall, returning a few minutes later with a nurse in blue scrubs. "This young lady seems to be in labor," Mary said.

The nurse's gaze turned to Mae. "She isn't due for eight more weeks," Mary went on, "and she had a miscarriage with her last pregnancy." Another contraction swelled, and with it Mae's despair. The nurse led Mae to a curtained area and instructed her to lie down on the padded table, then she left in search of a doctor. Mary stayed by her side, holding her hand. Trudy was there too, wearing that troubled expression.

"It's going to be okay, Mae," Trudy said. "You're just under a lot of stress. Rest right now."

"How can I?" Mae asked. "I keep thinking about Virginia and now the baby too . . ." Mary tucked a stray strand of Mae's long hair behind her ear and gazed deep into her eyes.

"You *have* to relax. That's an order." Mary smiled. She had been there when Mae had lost little Laura. Mae remembered her rebuke in the emergency room in Lake Emily, insisting that Mae ride in the wheelchair rather than walk. Her comfort had sustained Mae during that time. It still did.

Mae closed her eyes and commanded herself to be still, but stillness kept its distance. Another contraction swelled. A tear rolled from her eye into her ear.

An older man with a bulbous nose and a wide bald patch on the back of his head parted the curtain and introduced himself as Dr. McKenna. Then he bent with a stethoscope to listen to the baby's heartbeat. As he examined her, Mae remembered another doctor a little over a year and a half ago, the doctor who brought news that her baby girl was dead. The horror of that memory hovered.

Dr. McKenna lifted his face and smiled. "Your baby is fine right now," he said. Another contraction seized her. "Did the contractions just start, or have you been having them awhile?"

Mae thought. "I guess they started shortly after Virginia collapsed," she said once the pain subsided. The doctor looked questioningly at Trudy and Ella.

"She's the wife of Virginia Morgan's grandson," Trudy explained.

Dr. McKenna nodded knowingly, compassion in his dark eyes.

"You do seem to be in labor. We'll give you a shot of terbutaline to try to stop it and betamethasone to help mature the baby's lungs. We'll see what that does."

"Do you know how she is?" Mae said. "Virginia?"

"Mrs. Morgan is holding her own," he said. "But I need you to concentrate on this baby and taking care of yourself." The doctor turned to Trudy and Mary. "Is her husband here?"

"No. He's a farmer," Mary explained. "We're visiting from Lake Emily."

"I'll call him right away," Trudy said.

"Virginia's in good hands," Mary assured Mae.

"So are you," Trudy said.

Mae smiled despite herself. Then her frown returned.

"Stop it," Trudy said. "If you don't rest, I'll whack you with a rubber mallet."

Mae lay down and forced her eyes shut. She tried to focus on relaxing the muscles in her face. Another contraction hardened her belly.

A few minutes after the doctor left, a nurse came to take Mae to a more comfortable room. She gave Mae the shot to stop her contractions. Trudy went into the hallway to call Peter while Mary went for more detailed news on Virginia. In the solitude, Mae pleaded with God to spare both grandmother and baby.

four

Peter gripped the steering wheel. His knuckles were white. He stared hard at the damp road. Wipers swiped in rhythm before his face. *This can't be happening. Not another baby. Not Grandma, too.*

"God," his prayer shot toward heaven, "stop the labor. Keep Mae and the baby safe. Help Grandma pull through. I beg you. I need them all in my life." He exhaled a shuddering breath.

Mary Shrupp's was the first face he saw in the emergency waiting room. She met him with her kind gaze. "Peter," she said, drawing him to one of the padded chairs. Suzie Q's lingered, talking in low voices. Trudy was nowhere to be seen.

"I got here as quickly as I could."

"They're okay. At least for now. Your grandma's still in a coma, and Mae's labor has stopped." Peter sighed and lifted a hand to his blond-stubbled chin.

"What is the doctor saying about Grandma?" he asked.

Mary paused as if unsure of what to say. "She's still alive. They did an MRI. The stroke was caused by a blood clot, so it isn't likely any damage will continue. He hasn't told us much beyond that. Once she wakes up, they'll be able to assess the physical and mental damage. She's in ICU, so they'll only let one person in to see her ten minutes at a time each hour."

"At least I can see my wife," Peter said.

```
      #681   10-08-2016 12:00AM
Item(s) checked out to MACE, RICHARD DAL
```

TITLE: Charley Sunday's Texas outfit
BARCODE: 51010000539632
DUE DATE: 10-22-16

TITLE: The healer's touch [text (large p
BARCODE: 51010000517463
DUE DATE: 10-22-16

TITLE: Finding me [text (large print)] :
BARCODE: 51010000570116
DUE DATE: 10-22-16

TITLE: Proof of heaven [text (large prin
BARCODE: 51010000388386
DUE DATE: 10-22-16

TITLE: A girl to come home to [text (lar
BARCODE: 51010000494085
DUE DATE: 10-22-16

TITLE: Aprons on a clothesline [text (la
BARCODE: 51010000042363
DUE DATE: 10-22-16

                Vienna Public Library
                Please note due date

Mary nodded and led the way. They walked into the darkened room where Mae lay sleeping. Her face was turned away from him. Her silky dark hair spread across the pillow like a fan. When he drew closer, he saw that her mouth was open, and she made soft snoring sounds. A beeping monitor attached to her belly kept time with the baby's heartbeat.

Mary said, "I'll see what the ladies are going to do. Sounded like some were going to head back to Lake Emily." She excused herself and left.

Peter gazed at Mae's beautiful face. She was so peaceful. Their baby was safe. His heart swelled with gratitude. He touched a hand to her soft cheek. Her eyes fluttered open.

"Oh, Peter," she said. She reached for him. He held her and caressed her silky hair. She began to cry softly.

"It's over now," Peter said. "The baby's fine. Shh."

"How's Virginia?" She lay back against the crisp white pillow.

"She's alive, but we don't know much yet. Right now I'm just glad you and the baby are okay."

"I didn't know what to do," Mae said. She reached for a tissue from the bedside table and wiped her nose and cheeks. "I wanted to help her, but—"

Peter held a finger to her lips. "It's okay." He placed a hand on her belly and felt the child within shift. He smiled. "See. God's got it all under control."

"But Virginia—you should've seen her."

"Try not to think about that, okay?"

"You need to go to her," Mae said. "Your grandma needs you."

Multiple monitors lined the nurses' station in the intensive care unit, where a white-clad nurse kept a watchful eye. Rhythmic beeps from those monitors floated gently down the hall, and low lights created a restful atmosphere.

When Peter saw his grandmother, he barely recognized her. Her skin was ashen, and tubes grew from her arms and nose.

"Grandma," he whispered. There was no response, no fluttering of eyelids, not even a change in her breathing. Peter tenderly touched her hand, callused from years of hard labor. Blue veins wove paths across its back. "We need you here, Grandma," Peter said. "Don't leave us yet."

Peter heard footsteps by the door. He turned. A balding man in a white lab coat came in. "Are you the doctor?" Peter asked.

The man held out a hand. "Dr. McKenna. I've been with Mrs. Morgan since she was admitted. And you are?"

"Peter Morgan. Her grandson."

"Your wife is Mae?"

Peter nodded.

The doctor crossed his arms before beginning. "Your grandmother had a stroke. A blood clot broke loose and interrupted the flow to her brain. We won't know exactly what that means until she wakes up."

"Could she still die?" Peter asked.

The doctor's face was grave. "There's always that possibility. But she's gotten this far. There's reason to hope."

"And what about my wife?"

"She had a close call, but the terbutaline was effective in stopping her labor. Her water didn't break, and she isn't dilated at all. So she's in good shape. That baby sure seems active." That brought a smile to the doctor's face. "I'd like her to stay until supper just to keep an eye on her. We can discharge her tonight."

"Our last baby . . . ," Peter said.

Dr. McKenna nodded. "I'm aware of her history. She should keep to a very light activity level. Your regular doctor can help you figure out what she can and can't handle as far as her daily activities, but she needs to listen to her body. Take it easy. Get plenty of rest, plenty of fluids. No stress." With those words he raised an eyebrow. "And I mean *no* stress. If she feels even a twinge of pain, she needs to lie down. Another day like today and she'll be on full bed rest until her due date."

He reached for the chart at the head of Virginia's bed and studied it, forefinger to chin. He looked back at Peter. "I'll check on her later today. I'm on duty until five, so call if you need me." Then he dipped his head and left.

Peter drew up a chair beside his grandmother's bed and watched her peaceful face, her chest rising in rhythm with each breath. The heart monitor beeped while the cold April rains fell outside her window.

"Dad," Peter said into the phone. The hospital corridor seemed too bright after the dim halls of the ICU. Peter turned toward the wall as a nurse pushing a patient in a wheelchair passed him.

"Peter! It's good to hear your voice," David Morgan said brightly. "What's new back home?"

Peter wasn't sure how to tell his father that the woman who gave him life hung by a thin thread in the Austin ICU. "I have some bad news," Peter began.

"Yes?" A tentative note hung in his voice.

"Grandma had a stroke this morning." The line was silent. "Dad?"

"I'm here," his father replied. "Is she . . . ?"

"Alive? Yes. But she's in a coma. They won't know how bad it is until she wakes up."

"How did it happen?"

"She and Mae were with their Extension group at a museum. She collapsed right in front of Mae. It shook Mae up pretty bad."

"Is she okay?"

"She went into labor."

"Oh, Peter."

"She and the baby are fine," Peter assured.

"You didn't need that on top of everything else."

"It's okay, Dad. Mae's okay. She'll come home tonight, but there's no telling how long Grandma will be in the ICU or if she'll come out of the coma."

"I need to come home." Those words were a balm to

Peter's soul. He needed his dad's presence, his strength. "I'll look into flights right away. Maybe I could even get something today if I go standby. The orchestra can do without me for a few days."

"Do you want me to pick you up at the airport?" Peter said.

"You stay with Ma. I'll call Jerry Shrupp to come get me once I get everything figured out. I'll call your Aunt Sarah and let her know what's going on."

"Dad." Tears stung Peter's eyes. "Pray, okay?"

"I'm already praying."

ELLA ROSENBERG

Ella Rosenberg noticed the furtive glances Virginia gave her as she turned the white Oldsmobile into the driveway of Ella's tan-colored rambler. Virginia turned off the engine, and they sat in thick silence. Ella didn't dare speak; she knew she'd break down in tears. She dreaded going into the house to face the agony that awaited her there after every chemotherapy treatment: the nausea in unending swells, the sweating, the unfathomable weariness, and then the emptiness, the ache for her husband's arms. But he was gone. Dead five years already.

Virginia opened the driver's door and then moved into the house. Ella followed, but a wave of dizziness slowed her pace. She made it to the couch in the living room and collapsed. It wouldn't be long now. It never was. Virginia disappeared into the hall bathroom. Ella could hear her rummaging around for something. Ella closed her eyes and willed the nausea to stay away just this once. When she opened them, Virginia was beside her. She carried a pink bottle of Pepto-Bismol, a damp washcloth, and a plastic pail.

"Take this," Virginia instructed. She set down the pail and cloth next to the couch and poured out a dose of the medicine.

"That won't do any good," Ella said. "The doctor already gave me medicine to stop the nausea, but it never helps."

"Let's just try it, okay?" Virginia said. She leaned down, and Ella opened her mouth obediently. The liquid tasted of bubble gum and chalk. It coated her tongue and throat. She inhaled deeply and let her eyes fall closed again.

She awoke with a start and a heaving sensation. Sweat dripped from her brow. Her head pounded. But Virginia was there. She held the pail while Ella vomited. It was a violent thing, the way her body rebelled against her, first with the breast cancer and now with its remedy. Hadn't it been enough that the disease had taken her breast? Must it strip everything from her? Embarrassment flared. She hated throwing up in front of others. That was why Virginia was the only one she'd allowed to take her to these sessions; she didn't want anyone else to see her this way.

Virginia wiped the perspiration from Ella's face as she slumped back against the cushions.

"I can't do this," Ella moaned. Their gazes held in a bond that surpassed friendship and went to the core of their beings, a bond of suffering that those who'd never suffered couldn't comprehend.

"I'm here," Virginia said.

Her words gave Ella strength to go on.

f i v e

When Peter returned to his grandmother's room later, he found Ella Rosenberg sitting at her bedside. Her hair seemed rumpled, as if she had been up all night despite it being only four in the afternoon. "I'm sorry. I didn't know you were here," Peter said. "I can go."

"No, no," Ella said. "We can bend a few rules. Come sit down." She pointed to the vinyl chair across from her. The rest of the Suzie Q's had gone home with promises to call their various churches' prayer chains. Peter knew Ella would stay for as long as it took to will his grandmother to wholeness.

Peter glanced toward the door, then pulled up a chair alongside Ella's. "Any change?"

Ella shook her head. "She's a tough cookie, Peter. She'll pull through. She has to. What would I do without her? I could always depend on my dear friend Virginia." Her gaze fixed on his grandmother's face. "I had cancer. Did you know I had cancer?" She waved a hand in the air. "It was after my husband died. Virginia

35

drove me to every appointment. Then she stayed with me, held my head while I threw up. Now, what kind of a person is willing to do that? She was . . ." Ella exhaled and lifted glistening eyes to Peter. "She's a remarkable friend."

"A remarkable grandmother."

Virginia awakened, disoriented. Some sort of tube came from her nose and others from her arms. Then she saw the monitor alongside her bed and realized she was in the hospital. Ella sat at her bedside, dozing. Virginia remembered taking Mae's photograph with President Eisenhower at the SPAM Museum. And then incredible pain in her skull. Her head still throbbed. She tried to lift her left hand to the spot, but her hand was numb and wouldn't cooperate.

The room was dark, with blinds drawn closed. Rain plinked against the windowpanes, mixed with the monitor's soft beeps. She opened her mouth to speak, but her face felt heavy, numb like her hand. Her whole left side was a plastic mannequin. She moaned, and Ella lifted her head.

Her friend's eyes widened. "Virginia, I'm so glad you decided to come back. How are you feeling?" Virginia managed only a garble of syllables. "You had a stroke, dear." Ella stood up, then patted Virginia's shoulder and said, "I'm going to get the doctor and Peter, okay?" Virginia nodded ever so slightly.

Then Ella was gone. Virginia lifted her gaze to the ceiling.

Lord, what have you done? But there was no reply. Sleep beckoned. She obeyed its whisper.

Mae sat upright in bed and rested her hands on the roundness of her belly. Trudy had gone downstairs to the hospital gift shop in search of a crossword-puzzle book. Mae stared out the window at the gray gloom of day. She wished Peter would return. She hated waiting. If only she could go see Virginia for herself.

"Hey," Peter said from the doorway. She turned her face toward him. He held a tray in his hands. "How are you feeling?"

Mae shrugged. "I'm okay. So, what is that?"

"I brought us a little supper." He lifted the cafeteria dinner tray for her to see, then set the food on the table. He lifted the lid from the plate. Steam chased his hand. "Grilled chicken, mashed potatoes and gravy, and Jell-O. Mmm." He lifted his eyebrows.

"Sounds delectable," Mae deadpanned.

"Don't be so skeptical. Could be our best meal of the day."

"Where is that doctor?"

"Don't worry. He'll get around to discharging you. He's probably busy with some emergency."

"I hate waiting."

Peter sat next to her on the bed and reached for her hand. "You're going to have to get used to waiting. You have eight more weeks of it with this baby."

"Ugh! It's torture. I want to know how things turn out!"

"Let tomorrow take care of itself."

Mae's expression was doleful. "I'm just worried about Virginia."

"Worrying won't help anyone." Peter pulled the table on wheels closer to the bed and handed Mae her cutlery. "Dad's coming tonight. That'll help all of us feel better."

"Peter, we can't lose her."

"We won't. You have to believe that."

"Peter." Ella stood just inside the door. "Virginia's awake."

Doctors and nurses worked around Virginia's bed. They wrote in her chart, reviewed her blood pressure and heart rate, and spoke in hushed tones. Peter, Trudy, and Ella were careful to stand out of their way. Peter hadn't noticed before that the left side of her face seemed to droop. His grandma's gaze turned to them. Her pale eyes penetrated Peter's like a silent cry. She looked so helpless, so utterly lost. When the medical personnel finished, Dr. McKenna waved them over. "I'm sure Virginia wants to see all of you. Don't you, Mrs. Morgan?" They drew closer.

"Hey, Grandma," Peter said. He leaned to kiss her forehead. He wanted to reassure her that everything would turn out, that she'd be back to her old self soon, yet he held no guarantees. He reached for her hand and gave it a squeeze. It was cold, limp, a lifeless fish. If she could squeeze his hand in response, she didn't.

She opened her mouth, but no words came out,

merely grunts where words used to be. Frustration filled her eyes.

"It's pretty common to lose your speech, at least for a bit," Dr. McKenna told them when they gathered in the hall outside Virginia's room. "She could be talking normally in a matter of weeks, or longer, depending . . ." He turned to Peter. "She's paralyzed on the left side, but she seems to have some feeling. Walking will probably be a difficulty. Is she a pretty strong person—I mean, is she a fighter?"

"She's going on seventy-eight," Peter said, "but, yes, I'd call her a fighter."

"Good," the doctor said. "She needs to be in the coming weeks."

"She'll do it," Trudy offered, coming out of her unusual silence. She gave Peter a smile for encouragement. "She's a stubborn Minnesotan. She'll do it just to prove she can."

"When can she come home?" Peter said.

Dr. McKenna chewed his lower lip before answering. "That's something I wanted to talk to you about. I think it would be in her best interest to go into a nursing home, at least for a little while. I don't know what sort of long-term healthcare coverage she has, but she has a lot to relearn before she's ready to be on her own."

"She could live with us," Peter said.

The doctor shook his head. "I'm afraid not." His blue eyes held an apology. "I know you want to take care of her, but you're a farmer. You're going to be too busy in the fields once this rain lets up, and Mae shouldn't push herself like that, not with her history. It would put your baby at risk. I'm certain your primary-care physician would agree. I don't see any other way. Besides, Virginia would have around-the-clock care at a nursing home. Physical therapy would be right down the hall. Lake Emily has a fine facility. Once Virginia is walking and Mae's had that baby, then you could think about bringing her to your house. Even if Mae weren't pregnant, I doubt she could lift Virginia to help her do all she needs. I'm sorry."

Peter sighed. As much as he hated the thought, he knew the doctor was right. "I'll talk to my dad about it when he gets here," Peter said. "This is his decision and my Aunt Sarah's."

"Of course," the doctor said. "It will be a few days before she'll be stable enough to be moved anyway, although you need to find out if there's room for her and settle those details."

After he left, Peter and Trudy walked toward Mae's room while Ella kept Virginia company.

"What do you think?" Peter said.

"It's a hard one."

"He's right, though. What other choice do we have?" His words drifted to silence.

"What can I do to help?"

"Take care of Mae for me until my dad gets here." He looked his sister-in-law in the eye. "Take her home. Don't leave her. I don't know what else I can do, but I want her safe, not worried about all this."

"She understands." Trudy touched her brother-in-law's hand lightly. "She loves Virginia too."

"I know she does. I'll be home in the morning to milk. Dad's plane is coming in tomorrow morning, early if he can get on the flight he mentioned. We'll see what sort of arrangement we come up with then. I don't relish the thought of having to make these decisions alone."

"You're not alone," Trudy reminded. "And Bert can cover for you, you know. He's happy to milk your cows." They reached Mae's closed door.

"No. He has enough with his own herd and Fred gone."

"Stubborn boy," Trudy teased lightly.

"Peter, is that you?" Mae called from her bed.

"Thanks, Trudes. I mean that." He gave his sister-in-law a grateful smile. "I don't know what I'd do without you."

Trudy waved the compliment away. "Whatever. Don't get all sentimental on me."

six

Virginia was in prison. Her own body had become her jailer. Her loved ones spoke words of comfort, but she couldn't respond. She couldn't tell them how frustrated she felt, how afraid, how alone. She lay in the semidarkness, the bed half-reclined, as a television droned lowly near the ceiling in the corner. A single light shone over the sink along one wall. The glare irritated her eyes. Why didn't someone turn it out? Nurses moved with stealth, taking her blood pressure and temperature wordlessly, offering only looks of pity.

Emotions crashed over her in waves—frustration, fear, uncertainty, helplessness. Most of all she longed for Roy. The touch of his work-worn hands. The smell of hay and a day's sweat in his flannel shirts. The timbre of his voice that never failed to comfort a deep place within her. It wasn't right that she had to face this without him. She realized she was angry at him for not being there. And angry at her own frailty, angry for not seeing the symptoms sooner. She had ignored the headache that had stretched between her temples all morning. Guilt rode on the next wave. How could she place this burden on her family? Mae and Peter already had so much to contend with.

Then weariness rode in. She was too tired to endure another battle. Hadn't she suffered enough through Roy's cancer? Hadn't she paid her dues to the tornado that took her house? It wasn't right. It wasn't fair.

She closed her eyes.

Since when is life fair?

God, I'm too upset with you to talk right now, her heart replied.

The throbbing behind her eyes dimmed, yet she longed to sleep. In her sleep she was whole. Waking had become the nightmare.

The squeak of a door woke her. David was there! Her son. Her heart surged at the sight of him, despite his lined brow and the bags beneath his bloodshot eyes.

"Ma," he breathed as he drew close to her bedside.

She turned her face to reply, forgetting her traitorous tongue. A tear traced her cheek. David touched her hair, brushed the tear away, and bent to kiss her temple as he always did. She closed her eyes. Her David had come home.

"I got here as soon as I could," he said. He sat on the edge of the bed.

"Da-vid," Virginia managed to get out. Her first word, a baby's babble, the name of her elder child. She longed to hold him close. She lifted her right hand, and he clasped it to his heart.

"I called Sarah," David said. "She so wanted to be here. She and Tom send their love."

She'd rarely seen her daughter in the past few years. Tom's military career and then financial woes always stood in the way. But those felt like excuses today, trite excuses. Surely Sarah could borrow airfare to see her mother just this once. Virginia sighed as she realized her own selfishness. Yet it was there—the hurt that her own daughter wouldn't choose her during her time of need. She looked back at David.

I'm glad you came. The words ached to leave her throat. *At least you're here. My boy, my son.* She reached for him awkwardly, and he leaned forward. She kissed his cheek. His face was salty and damp.

"I love you, Ma."

She lifted her good hand in the motion of a conductor.

"I told them I need a little time off." David said of the Phoenix Symphony, of which he'd been conductor for the past year.

Virginia shook her head.

"They'll cover for me. At least for a few days. I had to come to make sure my best girl was okay."

Mae flicked on the bedside lamp and glanced at the alarm clock. Two o'clock. She hadn't gotten a wink of sleep, yet her body ached for rest. The baby shifted, and the familiar fluttering sensation traversed from her navel to her rib cage. She placed a hand on the spot and sighed. "I'm sorry I'm not sleeping, baby." But how could she when so much worry filled her mind?

Deciding to head to the bathroom, she slid her feet into fuzzy slippers alongside the bed and padded to the bathroom. The hall light slanted on Trudy's sleeping form in one of the guest bedrooms. Trudy had offered to sleep over so Mae wouldn't be alone, but Mae suspected Peter had asked Trudy to watch over her. Trudy was on her stomach, her mouth wide open, with a wet spot of drool on her pillow. One arm hung off the side to the floor. Trudy grunted and rolled onto her back. Mae smiled and slipped into the bathroom.

When she came out, headed back to bed, Mae gasped. Trudy stood in the hall, bearing two cups of steaming hot chocolate. "What are you doing up?" Mae asked.

"You take forever. I thought you'd died in there." She handed a cup to her sister. Mae gingerly took it.

"It's hard to sleep," Mae said. Trudy nodded. She led the way to the stuffed chairs in Mae's bedroom. After turning on the fringed lamp on the small table between the chairs, Trudy drew her legs under her. She wore hot pink footed p.j.'s, and her red curly hair was tied back in a short ponytail. Her hair had grown considerably since her Peter Pan pixie of the year before.

"You're not going to wear those pajamas after you get married, are you?" Mae pointed to the adult-sized toddler wear.

Trudy shrugged. "They're warm and comfy." She set her mug on the table.

"Bert won't think so. Did you call him tonight?" Mae held her fingers around the mug, warming her hands.

"From the waiting room. He said he would call the prayer chain."

"I wish I knew how Virginia was. I totally flipped out today, didn't I?"

"Don't beat yourself up." Trudy touched her sister's hand. "So, maybe you aren't cut out to be an emergency medical technician. You were afraid. We all were." She took another sip of her chocolate. It left a foamy mustache of brown across her upper lip. Trudy licked it off.

"I felt so powerless," Mae admitted.

"Thinking you *have* power, now that's the illusion in

45

life. The truth is, any one of us can be laid low in a heartbeat, just like Virginia."

"I didn't realize how true that was until today. I could've lost the baby."

"But you didn't," Trudy said. "You're not going to, either."

"I get so afraid," Mae confessed, "almost panicky sometimes, thinking about what I'd do if I lost this baby too."

"We all have our fears, honey. Some of us are just better at hiding them. You think I'm not terrified of being Lillian Biddle's daughter-in-law?"

Mae smiled. "Actually, Lillian surprised me today. She held together far better than I did."

"She did, didn't she? Of course, I'm well aware of her ability to boss people around. She's been sticking her nose in our wedding plans since day one. I finally gave in and told her we would hire Willie's nephew's polka band for the reception."

"Really?" Mae chuckled. "Mom will love that. Can you picture Catherine Larson doing the oompah-pah in Versace?"

"Definitely! It will make for some great photos."

Trudy set her empty cup down on the nightstand and released her hair from its ponytail. "You need your sleep, kid." She patted Mae's knee. "You want me to sleep with you like when we were kids?"

Mae smiled. "Sure, what the hey."

PETER MORGAN

Thirteen-year-old Peter Morgan sat on the bed in his parents' room. His father carefully laid out dress shoes and crisp, folded white shirts to add to his suitcase of suits and black socks. Peter still wore his black suit, his confirmation suit. But today was hardly the joyous event of those short weeks before. Peter wished he could cry, but his tears had been spent.

"Why do we have to go so soon?" Peter complained. "We just buried Mom today."

His father paused in his packing and sat beside Peter on the bed. He looked at the floor for a long time before speaking. When he did speak, his voice was quiet, measured. Talking down.

"We have to get back to living, Peter. The orchestra was kind to give me a leave of absence while Mom was so sick, but I have to get back to work."

"It's too soon. Why can't I stay here on the farm with Grandma and Grandpa? I can go to school in Lake Emily. I'm tired of always traveling. I don't want to forget Mom." He hadn't meant to sound so accusing.

His dad smiled sadly. "I'm not forgetting her, Peter. Living is a way of honoring her. Do you think Mom would want us to curl into a ball and cry for the rest of our lives?"

Peter knew the question was meant to have only one answer. But he wasn't talking about the rest of his life.

He didn't even have his funeral clothes off, and Dad was "moving on."

"Don't make me leave right now. The next tour. I can come on that one." His mother had always been with him on the road to fill the quiet hours while his dad played violin with the orchestra. Who would play Scrabble and Boggle with him now? Who would talk and laugh with him? No one. He'd be alone with the pain. How could he bear that? The thought strangled him, and the tears that had previously eluded him came. Why did his mom have to die? He'd asked that question a thousand times in the last three days.

"Peter," his dad said. "I need you. We're a family now, the two of us. I know you miss Mom. I do too. That's why we need to be together. I'm sorry this is the way it is, but it is."

"It wouldn't have to be this way if you had a normal job," Peter thought. "I could stay with Grandma and Grandpa and you. They're family too. We wouldn't have to always choose music above everything else."

s e v e n

The inky black of night pressed against the waiting room windows. Peter tried to doze in one of the chairs, but it was impossible to find a comfortable position, and his roiling thoughts kept him on edge. His dad was in with Grandma. Jerry Shrupp, his father's best friend since high school, had taken Ella back to Lake Emily.

Ella protested leaving Virginia's side, but Peter argued that she needed her rest or she'd end up in the hospital herself. She finally acquiesced, making promises to return in the morning.

Peter shifted and glanced at the nurse behind the receptionist's desk, her head bent over paperwork. Footsteps sounded in the long corridor. Peter's father appeared.

"Get any sleep?"

Peter shook his head and sat upright. "How does she look?"

David took the chair across from his son. His eyes were troubled. "I didn't expect her to look so . . . frail. And scared. What did the doctor say about her speech? Will she get that back?"

"Hard to say, but he seemed hopeful that it would return with time."

"Did he give any idea when she'll be released?"

"That's something I need to talk to you about. The doctor wants her to go into a nursing home for a while."

David raked his fingers through his graying hair. "I can't see Ma agreeing to that. You know how hard she fought to keep Dad home until the end."

"I know. But this isn't open ended like Grandpa's situation was. It would only be temporary. And there's no one to take care of her."

"What about you and Mae?"

Peter shrugged. "The doctor is concerned about the stress that would cause Mae. The physical demands could send her into labor again. And once I can get into the fields, I'll be gone day and night to make up for lost time."

"Have you mentioned all this to Ma?" David leaned forward, his elbows on his thighs.

Peter shook his head. "She's not even out of ICU." He glanced at his watch. "I wanted to talk to you first."

David sat back and sighed. "I guess we don't have a choice, do we?" He patted his son's knee. "I'll break the news to her in the morning."

"It *is* morning, Dad."

Peter slapped his cheek, trying to stay alert as he drove home in the predawn hours. He'd left the hospital at four o'clock, just after talking to his father about putting Grandma in a home. He needed to get back for the morning milking. Bert Biddle, Trudy's fiancé, had covered for him last night. But Peter wouldn't ask Bert to handle his own herd and Peter's seventy head of milk cows any longer. Plus, he needed to be with Mae now that Grandma was in his dad's care. It felt good to have him home. Peter hadn't realized how much he missed Dad's presence since he'd moved to Arizona. Was it only yesterday he got the call that his grandmother had the stroke? It seemed like weeks ago. His body ached with exhaustion.

As he passed through Waterville, the pale sun painted its shy blush across thin clouds that streaked the horizon. Peter yawned and forced his eyes open wider. Only another half hour and he'd be home.

When he'd left, Grandma was sleeping as his dad kept vigil beside her. The staff moved about as if he weren't breaking any hospital rules. When someone told him he needed to leave, David simply said, "She's my mother," and stayed put. Peter admired his father's confidence. He wondered where such nerve came from. Was it born of his years on the stage, or had his parents instilled it during his younger days? Or had the slow, painful death of Peter's mother taught David Morgan that lesson? Peter didn't know. There was so much about his father he wished he knew.

Peter flipped on the left-turn signal and pulled onto the gravel road that led to the Morgan farm. The rains had abated sometime during the night, but the fields would need at least a week to dry out before the tractor could get in and out for planting. Provided it didn't rain again. The forecasts were not on his side. Worry edged up, and Peter punched it down. He had enough to think about without fears of a poor crop toppling the heap.

The farmhouse came into view, a beautiful two-story yellow tan brick dwelling with a wraparound porch and red shutters. The red barn, with its row of white-trimmed windows, glowed in the morning light. Cows meandered in the muddy pasture, but most stood inside or at the door, eager for their morning milking. Peter killed the motor and sat in the silence. No beeping monitors here. No life-or-death decisions. Just a crisp dawn where the sunlight kissed the horizon. The place calmed his troubled thoughts and wooed him with its gentleness.

Scout, his grandpa's aged yellow Lab, bounded over to the truck. Peter stepped out and patted his head. Through the window Peter noticed that the kitchen light above the sink was on. Trudy waved at him.

He went inside quietly in case Mae was still asleep. But she sat in the built-in breakfast nook in the cheery yellow and white kitchen.

"I thought you'd still be in bed," Peter said.

"Oh, Peter," Mae said. She rose and moved to him. She held him in a fierce hug, her belly making them both lean their shoulders forward. "How is she?"

Peter glanced at Trudy. Her hair was frizzy and poked out at odd angles, and she wore footed pajamas. "Nice outfit."

She narrowed her eyes at him. Peter grinned before turning back to Mae.

"She's glad to have Dad with her, I think. It'll be a rough road, but she did manage to say Dad's name, so that's a good sign."

He took the mug of coffee Trudy handed him and sipped on the steaming drink before continuing. "She was so happy to see Dad." He stared at the floor and let the steam from his mug touch his nose. "It makes me realize how much she needed him when Grandpa died. He should've been here then, too, instead of touring in Asia with the orchestra."

"I thought you'd moved past all that," Mae warned.

"I have . . . This just brings it back. I wish Aunt Sarah could've come. She said she'd call later this morning."

"I'm sure Sarah would have come if she could. Virginia has her love and her prayers," Mae said. "Do you think it would be okay if I went back to see her today?"

He loved her for asking, but he shook his head.

"You need to lie low, okay? Wait until we get her back to the Lake Emily nursing home. You can see her then."

"Really? The nursing home?" Mae said.

"I know it's not what we want. Nothing about this situation is. But Dad agrees. Grandma needs constant care and physical therapy. It'll be right down the hall at the nursing home. And if anything were to happen, the hospital's right there in the next wing. I need to call the home and see if they have room."

"I can do that," Mae offered.

"Are you sure?"

"I need to do something useful."

Peter set the mug on the table, then motioned with a thumb toward the door. "Thanks. *I* need to milk."

"Have you slept at all?" Mae said.

"Sometimes sleep isn't relevant."

Jessie Wise rode her bike up the driveway to Virginia's house and pulled up to the garage. "Virginia," she called. But there was no answer. Jessie lifted her face to the sky. Dark clouds were rolling in. Thunder rumbled in the distance.

She tugged the garage's side door open and rolled the ten-speed in, in case it started raining again. The big white car was there, so Virginia should've been home.

Jessie went back outside and called Virginia's name again. The place was too quiet. Virginia usually kept the back door open with only the screen door closed, but both doors were shut. Jessie knocked and tried to turn the knob. It was locked. In all the times she had come to Virginia's after school, her door had never been locked. Jessie cupped her hands around her eyes to gaze inside. All was silent in the little two-story house.

There weren't any dishes in the sink, no scent of fresh-baked cookies or bread, no sewing project laid out on the dining-room table by the bay window to her left.

Jessie knocked louder. Maybe Virginia was taking a nap upstairs. Jessie called again. No answer. Where could she be? Virginia had always been there after school, always asked about her day and helped with homework, always made supper if Jessie's dad was going to be late. Jessie walked around to the front door. Maybe Virginia hadn't heard her. She was getting pretty old.

"Jessie, is that you?" Virginia's neighbor, Dee Marshall, peeked over a hedge. Jessie turned toward the woman. She was a skinny person with too-dark hair and an assortment of bangles on her wrist that jangled musically when she moved her hands.

"I was looking for Virginia," Jessie said.

"Didn't you hear?" Dee said. Her eyebrows formed a solid line with a crease in the middle. "Virginia had a stroke yesterday. I'm surprised no one called you."

"A stroke?" Jessie said. "What does that mean?" She'd heard the word before but couldn't recall what it was.

The woman's look turned to pity. "I'm sorry, Jessie. She's in the hospital in Austin, last I heard on the prayer chain. It doesn't sound like she's doing real well."

"Oh." Jessie felt very small. Virginia was sick in the hospital, and no one had called to tell her. "Thanks, Mrs. Marshall," she said. She returned to the garage as a loud clap of thunder cracked the sky. She got her bicycle and climbed on, not sure of where to go or what to do.

Virginia was sick. An image flashed—her mother dying after the car accident. It was still there in the deep parts of her memory, strong and painful. She remembered it all—the pictures, the sounds, even the smells of the hospital. She hated hospitals. Nothing good ever happened there. She thought of her father after the tornado, burned in the fire. The skin of his arm looked like thin, red paper, and he winced every time he moved. No, nothing good ever happened at hospitals, and now her best friend in the world lay in one in a town Jessie had only heard of. Jessie turned the bike up the street toward her house and pedaled for all she was worth.

Maybe if she rode fast enough she could outrace the awful truth.

Two days later Virginia was transferred to a hospital bed in Lake Emily. Virginia was relieved to be out of the privacy-invading ICU, and yet she feared that another stroke, like tremors after an earthquake, would end it all. How many times had she heard of folks who'd gone into the hospital for one stroke only to be killed by a secondary attack? She wished she could ask Dr. Mielke about it, yet he talked to David instead of her, as if she were still in a coma. They spoke of physical therapy and the eventual move down the hall to the nursing home. She tried to communicate to David that she didn't want that. Yet her lips were useless, and her handwriting was still illegible. David knew how she detested those places. He knew she'd done everything within her power to keep Roy out of those cold institutions. The thought that her son was entertaining this kind of talk worried her. She inhaled deeply and closed her eyes. Even so, she took comfort in David's reassuring presence. She reached for his hand and gave it a squeeze.

"You okay, Ma?" His blue eyes filled with concern.

Virginia nodded. "O-kay," she managed to force out.

"It'll be quieter here without those nurses interrupting your sleep every fifteen minutes." He turned to take in the new room.

Virginia patted his hand with her right hand. She didn't need to raise a fuss. David would take care of things. She just needed to trust him.

When Peter came in from milking the next night, he could tell from the look on his father's face that something was up.

"Dad, are you okay?"

David ran a hand through his salt-and-pepper hair and leaned against the kitchen counter. "I just got off the phone with my boss. I need to head out tomorrow."

"Already?" Peter's gaze moved to Mae, who sat in the nook.

"I'm afraid so. Two cellists resigned. I don't know what's going on, but he didn't sound happy." He crossed his arms over his chest.

"You can't leave. We haven't even put Grandma in the nursing home yet. You've only been here three days." His voice rose. "She needs you."

"She's doing better. There isn't a whole lot I can do for her, really. You know that I have responsibilities in Arizona." He lifted his eyes to Peter's.

"She's barely begun her recovery, Dad. How can you say that? You're her son. How can you just take off when Grandma needs you?"

"What am I supposed to do, Peter? This is my job. Those people need me too."

"Do they? You weren't here when Grandpa died, and now you're choosing your precious music over us again?" Peter was shouting now. He glanced at Mae again for support. Her eyes went to the mug between her hands.

"Peter, you have to understand—" David said.

Peter held up a hand. "I will never understand this, Dad. She's your mother. I would give up everything to be with *my* mother one last time." Peter knew the words cut deep, but they were true nonetheless. The room fell to silence.

The next morning David was gone.

e i g h t

The tall, thin stewardess passed David's row, collecting trash in a plastic bag. David ignored her. His mind was a thousand miles behind him, back in Minnesota with his mother. He tried to tell himself he'd made the right choice. He had to get back to Arizona, back to his orchestra. Didn't he? He was the conductor; who else would bear the burdens of the orchestra's success or failure? Even Peter left the hospital to milk his cows. Yet their argument played through his mind. *I would give up everything to be with my mother one last time.* Peter's words left a deep ache in David's heart. An ache for Laura and an ache for all that Peter had lost when she died. He knew Peter had hurled those hurtful words to get his attention, yet David had felt the same way every day since Laura's passing. Would his grief for his mother flow as deep as that well of pain?

His mother always said that she understood, that he should never apologize for the demands of his career. Yet gazing into her eyes at the hospital, he knew she wanted him there.

How many important family events had he missed because he had a concert to give? Too many. He understood Peter's bitterness. Yet what could he do? Give up the one thing that had sustained him through all his heartache?

Have I healed? Or have I simply outpaced the pain with my busy schedule?

He touched the wedding ring that still circled his finger. He was tired. Exhaustion was to blame for these doubts about going back to Arizona. Once he got a good night's sleep and his mother was back on her feet, he'd feel better.

Mae held her spring jacket closed despite the way it strained over her bulging belly. The rhythmic rumble and rattle of the milk machine made it hard to hear what Peter was saying. He squatted beside a Holstein, attaching the spiderlike tubes to the cow's teats as he talked. Mae cupped a hand behind her ear and motioned for him to come talk to her about this thing once and for all.

They turned toward the bleak day and gazed at the drizzling sky. Mae crossed her arms over her chest. Finally Peter said, "You know that I love my dad, but he was wrong to leave."

"You let him go without talking to him, without

making things right. You hurt him, Peter."

"Like Grandma isn't hurt by his leaving? Like I'm not hurt? I'm not going to apologize, Mae."

"But what choice did he have? He's responsible for the success of the orchestra. There was a crisis."

Peter held up a hand just as he had to his father. Mae bristled. "He's had a lot of choices in his life. His family always comes second. It's not my job to make him feel good about that."

"But you can't just leave it like this."

"I can and I will." Peter sighed. "For once he needs to understand what his choices do to the people he's supposed to love."

"I thought you were glad for him. When he took the conductorship in Arizona, you said that you under-stood, that you wanted him to be happy."

"I did. He was depressed about the arthritis. But now that Grandma's sick, we need him here. That changes things." Peter shrugged and turned to go back to milking.

"What about Virginia?" Mae said.

"We'll have to make up for his absence—again. Visit her more often. Her friends have already proven them-selves, especially Ella. At least she cares."

"Peter," Mae scolded. She reached for him. But he was beyond her grasp.

nine

David had deserted her, and now she'd been transferred to this hellhole.

It was her fault, his leaving. Hadn't she always told him not to apologize for what he did? Hadn't she reinforced his single-minded focus, his drive for perfection? Well, she regretted it now. She longed for a son's comfort. He'd been her rock those days right after the stroke, an anchor to hold her. It was almost like having Roy by her side. She sighed, hating the self-pity as much as the nursing home. Self-pity never led to anything but deeper self-pity, a downward spiral of black thoughts.

She closed her eyes and lifted her face to the ceiling. The television was black, silent in the corner. The sky outside her window was pewter, still crying for her.

She needed Roy, ached for his comfort. Everyone pasted on a smile and told her she should be encouraged. She'd made it past the critical stage. Already her speech was beginning to improve. Each day she managed a few new sounds. Even so, she missed her life, missed Jessie and all that they used to do together. Why hadn't the child come to see her yet? Had someone told her about the stroke? Or did she think Virginia had simply abandoned her? Virginia awkwardly reached for the paper and pen on her nightstand and scrawled a note: *Mae call Jessie.* She would ask Mae to do this the next time she visited. Virginia laid the pen and pad aside. Her ability to use her right hand seemed more improved—at least now she could hold objects without them slipping from her grasp. But her left side was still weak, and she could feel the droop in her face when she talked.

A nurse came in. "Good morning, Mrs. Morgan." She was a blonde with delicate features and piercing green eyes. Virginia had seen her before somewhere. She took hold of Virginia's arms and pulled her into an upright position. "How are you feeling?"

"O-kay," Virginia forced the word out.

"Your speech is good." She gazed kindly into Virginia's eyes. "And I'm not just saying that. You'll be back to your old self in no time."

Then it dawned on Virginia. Church. She had seen the girl at church. But her name eluded Virginia. With great effort Virginia ground out, "N-ame?"

"Anna Eastman. We worked together on the church bazaar last year, remember? You were in charge of the bake sale, and as I recall, you brought some amazing nut breads."

Virginia smiled lopsidedly, warmed by her praise. Then she went cold at the thought that she might never make those loaves again. Anna touched Virginia's hand. "I know this is a frustrating time for you, but don't get discouraged. That will only slow you down and keep you from recovering. We're all here for you. And from what I hear, there are a lot of folks who care about you. If you need anything, anything at all, press the nurse's button, and one of the nurses will come."

Virginia looked at her, puzzled. Anna laughed. "You thought I was your nurse, did you? Actually I'm your physical therapist. We'll get well acquainted in the coming days." Her smile was tender. Anna patted Virginia's hands. "I'm going to help you walk and talk again."

Virginia touched her numb left hand.

"I know," Anna said. "But it will get better, I promise. Can I take you for a ride, show you around the place?"

Virginia nodded.

Anna went outside to retrieve a wheelchair. A few minutes later she returned. She placed a wide transfer belt around Virginia's waist and then helped Virginia swing her legs off the edge of the bed. Once Anna had a firm grip on the belt, she and Virginia lifted up carefully and positioned her in the chair. Anna knelt to put the footrests down and placed a small tray between the arms in front of her.

"Are you ready?" Anna said. She pushed Virginia into the bright corridors of the Lake Emily nursing home. Other residents sat here and there, many in a world all their own, talking to walls or ghosts—Virginia couldn't tell which. One woman said hello, but Virginia's stubborn throat couldn't respond before they had passed her. They went into the fellowship hall, a large room with round tables and a fireplace at one end. A bank of windows revealed the rainy day outside.

"It's usually pretty cheery in here," Anna said. "At

least it is when the sun cooperates. Many of the residents come to play board games and visit. And the activities director holds interesting events in here like craft projects and sing-alongs, all kinds of things."

To Virginia it sounded more like a child's day camp. She knew the girl was trying to make her feel welcome, but her words only fixed the roots of Virginia's gloom deeper.

Next they moved to the physical therapy room. "This is where we'll be spending our time together," Anna said. "That's Kathy." She waved at a woman with thick, wavy brown hair. "She's the other physical therapist here." She showed Virginia around the room that held a weight set, parallel bars, mats, and the assorted paraphernalia of recovery, then wheeled her back into the hall. Virginia looked at the girl questioningly, wondering why they hadn't done any exercises.

Anna laughed. "This is all your therapy for now." She patted the handles of the wheelchair. "Learning to get in and out of this thing is enough for one day, don't you think?"

By the time they returned to her room, Virginia was amazed how tired she was. A large nurse came to help Anna get her back onto her bed. After Anna left, all Virginia wanted to do was sleep.

ten

Late the next afternoon a knock sounded on Virginia's door. The last thing she wanted was more company. First, Ella had come to read the paper with her, then half the Suzie Q's poured in, chattering about this and that, and then Mae and Trudy followed with their excitement about babies and weddings. It seemed life had no compunction about going on without her. Virginia knew that they meant well, that they were offering encouragement, but all she wanted was quiet. She was more than tired from the day's physical therapy.

The door cracked open, revealing Jessie Wise. Her father stood just behind her in the doorway. She chewed her lower lip and twisted her hands in front of herself.

"We hope we aren't interrupting," Steve said.

"Jessie," Virginia breathed, feeling as though a ray of sunshine had just shot into the room. She smiled, conscious that the left half of her face drooped, and waved them in.

Jessie crossed her arms over her chest and took two steps forward. Her father gave her a nudge and an apologetic smile to Virginia. "I don't know what's up with her," he explained.

Jessie let her hands drop to her side and asked in a timid voice, "Are you feeling okay?"

Before Virginia could attempt an answer, another

knock sounded, and Anna Eastman came in. "Virginia, your nurse asked me to bring you your—" Then she looked up and realized Virginia had company. "Oh, I'm sorry. I haven't met these visitors before."

Jessie lifted her fingers in a wave. "I'm Jessie," she said.

"Granddaughter?"

Jessie shook her head. "Friend." The word meant more to Virginia than anything she'd heard in a very long time.

"Ah, just as good." Anna offered a warm smile.

"I was asking Virginia how she's feeling," Jessie said.

"She still has a hard time talking," Anna explained. Virginia saw the way Jessie's shoulders sagged at the pronouncement, and Virginia's heart—weak, feeble, old—fell with them. "But it's coming back quickly," Anna went on. "How did you meet Mrs. Morgan?"

"Virginia was my book buddy at the library," Jessie said in a too-quiet voice. "I go to her house after school every day. I mean . . . I did, before . . ." The fear in the girl's face made Virginia long to hold her, to tell her everything would be just fine. "Can you talk at all, Virginia?" Jessie turned back to Virginia.

"Lit-tle," the word came out garbled, disfigured.

"Does it hurt?" Jessie said.

Virginia shook her head. Jessie uncrossed and crossed her arms again as if she couldn't think of another thing to say. Virginia closed her eyes, wishing she could speak, wishing she could tell Jessie not to be afraid.

"Mrs. Morgan and I get to do physical therapy together every day," Anna filled the silence.

"So,"—Steve turned to Anna—"any idea how long she'll be staying here?"

Anna offered a smile at Virginia. "It shouldn't be too long once she's walking again . . ." Her words trailed like crumbs before a starving person. "Well, I'll drop by after you're done visiting, okay, Virginia?" Then she left.

Jessie's sniffles drew Virginia's gaze. Virginia motioned with her right hand for Jessie to come closer. She pushed the girl's bangs back and wiped a tear from her cheek.

"You can't die, Virginia," Jessie said. "You just can't."

"She's been weepy like that since she heard about the stroke," Steve said.

Virginia gazed tenderly at the girl. Oh, to be whole, to be back in her sunny little kitchen baking chocolate-chip cookies and helping Jessie with her 4-H project. But she wasn't certain of anything these days, and she wasn't about to make promises that would turn to lies.

When Jessie and Steve were gone, the silence of the room cocooned her. She wasn't afraid of the quiet usually. At home she relished the chance to restore her soul, to pray and find rest. But today loneliness taunted like a playground bully, a loneliness of living inside the walls of her weak body. No one could reach her there.

God can.

A prayer resounded in her heart. *I want to be with you, Jesus. This world is painful. No one needs me, not really. Even Jessie is beyond my reach. I saw the fear in her eyes, and I'm powerless to take that fear away. It's the same fear I carry with me. I have no reason to continue. Roy is gone. Why can't I come now? Please. I'm a burden to everyone. My own son and daughter have left me.*

What about me? the inner voice argued.

What about you? I can love you as much—no, more there as here. Death is not a bad thing. At least not from where I sit. My family will have to deal with my death eventually. This way they can remember me the way I used to be—healthy, strong, productive. I don't have a purpose.

You have purpose.

She scoffed. *Lying here, mute and helpless. I'm warming a bed; that's all. I'd rather die, Lord. I'd rather die. It would be the merciful thing. Just take me home.*

Sleepiness crept over her again. Or maybe it had never left, this longing to sleep all day and never awaken to this reality.

Who really cares? You're supposed to, God—I know that. Yet all I hear are clichés and platitudes. No one understands. No one. I long to be set free, and yet I don't see how I possibly can be. Not short of death anyway. Please don't forget me here. I beg you.

She sighed, and a tear trickled down her cheek.

You're cruel. You tease me with promises of comfort,

joy, peace. You say there's nothing I can't handle with you, and yet I am alone. In my heart of hearts I am alone. Let me die. Let me see Roy and my parents. Let me see you. Is that so wrong, to want to see you? Because as mad as I am at you, Lord, I do still love you.

e l e v e n

The audience applauded, and the curtain closed. When it opened again, David Morgan took a bow from his platform, then extended his hand to the orchestra behind him. The deafening sound grew. The audience wanted an encore; they always wanted an encore. Finally he turned, a signal to the orchestra that they would play another song.

He lifted his baton and motioned for the flutes to take flight. The oboes followed and then the strings. David heard little more than a distant, faded melody in the glorious song. His hands moved by rote, not from any deep stirring.

His mother had been in the nursing home for two weeks. How was she really? Whenever he called, Mae assured him that his mother was fine. But a hesitance in her voice left him unsure. What kind of son was he not to be there? Peter's accusations barked at him. But there was nothing more he could do for his mother, David argued. She was being well cared for. What more did Peter want?

He lifted his arms to signify the music's swell like a wave rushing toward the shore.

Finally the song ended, and the curtain closed. Musicians congratulated each other as they gathered music. David nodded and put on a fake smile for those who praised the performance.

The hole bored into his heart by his mother's stroke grew deeper and wider daily. Yet it seemed to him the hollow had existed for much longer. Probably since Laura's death. His beautiful bride.

When he reached home, the clock read 11:25. It would be too late to call Peter. He needed to talk to his son, to make him understand. He glanced at his phone and noticed the answering machine's blinking light. He pushed the Play button, and Peter's strong voice quenched the silence: "Dad, just wanted to update you on Grandma." Terse as the day they'd argued. "She's still . . . adjusting. I don't know. She was never happy about going into the home. Her speech seems to be better. Anyway, I thought you'd want to know." Then he reminded his father of Virginia's address and phone numbers at the home and said, "Give her a call. I know she wants to hear from you." The line clicked to silence.

You weren't here when Grandpa died. . . . How can you just take off when Grandma needs you? Again! . . . Your precious music has always been more important than we are. . . . I would give up everything to be with my mother one last time.

"I would too, Peter," David whispered. He glanced at

70

the gold band on his finger, then at the empty apartment with its stunning view of the twinkling city lights.

Is music more important to me than my family? Peter had accused him of that before, in his growing-up years, but David had never really considered whether it was true.

Peter had hated traveling from town to town as a child. He wanted roots, friends. David supposed that was why he jumped at the chance to take over the farm.

But David wasn't a single father raising a child anymore. He was a grown man following a lifelong dream.

But where had his dream left him?

May days turned warm with the promise of summer. Virginia, though reluctant to push herself physically, had regained most of her speech. Only a slight lisp remained. Yet the wheelchair still held her captive—part of the reason for her moodiness, Peter knew.

Peter had his own reasons for moodiness. It had been raining for two solid weeks. After the morning's chores were done, he climbed the stairs to the bedroom. Mae was reading in the overstuffed chair, as had become her morning ritual of late. Her feet rested on the matching stuffed ottoman.

"How you feeling?" he asked.

Mae gazed dolefully at her ankles. "The swelling's gone down some. At least they don't hurt like they did before." She pressed a hand into her side. Peter saw the lump in her abdomen shift. "He keeps kicking my bladder. I've run to the bathroom three times in the last half hour!"

Peter laughed. "So you probably wouldn't want to come to the Chuckwagon with me for lunch, then?"

"Are you kidding? I'd love to. I need to get out of the house. This rain is driving me nuts."

"You too?" Peter said. "It's going to put us under if it doesn't stop."

"Peter, it has to stop raining sometime."

"No, it doesn't."

Mae laughed. "Okay, mister. Let's go. At least the Chuckwagon has a bathroom!" She stretched her back, then pressed against the armrests to stand. "I'll be so glad not to be pregnant. I told Ella that I wanted my waist back. She said she's been waiting forty-seven years to get her waist back, so I'd better not hold my breath."

"When did you see Ella?" They descended the stairs into the kitchen.

"Yesterday when I went to see Virginia. She's there constantly, along with Minnie Wilkes and Lillian Biddle. I hope I have friends like them in my old age."

"Lillian Biddle?" Peter said. "You sure you want friends like her?"

"I'll have Trudy."

"True enough." Peter laughed.

They dashed between rain droplets and climbed into Peter's green Chevy pickup. "There is a bright side to all this rain," Mae said. Peter lifted an eyebrow. "Time to be together before the baby takes over our lives; a month from yesterday is my due date."

Peter started the motor, then gave Mae's hand a squeeze. He backed out of the driveway. "What are we going to name this kid?"

"Peter, we keep going around on this. If you'd just let me pick names, we wouldn't have any of this argument."

"Sure, but I'd have to call my kid Evangeline for the rest of my life."

"Whatever! Even that's better than Electra. How many Electras have you met?"

"That's my point. It's unusual. People won't have a stereotype in mind when they hear it. She'll be free to be herself."

"Are you kidding? They'll expect Superwoman with electrical powers!"

It felt good to banter as they used to, without the weighty thoughts of the past few weeks. Peter reached for Mae's hand again and kissed the knuckles.

"Maybe we can go see Virginia after lunch," Mae said with a sigh.

Peter nodded. "I need to check on her house, too, maybe get her some books from home."

The Chuckwagon bustled with activity. The bankers from First Farmers filled one table. Several booths that flanked the tall windows held a gaggle of widows on their weekly outing. A couple with their preschool daughter sat amid the regulars lined up at the counter.

"It's the Morgans," Jim Miller, the proprietor, said with a grin. He was a large man with an ample waistline and a head of thick black hair. When he laughed, he could be heard throughout the restaurant, even when he was slaving over the griddle in the back. Jim Miller's ready joy was one of the things Peter liked most about this mom-and-pop place. Jim led the way to a booth with a wide view of a damp Main Street.

Jody, the fifty-something waitress with dark roots, panted past, then sloshed two glasses of water onto the table along with menus. "Be right back," she said and was off again.

"I guess that gives us time to decide," Peter whispered to Mae.

Mae went to slide into the booth only to discover that her pregnant girth didn't fit between the seat back and table. She turned sideways and scooted in. Peter chuckled.

"It's not funny!" She smacked his hand playfully. Then Mae's expression turned sober.

"What's wrong?" he said, baffled at her quick mood change.

Mae sighed and shook her head.

"Tell me." Peter leaned forward. "It's not because you don't fit in the booth, is it?"

"No." She smiled despite herself. "I wish this time wasn't so bittersweet. We're having our first baby, and that's wonderful. But without your grandma here to share it . . . I want her to get better soon. I wish I could do it all for her," Mae said. "Her speech has come so far, but . . . but it's hard."

"I know."

"I get the feeling that she almost doesn't want me to come see her."

"You know she appreciates your visits."

Mae shook her head. "It's just a feeling, but . . . I don't know. I worry about her."

Thunder cracked outside the window, and both Mae and Peter turned to look. Few cars wandered the rain-drenched street. A pedestrian dashed from the newly rebuilt Ott's Drugstore across the street to Hardware Hank. The hardware store looked bare without the tall, leafy oak that had towered there before the tornado. Peter glanced up at the drugstore's second story, where Trudy lived. The curtains in her front window fluttered slightly with the breeze.

"Looks like your sister's home. She leaves her windows open in the rain."

"She's probably too preoccupied putting the finishing touches on her wedding dress to even notice."

"Do you think she and Bert are ready?"

"Who's ever ready for married life?"

"True," Peter said. "For a good month after our wedding, I was in a state of shock."

"Hey!" Mae gaped in mock protest.

Jody returned for their orders. "What'll it be, kids?"

"What's the soup today?" Mae asked.

"Wild rice or clam chowder."

"Ooh, that sounds good," Mae said. "Can I get a bowl of each? And some breadsticks?"

"You want two bowls of soup?" Jody confirmed with a raised eyebrow.

"It's the pregnancy, Jody. Just humor her."

"As long as you're happy, honey, I'll bring you a whole tureen of soup." Jody winked. She turned to Peter. "How about you, bub? What'll it be?"

"Let's go with my usual."

"Reuben and a dinner salad with poppy-seed dressing," Jody finished for him. She disappeared to place the order, hollering to the cook over the hum of the café.

He gazed back at the window, where rain streaked the glass. "Stop worrying," Mae scolded.

Peter shrugged. "I can't help but wonder what all this rain means for the farm." He'd been thinking it for several weeks. "If I can't get the peas planted soon, I may as well forget them altogether. And the corn and beans—"

"Every other farmer in the county is in the same boat."

"Except that most of our neighbors own their land outright. Renting acreage from Grandma will kill us if there's no crop to sell. And Grandma needs money now more than ever." He shook his head. "I don't know what we can do. That nursing home isn't cheap. She has some coverage, but nothing for the long term. We'll have to start paying out of pocket if she doesn't come home soon."

"Do you think I was wrong to quit my job at the courthouse?"

Peter shook his head. "With a baby coming, no. We agreed that you should stay home and work the farm

76

with me when I need the help. Besides, day care and work expenses would eat up most of the benefit of that. No. We need to look for another solution. Getting Grandma out of that nursing home as soon as we can . . ." He shrugged.

"Getting her healthy—for her own sake as much as for ours," Mae added.

twelve

The invitations were ready to go out. The flowers and cake were ordered. The caterer was set to go. The reception hall and church had been booked over six months ago. The tuxedos and bridesmaid dresses had been altered and wrapped in plastic bags. All that remained was for Trudy to sew the white sequins on the crown of her veil. A long train of tulle would trail behind her, just like Julie Andrews's train in *The Sound of Music*. Ever since Trudy had seen that movie at age ten, she'd wanted one just like it, along with "How Do You Solve a Problem Like Maria?" as her recessional.

Rain pattered outside, under the occasional crack of thunder. A cool breeze touched Trudy's cheeks from the open window as she stitched with needle and thread. A pincushion with a plastic wrist clip held pins at the ready as she stitched back and forth. She wanted the veil just so and was deliberate about where she placed each sequin.

Swap Shop came on the old brown RCA Victor radio

Trudy had bought at the thrift store. "Welcome to *Swap Shop*, where listeners call in with items to buy, sell, trade, or give away. We'll be taking your calls for the next half hour." The announcer gave the phone number and opened the line for callers. Trudy turned the volume up. She liked to listen, not because she ever bought anything, but because it amazed her how much "stuff" people wanted to unload. She smiled and lifted another sequin onto the needle. She'd learned about "stuff" this past year and how little she needed to be truly happy. All her belongings had blown away in the May tornado, all her possessions, treasures she'd had since childhood. Yet she was filled with a deep sense of joy that came from a strengthened faith in God. He met her needs without fail, both emotional and physical. Knowing he wouldn't bail on her gave her a new freedom. Also, Bert's entry into the quiet of her heart affirmed his true acceptance of her. Having chosen to share the deep lonely places with Bert, the hurts of her past, of her father's rejection, she'd found a healing unequaled in her life based on pure, unconditional love. It filled her, made her alive, made her believe she could do whatever she wanted.

Trudy sighed happily as a knock sounded on the door down the hall. "Come i-in," she sing-songed.

"Hey," Bert's voice sounded. He came down the shotgun-style apartment to the "studio" at the front where Trudy sat. He wore his green seed cap on his head. Dishwater blond curls jutted from beneath the back. His deep blue eyes sparkled when they met hers.

Trudy shoved the needle into the pincushion on her wrist and moved across the room into his embrace. Their kiss was long, slow, delicious.

"Only one more week. I can hardly wait," Trudy breathed, leaning in for a lingering moment. When she pulled back, she saw that Bert had turned red. Trudy kissed his nose. "Any word from your brother?" She flopped onto the couch.

Fred Biddle, Bert's twin, had deserted the family farm over a year ago in favor of the warmth and glamour of Walt Disney World, far from Lillian's nagging. Fred's lingering absence was a sore spot for Bert's father, and Bert hoped the wedding could bring the prodigal home. But so far Fred hadn't even acknowledged that the wedding was on his radar.

"Not exactly." Bert held out the letter they'd sent to Fred with "Return to Sender" and "No Forwarding Address" stamped on the front. Trudy reached for it.

"No forwarding address. What does that mean? That he isn't at Disney World anymore?"

"I think he's jealous." Bert said. "He wanted you for himself." He sat next to Trudy on the small couch.

"That's ridiculous," Trudy said. "Fred and I were never serious about each other. We went out a couple of times, that's all. If he thought he stood a chance, he's nuts."

"If he doesn't come to the wedding, it'll kill Ma." Bert sighed. "It's just like him to think only of himself. Looks like Peter will be my best man after all."

Trudy snuggled close to him, and Bert lifted an arm

across her shoulder. "This isn't just about your ma. You want your brother to come. You don't have to pretend with me, Bert. He's your *brother*. I'd feel the same way if Mae weren't coming."

"Sure, he's my brother, but I get tired of these kinds of stunts."

"Hey, at least we're getting married, right? That's cause for celebration."

"I'm sorry." Bert kissed her cheek.

"You never know, he just might surprise you."

"It hurts," Virginia complained. Tears seeped from her eyes. They seemed to come all the time lately. This uncontrollable weepiness.

"I'm sorry, Virginia," Anna said as she moved Virginia's arms back and forth. "But your elbows and shoulders are stiff from lack of exercise. If I don't work them, the pain will only get worse."

The ache radiated down Virginia's arm and into her upper chest. Anna slowly bent and straightened her left arm ten times, then returned to her right. Virginia closed her eyes, trying to shut out the shards of glass that sliced her shoulder.

"Your right arm is much stronger than the left," Anna said. "So we'll have to work the left a little longer, okay? We need to keep those tendons and ligaments limber for when you start doing these things on your own again."

She wiped Virginia's perspiring brow. "I know it's hard, Virginia. Just hang in there with me, okay?"

The girl offered a hopeful smile that heightened Virginia's guilt for not being capable of doing more. "You're doing great, Virginia."

Virginia smiled tentatively. But nothing could erase the pain.

"Can we be done?" Virginia finally said.

"Okay," Anna said. She laid Virginia's arm by her side. "I should have told you that PT stands for 'pain and torture,' huh?"

"Is Virginia giving you a hard time?" Ella Rosenberg's voice sounded from the doorway. Every day at one thirty, right after physical therapy, she showed up like clockwork. Faithful, true to the end. And irritating as all get-out. Virginia had never noticed before now how bossy the woman could be.

"Oh no, Mrs. Rosenberg," Anna answered with a wink to Virginia. "Virginia's a model patient. We were just finishing up. Weren't we, Virginia?" She called the other therapist to help her move Virginia into the wheelchair. They hadn't tried walking yet, though Virginia knew she wasn't ready for that feat. Her body was still weak, uncooperative.

Ella released the brake and pushed Virginia into the corridor and down to the fellowship hall. Once she settled Virginia alongside the fireplace, Ella held up the latest issue of the *Lake Emily Herald*. "I thought we could read the paper together again," she said.

Virginia nodded her consent. It wasn't as if she could stop the woman. Ella sank into the chair beside her.

"Looks like the school board is up to their usual hoo-ha," Ella commented. She read the front-page article about combining the girls' tennis teams with a neighboring school's teams and the elimination of all foreign languages but Spanish from the high-school curriculum. "Oh, look at this." She held up the announcements: weddings, births, obituaries.

"Who died now?" Virginia added under her breath, "Lucky stiff."

"What's gotten into you? I was showing you Bert and Trudy's engagement announcement."

Shame flashed through Virginia.

"Virginia." Ella gazed at her, concern in her dark eyes. "What's wrong?" She leaned closer.

Virginia shook her head. "Nothing. It's nothing."

She wished it were nothing.

JESSIE WISE

The house was a wreck. It had been a wreck ever since the accident. Dirty dishes cluttered the countertops, so there was no place to lay her papers from school. Nine-year-old Jessie Wise tossed her backpack and coat onto the floor, which was every bit as messy, and went in search of her father.

"Da-ad," she called. It was so weird to call his name instead of her mother's. She puffed out her cheeks at the thought. The house had never looked like this when Mom was alive. She had kept everything sparkling. And there was lots of good food in the cupboards and

the smell of roasts and tacos and fried chicken to make her mouth water. There was music, too—beautiful music from her mom's old piano. Dad sold it the week after the funeral. Jessie bit her lower lip and went into the living room. The television blared at no one from the corner. She flicked it off and stood in the stark silence.

"Dad," Jessie called again. Where was he? Worry nibbled at her.

He'd been coming home later and later. Sometimes he didn't . . . smell too good. The odor of beer and smoke clung to him. His eyes were dull and sad.

Jessie dropped down onto the cornflower blue couch and pulled an afghan—the one her mother had made in pretty shades of blue and green—around her shoulders. Darkness gathered at the windows. She peered at them, wishing the day would last a little longer, that her dad would come before she was swallowed by the black. But he didn't come.

When she awoke, a single light in the kitchen cut a bright path across the dark room, letting her know that her father had come home.

Jessie crept to his bedroom. He lay on top of the covers, his clothes and shoes still on. Jessie lifted the afghan from her shoulders and went to cover him when he stirred.

"Oh, Jess, you don't have to do that," he said. "I'm sorry I was so late. I got hung up at work. Did you get something to eat?"

Jessie didn't answer. She climbed onto the bed with

him and snuggled by his side. Her dad put an arm across her shoulders. She could smell the beer. But it didn't matter. He was her dad, and she loved him.

thirteen

Steve Wise had been to church twice in the past three years. First for his wife's funeral, and second to see Jessie in the Christmas pageant.

Of course, the latter had been Virginia Morgan's doing. Jessie was so proud to speak her few lines as Mary in the play. When Steve saw the joy on his daughter's face, he knew his drinking had cheated her yet again of the heritage his wife had offered. Jessie had begged him to go to church ever since, and still he said no. Setting foot in that building had lost all appeal after Caroline died. But lately he'd felt that tug again.

Maybe Virginia's stroke was responsible. Without her, their life seemed empty somehow. He told Jessie she could visit Virginia anytime, but the girl refused to go. When he questioned her about it, she just shrugged her shoulders. He couldn't figure it out. He knew Jessie missed Virginia. She prayed for her every night before bed, talked incessantly about "when Virginia is better," and yet something held her back.

Virginia's words of long ago reverberated. *You still have choices. To be Jessie's father, to love her and to let her love you. Love—real love—is given when we least deserve it. It's the love God has for you, too, like*

Jessie. Those words gave him more courage than he had imagined they could. They came in the quiet hours and quelled the raging loneliness that drove him to drink. It was such a simple notion—that God could accept him, flaws and all. Yet it comforted, gave him strength to turn away from the weaknesses of the past.

Steve awoke early, showered, put on dress slacks and a white shirt, then went to wake Jessie. He shook her shoulder. "Come on, punkin. Wake up. We're going to church today."

"Church?" Jessie's eyes opened wide. "Do you mean it? Can I go to Sunday school, too?"

Steve laughed. "Let's start with church and work our way up to Sunday school, okay?"

"Okay!" Jessie shot out of bed. "I wonder if Susan Warner will be there," Steve heard her say as she dug through her messy dresser for something to wear. Within fifteen minutes she was dressed in a clean pair of jeans and a striped cotton shirt. She came into the bathroom to brush her teeth, then stood in front of Steve with a brush and ponytail holder in hand. Her blond locks had grown long in the last two years, reminding Steve of Caroline's golden hair. Somehow those reminders didn't kill him like they used to. More often now they brought him joy. He gently ran the brush through the ends, working his way higher with each stroke. "Ouch!" Jessie complained, grabbing the top of her head.

"I'm not trying to hurt you, but you've got snarls."

Jessie lowered her hand, and Steve resumed his task. It was such a basic thing, brushing his daughter's hair. Yet basic acts like this bound them as father and daughter. He wondered what simple yet priceless connections he'd missed when he'd been drinking.

He'd been sober a full eleven months. Some days it was all he could do not to stop in at the bar just for a taste. It called to him, especially when he felt weak. But it called during the good times too. *Just one drink to celebrate.*

He prayed he'd always have the strength to say no to that demon.

The church loomed ahead. Jessie's dad parked the car in the blacktopped parking lot, and they gazed up at the stone structure. Jessie grinned and hopped out. When she realized her father wasn't behind her, she turned around and said, "Come on, Dad."

Her dad looked nervous. His fingers remained wrapped around the steering wheel.

"Come on, Dad. What's wrong?"

"Maybe this is a bad idea."

"Please," she started to beg.

"Hello!"

Jessie whirled. A pretty blonde bent her head down and gave a little wave to Jessie's dad. Then she straightened and placed a hand on Jessie's arm. Anna, Virginia's physical therapist. She had a nice smile. Jessie's dad rolled down his window.

"I didn't know you went to church here," Anna said.

"We . . . uh . . . don't go to church anywhere," Jessie said.

"Well then, allow me to do the honors. It's not so bad if you have an escort." Anna stepped back from the car door. Jessie liked her—she seemed to understand her dad's mood. He climbed out, calmer now.

"I haven't gone here for long myself," Anna admitted as they walked toward the doors. "I only moved to Lake Emily a year and a half ago. I grew up in Truman."

They entered the church through the tall raspberry-colored door. Jessie saw Anna smile at her dad and heard him take a deep breath.

"It's been a while," he said.

"I couldn't tell." Her voice was light.

The head usher—"Mel Johnson," his nametag read—was a short man with a lined face. He held out a hand to Jessie's dad. His skin was a grayish color that matched his gray crew cut. "It's Wise, isn't it?" Mel said.

Jessie's dad nodded, then he looked at Jessie with lifted eyebrows as if to say he was amazed that the man remembered his name.

"And Jessie?" The old man shook hands with the ten-year-old. Jessie beamed.

"They're visiting today," Anna informed him.

"I have just the thing." He handed Jessie a bulletin that contained a crossword search, a page to color, and a word game. "It's all about the sermon, so you won't miss out on the message. Just a little easier to follow."

He winked at her. "I like to do them myself when Pastor Hickey gets boring."

Jessie giggled.

"Let's head in," Anna prompted with an easy smile. "I'll sit with you, okay, Jessie?"

"That'd be great," Jessie said.

Thick wooden beams like the ribs of a giant whale lifted the high ceiling. Stained-glass windows of men in long robes seemed to fill the room with multicolored lava-lamp light. Anna led them to a row toward the back along the left wall. Jessie perched in the middle and glanced up at her dad. His face was relaxed, almost happy. She liked the look. Then Jessie glanced at Anna, who smiled down at her.

"Have you visited Virginia lately?" Anna said.

Jessie shook her head. Her stomach churned. If only Virginia would get out of that awful place. If only Jessie could believe she'd be okay. "Is she doing better?" Jessie asked in a small voice.

Anna put an arm around the girl. "She's getting better every day. She'll be back to her old self in no time."

"Back to helping me with my homework?"

Anna smiled. "Does Virginia help you with your homework?"

"I used to go to her house after school every day. She'd make me treats and help me with my 4-H projects. But I had to bring my rabbit to my house after she had the stroke."

Anna's eyes lifted to Jessie's dad's. They were kind

eyes, not the judgmental, suspicious eyes that a lot of people had. They sparkled with joy and something else. Jessie wasn't sure what. The organ began to play.

"Would you two care to join me for lunch after church?" Anna whispered as the service drew to a close and people began to file out. "I have some pizzas in the freezer."

"Can we, Dad?" Jessie's expression was pleading.

"Sure," Steve said. "It'll save us from my cooking." He winked at Jessie. Then he smiled at Anna. Jessie secretly hoped it meant more than just thank you.

Anna's cute little cottage boasted a sparkling view of Lake Emily and a long, sloping lawn to a private dock. Jessie's dad stood gazing through the bank of windows that overlooked the lake while Jessie jabbered at Anna in the kitchen. They got out dishes to set the table and put extra cheese and pepperoni slices on the frozen pizzas.

"My mom used to do this when I was a kid," Anna said. She got out a container of oregano and sprinkled some across the pizzas. "She said it made them better." Jessie liked the way her eyes crinkled when she smiled.

"Too bad it's raining again," Anna said as she led the way into the dining room.

The dining room and living room formed one big room with furniture and area rugs arranged in cozy groups. The table was small, seating only four. Yet it felt comfortable. Anna set the plates and cloth napkins on the white lace tablecloth. Jessie followed, bearing three glasses, and set one at each place.

Her dad turned back to the view. "Yes, I thought we might actually have a dry day today. At least the rain waited until after church."

"I feel bad for the farmers," Anna said. "It must be frustrating." She disappeared into the kitchen and returned with a trivet, which she placed in the center of the table. "Oh, Jessie, could you get the garlic powder I left on that tray on the counter?"

She heard Anna say as she left, "You have a great kid."

"That she is." When Jessie returned, she saw the kind expression on Anna's face and knew they'd been talking about Jessie's mom.

"I'm sorry," Anna was saying. "It must be difficult for you both."

Her kind words made Jessie want to cry. Sometimes it seemed everyone had forgotten their loss, going on as if nothing had happened, while Jessie and her dad lived with that loss every day. Every supper for two, every load of laundry that held nothing frilly or feminine, reminded them of Mom.

"Something smells good." Jessie's dad broke the spell.

"I better check on those pizzas." Anna disappeared into the kitchen again.

"Are you having fun, Daddy?"

"Sure, punkin. How about you?"

Jessie nodded. "Anna's really nice. She said that when the weather gets warmer, we can come have a picnic and swim from the dock."

"That'd be fun."

The enticing scent of pizza told them Anna was back.

Each took a seat, and Anna reached for their hands before bowing her head in prayer. "Father," Anna began, "you give us wonderful things, like rainy days and new friends. Thank you, Lord, for the food we eat. Thank you for the friend we share in Virginia Morgan. She's having a hard time. Encourage her and remind her of your love. Remind us, too. Amen."

Besides Virginia, Jessie had never heard anyone pray like that. Anna talked to God as if he was right in the room, like a friend. They lifted their heads, and Jessie said, "You think Virginia's having a hard time?"

Anna nodded and reached for Jessie's plate. "I think so. She won't talk about it, but I think she misses her husband." Anna placed two slices of pizza onto the plate and handed it back.

"It must be hard," Jessie said.

"What must be hard?" Dad said. He handed his plate to Anna.

"Getting old. I'd think about dying all the time. Don't you?"

The adults both laughed. "Are you calling us old?" Anna said.

Jessie's face warmed. "I didn't mean—"

Anna patted her shoulder. "Don't worry about it. Say"—she turned to Jessie's dad—"I was telling Jessie you two should come swimming when it's warmer." Anna reached for a slice of pizza for herself.

"She was saying that."

"I love to swim," Jessie said. "I'm in level five in swimming lessons. My friend Mandy is still in level four." She took a bite of pizza. Then she pointed with it as she talked. "My mom used to take me to the pool every afternoon in the summer . . ." Afraid she'd said something she shouldn't have, Jessie's voice trailed away.

"My mom used to take me swimming too," Anna said. A look passed between her father and this stranger who seemed to care. It held understanding, compassion, connection. "It's one of the favorite things we used to do. You know what I always loved to do with my mom on Sunday afternoons?"

Jessie shook her head.

"Board games—all kinds. We played Boggle, Chinese checkers, Mouse Trap. You name it. And we put together more puzzles. We still play games whenever I visit her."

"My mom liked to put puzzles together with me," Jessie said. "But she really loved Scrabble, didn't she, Dad?"

Her dad nodded.

"I adore Scrabble!" Anna said. "Would you like to play after we finish up here?"

Jessie looked to her father for permission. When he nodded, Jessie clapped her hands. Who was this person who could be a good friend after only one meal?

• • •

"What kind of word is *luff?*" Anna pointed to Jessie's dad's tiles.

"Are you challenging me?" He raised an eyebrow, which caused Jessie to giggle.

Anna winked at Jessie. "Yes sir, I'm calling you on the carpet. *Luff* is not a word. You made it up!"

He placed a hand on his chest in mock offense. "I will not be unjustly accused. Jessie, hand me the dictionary." He flipped through the pages.

Anna leaned toward Jessie. "Now he's making me nervous!" He laid the thick volume out and pointed to his evidence.

" 'Luff,' " he read, " 'the forward edge of a fore-and-aft sail.' Ha!" Then he shut the book and handed it to Anna.

Anna's mouth dropped open. "It didn't *sound* like a word! That was a lucky guess!"

He smiled sheepishly. "Maybe . . ."

"That's not fair! Can you believe your dad?"

Jessie grinned. "Yes. He does that to me all the time. Once he said *ooph* was a word, but I caught him."

"Good for you, Jessie." Anna closed her eyes to slits. "He's a slick one, isn't he?"

Jessie's dad turned dark red and threw up his hands in surrender. "Ganged up on by women!"

Jessie couldn't remember the last time she and her dad had had more fun. They spent the rainy afternoon playing games, talking, and enjoying leftover pie from Baker's Square. She gazed at her father's light-filled eyes. He'd been so sad for so long. It was good to see that smile again.

He glanced at his watch, and Jessie's heart fell. "Where did the time go? We've taken up your whole day."

"I'm glad you did. I didn't have any other plans, and, besides, we had fun."

"We did," Jessie chimed in. "Can we see Anna again sometime? Please." She clasped her hands in full begging pose.

"I'd love to see you again real soon," Anna said. Jessie's smile was triumphant. Her dad tousled her hair and then extended a hand to Anna. "Thank you for having us. It was really nice getting to know you."

She took his hand and said, "It was nice getting to know you, too." She gazed down at Jessie. "And I'm serious about you coming to swim, okay?"

"Okay." Jessie grinned.

After they climbed into their car and turned toward home, Jessie said, "Daddy, do you like Anna?"

He gazed at her a long moment, then said, "Yes, sweetheart. I like Anna a lot."

Virginia missed Jessie. She missed the quiet afternoons together after school, helping the child with her homework, watching her play with her bunny in the backyard. She ached for those serene days she'd taken so much for granted. Did Jessie miss her as much? Was she staring out the window with this same longing?

Virginia lifted her face to the darkened ceiling. The

curtains were closed against the afternoon light. Her gaze shifted to the wall clock—four o'clock. Jessie would be home from school. If only Virginia could hear her voice. If only she could find out how the child was.

Lifting the phone's receiver, she dialed the Wises' number. After the fourth ring, Steve answered. "Hello?" He sounded winded.

"Steve. It's Virginia Morgan. Is Jessie there?"

"Oh, Virginia. It's good to hear your voice. Jessie isn't around. She went over to Anna's after school."

"Anna?"

"Your physical therapist. We spent some time with her after church last weekend. We really had a great time. She's such a nice person. Jessie's been going there after school many days. I was just about to go get her."

Virginia's heart fell. Apparently Jessie was fine without her. She'd found another to fill the void. Someone Steve really liked. Who needed this old woman? Jessie had gone on, just like everyone else in her life. Like her son and her daughter.

"Do you want me to have her give you a call?" Steve was saying.

"No," Virginia mumbled. "Don't bother. I'm just glad to hear she's doing so well."

"Okay . . ." He said it as if he sensed the pain in her words. After a silence he said, "I don't want you worrying about Jessie, Virginia. You've meant a lot to her, really. But she's okay. She really is. I'm taking care of

95

her like she deserves. And, well, you need some time to take care of yourself. Okay?"

It was the final blow.

f o u r t e e n

Sunshine finally broke through as May became June. Lilacs and peonies lifted their radiant faces to its warmth. Birds sang the "Hallelujah!" chorus. The farmers celebrated by breaking out their plows and seed.

Trudy couldn't imagine a more perfect day for a wedding. She and Mae admired each other before the full-length mirror in the Methodist church's nursery, which doubled as a dressing room for brides-to-be. Trudy's pure white gown featured a simple cut with crisp lines and an off-the-shoulder neckline. Her hair was pulled up, yet ringlets of red curls kissed her shoulders and framed her freckled face. She laid the veil across a toddler-sized chair. She would put it on just before going down the aisle. It was so long she didn't want to risk getting it dirty or tearing it.

Mae wore an icy pink satin bridesmaid dress with a similar neckline. Of course the cut had been modified to accommodate her growing girth, but she still looked adorable.

Trudy leaned close to the basketball that was Mae's belly and said, "Hey, little squirt, this is your Aunt Trudy. You can't be born today, do you hear me? Just let Mommy be, and stay warm in your little space there, because Aunt Trudy is getting married today." She straightened up and gave her sister a cheesy smile. "That should take care of it."

"I'm going to humor you today," Mae said with a raised eyebrow. "How are you feeling?"

Trudy sighed happily and said, "Numb, but I'm okay. I hope Bert doesn't back out of it. It would be a waste of a good polka band!"

"Bert isn't the one I'm nervous about."

"What? I'm not so fickle that I'd change my mind on my wedding day! I love this dude, you know."

"He's a great guy." Mae reached for her sister's hand and gave it a squeeze. "I'm so happy for you."

Trudy smiled. No one in her entire life had been there for her the way Mae had. Mae always found room in her life for her big sister. Once again, the security of unconditional love surrounded Trudy, reassuring her. She supposed her mother loved her that way. Her father . . . well, with him she couldn't be sure of anything. She hadn't seen or heard from him since she was fourteen years old. Trudy let out a melancholy sigh.

"What's wrong?" Mae said.

"I keep thinking about Dad," Trudy said. "Did you think about him on your wedding day?"

Mae shook her head. "I don't remember him very well. I was so little when he left."

"I wonder where he is." Trudy glanced out at the green church lawn. "I wonder if he ever thinks about us, if he knows what he's missing." Her eyes began to mist.

Mae dabbed her sister's cheeks. "No crying before the wedding," she scolded. "Your mascara will run! Then Bert *will* back out of it."

Trudy smiled. "Okay, I'll be good. Lillian thinks it's ridiculous that we're getting married during the summer, but I always dreamed of a June wedding. Who knew Bert wouldn't be done planting yet?" She shrugged.

"You're so stubborn!" Mae pointed out.

"Me?" Trudy objected. "You're the one who didn't tell anyone you were pregnant until after I'd booked the reception hall."

"You could've changed it, you know."

"And miss out on the fun of seeing you waddle down the aisle?"

Mae batted her on the arm. "You're lucky Bert's willing to take you on any kind of a honeymoon is all I can say. Peter would be fretting about planting the whole time. Has he told you where you're going yet?"

"No. But he promised no man sports."

"Ouch!" Mae jumped.

"It wasn't that big a deal." Trudy gazed curiously at her sister.

Mae pushed at the side of her belly. "Big kick. He must be a hockey fan." Trudy groaned just as their mother entered the small dressing room. She was a petite woman with Mae's dark good looks.

Catherine Larson stood back to admire her elder

daughter. "You're lovely."

Trudy blushed and grinned at the same time. "Thanks, Ma."

"Mother," Catherine corrected. "You know how I abhor 'Ma.'" She wore a lavender dress with a fitted bodice that showed off her trim figure. She touched the lace of Trudy's veil where it rested across the chair. "But still, he is a farmer. If you're not completely sure . . ."

Trudy rolled her eyes. "Mom, I'm marrying Bert. Deal with it. He's the nicest guy on the planet, and I love him. I'd be insane not to marry him."

Catherine held up a hand of surrender. "As long as you're sure." She walked behind Trudy and fidgeted with Trudy's sleeves. "Your future mother-in-law is out there bossing everyone on our side of the family. She's a very pushy person!" At that Trudy began to laugh.

"Well, she is." Catherine placed hands on her hips. "You're going to have to put up with that for the rest of your life, you know."

"Bert will too, Mom," Trudy said.

Catherine straightened and gave her a puzzled look. "Well, of course. Bert would have to put up with her whether you married him or not."

Trudy and Mae exchanged looks. "His ma and I have come to a truce. She doesn't get in my way, and I don't get in hers."

"You let me know how that works out for you, will you?" Catherine said.

• • •

The sanctuary of the United Methodist Church glowed in candlelight. Sconces lined the center aisle. Yellow roses scented the air. Butterflies fluttered inside Trudy's stomach as she waited behind Mae and the three bridesmaids—Ellen, her former roommate from St. Paul; Maria, a girlfriend since high-school days, and Rosemary Johnson, a co-worker at Lake Emily High School. Trudy's stepfather, Paul Larson, stood at her side looking Robert-Redford perfect with his feathered blond hair and pale blue eyes.

Bert escorted his mother up the center aisle to her seat at the front beside Willie. Then he returned to escort Catherine to her place of honor. He looked so handsome in his black tuxedo that Trudy caught her breath when he turned around. Bert's dishwater blond hair was freshly cut, transforming his curly locks into sexy waves. His blue eyes sparkled. Trudy's mouth went dry. Their gazes locked for a moment. Then he moved out of her view. She turned and smiled at her stepdad.

He patted her gloved hand, which was tucked into the crook of his elbow. "Nervous?" he whispered.

Trudy shook her head. "Just happy." His eyes smiled at her, and she noticed a tear glistened there. "What's wrong?"

Paul shrugged. "I'm just sorry I'm not your dad."

"I'm not wishing he were here instead of you," Trudy whispered.

"No, you don't understand. I love you like a dad; I

wish I *were* your dad." His tender expression made Trudy choke up.

"Don't do that!" she scolded. "Mae warned me not to wreck my mascara." She took a deep breath, then looked him in the eye. "I'll admit, I have thought about Dad today. But even if he were here, you'd still be the one giving me away. You've been more of a true dad to me, even through all my craziness, even when I wasn't so nice to you. I've never told you how much I appreciated that."

He squeezed her hand, and the processional music began. Petite Ellen started down the aisle in her halting walk to the front. Her pale hair glistened in the candlelight's glow. Trudy could see Tony, Ellen's groom of a year and a half, beaming with pride from his spot near the back. Next came Maria, followed by Rosemary. The older spinster had protested the idea of being a bridesmaid at her age—her mid-fifties—but when Trudy insisted that Rosemary was her dearest friend in Lake Emily, Rosemary couldn't argue. And it didn't hurt that Bert had chosen Bob Ott—Lake Emily's bachelor pharmacist and Trudy's landlord—to stand opposite her. The two had become inseparable since the tornado. It wouldn't surprise Trudy one bit if they announced their own nuptials soon.

Mae turned and gave Trudy a thumbs-up. "Ready?" she whispered.

"Just don't trip!"

Mae began her march. Even from where she stood,

Trudy could see Peter's eyes locked on his beautiful wife. Trudy's gaze moved to Bert. He, too, stared at his bride. Trudy felt her face flame, and Bert grinned.

Mae reached the altar, and Peter joined her to walk up the steps. The organist played the fanfare that signaled Trudy's entrance. Her heart hammered in her chest. She and her stepfather began their walk. The audience rose to their feet. Heads turned to smile. Her aunts had come from Big Lake and Sioux Falls. Her uncle from Ely and her many cousins were scattered through the crowd. Her smile was so big she felt certain her face would crack, but she couldn't help it. She was too happy to help it.

As she neared the front, Bert walked to her, and Paul released Trudy's hand. Bert unhurriedly tucked the other into the crook of his arm, and they turned to walk the three steps to where Pastor Hickey and the rest of the party stood. Trudy took a deep breath. She wanted to imprint this moment in her memory—the glow in her heart, the joy shining in Bert's eyes, the sweet smell of roses from her bouquet, every nuance—so she'd be able to tell her children about it someday.

"Who gives this woman to be wed?" Pastor Hickey said.

"Her mother and I do," she heard Paul say from his spot behind Trudy and Bert. Then Paul took his place beside Catherine.

The pastor began with a prayer, which was followed by a hymn. Then Mae and Rosemary handed their bouquets to Ellen and walked to the grand piano and Mae's

102

cello, which waited in its stand. Once Rosemary was settled on the piano bench and Mae was in position, they began to play Johann Sebastian Bach's "Air." The roundness of Mae's belly forced her to lean far forward to place the bow on the strings. When the song ended, a sense of reverence settled over the room. Trudy noticed Mae's eyes widen. She wondered what had happened, if perhaps Mae had made a mistake in the song. Certainly Trudy hadn't noticed anything wrong with it. Rosemary made her way back to her post at the altar, but Mae stayed put. Something wasn't right. Trudy mouthed, "What's wrong?" but Mae shook her head slightly and motioned to go ahead with the service.

Pastor Hickey leaned to say something to Peter, who stood on Bert's other side, then the pastor began his sermon while Peter walked quickly to his wife. Peter bent down to whisper to her. Trudy tried to concentrate on what the tall, beanpole pastor said, but she kept glancing at Mae.

"What's up with Mae?" Bert whispered.

Trudy shrugged. A moment later Peter returned to his spot behind Bert and stood with hands clasped as if nothing were amiss. Bert leaned toward Peter while Pastor Hickey kept on. When he turned forward, Trudy said, "So?"

"When two people come together in marriage, they are making a statement to the world," Pastor Hickey said.

"Her water broke," Bert replied. Trudy's mouth

dropped open. "Mae wants to stay right there until we're all done."

Trudy's eyes shot to her sister's. Mae wore a mortified look. Trudy felt the urge to laugh. Her shoulders began to shake. Bert's eyes warned her to be good. His face deepened in redness. Yet Pastor Hickey kept going.

Trudy tried to concentrate on Bert's face during the vows. But her mind kept wandering to her uncomfortable wet sister behind the cello.

Bert seemed to have put the whole thing out of his head. He made his promises to her effortlessly as he gazed deep into her eyes. Trudy's smile widened.

"I, Albert Charles Biddle, do solemnly vow . . ." He squeezed her hand as he went on. Then it was Trudy's turn.

"I, Trudy Elaine Ploog . . ." As she spoke, the importance of each word pressed upon her. She believed every syllable, and she knew that these words would change her life in more ways than she could comprehend. Yet she felt no fear for what they would bring, because she knew that Bert stood on the other side of those promises. She trusted him with her very life.

Finally the announcement came. "Ladies and gentlemen, I present to you Mr. and Mrs. Albert Charles Biddle." The audience applauded, and a few of Bert's hockey buddies whooped and whistled from the back row.

Trudy and Bert kissed as real married people.

• • •

Peter watched Mae throughout the ceremony. She wore a pleasant enough smile, but he wasn't fooled. She was scared, and, worse, the stubborn girl was so worried about ruining her sister's big day that she wouldn't even allow him to take her straight to the hospital. He fidgeted with his sleeve, which was just a little too long. His gaze wandered to Mae again. She smiled at him nervously. He glanced down at his watch. Only fifteen minutes since her water had broken, yet it seemed forever.

When Bert and Trudy finally descended the steps as man and wife and the organ boldly played "How Do You Solve a Problem Like Maria?" Peter returned to Mae's side.

"Are you having contractions?" he said.

Mae nodded. "Just three, though." Her voice was tense, frightened.

"In fifteen minutes? That's a lot. Let's get you to the hospital." Peter glanced around for a quick escape route. Some way that wouldn't take them through the masses. The door to Pastor Hickey's office at the front was clear. The other groomsmen and bridesmaids made their exit with glances over their shoulders. Peter waved them on, then reached for Mae's hand to help her stand. She rose slowly, then took a deep breath.

"What is it?"

"I'm having another contraction." They waited for it to pass.

"Let's walk," Mae whispered through clenched teeth.

"That's the fourth in sixteen minutes," Peter said.

Mae nodded. The ushers came up to dismiss the guests, moving row by row.

"Take it slow," Peter reassured. Mae breathed in and out. Her hand rested on her belly. Peter put an arm around her back, but Mae quickly pushed it away.

"I'm all wet," she explained. "I'm nervous, Peter. They're every four minutes."

Peter smiled. "We're going to have a baby today." He squeezed her hand. "Can you feel him moving?"

Catherine was there then. "What's going on?" she said.

"My water broke," Mae said.

Catherine looked concerned. "Do you need me to come along?" She placed a hand on Mae's arm. Peter had never seen this much affection from the woman. He knew it would warm Mae.

"No. Stay here with Trudy. Tell her I'm sorry about wrecking her wedding!" Mae said.

"You haven't wrecked anything. You're having a baby. She'll understand." Catherine laughed. "I really think I should come with you."

"It could be hours before the baby comes. Trudy needs you now. We'll call and keep you updated, okay? You go enjoy the reception. Dance a dance for me." Her eyes met Peter's.

"Okay." Catherine turned to Peter. "Take care of her?"

"Do you need to ask?"

Mae and Peter opened the door to the parking lot and moved quickly to the Jeep. Peter reached for the thick terry towel they kept under the backseat of the Jeep for just such a scenario and placed it on the passenger's seat before Mae climbed in. He sighed, anxiety rising.

Mae touched his hand. "The baby's fine. He's doing somersaults in there, but it hurts!"

Peter reached for his cell phone and dialed the hospital as he turned the key in the ignition. "Hello. This is Peter Morgan. My wife's water broke, and I'm bringing her in. Dr. Mielke. Yes. She seems fine." His gaze traveled to Mae. "She's just fine."

Trudy kept watching for Mae at the reception but was soon distracted by the crowd of well-wishers. Finally Catherine appeared. "Mae and Peter left for the hospital," she told them. Bert leaned close to hear the news.

"So she's going to miss the whole reception?" Trudy said.

"I'm afraid so. But she said to enjoy ourselves, and they'd call with any news."

Trudy moaned. "It won't be the same without Maeflower." Catherine patted her shoulder.

Trudy worried about her little sister. Was she afraid of losing another baby? Or had that memory flitted away with this new hope? She leaned in to Bert, and he kissed the top of her head.

"We'll go to the hospital as soon as we hear, okay?" Bert said.

She loved him all the more for saying it. Then she realized—this was her husband! Trudy raised herself up on her high heels and kissed him firmly. The crowd cheered.

"You're ready to push," the swarthy nurse with a faint mustache said as she checked the blood pressure cuff on Mae's arm.

"On the next contraction, give it a try," Dr. Mielke said from his spot at the foot of the bed. Mae kept her eyes on him because she found herself irked at the nurse, who wouldn't stop fidgeting with Mae's medical equipment. First the heart monitor kept slipping out of position on the roundness of her midsection; then she readjusted the blood pressure cuff; then the woman jangled the instruments noisily.

"It's going to start soon," she announced before the pain even began. Mae imagined giving the woman a hard pinch on the nose. The contraction began then. Her abdomen grew hard. Mae bore down, and an intense heat came over her.

"Push," Peter murmured near her ear. "You're doing great. This will be over before you know it, and you'll be holding our baby."

"Shh," Mae scolded. She needed to concentrate on the pain. He held her hand. Mae squeezed until Peter finally pulled his fingers away. She felt the baby shift down. Then the automatic blood pressure cuff tightened. Its hum filled the air. In one swift motion, Mae tore the Velcro fastener apart and flung the cuff away.

"You're not supposed to—," the nurse sputtered. Mae dared her with a stare to say another word.

The next contraction seemed to last forever. And it was so intense Mae felt as though the blood vessels in her eyes were popping as she pushed.

"You're doing great." Peter wiped her forehead with a white bath towel once the contraction finally ended. She gazed into his tender face.

"I don't feel like I'm doing great," she said. She touched her cheeks. "My nose is tingling."

"You might be hyperventilating. Just breathe easy." He tucked her hair behind an ear. The pain swelled again, less than a minute since the prior contraction. Mae grabbed Peter's hand again and pushed with all her might. She felt her face grow red with the effort, but she didn't care. This was going to hurt, and there was no way around that fact. With that realization, she pushed harder yet.

"I can see the top of the head," Dr. Mielke said. Those words gave her courage to keep going. The fiery heat intensified, a searing pain. And then the baby was out. Instant relief spread through her. It was over. Just like that.

A cry filled the room. "It's a boy," Dr. Mielke said. "And he looks great."

Tears filled Mae's eyes.

She wanted to memorize this moment, to take in

everything so she could tell her son about it as he grew—the joy at his arrival, how amazingly beautiful he was, the pride in Peter's eyes. The room seemed so bright, as if it, too, glowed with the good news.

The doctor held up the red-faced baby boy, who squalled loudly. The nurse offered a smile of congratulations. She toweled the baby off and wrapped him in a fresh blanket. Mae wondered what she had found so irritating about the woman just a few short moments before. The nurse laid the crying babe on Mae's chest. His tiny body was warm and squirmy.

"Hey, little one," Mae said. "I'm your mommy." His eyes were dark, and the instant he heard his mother's voice, he calmed and gazed at her. Mae stroked his velvet hair and the soft skin of his neck and back. Peter was there too. When Mae glanced up at him, she saw tears in his eyes. "You have a son, Mr. Morgan," Mae said.

The expression on Peter's face reflected her own feelings of that moment—pure rapture. They were no longer bound by the confines of time and place on a temporary earth. In that moment, they had simply become a mother and a father and a son.

And it was good.

fifteen

When the last of the guests drove off, Trudy and Bert along with Catherine and Paul ducked into their cars and made a beeline for the hospital. The bride and groom still wore wedding attire. Rice from old-fashioned guests and birdseed from the "green" party-goers clung to hair and lace. It was ten o'clock by the time they arrived, exhausted and yet floating on a supernatural energy source.

High heels clicked on the tiled floor as they looked for Mae's room. All was quiet in the maternity ward.

"Which room did Mae say, Mom?"

"Room 102," Catherine replied.

Bert asked a passing nurse for directions. She pointed two doors down and said, "We've only got one baby, so that has to be it."

They opened the door quietly. Mae's and Peter's heads were bent over the sleeping cherub Mae held, a tiny fist tucked under his chin. Trudy was struck by the solemnity of the moment, the way her sister glowed with joy even though she looked tired. She felt a stab of envy. She reached for Bert's hand as Mae lifted her face in a smile.

"Hey," Trudy said. She and Bert stood alongside the bed.

"It's so late. Is it okay that we're here?" Paul said.

"There isn't anyone else in the whole wing," Mae said. "No need to worry."

Trudy sat on the edge of the bed. She leaned in to see her new nephew. "He's perfect," she whispered.

"A new baby and a new brother-in-law all in one day," Mae said. "Are you mad at me for wrecking your wedding?"

"Are you kidding?" Trudy said. "It will make for a great story. Besides, how could I be mad about something as beautiful as he is?"

Peter smiled at Bert. "Has it sunk in yet? I mean that you're actually married to Pippi here?"

Bert grinned. "No. But we'll make that right as soon as possible."

Trudy feigned shock. "What does he mean by that, I wonder!"

"Hand my grandson over." Catherine leaned her petite frame past Trudy with arms out to take the baby. Mae gently deposited him in his grandmother's arms. Pure adoration filled Catherine's gaze. Trudy wondered if she'd looked at Mae and her that way when they were born. Catherine lightly stroked his cheek, and the infant turned his head as if to suck. His eyes remained closed in sleep. "What are you going to name him?" Catherine said without lifting her eyes.

Mae looked to Peter before answering, "Christopher David, after Peter's dad."

"He looks like you, Mae," Catherine said, "with that shock of black hair and the dimples in his cheek. You looked like a little Hispanic baby when you were born."

"Do I get a turn?" Trudy complained. "It is my wedding day!"

"After Grandma is all done," Catherine said with a smile. "And I'm not done yet."

"She's paying me back for the whole polka-band thing," Trudy said in a stage whisper.

The baby squirmed, and everyone watched. When he settled again, they exchanged dopey grins. Finally Catherine kissed his forehead and turned to Trudy. "Okay. It's your turn."

Trudy lifted her hands to take him.

"No, I mean it's your turn to have a baby. Mae's done her part."

"I just got married! Would you give a girl a break?"

Catherine carefully laid Christopher in his aunt's arms. He felt warm and oh so tiny. His little lips puckered as if he were about to kiss her. Trudy touched his silky hair.

Paul moved next to the bed and leaned over to gaze at the baby. He said to Mae, "Did your water break during the song or after?"

Mae blushed. "During. That odd-sounding glissando wasn't written into the music!"

"The expression on your face was priceless!" Trudy said. "It's all on the videotape, I'm sure. We'll be sure to get you a copy for Christopher David here." She snugged the blanket around his body. "Can we bring him on our honeymoon?" she said to Bert.

"His ma might not like that idea," Bert said. He touched Christopher's shoulder.

"It's getting late." Peter pointed to his watch. "And this lady has had a very long day."

"We all have," Trudy agreed. She handed the baby back to Mae.

"Maybe we could continue this tomorrow?" Catherine said.

Mae nodded.

"We'll be off to *wherever* it is we're going on our honeymoon," Trudy said with a pointed look at Bert. "So I guess this is good-bye for us."

The visitors stood. Trudy kissed her baby sister on the forehead. "You did real good, Maeflower."

Mae's eyes welled. "I love you, Trudes. Congratulations to you, too, Mrs. Biddle."

"That's going to take some getting used to, at least without envisioning Lillian every time I hear it!"

Next came Catherine. She held Mae's free hand and smiled down at her. "I love you." They were words that came on the rarest occasions. Mae smiled tenderly.

Tears flowed then. Tears of healing, forgiveness. Tears for a new start.

Once everyone had gone and the stillness of the corridor resumed, Mae lay back. The baby was asleep, propped on his side in the clear plastic bassinet alongside her bed. Peter had gone home to get some rest and milk the cows in the morning.

Mae was exhausted beyond words, and yet she was content. After all her worry and fear, her baby was here. He was a living, breathing person, someone she had yet to know really. She was eager to begin that journey of discovering who her son was, what his qualities were, who he would become.

Peace of a new kind filled her with fullness, meaning, purpose. She prayed it would never disappear.

Because Christopher David had made his appearance so late in the day, Mae and Peter decided to take him to meet his great-grandmother right after her physical therapy session the next morning. And because the nursing home was a separate wing of the Lake Emily Hospital, Virginia was only a short wheelchair ride away. Mae showered and dressed in ritual fashion. She felt rested, although she was still sore. Dr. Mielke said he'd rarely seen a delivery go so effortlessly. Definitely the words of a man.

Peter arrived at nine, looking freshly showered and invigorated. He pushed an empty wheelchair.

"I can walk," Mae said.

Peter shook his head. "No reason to when pampering is available. Grandma's on the other side of the hospital, so sit!"

Mae kissed her husband's cheek. The baby wriggled in his bed. "He wants to go see Grandma," Peter said. Mae eased into the wheelchair, and Peter placed Christopher in her arms and backed the chair into the hallway.

Virginia stared at tiny Christopher David Morgan. His pink face puckered as his lips searched for his clenched fist. "What do you think, Grandma?" Peter said.

"He's beautiful," she murmured. She longed to hold him, but the therapy session had taken the strength from her hands. She had wondered if she'd live to see this child, and now that he was here she felt . . . humbled. A tear slipped down her cheek, then another.

"Are you okay?" Peter squatted next to Virginia's chair.

Virginia nodded. "He's just . . . so wonderful."

Peter lifted the baby into her lap. "I'll drop him," she protested.

"He's just fine, Grandma," Peter said. Christopher smacked contentedly. "See." Wide dark eyes ringed in thick lashes stared up at her. Deep dimples cut parentheses in his cheeks.

"I'm glad I stayed around to see this day."

"You're going to live to see many more days, Grandma. And many more great-grandchildren." She wanted to believe him. Peter had good intentions, but he was young and invincible. Truth was, he couldn't promise her even a single breath.

David Morgan tapped the baton to get the orchestra's attention. Today's rehearsals had run longer than usual, but he was determined to perfect Robert Schumann's "The Merry Farmer" from his *Album for the Young*.

"Let's pick it up at measure fifteen. And remember, allegro animato—keep it light and animated." David lifted the baton and gave the orchestra a count of four. His arthritis was acting up again, which didn't help his mood. The violins began their dance, but instead of light-footed ballerinas, they gave the impression of lumbering rhinos. Four measures later David tapped the baton again. The music petered off. "Violas, you're missing that eighth rest in measure seventeen. That's why you're coming in early there. Let's do it again; this time let's be light, airy. This is a fun piece. One, two, three, four . . ."

Two hours later he dismissed the musicians with reminders to work on the problem sections before the next rehearsal.

"David."

Philip Randall made his way to David on center stage while the remaining musicians filtered out.

David lifted his gaze to his boss, a slight man with thin lips and piercing blue eyes, as he gathered his music and put it into his leather briefcase. He gave a quick nod.

"Sounds like you're making progress with the new musicians. I wanted to touch base before the next board meeting. With ticket sales down, we need to put our heads together for some possible fund-raisers, as you know. I hope you don't mind, but I made an appointment for you to meet with Bob Tungren. He's president of the Kaisler Foundation. They've been looking for a few good charities . . . Well, you know the rundown."

David nodded. He'd learned "the rundown" all too well in the last year. Instead of focusing on his craft, he'd been constantly pushed into such blind dates, begging for money for the orchestra. Philip handed him a slip with all the details for this latest rendezvous. David slid it into the front pocket of his briefcase and turned to go.

"David," Philip said to his back. David turned. "We don't have a problem here, do we?" The thin lips formed a line.

"No sir," David said. "No problem at all."

By the time he got back to his sparsely furnished apartment, David was spent. He tossed his keys into the bowl on the hall table and kicked off his black dress shoes. He wandered into the kitchen. The refrigerator was mostly empty except for a pitcher of orange juice. He poured himself a glass, then pulled a frozen single-serving lasagna from the freezer and turned the oven to 350 degrees.

His thoughts turned to Lake Emily. Home. How was his mother doing? He hadn't heard anything in a long while, and he often didn't think of calling until it was too late in the evening.

The phone rang. David jumped, then answered it. "Hello, this is David Morgan."

"Hey, Dad, it's Peter. I've been trying to get ahold of you all day, but—"

"I left my cell phone at home this morning," David explained. He glanced at the phone that still sat in its charger.

"I have some news for you."

David's heart skipped. "It's not Ma—"

"Oh no. It's good news, Dad."

"Mae had the baby!" David clapped a hand across his chest.

"It's a boy. Christopher David Morgan, seven pounds, eight ounces, twenty-two inches long."

David's eyes stung with sudden tears.

"He's beautiful, Dad, and healthy. He was born late last night. Mae did great."

"I can't tell you how happy I am to hear that. Christopher David, huh?" David felt that pang again. "Has Ma seen him?"

"We took him down this morning. She's thrilled."

"I wish I could come."

"When do you think you could get away?" Peter's voice sounded hopeful.

"I'm sorry, Peter. The orchestra is leaving day after tomorrow for a week in Austria and another week in Switzerland. I wish I could get away."

The phone line hummed.

"I'm sorry, Peter."

"Sure," Peter mumbled. "I understand. We'll send pictures."

David knew what Peter wanted to say. They were the very words he said to himself as he wandered his lonely apartment lately, words that accused him for his poor choices.

He wanted nothing more than to make the right choice.

And yet he was powerless to comply.

Peter felt as if the joy had been gut-punched out of

him. His dad had become the same self-consumed musician Peter had resented as a child. They'd made so much progress since Peter and Mae had moved to the farm. He'd felt at peace with his father's decision to move. He even felt as though he'd come to terms with his lonely childhood. But music invariably brought these choices to the fore, as if they were caught in an episode of *Twilight Zone*, taking the same test day after day and always choosing incorrectly. Grandma and Grandpa had excused his father's absences, but they were part of nurturing the dream. They encouraged David to pursue music above all else. Peter played no part in it. He was simply the second choice, always second.

He walked the hospital corridor toward Mae's room. He wouldn't do that to his own son. He wouldn't make Christopher David feel like a second choice. Not ever.

sixteen

The sun beamed its happy smile, warming the earth and promising better days. The fields were finally dry enough to get machinery in and out without needing a tow. Trudy knew Bert had misgivings about being gone when he should be finishing the planting, but Bert's dad had promised to plant in his stead and look after the dairy herd, so the newlyweds headed out for a three-day honeymoon.

Bert gave no clue about where they were going, only

a mysterious lift of the eyebrow as he pointed the pickup north.

"We're going to the Cities," Trudy guessed.

Bert shook his head.

"Mall of America?"

"Nope."

"Hinckley? Aitkin? Hill City?"

Bert grinned mischievously. He was enjoying this entirely too much. "I'll tickle it out of you," Trudy threatened.

"Like last night?" Bert said. Trudy blushed with embarrassment.

Who could have thought that a bashful farmer could be so gentle yet so . . . satisfying? Trudy inhaled a contented breath and gazed out the side window as they passed the damp fields. One overeager John Deere tractor, up to its axles in mud, sat as testimony to the soggy season's perils. Another tractor was pulling it free. "Now, that wasn't too smart," Bert observed. "Not that I haven't done the same thing myself."

"You're going to be really behind this year, aren't you?"

"No more behind than anyone else. But I don't want to think about it today. I'm on my honeymoon."

Trudy's gaze turned to his strong profile. She removed her hand from his and held her hand out, turning it from side to side so the diamond caught the light.

"It's going to take some getting used to, isn't it?" she said.

"Sure is, Mrs. Biddle."

"Oh, don't call me that. It makes me think of your mother."

Bert laughed. "Still, it's your name now."

Trudy scooted closer to him on the seat and rested her head on Bert's shoulder. "Mmm," she murmured. "I can see why you insisted on bringing the truck. The gearshift in the Pacer would've gotten in our way."

It was Bert's turn to blush.

They stopped for lunch at a truck stop in Hinckley, site of the great fire of 1894. Framed newspaper accounts of the event hung on the restaurant's dark-paneled walls. Bert and Trudy waited as their eyes adjusted to the dim interior. Then a matronly woman with high hair led them to a booth in one of several rows of booths. The waitresses buzzed up the aisles like speedboats in a marina. The hostess handed out menus, then left to escort the next guests. Trudy leaned forward and whispered to Bert, "Do you think she can tell that we're newlyweds?"

Bert glanced at the woman. "How can she not? We're smiling like goons!"

"I feel like everyone's staring." Trudy reached for his left hand and toyed with the gold band on his ring finger.

"You ready to order?" A twentyish waitress with pale pink lip gloss and baby blue eye shadow appeared from nowhere. Realizing she hadn't looked at the menu yet, Trudy picked it up. She was *hungry*.

"What's the special?" Bert said.

"Ham with scalloped potatoes for $5.95. And the soup is beef barley."

Bert looked to Trudy for her opinion. She nodded, and he said, "We'll take two of those."

"Which—the special or the soup?"

"The special."

"Okey-doke." She jotted it down, clicked her pen closed, and shoved it onto her pad before motoring back up her lane.

"Oh yeah," Bert said to Trudy. "She could tell we're newlyweds, all right."

Trudy tapped his hand. "I've never seen your sarcastic side before, Mr. Biddle."

"There's a lot about me yet to discover, Mrs. Biddle."

Mae put the last of her clothes into the overnight bag and straightened to peruse the hospital room. Midmorning sunlight streamed through the miniblinds, creating stripes on the white tile floor. Christopher looked spiffy in a blue layette. His tiny mouth drew his fist like a magnet, and he sucked away.

"That's it?" Mae said to Peter, who stood over the baby, mesmerized. "We just take him home?"

"The nurse said we're free to go." He reached into the bassinet and lifted Christopher to his shoulder.

"But it doesn't seem right. Shouldn't we have to *know* something before we're given such a huge responsibility? We should at least have to sign some paperwork, a contract stating that we'll love him."

Peter laughed. He turned to gaze at his wife.

"Well, it *doesn't* seem . . . right, does it? How do we know we'll be any good as parents? I have no clue what I'm doing. He's so dependent on us. What if I forget to feed him or something?"

"You'll be just fine. I promise. We have friends and family to give us lots of advice, and Christopher will let us know if he's hungry." The tension on Mae's face eased.

The nurse came in with a wheelchair to take Mae and the baby to the car. "Hospital policy," she said. "You'll need your energy once you get the baby home." Mae gave Peter another worried look, then she climbed in the chair, and they wheeled toward the entrance, where Peter had parked the Jeep. Everyone they passed—nurses, doctors, orderlies, fellow patients—offered grins and wistful glances. Peter hadn't felt so proud in his whole life. He was a father. He'd never imagined he could feel such powerful emotions for a tiny child after a mere day and a half, and yet the allegiance in his heart was unparalleled. The love in his heart for Mae had multiplied as well, although how that could be possible he didn't know. They'd been together through so much, not just the physical pain of childbirth and the long pregnancy before that, but through the worries about the farm and the grief of losing baby Laura. Mae had been there to comfort and encourage.

They reached the car, and Peter opened the door. Mae secured the baby in his car seat.

"He seems too small for this seat to do much good," Mae said.

"He'll grow into it before you know it, and you'll be buying a bigger one," the nurse said knowingly. She handed Mae the packet of pamphlets they'd reviewed together—tips for breast-feeding and bathing and symptoms of problems to watch for. "The nurse's help-line number is right there." She pointed to a pink sheet of paper on the top. "Don't hesitate to call if you have any concerns." Mae's gaze moved to Peter, and he squeezed her arm. The nurse said farewell, and Peter and Mae and Christopher started toward home.

"It's a perfect day for a homecoming," Peter said when the warm June sunshine spilled across the front seat. Mae turned her head to check on little Christopher. His eyes were closed in contented rest.

"He's fine," Peter said. He reached for Mae's hand. "Relax. I have a surprise for you at home."

"What kind of surprise?"

"A nice one."

They enjoyed the quiet as Highway 36 spread out before them. The fields were no longer the flooded plains of May. With two solid weeks of sunshine and a steady breeze to whisk moisture away, they'd started planting May 15. It was a month later than their usual start date, but Peter was glad to be planting at all.

"You're going to want to get back into the fields, aren't you?"

"I'm dreading it now. I'd rather be home with you and Christopher."

Mae squeezed his hand. "Do you think we'll be able to bring Grandma home soon?" Mae asked.

Peter shook his head. "You're still recovering, and from what I hear, we won't be getting much sleep in the coming weeks."

"I miss her."

"I want Grandma home too, but we need to be realistic about what you can and can't handle. It's still too much, and Grandma isn't exactly mobile yet."

Mae sighed. "It's not the same," she said. "I've been looking forward to having her with me during this time. I wanted to share it with her, have her words of wisdom, and now—"

"Give it time. She'll be back. We've got to believe that."

Peter pulled into the driveway. Mae noticed her mother's car immediately. She looked at Peter. "This is the surprise?"

He nodded. "Are you okay with it?"

Mae's lips twisted as if she wasn't completely sure.

"She really wants to be here for you and the baby."

"Really?" Hope bubbled beneath her small voice.

"Really. Maybe this is the fresh start you've been praying for."

He had left. Just like that. As if Catherine and Trudy and Mae never existed, didn't matter to him at all. They were an afterthought. An unnecessary extension of him.

Catherine stared out her St. Paul apartment window at seven-year-old Trudy, who was playing on the inner courtyard's swing set. She'd have to tell Trudy that her dad wasn't coming back, that they'd have to find a way to live on their own. Mae was too little to understand. Catherine drew in a thick, shuddering breath. This wasn't right, wasn't fair to them. The tears spilled from her reddened eyes again.

How could she possibly raise these girls on her own? She had no skills to fall back on. She'd married straight out of high school. Michael had been the breadwinner. She was supposed to be the mother.

She heard the apartment door open and close. "Trudy," she called, "I need you to come into the kitchen." Two-year-old Mae, awakened from her nap, toddled down the hall behind her sister, wiping sleepy eyes.

"Are you hungry?" Catherine said to them both. She picked up Mae, gave her a kiss on the forehead, and held her tight, drawing hope from the innocent child. It didn't last beyond the hug. She tucked Mae into her padded highchair.

"Can I have chips?" Trudy said. She pulled out a

chair at the table and climbed up.

Catherine opened the cupboards. There wasn't much to choose from. A jar of Wyler's chicken-bouillon cubes, flour, a little sugar, some spaghetti noodles, and a box of Cheerios. She'd have to go shopping. Not that she had any money. She reached for the Cheerios and pulled down two bowls. She handed a bowl of dry cereal to each of her daughters, then took a chair at the table with Trudy.

"I have something to tell you," Catherine began.

"Where's Daddy?" Trudy said, looking around.

Catherine swallowed. She would not break down. She wouldn't be able to get through this if she did.

"That's kind of what I need to talk to you about. Daddy decided to go live somewhere else. He's not going to live with us anymore."

The bewildered look on Trudy's face broke Catherine's heart. "What do you mean? Daddy's coming back. Daddy has to come back!"

Catherine shook her head. "No, honey. He isn't."

"But he loves us. When you love someone, you don't go away."

"I know," Catherine said. She touched the top of her daughter's fiery red hair. "I know."

atherine wore one of Mae's gingham aprons. The mouth-watering smell of spaghetti and meatballs filled the kitchen. She cooed over her grandson while Peter brought in the bags. She tugged the blanket away from his sleeping face.

"Look at him," she breathed. Her eyes met Mae's. An understanding only mothers could share passed between them; in it was wrapped a deep connection to this tiny person, deeper than any relationship Mae had ever known.

"I thought you'd like a home-cooked meal," Catherine whispered with a smile.

"Mmm. My favorite, too. You always did make the best spaghetti and meatballs."

"I brought Herschlebs chocolate-peanut-butter-cup ice cream, too. I know how much you like that."

"Thank you," Mae mouthed. Catherine's gaze returned to Christopher in her arms.

"It's the least I could do."

"Virginia, what's wrong?" Anna pointed to Virginia's untouched plate of food.

"I'm not hungry." Virginia rubbed her left hand, trying to massage the numbness from it.

"You need to eat."

Virginia shrugged. "I'm eating just fine."

Anna stared at her long and hard. Virginia felt her

gaze but didn't lift her eyes to the girl. She didn't want to see the judgment there. Finally Anna said in a soft tone, "You need to take care of yourself, Virginia. We can't do this for you. You want to go home soon, don't you?"

"Of course I do."

"That new great-grandbaby needs you too, you know."

Really? Mae and Peter and Christopher would go on living with or without her. What did it matter if she was in a nursing home? What did it matter if she got better or if she didn't? It wasn't as if her children had rallied to her side.

Anna pushed the wheelchair alongside the bed. "Getting out of this stuffy room will do you a world of good. Let's head to PT. Get those legs pumping."

"I don't feel like it." Virginia was tired of trying, of working so hard to regain her mobility and making such little progress.

"I know you don't, but you have to do it anyway. I'll be there every minute, Virginia, and if you get too tired, I promise to bring you right back to your room, okay?"

Virginia sighed. She scooted to the edge of the bed and put an arm around Anna's shoulders. On the count of three, they moved together to reach the chair. It was the same every morning: A nurse came to get her dressed and to the toilet, and then she ate breakfast, and then she went to physical therapy with Anna. She despised the invasive, humiliating routine.

Once Anna positioned Virginia's feet on the footrests, she wheeled her down the hall toward the physical therapy room. Virginia stared, unseeing, ahead.

"Jessie and Steve came over again last weekend," Anna said. Virginia lifted her face with a puzzled expression. "Your friends? Remember I met them when they came to visit you? They were at church last month, so I invited them for lunch."

"How is she?" Virginia asked.

"Okay, I think. She comes over a lot, actually. Rides her bike to my place after school. She's a great kid. She asked about you," Anna said.

"H'm."

"Jessie's mom died a little over two years ago?" Anna probed.

"Yes. Died in a car accident."

"How horrible. That must've been so hard for them."

They reached the swinging door. Anna turned the wheelchair around and backed through.

Kathy met them, her dark hair swinging. "Good morning, Virginia. We're going to get you standing today." Virginia found her much too bright for this dreary place.

"Standing?" Virginia said. "I'm too weak—"

Anna held up a hand. "We'll do all the work for you, okay? You don't have to do more than you're comfortable with." She looked so annoyingly earnest. Virginia took a deep breath.

"Doesn't hurt to try, does it?" Anna said.

Virginia gazed into her eyes. She longed to have Anna's courage and conviction, yet her well had run dry. She bit back the tears that wanted to run and decided to at least put on a brave face. Anna buckled the transfer belt around Virginia's waist and helped her up while Kathy held the wheelchair in place in case they needed to lower her into it.

"Okay, Virginia," Anna said. "Shift your weight to your right leg first. Then, once you feel confident, we'll let you go."

Virginia took a deep breath. She closed her eyes and leaned slightly forward, then pushed up.

"You're getting there," Anna encouraged. Virginia was upright. A surge of pride swelled. She shifted to center but suddenly heaved backward. The therapists braced against the fall, but it was no use. Virginia plopped heavily into the chair, which scooted back slightly with the force.

Defeat fell on top of her.

Anna crouched by her side and made sure she hadn't been injured. "That's okay," Anna soothed. "It was just the first try. It will get easier with time."

"Take me back," Virginia murmured. "Just take me to my room." It was too much. Simply too much. Virginia was too old, too tired for new beginnings. At her age, she was ready for final endings.

Christopher's cradle looked somehow "right" at the foot of Mae and Peter's bed. It rocked slightly as the baby moved within it. Peter glanced at the clock—two in the morning. Mae shifted on her side of the bed. Within moments Christopher's tiny mew began, then grew to a full battle cry. Mae crawled out of bed, pulled her robe on, and stumbled to turn on the light beside the stuffed chair. Peter plumped his pillow and watched as Mae bent over the baby. Her long dark hair fell in a curtain. She tucked it behind her ears, then she tenderly lifted the newborn. She kissed his troubled brow and took him to the chair. His crying ceased for a moment only to renew its strength a few seconds later. His fingers splayed beside chubby cheeks, and he turned his head back and forth while his mouth opened in search of food.

Mae settled into the chair patiently, and soon the baby's cries ceased. Mae gazed down at him as if the two of them were the only people in the world. Her expression held utter contentment. Pure joy. It was the most beautiful thing Peter had ever seen.

e i g h t e e n

Bert unlocked the apartment door as Trudy watched from behind. It felt weird to have him place the key in the door that had been hers alone, but it was his place now too. Their honeymoon had been a glorious three days—kayaking along Lake Superior's rugged shores, exploring the quaint town of Bayfield, Wisconsin, and the Apostle Islands, watching Bert fish while she sat in the bow of a rowboat and sketched. Reading for the pure pleasure of it. Painting as the sun cast its colors across the shimmering waters on the far side of the lake. Drinking in the pleasures of married life, enjoying companionship, listening as Bert played bluegrass on his banjo.

"Shall I carry you across the threshold, Mrs. Biddle?" Bert drew her attention to the present. Trudy grinned and wrapped her arms around his neck. He lifted her effortlessly, like a bale of dry hay, and stepped across the room, then plopped her onto the couch in the small living room.

"Hey!" She protested the unceremonious deposit. Bert laughed and went back to the landing to retrieve their suitcases. "I guess the honeymoon's over!" Trudy hollered. Bert returned with the bags and gave her a grin. He set them down next to the piles of unopened boxes he'd brought over before the wedding and then wandered into the kitchen, where he opened cupboards in search of something.

"What are you looking for?"

"Something to eat. I'm starving after that long drive."

"I haven't gone shopping."

Bert poked his head back into the living room. "What do you mean?"

"I mean, we don't have any food. We've been gone for three days. Remember?"

Bert's expression said he couldn't comprehend her words. Trudy laughed. "I can see already I'm going to have to take shopping lessons from your ma!"

Bert turned red. "I'm just used to always having *something* to eat."

"I'll run to the grocery in a few minutes, okay? It's just down the street. See, there are advantages to living in town." She patted the seat next to her on the couch. Bert snuggled up. She pointed to the boxes of Bert's belongings that lined the entire wall of the small living room. "We'll have to figure out where to put everything. I want this to feel like your home too." She paused in thought. "You aren't going to want your hockey trophies up, are you?"

"That's nice!" Bert sputtered and inched away.

Trudy pulled him back. "I was just kidding. Of course I'll find a spot for your sports memorabilia."

Bert grinned. "You must love me." He kissed the end of her nose and said, "If you want to leave them in boxes, I don't care. I'd be happy to live with you in a paper sack."

"You're so sweet." She leaned her head against his shoulder. Bert's stomach growled.

"All right, all right already. We'll hit that grocery store, Jethro Bodine." Trudy grabbed a red silk purse with dragons stitched in an Asian style. The two headed downstairs, Bert in the lead.

He looked back at her. His strong face was so handsome. His expression was filled with the glow she felt. She wanted this feeling to last forever.

Once on the sidewalk, Bert pulled her close. She tucked her hand into his.

"What are you thinking?" she said.

"I don't know."

"Come on, tell."

"Well . . . I *should* get back into the swing of things."

"You mean work? You're thinking about work?"

Bert nodded.

"When?"

"Tonight?" Bert said.

"It's too soon. We're still on our honeymoon!"

"Dad's done so much already," Bert said. "It's bad enough he had to milk, but to expect him to be in the fields . . . There's no avoiding it. I have to go back sometime."

"But we haven't even been home one night. I had plans for you tonight." She pulled him close.

Bert blushed and cleared his throat. "Plowing can wait until tomorrow, I guess."

Trudy sighed. "I wish you never had to go back to work."

Peter was back in the trenches. Milking and feeding the cows from five to eight, a quick breakfast, then into the fields with a paper-sack lunch in hand, plowing and planting until supper. Another milking session followed, as did more field work, until it was time to come home for bed. The baby had been home all of one full day. Mae knew she wouldn't see Peter for weeks other than on his way to bed or as he passed through to stuff a meal into his mouth. He was weeks behind already. He'd be living in his tractor and

136

rushing through milkings until exhaustion overcame him. He'd already lost too much of the season to plant peas.

Mae knew he worried about that and that he missed Christopher and her. But farming was the life they'd chosen, and his absence during the summer was its price. They needed the income, and a poor crop would be worse than no crop in lost time and resources. At least he could plant beans and have one good harvest, as long as the rains didn't return.

Christopher gave a cry. Mae heard it through the baby monitor as she washed breakfast dishes in the kitchen. She dried her hands to go get him when her mother's voice came over the speaker.

"Hey, little wonder," Catherine said. "It's your grandma." The baby's cries melted. Mae's heart warmed. These past two days could only be considered a miracle. The tiny child had transformed Mae's mother, showing Mae a side she'd never seen. Mae wondered what other secrets her mother kept.

A few moments later Catherine appeared at the head of the stairs, carrying Christopher at her shoulder.

"Look who's finally up from his nap. He has a fresh diaper, but I think he wants his mama. There's only so much Grandma can do."

Mae glanced at the wall clock. "It's been two and a half hours since he last ate. He's a regular timer."

"You were the same way—still are. Predictable, steady Mae. Trudy, on the other hand, never held to any kind of a schedule."

"You expected her to?"

Catherine chuckled and handed the baby to Mae, who took him to the sun-dappled living room. Catherine settled onto the couch across from her.

"How is Paul faring without you at home?"

"He's okay. At least until the TV dinners run out."

"You've never bought a TV dinner in your life, Mom!"

"Oh, but Paul likes them. I think they bring back his bachelor days." Catherine sat back, her arms crossed over her chest. She sighed contentedly. "I probably should head home next weekend, though. I'm enjoying this time so much with Christopher . . . and with you." Mae ran a finger along her son's fine dark hair as he nursed. The baby grasped her pinkie and held on firmly. "You've got this covered just fine," Catherine said softly. Mae lifted her eyes to her mother's. Catherine offered no more words, but Mae knew it was her mother's way of reaching out, of saying she was proud of her. A lump stuck in Mae's throat. She trained her gaze on her son.

"It's been good having you here," Mae said.

When Anna came to get Virginia for physical therapy, she was reading her Bible—something she hadn't done much since the stroke. God was elusive lately, hiding behind bushes. She longed for the closeness she shared with him before the stroke.

"What are you reading?" Anna said.

Virginia lifted her gaze. "The book of Job. I have

renewed respect for that man."

Anna gazed at the open book and lightly touched Virginia's back. "Because he never turned his back on God?"

"Sure, that. But also because he wasn't in denial about how awful his situation was."

"Are we making comparisons?" Anna moved to the chair alongside Virginia's bed.

Virginia absently rubbed her left hand. "It's such a roller coaster," she admitted. "I get tired of that. One day I'm encouraged, the next, well . . . I was never one to feel sorry for myself before. Oh, a little but not like lately." She sighed.

"We all have those days, don't you think?"

"I'm tired of being in a wheelchair."

"We can work on that."

There they were again—meaningless platitudes. Virginia glanced at the girl. She couldn't understand what Virginia felt. She'd probably never had a dark day in her short life. Frustration boiled. She snapped the Bible shut. "I'm tired of working," Virginia said. "I'm tired of feeling alone even though I'm surrounded by people. I'm tired of missing my husband. I'm just tired. I'm supposed to put on a Pollyanna smile and pretend to be dandy. But I'm *not* dandy. I just want to die. I want to go be with Roy once and for all!"

A small knock sounded on the door. "Go away!" she growled and lay back against her pillows. "Everyone just leave me be!"

139

She turned her head away from Anna and let the Bible fall to the floor.

Jessie spent all week working up her courage to go see Virginia. She missed the older woman desperately, and yet the strange smells and odd-looking residents at the nursing home scared her. They stared from their wheelchairs and drooled or said weird things to her.

Her dad had said Virginia needed her, that a real friend would go to visit anyway.

So, after he left for work, Jessie got on her ten-speed and rode to the tan brick nursing home. The June air was muggy and hot already this morning. Jessie put the kickstand down and took a deep breath. She could see people inside the wide glass doors of the nursing home. They walked hunched over in hospital gowns, shuffling at a snail's pace. Their cardigan sweaters drooped from their shoulders. Some sat in wheelchairs.

Her dad's words echoed. She took a deep breath and went inside. A nurse asked if she needed help, but Jessie shook her head and made her way to Virginia's door.

Someone was shouting inside. It sounded like Virginia. Jessie timidly knocked.

A moment later Virginia's voice echoed, "Go away! Everyone just leave me be!"

Jessie stood stunned in the bright hall, her feet glued to the floor. Virginia didn't want to see her. Her father was wrong. She turned to leave. Faces of deranged old people stared, crowded in on her. Her pace quickened.

140

And she began to run. Tears streaked her cheeks. She turned the corner and flung the doors wide.

Jessie clutched her arms around herself, and the tears fell full force then.

Virginia didn't need her. Jessie swiped the tears away with the back of her hand. Longing for her mother's comforting arms rose and with it the image of Anna.

n i n e t e e n

The curtains in Virginia's room were drawn. The television was dark, silent. Mae didn't see Virginia there, so she decided to head toward the physical therapy room. But as Mae turned, the sound of Virginia's heavy breathing pulled her back. She studied the dark room. Then she saw her. Virginia sat in a corner chair that faced the rumpled bed. Her head was down as if she were sleeping, but her eyes stared straight ahead.

"Virginia?" Mae said. Virginia's eyes lifted, bearing mournful sadness. "What's wrong?"

Virginia waved a hand in the air. "I'm all right. A little tired is all." But Mae knew she was lying. "Where's the baby?" Virginia asked.

"Trudy has him." Mae crossed to the window and opened the curtains. Bright light flooded the room.

Virginia squinted. "Why would you do that? It hurts my eyes."

"It's more cheerful, don't you think?" Mae sat on the

bed and inspected Virginia's sallow face. She reached across the span that separated them and grasped Virginia's wrinkled hand. "Are you feeling down?" The older woman's lips faked a smile. "Have you had many visitors?"

Virginia nodded. "More than I care for." She pulled her hand free of Mae's and drew the blanket on her legs up higher.

"What is it, then?"

"Why do you keep asking that? I'm fine." Mae backed off uneasily. The cocoon around Virginia thickened, and this time Mae was powerless to break through.

After seeing Virginia, Mae went looking for Anna Eastman, who referred her to Dr. Mielke. The tall, white-haired doctor leaned forward in his office chair. His gaze held that kind, comforting quality Mae had so appreciated during her miscarriage.

"I'm glad you came by," Dr. Mielke said. "Virginia has become very withdrawn in the past few days. She protests going to physical therapy. She sits in her room with the shades drawn. She doesn't eat."

"What are you telling me? That she's depressed?"

The doctor nodded. "It's common for depression to set in after a stroke, but to be honest, I hadn't expected it of Virginia. She has a strong support system and a fairly optimistic prognosis. But if she just gives up—"

"What do you mean, if she gives up?"

Dr. Mielke leaned back now and crossed his arms over his chest. "Has she ever talked with you about death? I mean about wanting to die?"

"You're afraid she's suicidal?"

The doctor held up a hand. "It could be nothing. She made a comment to Miss Eastman, and frankly I'm concerned about her."

"So, what can we do?" Mae's pulse raced as she thought of Virginia being suicidal.

"Counseling, to start. I'll give your pastor a call, see if he can talk to her. It's Pastor Hickey at the United Methodist Church, right?"

Mae nodded.

"I'd also like to prescribe Wellbutrin; it's an antidepressant. Just temporarily, to get her past this rough spot."

"If you can get her to take it. She's reluctant to even take Tylenol."

Dr. Mielke pursed his lips. "We need to get her past this hurdle. Depression will only delay her recovery."

"Maybe she needs to come home now. I've had the baby. Maybe if she's back at the farm . . ."

He shook his head. "I wish I could say yes, but she's not ready to leave, at least not for good. An afternoon visit might be helpful, but I want her to be more mobile, able to walk, go to the bathroom by herself before she goes home. Not that you couldn't help her some. But we're just better equipped to handle such needs."

"A day visit—that would be okay?"

"Sure, as long as there's someone with a strong back to help her around."

"Maybe it'll perk her up. A whole afternoon around her great-grandson might do her worlds of good."

"In the meantime I'll see that she gets that medication."

t w e n t y

The milk machine's loud clatter forced Mae to shout so Peter could hear her. He bent beside a black-and-white Holstein, placing black rubber tubes on each teat. He straightened to face Mae. The cow swatted him with her tail, and Peter rested a hand on her rump. "I can't spare the time right now, honey. I wish I could, but—"

"This is your grandmother we're talking about, Peter. It's important! You didn't hear the doctor—"

"I know it's important, and I wish I could do it for her, but you know how this year is. Every minute out of the fields puts us that much closer to a failing season."

"Maybe I could bring her home for a visit on my own."

"You know you can't. How will you get her up the stairs into the house?" Peter bent to attend the next cow.

"Peter!" Mae said. Her face flushed with heat. Tears threatened. "How can you do this? After all your preaching to your dad about putting family first, how can you do the same thing to your grandmother?"

Peter straightened. His face reddened. "This isn't the same!"

Mae crossed her arms over her chest. "You could've fooled me." She turned and stormed from the dark barn.

The June sunlight warmed Mae's face as the tears fell. A blue jay darted to the bird feeder along the side lawn. He chattered angrily. Mae hugged her arms around herself. "I know how you feel," she whispered.

Mae went in through the mud room to splash water on her face before going inside. Christopher was bellowing loudly from his playpen in the living room, where Mae had laid him down for his nap.

"Mama's coming," Mae said. Her breasts felt full, so she knew he must be ravenous. When Christopher heard her voice, he started crying harder. The phone clanged in on the chorus.

Mae lifted her son, then went to answer the phone. Christopher's cries escalated. "Hang on," Mae shouted into the receiver. Then she settled into a chair in the living room and set the baby to her breast.

She cradled the cordless phone between her ear and shoulder. "Hello?"

"That was quite a welcome," Trudy said. "What's up?"

Mae longed to blurt out her frustration, but instead she said, "I'm sorry. I'm just . . ." Her words ended on a sigh.

"That good, huh?"

Mae tried to collect herself and put the argument behind her. She felt so alone and in need of some friendship since her best friend was being a pill.

"You want to come over? I could use the company."

"I'd love to. I've been married eleven days, and I'm tired of being a farm widow already!"

"Tell me about it." Mae didn't try to hide her sarcasm. She glanced toward her son, who placed a tiny clenched fist on her chest.

"How do you handle it?" Trudy went on. "We weren't back two minutes, and he was talking about getting in the fields!"

"I know."

"Am I ever going to see him again?"

"Wait till October or, more likely, November."

"You're a big comfort. Okay—your turn. And don't tell me it's nothing; I know your tones."

"I just came back from seeing Virginia. The doctor thinks she might be depressed, maybe even suicidal."

"Suicidal?" Trudy's voice rose.

"I'm scared. I don't know what to do."

"I'll be right over."

By the time Trudy arrived, Mae had calmed down considerably, although the question of what to do for Virginia still needed an answer. In the meantime, Mae decided, she would keep up her chores and trust that the solution would come to her. It had to, because she was fresh out of ideas.

Trudy's multicolored, Minnesota-themed AMC Pacer pulled into the gravel drive. Mae heard the car door slam and Scout's bark of greeting before her sister appeared through the back door.

"What's that? Trudy pointed to the cloth contraption, like a backpack with holes, that Mae wore across her chest.

"A Snugglie," Mae said. "I can carry the baby and still have my hands free. I need to feed the chickens." She lifted Christopher from his baby seat and gently tucked his arms and legs into their appointed slots.

"I could feed the chickens for you."

"No thanks. This is all part of me learning to adjust to motherhood."

Trudy crossed her arms over her chest and snorted.

"I can't very well call you every day to feed my chickens, can I?"

"Do what you like. Take him into that filthy chicken coop. Hey, dip him in mud while we're there."

Mae rolled her eyes. Why was Trudy being so ornery? It was true that her sister had an opinion on most every topic whether she was well informed or not, but it usually didn't grate on Mae so. Mae brushed it off, deciding her irritation was a remnant from her fight with Peter. Mae tightened the straps that secured Christopher in place and then patted his back. Dark eyes peered up at her, and she felt herself relax. Something about his wise face put everything into perspective.

"Ready?" Trudy asked.

Mae followed Trudy out the back screen door. The spring squealed in protest as it stretched, then the door slammed shut. They crossed the drive and went to the squat, white henhouse. Inside twin circles from the heat lamps' lights, the little birds cheeped in a comforting riff. Mae and Virginia had shared this experience every year since her move to the farm. The tears came then.

"Virginia will be okay," Trudy assured.

"I want to bring her home at least for a day visit, to cheer her up, you know? But Peter . . ."

"Let me guess—he's eating and breathing field work."

Mae nodded.

Trudy pulled her sister closer. "I'll help you bring her home for a visit. Between the two of us, we can manage."

"Do you think so?"

One of the chicks hopped up onto the feed tray and tilted its head at Trudy. "We'll be just fine."

Hope stopped the flow of Mae's tears.

Trudy smiled at Mae. "So, what do you know about shopping for groceries in bulk?"

The diesel engine of the John Deere tractor rumbled as Peter moved up and down the rows. It was June, and he was still planting. He should be finished by now. And the fields needed another application of fertilizer since the rains had washed away last fall's supply.

The sun lowered its face in the west. Peter hadn't bothered to go in for supper. He hadn't wanted to see Mae's accusing eyes. How could she say such a thing? Comparing him to his father.

Mae acted as though he had a choice in the matter. Didn't she understand that this was what a man did to care for his family? That they would lose the farm, everything they'd worked so hard for, if he didn't stay the course? It was more important now than ever that he succeed. He wanted to leave a legacy for Christopher. He wanted Christopher to have the choices he didn't have, a childhood without the fears he'd had as a boy.

He turned the tractor up the next row, and his own words to his father pricked him. *You're choosing your precious music over us again.* Then Mae's accusation. *After all your preaching to your dad about putting family first, how can you do the same thing to your grandmother?*

This was different. He hadn't abandoned his family. He was here with them, wasn't he? And he sure wasn't working this hard for his own good pleasure. He'd seized the opportunity his father had lost, all for the sake of the family that he loved. There was more at stake here.

Wasn't there?

ALAN HICKEY

Pastor Alan Hickey stared at his reflection in the full-length mirror. He adjusted his robe and stole. Why was he so nervous? It wasn't as if this role was new to him. He'd served the Methodist church in Fergus Falls four years and never once felt this way. His stomach rolled and then gave a growl. The last thing he needed was for the entire church to hear his belly rumbling. He took a sip of water from the glass he'd set on the church secretary's desk.

A knock sounded on the door. He motioned his wife, Arlene, in. The sound of organ music floated in with her.

"Are you okay?" she said.

He forced a smile. Arlene placed a hand on her hip and pierced him with her vivid green eyes. "Everyone's waiting for you to make your appearance. What's wrong?"

"I'm . . ." He sighed heavily. "Terrified to go out there!"

"Why? This is your home church. You grew up with these people."

"I know. That was why I wanted to take the pastorate here, but I just . . . People remember who I used to be."

"So? You're afraid they won't let you break out of that box? You're a grownup now, Alan. A mature man of God. If people think of you as a rebellious teenager, that's their problem. You'll just have to show them dif-

150

ferent. The good news is people already love you here. Love forgives." She offered a sweet smile and touched his cheek. Alan closed his eyes and allowed her words to penetrate deep.

"You're right," he said finally.

When he entered the sanctuary and took his seat at the front, Virginia Morgan caught his eye from her place in the front pew. She held her hymnal high as they sang "O the Deep, Deep Love of Jesus." Then she smiled at him with a smile that said she was proud of him, that he was part of the family.

He stepped to the podium. "Good morning, and welcome to the United Methodist Church of Lake Emily . . ."

twenty-one

He'd come to visit on several occasions, whether Virginia wanted him there or not. She knew Pastor Hickey meant well, that he was just doing his job, but she wished the tall, loud-voiced pastor would leave her alone.

"Virginia." He stood alongside her bed and lightly touched her shoulder. Virginia pretended to be napping, but the man kept talking. Virginia wondered if he had a quota of drivel to pass along in any given day. "I need to talk to you." Virginia let loose a fake snore. "The doctor tells me you aren't eating well. And that you've been talking about wanting to die."

151

Well of all the . . . Virginia opened her eyes. "What's wrong with talking about wanting to die?" She rolled onto her back.

"There's nothing wrong with contemplating your heavenly reward, but a lot of people are concerned about you. Have you been saying you want to be with Roy now?"

"I don't see a thing wrong with that. I loved my husband. Why wouldn't I want to be with him? King David asked God to take his life many times, didn't he?"

"Your loved ones are worried about you, that's all. You can't dwell on wanting to die; it isn't healthy. You need to be concentrating on getting better."

"Oh, let them worry! I'm not going to kill myself, if that's what they think. I'm surprised at you, Pastor. You preach it week after week, that we should anticipate being with Jesus. That's all I'm doing. So what's wrong with my asking God to hurry it up a little?"

"Virginia."

"Oh, 'Virginia' yourself. I'm right, and you know it. Don't be a hypocrite. Even the apostle Paul said to die was gain. Well, I for one believe that. If you don't, maybe you should take that up with God."

Trudy couldn't get her mind off Virginia. All day she thought about her, considered what she would do if she were in the same situation. She was supposed to be unpacking Bert's belongings, but her mood wouldn't allow it.

As approaching dusk dimmed her apartment, Trudy decided to go out for a little walk, maybe do a little sketching. Perhaps that would clear her mind and give her the wisdom she lacked. She gathered her pad of paper and charcoal pencils in their leather case and descended the stairs.

There had to be some other ways to encourage Virginia in addition to an afternoon of visiting. Truth was, Trudy was glad for the distraction. It kept her from thinking about how much she missed Bert while he worked night and day. A light clicked on in her brain. A distraction might allow Virginia to heal instead of dwelling on how awful she felt. But what could possibly suffice? The woman had plenty of visitors, so that wasn't the answer, and her physical limitations kept her from the hobbies she used to enjoy, like needlework and baking.

Trudy reached the bottom of the enclosed staircase and came out into the beauty of a waning summer day. The sky was a cerulean blue. Not a cloud in sight. The fading sun was warm but not stifling. Trudy inhaled deeply. What was it about a clear day that could so invigorate?

Bob Ott, the fifty-something pharmacist who rented the apartment to Trudy, was washing the windows of the newly rebuilt building.

"Hey, Mr. Ott." Trudy waved. "I thought you'd just cleaned those windows."

"Bob. Call me Bob, *Mrs. Biddle*. They looked dirty again!"

Trudy smiled.

"So, what are the big plans for your evening?" Trudy said.

Bob lifted his eyes to the sky. "You never can tell, Trudy. You never can tell."

The mischief in his eyes piqued Trudy's curiosity.

"Does it have anything to do with Rosemary Johnson?"

Bob wasn't biting. He merely grinned and wiped the plate-glass window with his rag.

Trudy meandered down Main toward Lion's Park. Her thoughts flitted from missing Bert to Bob Ott's romance with Rosemary Johnson to what to do for Virginia.

She passed Hardware Hank and the bakery. The single-screen theater across the street had kept a firm foot in a bygone era even after the tornado damage was repaired. The refurbished marquee and posters alongside the box office declared the week's attraction as well as those coming soon. Trudy loved the romance surrounding that majestic place. Now that summer was here, movies ran nightly at seven, but during the school year the owners kept showings to Friday, Saturday, and Sunday only.

Trudy waved at Coach Miller, the high-school football coach, who walked into Buzz Johnson's barbershop across the street. She passed the floral shop, with its green awning and hanging flower baskets, and State Farm Insurance. The Methodist church loomed ahead on the left, and Trudy smiled at the memory of her wedding day.

Across the street from the church, Lion's Park stood on the shores of Lake Emily, a picturesque photograph framed by ancient oak trees. Children in T-shirts played kickball in the field on the far side of the park. They shouted and squealed as a heavyset boy with a crew cut rounded the bases. An elderly gentleman with a thick head of white hair sat on a bench enjoying the game. Trudy settled next to him.

"Good evening." He tipped his head to her. She smiled in return. "That's my grandson," he said. "Ben, over there." He pointed toward a scrawny boy of seven or eight. "Not much of a ballplayer, but it's a miracle he's running at all. I'm August." The man held out a hand.

"Do I know you? You look familiar." Trudy shook hands with him.

"Hard to say. What's your name?"

"Trudy Ploog. I mean Biddle. I just got married. I teach art at the schools in town."

"Ah." The man nodded with a knowing look. "I know who you are."

Trudy grimaced, imagining what gossip he'd likely encountered. It seemed everyone knew of her after the letter-to-the-editor fiasco when she accused the school board of favoring the sports program with no thought for other programs that were more beneficial. It hadn't made the sports buffs in town happy with her.

"I . . . uh . . ." She had yet to figure out the best way to explain the letter that had caused an uproar and her arrest for vandalism, but the man held up a hand.

"You're Mae Morgan's sister. I was her boss at the courthouse. August Cleworth?"

"Oh sure. Now I remember. How's it been without Mae?"

"Never the same. She's a good kid. She had a baby, I hear."

Trudy nodded. "A boy. Christopher David."

"Good for her!" He winked at her.

Trudy leaned back against the bench and glanced sideways at August. What was it that caused one person to become gracious and kind in old age and another to turn bitter and brokenhearted? She envisioned Virginia in the nursing home. Had life simply been more kind to Mr. Cleworth, or had he chosen different responses to life's hardships along the way?

Twilight flitted across the lake in a million sparkles. Pines, birches, and oaks shifted in the breeze, their leaves waving hands in a parade. Trudy consciously inhaled.

"It got you, too." August broke the spell.

"Excuse me?" Trudy leaned toward him.

"Summer is a temptress. There's no telling what it can make a person do. I knew a boy who loved summer so much he went off to World War II just so he could spend time in the South Pacific."

"You?"

"About got me killed." He laughed. His wrinkled eyes held a boyish glint. "I was foolish, but it was still good. Did things I never would've done otherwise."

"Have you always been so carefree?"

"I don't know that I'm carefree. But I do like to look at the positive. Too many people focus on what's wrong in their lives." Then he shook his head. "Before my wife, Willa, died, I wasn't that way." His smile deepened. "But losing her taught me that one can't find meaning without taking a few risks every now and again." His gaze spoke of a distant place filled with longing. "She taught me about love. I took it for granted, and then it was too late. I think that's why I try to enjoy such things as watching my grandson play kickball on a summer evening . . . because she left me so much."

Hadn't Virginia lived much like this before her stroke, with a willing heart, a layer of gratefulness under every moment? What had happened? Had she simply forgotten?

"Mr. Cleworth, would you consider talking to a friend of mine?"

VIRGINIA MORGAN

Virginia Bjork Morgan was a simple woman. She didn't ask for much—a roof over her head, a husband to cherish, and someday healthy children she and Roy could raise together. Or perhaps that was too much. It seemed so now, as the foreboding locomotive pulled into view. Roy's pale eyes peered into her soul. He lifted her hand and kissed it. Virginia held back a sob.

How could he leave her just a week after their wedding at his parents' farm? It wasn't right. It wasn't fair. They should be together, setting up a home, a life. They shouldn't be torn apart like this with the specter of war hovering over them.

"I can't bear this," Virginia said, her heart slipping with the admission. "What am I supposed to do while you're gone?"

"Pray that I come back in one piece." The joke fell flat.

"I'll worry about you every moment."

"I'm counting on that, Mrs. Morgan."

The still-unfamiliar name brought a smile to Virginia's face. "Were we crazy? Getting married a week before you leave. What if—"

Roy placed a finger on her lips. "You've given me something to hold on to." He leaned close to her. She memorized the scent of his aftershave, the way his hands were both rugged and gentle. She wished this moment would last. She wished she could hold the worrying at bay.

But the whistle blew, and Roy's gaze shifted. Virginia reached for him in a long, slow kiss. His stubbled chin was rough against her cheeks. She rested her head against his wool overcoat, savoring his warmth this one last time.

"I hate good-byes," Virginia whispered.

"Can't have hellos without good-byes." His eyes twinkled. "I'll write every day. Can't guarantee I'll be able to mail 'em, but I'll write." His eyes searched

hers, and she saw the worry he tried so hard to hide. He needed her to be strong now, to hold things together here at home until he came back. She promised herself she'd do just that. She would take care of Roy's folks, do her part to keep the farm afloat while he was gone. She'd be the wife he needed.

The train whistle blew again, and Roy bent to lift his suitcase. Virginia held his arm as they moved silently toward the steps that would take him away. Roy turned. "I'll love you forever, my girl." He touched the end of her nose with a forefinger.

Virginia's vision blurred under tears. She wiped them away and said, "Come back to me."

Then he was gone, enveloped in the train's dark depths. Virginia wrapped her arms around herself and watched as the train became a speck on its way north to Fort Snelling. She shivered in the chill Minnesota air. Pregnant clouds hovered low, promising an early snow. But Roy would not be there to warm her on the cold days to come. Those days she would have to face alone, his memory giving substance to the hope in her heart.

twenty-two

Virginia wasn't sure she liked the idea. She knew what Mae was trying to do. Truth be told, she'd probably do the same if someone she cared about was feeling down. But Virginia was plain tired of good intentions, of everyone's trying to find the easy cure for her blues. So she was sad. So was everyone now and then. Why did they act as though sadness were something to be cured?

What's wrong with you, Virginia? They care about you. She'd been scolding herself constantly lately, yet it only sent her further into the abyss of guilt.

She stared at the passing fields, Roy's fields, as they drove toward the farm. She could see where Peter's plow had dug its fingers, leaving black furrows and pale sprouts. She pictured Roy out there, his weathered, strong face tanned from the sun, his flannel shirt smelling of earth and a faint trace of diesel fuel. If only she could bury her face in that shirt and breathe in the scent of him again. Oh, to smell him just once more, to kiss those dark cheeks and feel the warmth of him. She closed her eyes, imagining.

Mae pulled the Jeep onto the gravel drive. Scout bounded over and barked as Mae turned off the engine.

"You ready?" Mae asked, turning back toward Virginia.

"As I'll ever be," Virginia said.

"Let me get the wheelchair out first," Mae said.

She and Trudy got out. Virginia glanced at Christopher, who slept beside her in his rear-facing car seat. His tiny lips puckered, and his pale brow moved as if he were dreaming. Virginia touched his cheek tenderly.

Her door opened. Trudy moved the wheelchair into place and set the brake. "Here we go." Trudy leaned in toward her just as Anna had instructed. Virginia placed

160

her arms around the girl's neck. Once they were past the door, Mae helped support her while they settled Virginia into the chair.

Virginia glanced toward the pasture, where the cows watched curiously. One girl ambled to the fence. Her skin flicked where a fly landed. Virginia stared into her dark, luminous eyes. This was home. Her Cape Cod in town could never compare to this place, where she and Roy created their life together, where she experienced her deepest sorrows and her highest joys. She closed her eyes to feel the full weight of summer's glory on her face.

Mae interrupted. "I'll take the baby in first, then we can work on getting you inside, okay?"

Virginia nodded. Mae bent back into the car, while Trudy wheeled Virginia closer to the fenced pasture. Scout stayed at Virginia's side, and she patted his head.

So many images filled Virginia's mind. Bringing David home as a baby. His bout with pneumonia at six months of age. Sarah running up the drive after school, braids flying. Summer days on the porch, watching the kids chase each other through the sprinkler. Laughter echoing on warm days. Snow fights and forts.

Melancholy blanketed her heart.

Virginia, you've got to stop. Even here the sadness smothered. She wearied of its stifling embrace, too tired to fight it. It would be so much easier to allow that blanket to snuff her out.

twenty-three

As the afternoon wore on, Virginia was able to set her woes aside. They lurked, never far away, but she determined to ignore them, if only for Mae and Trudy. The sweet girls had done so much for her.

The table in the dining room was set with Mae's pink-flowered wedding china and crystal. The centerpiece of yellow daisies added a touch of brightness, and fresh-baked scones and Snoodle Doodle coffee from her favorite coffee shop in Montgomery filled the farmhouse with heavenly aromas.

They relaxed around the table leisurely, just like old times before Virginia had moved to town.

"Has Jessie been to visit lately?" Mae asked. "Weren't you helping her make an apron for 4-H?" She cradled Christopher in the nook of her arm. His little chest rose and fell as he slept peacefully.

"Jessie." Virginia set her cup down and absently rubbed her left hand. "She hasn't come since that first time with her dad. From what Anna tells me, she's busy enough, though."

"What makes you say that?" Trudy asked.

Virginia shrugged, aware of the lurking gloom. "She's that age." She said it as if it were only natural for Jessie to grow away from her, yet she knew it was a lie. Or maybe the truth was that she needed Jessie more than the girl needed her, and Virginia had used the girl to get the sense of purpose she craved. Virginia lifted her cup and sipped, trying to mask her troubled thoughts.

The crunch of tires on gravel drew their attention.

"Is Peter back?" Virginia asked.

"No," Trudy said. "Actually, I invited another guest. Do you remember Mae's boss at the courthouse? He mentioned that you were acquaintances."

"August Cleworth? I know him a little. I knew his wife better. Willa was in a Le Center Extension group, so we'd run into each other every now and again. Why is he here?"

Trudy shrugged. "I saw him in the park the other day. He's a nice guy."

Virginia wasn't sure what the girl was up to, but she certainly didn't like it. Not one bit. "I'm far too old for your matchmaking. Tell him to go back home."

Mae looked embarrassed, but Trudy didn't notice. "I promise I'm not matchmaking."

Mae cleared her throat. "What can it hurt to chat?"

Virginia grunted in disgust and crossed her arms. Mae gently touched her forearm as Trudy left to let August in. "Please don't be angry. You know how Trudy is. She doesn't mean any harm."

"I'll talk to him. But this is not funny!"

"We're not trying to be funny, Virginia. I promise you that. If you're uncomfortable, we can ask August to go."

"Well." She picked up her coffee cup. "I guess there's no point in being rude."

August looked as Virginia remembered him from the

few times they'd met. She found herself looking for Willa, his petite wife. The picture of him somehow wasn't right without her nearby. August dipped his head in greeting. "Virginia."

"How are you, August?"

"Holding my own, I suppose. Are you ladies having a nice visit?" He took the chair opposite Virginia. She hadn't recalled him being such a handsome man. He had clear blue eyes and a strong chin and nose that gave him a manly air. Virginia rubbed her left hand. "I'm sorry to hear you've been having a rough go of it," he said.

"You haven't had it easy either," Virginia said. August's eyes clouded with the words. "I'm sorry. Willa was such a lovely lady."

"Unless you got her Irish up. Then look out!" He chuckled. "She'd pinch me under the table if I got out of hand."

"Sounds like you had a wonderful friendship," Mae said.

"That we did. Ups and downs though, like any marriage. I'm sure Virginia has her stories. Don't you, Virginia?"

"I sure do." She recalled Roy coming in from milking, washing his hands in the mud-room sink. "Roy never knew how to put a towel back in its place. Used to drive me crazy."

For a few brief moments, the specter left the room.

August helped Mae and Trudy get Virginia into the car.

Having secured her in the backseat, he leaned in and said, "Would it be all right if I came to visit you?"

Virginia's heart skipped a beat, jumping over uncertainty. What did he want from her? She sank back into the seat and looked into his eyes. "I just lost Roy—"

"Nothing like that," he interrupted. "Just to visit as friends, that's all."

Her hesitation lingered, but she said, "As friends, I suppose."

Her heart didn't know what to make of it.

Peter didn't come in until after Virginia had gone. Mae was changing Christopher's diaper upstairs when she heard the back screen door slam shut. The two had barely spoken to each other since their argument. The man could be so stubborn! Why couldn't he see how wrong he was? Why couldn't he admit that he was being a hypocrite?

She turned her shoulder away as he came into the bedroom.

"Is Grandma gone already?"

"Why would you want to know?"

He touched a hand to her arm. "Come on, Mae."

Mae moved away and finished fastening the snaps on Christopher's sleeper.

"How long are you going to be mad at me?"

Mae's anger boiled. "Don't make this my problem! You're the one who couldn't make time for your grandmother!"

Peter sighed and raked a hand through his blond hair.

"Mae, I love Grandma. You know I do. I would've helped out if I could have. Did she have a good visit?" His tone was calm, which was especially pronounced beside Mae's ranting. That always irked her. She lifted her eyes to his and saw concern there. It ate away her resolve.

"I think she had a good time. At least she was able to forget her troubles for a little while."

"Good," he said sincerely. "That's good."

The headlights of the tractor glowed like a UFO making crop circles. Bert was spent. He'd been up since five o'clock, and it was now past midnight. There was no point in going on when he couldn't even keep his eyes open. He turned the tractor toward the gravel road and left the tall John Deere on the field approach. He climbed into his blue pickup and headed toward home. Halfway to the farm, he remembered that he lived in town. He opened his eyes wider and slapped his cheeks, trying to wake himself up. Then he made a U-turn and drove toward Lake Emily.

The light outside their apartment door illuminated the private landing. Bert smiled at Trudy's thoughtfulness. He fumbled with his keys only to discover that the door was unlocked. The apartment was quiet. Bert crept to the tiny bathroom off the living room to clean up and then went down the shotgun-style apartment to the bedroom. Trudy lay in a glow of moonlight. Her shoulder-length curly red hair spread across her pillow. Bert touched it lightly, and Trudy shifted.

"Hey," she said.

"I didn't mean to wake you."

Trudy stretched. "What time is it?"

"It's 12:32." Bert sat on the edge of the bed and took off his shoes, then started looking through the boxes along the wall for a pair of p.j.'s.

"Aren't you exhausted?"

"Sure am. Where are my clothes?"

Trudy pointed to the built-in dresser opposite the bed. Bert slipped into his pajamas, then Trudy held up the covers for him to climb under. "I've missed you." Trudy snuggled close and kissed the back of his neck, but the weariness of the day and the softness of the bed won him over before Trudy's seductions could have their way.

twenty-four

Three days after his visit to the farm August Cleworth decided to go to the nursing home to call on Virginia. He wasn't exactly sure why he felt compelled to go. Truth was, he barely knew Virginia Morgan. But he understood her pain. He'd seen the expression in her eyes before—in the mirror after Willa died. He'd all but given up on everything. Yet somehow he'd found the strength to go on, even to find joy in life again.

Maybe he could help Virginia, maybe not. The least he could do was try.

When August opened the door to Virginia's room, she looked ready to throw something. "Knock, knock," he said. "Don't you look cheery?"

Virginia crossed her arms over her chest. "Why are you here?" she said. "You don't owe me a thing, you know."

"I know." August took a chair beside her.

"I have friends."

"I know you do." He leaned forward, elbows on knees. "You ever think maybe I could use a friend?"

Virginia's tense shoulders softened. "I'm sorry. It's not you. I'm just frustrated with how slowly I seem to be progressing."

"How long has it been since the stroke?"

"Nine weeks. Nine weeks of waiting for a breakthrough. I'm sick of being weak."

"So tell your physical therapists you want to do more. You're in charge of your own recovery. Just don't allow yourself to become one of those nasty old people who complain and give the rest of us a bad name." He kept his tone kind. "You have a choice right now. You have to decide how to respond to your circumstances—take charge or grumble."

She looked as though she wanted to be indignant but couldn't be. He guessed that it was because deep down she knew he was right. She had been dwelling on her sad state, yet she'd done nothing to change it.

"I'll help if you'll let me," August said. "And I don't mean that I'll tell you what to do. Heaven knows, I'm inadequate on that count. But I like you, Virginia

Morgan. We'll have you up and dancing by summer's end."

Virginia laughed at that. "Dancing? What makes you think I want to dance?"

He grinned at her. She was a coy one, all right. A good sign. "You want to up here," August said, pointing to his temple. "Dancing starts in the mind."

A week after he'd forgotten he lived in town, Bert finally made it home for supper at a decent hour. With the field work done for now and the first haying behind him, he'd actually have a little time in the evenings for his new bride. He looked forward to that.

"Hey," he said as he clomped into the apartment. Dry bits of grass clung to his jeans and T-shirt. Hay clung to his green seed cap. Bert lifted it off his head and brushed the particles away.

"Hey." Trudy met him at the door with a kiss. His face turned red. "I love it that you still blush when we kiss." Trudy offered another morsel. "Mmm, your lips taste salty. Come, I have something to show you."

Trudy led him to a piece of furniture cloaked in a white sheet along the living room wall. It was a good five feet tall. She carefully removed the sheet to reveal a Hoosier cabinet painted white and filled with Bert's sports trophies and memorabilia. Pennants hung along the sides.

"So, tell me what you think."

Bert was speechless.

"I managed to get every last trophy on. It wasn't easy; you have a lot!"

He scratched his head. This wife of his was constantly surprising him, but this gesture took the cake. He knew how much she hated competitive sports, especially hockey.

"Really, what do you think?" Trudy said. "I got the hutch at a garage sale for forty-five dollars. Isn't that great?"

He lifted her in a bear hug.

"Hey!" she squealed, the biggest smile on her face.

"Thanks," he said as he put her down. "I know how hard this must've been for you."

Trudy waved the comment aside. "I love you."

Bert turned back to admire the homage to his younger days. "How'd you get it up here?"

"Oh, I have friends." Trudy raised an eyebrow.

"You think they could help take it back down?"

"Why? I thought you liked it."

"No. I like it just fine." Bert kissed her temple. "It's just that Ma and Dad are thinking of buying a place in town."

twenty-five

*T*own? Bert couldn't possibly mean what Trudy thought he meant. She straightened and placed her hands on her hips. "Would they rent the farmhouse out then?"

"No . . . They were thinking that you and I would move in."

She knew it! "What! And did they consult us about this? What did you say to them? I didn't think Lillian would ever consider giving up control of the farm. What would she do in town?" Trudy stomped into the kitchen.

"She sounded like she was looking forward to it. It makes the most sense. Dad's ready to be done with farming. His time working during our honeymoon taught him that he's just too old. If they sold off some acres, they could afford to buy a house in town and have a little left over."

"Do you *want* to live at the farm?" She knew his answer before she even asked, yet she had to hear him say it.

Bert looked kindly into her eyes. "I want you to be happy first."

"And?"

Bert leaned a shoulder against the refrigerator. "Well, with my parents gone, it wouldn't be so bad, would it? We wouldn't have to pay rent on an apartment. I'd be close by to tend to the animals. Ma wouldn't be under-foot to rub you the wrong way."

Trudy could see his point, and yet she wasn't sure. She liked the constant motion of town. It was much like life in St. Paul, if on a smaller scale. Always people to see, things to do. She pictured herself sitting alone in that big house all summer long while Bert was out in the fields or in the barn milking cows. In many ways it was appealing—a quiet, simple life. Yet . . . she wasn't exactly a quiet, simple girl.

Bert moved closer and stared into her eyes. She lifted on her toes to kiss him again. "I guess it wouldn't be so bad," she admitted.

Bert broke into a smile. "It'll be a while yet. The sale of the land would have to be a done deal before Ma and Dad would even look for a place in town. Dad's pretty particular about that."

That brought some comfort. Maybe Lillian and Willie would sit on the idea indefinitely. No sense in panicking over something that might never happen.

ROSEMARY JOHNSON

Rosemary Johnson quietly entered the sanitarium's atrium, where her mother sat staring through the wide windows. Vibrant sunshine flooded in and warmed the room. Violet turned her head to acknowledge her daughter's presence.

"Hey, Mom," Rosemary said.

"Good morning," her mother said. She wore that placid look that seemed pasted on; it lacked depth, true joy. Rosemary wondered if they'd put her on another antidepressant. She'd no doubt need a double dose of it after today.

Violet had been in the sanitarium since Rosemary was ten. She could barely recall a time when her mother hadn't been here. They'd tried on several occa-

sions to bring her home, but invariably something sent her back over the edge. At first it had been the suicide of Violet's sister, but after that, even minuscule events could send her fragile inner self toppling. Once some news piece she'd seen on television sent her into a screaming rage; another time, she fell apart over the news that Rosemary's brother, Henry, was joining the military. They eventually gave up hope of ever bringing Violet back to them. She was at peace in the sanitarium. It was safe there—quiet, manageable.

"How are you today, dear?" Violet said. She gave her daughter a peck on the cheek.

"I'm not doing so well, Mother," Rosemary said.

She saw the clouds gather in her mother's eyes. Rosemary looked around to make sure that the nurse was still at the door. She stood at the ready.

"What is it?"

Rosemary took her mother's hand. "It's about Father. He had a heart attack yesterday, Mother."

Violet's hand flew to her mouth. Pain lined her brow.

"He died, Mom," Rosemary said. Her own pain was a sword in her side.

"It can't be," Violet breathed. Her gaze turned back to the window. Rosemary's father had been a rock for his fragile wife. She expected her mother to shout, to rage as she always did when she couldn't cope. Yet this time she withdrew into herself, closing the curtains over her eyes.

"Mother." Rosemary placed a hand on Violet's shoulder.

But Violet said nothing. She would never speak again.

twenty-six

Residents of the Lake Emily nursing home sang in discordant chorus as Ronnie O'Brien, the activities coordinator, led them in a rousing version of "California Dreamin' " on her autoharp. She wove around the circle of wheelchairs and sang to each gray-haired participant as he or she shook an egg shaker or tambourine.

Virginia's instrument lay dormant in her lap. She refused to act like a child at Kindermusik. She crossed her arms over her chest and turned her gaze toward the door. August's words came back to her: *Dancing starts in the mind.* Easy for him to say when his body was still within his control.

A smallish woman with a pageboy cut came in the side door. Virginia didn't recognize her at first. She turned, and Virginia realized it was Rosemary Johnson, the high-school music teacher. They had gotten to know each other a little during last year's production of *Oklahoma!* when Virginia had volunteered with Jessie to paint sets. The memory stirred her longing for the child's company.

Rosemary made her way down the hall, apparently to visit someone. Virginia wondered whom. Rosemary walked purposefully. She never sauntered or sashayed.

She turned the corner into the Alzheimer's wing and out of Virginia's view.

"Nurse," Virginia said to a nearby woman who was clapping along with the song. The woman bent down to hear. "Can you wheel me over there? A friend of mine is here." She pointed to where Rosemary had gone and handed the nurse the tambourine.

"Don't you want to stay for the rest of the sing-along?"

Virginia gave her an are-you-kidding-me look. The nurse unlocked her wheels and did as Virginia requested and headed down the hall. When they passed a door that stood slightly ajar, Virginia spied Rosemary.

"Right here," Virginia said in a hoarse whisper.

Rosemary stood alongside a bed and reached for the weathered, lined hand. "Mother." She stroked her mother's hand. "It's Rosemary." The woman didn't respond, though she seemed fully awake. Wide eyes stared off into space.

"Do you want to go in?" the nurse asked.

Virginia realized that she had no idea what she'd say to Rosemary and felt suddenly embarrassed at her nosiness. Virginia shook her head. "No, I should go."

Rosemary must have heard them because she came out to the hallway. "Virginia," she said, "I'd heard you were here. How are you doing?"

Virginia's face flamed as she realized she'd been caught spying. "I'm sorry. I saw you come in. I didn't mean to intrude."

"Would you like to meet my mother?" Rosemary pointed back toward the room.

"Of course."

Rosemary took the chair from the nurse, who went back down the hall. Rosemary had never spoken of her mother being in Lake Emily, much less the nursing home. Virginia wondered why.

"You're going to have to excuse my mother; she hasn't been real talkative these past few years," Rosemary said when Virginia's eyes met hers. "She stopped talking when Daddy died. I think it was just too much for her."

Rosemary positioned Virginia beside the hospital bed. "Mother," Rosemary said in a louder voice. The woman's blank gaze stared straight ahead. "This is Virginia Morgan, Mother. She's here at the nursing home for a little while too." The woman didn't blink. Her eyes watered, and a thin line of drool traced her chin. Rosemary told Virginia, "Her name's Violet. I had her moved here after my father and younger brother died so I could visit more often. She was at a sanitarium in Wisconsin when I was a girl." Rosemary sighed and looked at her mother with a wistful expression. "She likes it here now. Don't you, Mother?" Rosemary wiped her mother's chin with a Kleenex from the tray beside her bed. "She'll be ninety in August."

Rosemary beheld her mother with tenderness, as if they shared a close bond. Rosemary's gaze turned to Virginia. "I'm all she has now that Daddy and Henry are gone," Rosemary whispered. Rosemary smoothed her mother's white hair. It struck Virginia as one of the most beautiful scenes she'd ever seen, a daughter caring for her mother. "I'm sorry she isn't more sociable," Rosemary said.

August's words came again. *You have to decide how to respond to your circumstances, Virginia.* Rosemary had chosen to rise above them, to be a beautiful person despite her mother's illness. Such courage intrigued Virginia and illuminated her own frailty of character.

"Would you mind if I visited her from time to time?" Virginia said. She didn't know why she'd said it. She only knew that she needed to apply herself to something beyond herself, and whatever the reason, she knew it was right.

"I'm sure Mother would like that, wouldn't you, Mother?" Rosemary said.

Violet was unflinching.

At least it would give Virginia something to do besides sit around feeling sorry for herself.

The following day after her physical therapy session and a visit from Minnie Wilkes, Virginia asked to be wheeled to Violet's room. Heavy curtains shrouded the tall windows again, standing guard against the sunny day. A silent television flashed its pictures in the corner. Violet stared at the set, unaware anyone had entered the room. Her hair was a matted web, and drool glimmered on her chin.

The nurse positioned Virginia's wheelchair alongside the bed and instructed her to push the call button when she wanted to leave. Once the door closed behind her, Virginia looked tentatively at the silent woman propped up beneath the blankets.

"Hello, Violet. Remember me? I was here yesterday." The woman's gaze into nowhere remained. "You're probably wondering why I'm here. Truth is, I'm wondering the same thing." She paused and studied Violet's profile. She was a pretty woman, despite her advanced age. She had a turned-up nose and wide-set blue eyes beneath a high forehead.

Virginia allowed herself to feel the comfort of the silent room. There were no struggles here, no battles to be better or to overcome odds or to be loved. She simply *was*; there was a certain beauty in that. A certain restfulness.

Yet a perpetual frown cut Violet's troubled face. Her eyes squinted, creating a crease between her brows, and her lips were a thin white line.

"Who are you?" Virginia said.

Violet made no attempt to answer.

Finally Virginia went on, "How did you get to this point? What pushed you over the edge? Was it something extraordinary, or was it something common? Some everyday occurrence that was just too much for you? And if it was something common, could I be susceptible like you were? That's what fascinates me." Virginia sighed and lifted her gaze to the ceiling. "I'm not criticizing, mind you. In some ways I suppose I'm envious. That sounds odd, doesn't it? But I know what it is to be weary, tired of fighting, tired of losing so much. I'm not ready to die. I thought I was, but I'm not. It would be so easy to quit rather than face my challenges. I guess I just can't give myself that permission. What did you tell yourself in your quiet hours that gave you permission to leave the real world for the place you live in now? Is it better where you are? More peaceful?"

She gazed at Violet's lined face. Fear seemed etched in every crevice. How could she find peace in such a life? Peace forever eludes without the Giver of true peace. Impostors always promised but couldn't deliver. Without Jesus whispering his love in her ear, how could Violet know that peace?

Has peace been ruling your heart, Virginia?

No, she'd been ungrateful. Through all her difficulties, God had been near, showing himself in the people who cared, in the comfort she felt even in her darkness. Yet she'd grumbled. God's whisper remained, yet she chose to gripe. August was right.

"God, forgive me for my selfishness. I forgot that you love me. I've felt sorry for myself. Yet I know that I'm weak, that I'll feel this way tomorrow or the day after that. I try to get it right, but I inevitably fail. I don't deserve your kindness. I guess that's what makes your kindness so powerful—that I can't do a thing to deserve it. Help me when I'm weak, and I'm always weak."

When she lifted her eyes, she realized she'd spoken the prayer aloud. Violet's eyes were on her. Eyes that hadn't connected with another soul in forty years were

179

gazing into Virginia's, and a tear traced her cheek.

Virginia felt suddenly guilty for her selfishness. Violet didn't deserve to be her captive confessional. "Forgive me," she whispered and pushed the button to call the nurse.

"Virginia?" a voice called at her door later that day. Virginia flicked off the television and turned to see Rosemary Johnson. "May I come in?" she said.

Virginia nodded. Rosemary moved to one of the two green vinyl chairs beside the bed. "The nurse said you'd been in to see Mother today."

"Yes . . ." She tried to read Rosemary's expression to see if she was upset over what had happened with her mother, but her face gave away nothing.

"What happened? The nurse said she was crying."

"About that, I'm sorry. I didn't mean to upset her."

"No. You don't understand." A smile touched Rosemary's lips. Virginia noticed how much she looked like Violet. "It's a good thing." Virginia met her eyes. The younger woman took a deep breath. "My mother hasn't responded to anyone since . . . I can't remember when. But you—somehow you broke through to her."

Virginia sat back against her pillows, trying to remember what she'd said to the woman. She'd been selfish just as August had accused, and still her words had met some need in the woman. How could that be?

"I was hoping," Rosemary went on, "you'd be willing to visit her some more. It's been so long since I've held out any hope."

Rosemary squinted her eyes as if a long-forgotten memory flickered behind them. "I've been without family for a long time. When I was a girl, I came home from school one day to find my mother sitting in a pile of cut-up photographs. Her sister had committed suicide that day, and it tore her up. She blamed their father. Cut his face out of every picture. For some reason when I came in, she saw him instead of me. She came after me with the scissors. I didn't understand. What child would understand such a thing? But I loved my mother. That's what daughters do . . ." Her story trailed away.

"I'd be happy to visit her again. More than happy."

The following Sunday, the last Sunday of June, Jessie awoke early to the sound of her father singing in the shower. She couldn't remember ever hearing him sing in the shower before. She lay between the covers listening until the water turned off and the door opened.

"Punkin," he called through her closed door, "time to get up, sleepyhead. Gotta get ready for church." The door cracked open. "Jessie?"

The girl giggled. "You were singing." Jessie pulled the covers from her face.

"What did you think? Am I ready for the big time?" Jessie shook her head, then burst out laughing. "Hey!" Her dad placed a hand on his chest, feigning indignation. "Come on." His voice turned serious. "We leave for church in half an hour."

"Are we going to Anna's again afterward?" They'd

gone to Anna's every Sunday for the past two months. Anna had proved she could make wonderful meals as well as frozen pizza. They played board games, and on sunny afternoons they went swimming from Anna's dock. For Jessie, Anna's home was heaven or at least the closest thing to it. She imagined that Anna was her mother and that Anna loved her father and that every day could be like those Sundays of laughter.

"No," her dad said, "we aren't going to Anna's this week."

Jessie groaned.

"I invited her to come to the Chuckwagon with us instead."

Jessie threw her pillow at her dad. "You're so mean!" She grinned. She climbed out of bed and opened her dresser while her father returned to his bathroom. Jessie could hear his shaver's buzz.

What did it mean that he had asked Anna to lunch? Did Dad like Anna as more than a friend? She hoped so. Jessie picked up her brush and drew it through her blond hair in long strokes. What would it be like to have a new mother? Longing rose, and guilt's arrow pierced it. Was it right to wish for a new mother? She still loved her mother beyond words. She fingered the locket at her throat that bore her mother's fading smile. How could she so quickly betray the mother she adored? Sure, Anna was pretty and kind, but she wasn't Mom.

If only she could ask Virginia about it, but Virginia had made herself clear. She didn't want anyone coming around. She had enough to think about without some pesky kid annoying her.

Jessie stirred the chocolate malt slowly, giving it far more attention than the task required. Her dad was telling Anna about his new job at the motorcycle shop. Jessie watched her with sidelong glances. *What kind of mother would she be?* Jessie stared harder at the malt.

"What made you decide to become a physical therapist?" her dad asked.

Anna tucked her long blond hair behind her ears and took a sip of her malt. "When I was sixteen, my mom was in a bad car accident."

Jessie lifted her eyes to Anna. "We didn't think she'd ever walk again. It was really hard. She was so discouraged, but her therapists encouraged her to keep trying. If they hadn't been there, I don't know what she would've done. Now she leads a normal, happy life." Anna winked at Jessie. Jessie felt her face warm.

"What about you, Jessie?" Anna said. "What do you think you'd like to be when you get older?"

"Maybe an artist." Jessie thought about Miss Ploog—now Mrs. Biddle—and how she bragged about the drawings Jessie had done for 4-H. Then she thought about how much she'd liked taking care of her lambs and rabbit. "Or maybe a farmer or a vet. I like to spend time with my sheep, although I haven't been out to see them in a long time."

"Where do you board them?" Anna said.

"Out at Mae and Peter Morgan's farm." Jessie looked into Anna's green eyes. She was smiling at Jessie. It felt good to be smiled at.

"Would you show them to me sometime?"

Jessie nodded. "I used to go see them every day before Virginia had her stroke."

"With my new job and all, I just haven't had time to take her," Jessie's dad explained.

"I can take you after work," Anna offered.

"That would be nice," Jessie said. She felt like a traitor saying it. Yet Anna was so kind. Even if she wasn't Virginia. Or Mom.

twenty-seven

It's rare when you aren't working these days, and we're eating supper with your *folks?*" Trudy complained as she and Bert sped in his pickup along the dusty road. The July day was muggy and stifling. Fields drenched two months ago were now dry and thirsty and begging to be quenched.

"They said they have something to tell us."

Bert pulled the blue pickup into the long gravel driveway. White sheets flapped in the breeze on the clothesline. Lillian's rhubarb had gone to seed—odd-looking shoots with clusters of seeds rose above the thick green leaves. The rest of the garden was a veritable produce aisle of beets, okra, tomatoes, peppers, beans, cabbage, lettuce, peas, potatoes, and onions. Sweet corn was knee high. Squashes and pumpkins sent out their tentacles. Grapevines wove along the trellis on the far end. Lillian was bent over, her wide rump pointed skyward as she pulled beets and sliced off the green leaves. She tossed the stems into a heap in the grass beside the garden and dropped the thick burgundy vegetables into a plastic pail at her feet.

Bert killed the motor, then looked at Trudy. She crossed her arms over her chest.

"We won't stay long," he promised.

"Only because you have to get back to work. What excuse do I have to get out of here?" With a forefinger Bert lifted her chin. When their eyes met, Trudy sighed and said, "I'll be good." He kissed the tip of her nose, and they climbed out.

Lillian straightened and wiped an arm across her forehead. "I was beginning to think you wanted me to bring your meal to the truck!"

Trudy sent Bert a pleading look asking permission to make a wisecrack. Bert shook his head despite the grin on his face. Lillian wiped her hands on the full-body apron that crisscrossed her back, then she pulled the garment off over her head. "Supper's ready. Come on in." She led the way into the rambling Biddle farmhouse.

The back porch sagged a little, and the paint was starting to peel. She hadn't noticed that before. But then she'd never thought she'd be living here. Piles of clutter—magazines, newspapers, old clothes, an unplugged freezer, and an old wringer washer—overflowed the mud room. A path through the middle led to the back door.

Willie Biddle sat at the Formica and chrome-legged kitchen table reading a copy of *The Land* magazine. He set it down when Trudy and Bert came in. "Couldn't resist Lillian's goulash, huh?"

"Yep," Trudy said. "You know me, Will, I'm a goulash freak."

Willie gave his daughter-in-law a puzzled look that turned into a smile holding the same spark as Bert's. Trudy patted his shoulder. She was just about to sit down with him when Lillian shoved a casserole dish into her hands.

"Take this Jell-O salad to the dining room for me." Pieces of marshmallow and banana quavered in the translucent red gel.

"Uh . . . okay." Willie grinned a little too broadly. He lifted the magazine to cover his face again. "Men!" Trudy muttered.

Lillian followed her and placed a steaming dish—a mixture of noodles, hamburger, tomatoes, and paprika—on the table. "I can give you this recipe," Lillian said. "It's Bert's favorite."

"It is?"

"I'll write it on an index card later. You do have a recipe file, don't you?"

"Who? Me? Of course I have a recipe file." Lillian harrumphed doubtfully and disappeared back into the kitchen. "I do too have a recipe file!" Trudy whispered to her back. She stuck out her tongue just as Bert came into the room with his dad. Trudy quickly put her tongue away and pointed her father-in-law to his chair. But the tilt of his chin told her he'd seen. Lillian returned bearing rolls in a cloth-napkin-lined basket.

Trudy leaned toward Bert and whispered, "Is goulash one of your favorite meals?"

"*The* favorite," Bert said.

Lillian gave Trudy a triumphant smirk.

After grace was said and the food began its rounds, Willie spoke in his quiet way. "We asked you two here for a reason. We've been talking about selling some acres and moving to town, as you know." Bert nodded and tilted his chair back on its rear legs. "With Fred gone, it seems more important than ever to take some action. We have more acres than you can manage on your own, Bert, and if we sell, we can pay cash for a house without impacting the farm greatly. It's going to be a rough year as it is with the rains and now the drought. Your brother hasn't made it any easier." He shook his head, then laced his fingers together and placed them on the table. He glanced at Lillian, who was mysteriously silent. "I found a buyer for the five hundred acres on the north end."

"A buyer? Already?" Bert said. Goulash stuck in Trudy's throat.

"Mack Weber. You remember him. He used to help bale. His boy, Samuel, is taking over for him, and they've been wanting to expand."

"You get a good price?"

Willie nodded. "A little over thirty-five hundred dollars an acre. That brings me to another thing." He paused, seeming to search for the right words. "Ma and I have been talking about our wills and making a living trust and such. It only makes sense with us moving to town. Well, I'm leaving the farm to you." Will ran a hand through his hair. "Nothing is as important to us as seeing this farm survive in our family. Who knows if your brother will ever come back or if he'd even want to pick up farming again. He's been gone over a year . . . Even if he did come back, I don't know if I could trust him, taking off like he did." The pain of his words was etched in his pale blue eyes and in the set of his brows.

"Not even coming back for his own brother's wedding," Lillian added under her breath.

"You're loyal, dependable, Bert . . ." Willie's voice trailed off. "A good son."

"It's only right you should have it," Lillian said.

Silence descended. Even Trudy couldn't think of a thing to say.

Finally Bert said, "Fred's going to be hurt."

"I don't much care how Fred feels about it," Willie said. "He wasn't thinking about how we'd feel when he left. No. He made his choices. That's all there is to it."

"You two should move in here as soon as you can," Lillian voiced the words Trudy dreaded.

"Ma," Bert warned.

"Well, it's a crime to throw money at that pharmacist when you can have a place for free! There's plenty of room for us all here." They'd had this fight before; it had almost split Bert and Trudy for good.

Bert held up a hand. "We appreciate that, Ma. But we've talked this through." His gaze met Trudy's, and she felt the glow his words of support brought.

"Well, once we find a place in town, then," Lillian conceded.

"We'll figure that out when the time comes." Bert looked over at Trudy. "We'll work it out," he said. He squeezed Trudy's hand beneath the table, then he turned to his father. "I don't know what to say about all this, Dad."

"It's the right thing," Willie said. "And making a trust now will keep it out of probate later."

Trudy wasn't certain of all the implications of what had just happened, but she knew she wasn't ready for it. No, she wasn't ready just yet to give up her place in town for this too-quiet life. She would have to make that clear to Bert.

MINNIE WILKES

Minnie Wilkes pushed the On button of the loud canister vacuum and bent to her work. She had to get the place cleaned for the meeting of the Suzie Q's that Thursday evening. She'd even taken her daughter, Meredith, to a sitter so she wouldn't be underfoot. Minnie hefted the rust-colored couch away from the wall to vacuum behind it.

So much weighed heavy on her mind lately. It would be good to have the ladies over. Their company would give her the distraction she so needed from the worries of the farm and her worries about her son, Warren. Every time Walter Cronkite came on the air with the latest news on the war, her heart twisted with fear. Was Warren in the thick of that latest battle in Vietnam?

When she returned the couch to its spot and turned off the vacuum, she heard the insistent buzz of the doorbell. She hurried to answer it, taking off her apron as she moved through the kitchen to the door. The kitchen smelled of pumpkin pie—her dessert for Extension that night.

"I'm sorry," she said, opening the door. "I didn't hear—" She saw the deep blue of the man's uniform, the sharp-looking hat, the sympathetic gaze. Minnie's hand flew to her chest.

"Mrs. Wilkes, I'm Staff Sergeant John Barry. May I come in? Is your husband here?" She pushed the screen door open for him. He looked around the small kitchen as he entered. He was a tall, skinny man, more of a boy really, with that clean-shaven face.

"My husband's working in the fields," Minnie said.

"Is there any way to get ahold of him?"

Minnie shook her head, dread rising. "It's Warren, isn't it?"

"I'm sorry," Sergeant Barry said. He reached into his briefcase for a slip of paper that he handed to Minnie.

"The War Department regrets to inform you that your

son, Airman First Class Warren Wilkes, was reported missing in action when his plane went down . . ."

Beyond that, the words ceased to have meaning. Minnie stared at them, unwilling to believe.

"We'll let you know if there's a change in his status, ma'am, if a . . . body is recovered," the man said. "It sounded like your son was a good man, a good pilot." How could he be talking about Warren in the past tense? Minnie's eyes burned.

"How?" she said. She lifted her face to the man's dark, compassionate eyes. He was so young, Minnie thought again, someone else's son. Except he was still here, still alive. Her chest ached.

"He was flying a mission over Haiphong. He was supposed to drop his load but was hit before he had a chance . . ."

"So the likelihood that a body will be recovered . . ."

The man just shook his head.

Minnie hugged her arms around herself. She wished her husband were here. She really needed Otto with her right now.

"Maybe you should sit down, ma'am."

Minnie walked numbly to the living room. The soldier held her arm to support her. The cord from the vacuum lay in a tangle across the floor. She stared at it without comprehending. Nothing made sense. This wasn't real. He helped her sit, said something.

Minnie lifted her face. Had he just spoken? "Whom can I call for you?" he repeated.

"Virginia. Virginia Morgan will be home."

191

twenty-eight

Minnie Wilkes's plump cheeks and deep dimples made her appear perpetually happy. That was one of the things Virginia had always liked about the short, round woman. Since Virginia had gone to the Lake Emily nursing home, Minnie, like the rest of the Suzie Q's, had visited faithfully.

She and Virginia sat in the sunny lunchroom beside the huge picture window. Minnie was telling Virginia about her great-granddaughter's latest antics. An occasional car meandered up Fourth Street's oak-lined path. A robin hopped on the lawn, then bent and poked its beak into the dark earth. When it straightened, a long, squirming earthworm dangled from its mouth. For some reason the sight struck Virginia as humorous.

"What's so funny?" Minnie asked.

Virginia realized she hadn't heard anything her friend had said. "I'm sorry. I was watching that robin out there. Isn't it amazing how they can just know where those worms are?"

"You sound like you're feeling better."

"Encouragement comes and goes, but, yes, I am feeling better. Maybe it's the sunshine." In truth, she'd been feeling lighter ever since August Cleworth had started visiting. And since she'd started paying her own visits to Violet Johnson, not that the woman ever said anything. Virginia had gone every day since that first visit, sometimes just to sit. At other times she talked about her life, how much she missed Roy. She'd finally gotten the focus off of herself, and somehow that eased her burden. She'd even told Anna and Kathy that she was ready to stand. And she was. Just saying it out loud gave her the courage to try.

"Any idea when you'll be ready to go home?"

Virginia shook her head. "I'm getting there, but . . ." She paused. "I don't know if I'll ever be able to move back to the Cape Cod. The stairs are going to be a challenge, and living alone . . . The doctor is worried about what would happen if I fell or had another stroke."

"You could turn the den into a downstairs bedroom."

"But the bathroom is upstairs."

"That *is* a problem." Minnie thought on it. "Don't you think you'll be able to manage stairs eventually?"

"I'm going to be seventy-eight years old in January. Who knows if I'll ever be strong enough for that."

"What do Peter and Mae say?"

Virginia shook her head. "They have enough on their plate without an old woman to take care of."

"Their words or yours?" Minnie's eyes scolded. "Don't underestimate them. They love you."

"I know they do. It just isn't . . . right for me to expect them to take care of me. They're just starting out with that new baby. They have all the cares of the farm—"

"You always were a proud woman, Virginia Morgan." Compassion tempered the harshness of the words. "I'd be the same, no doubt, if I were in your shoes." She placed a hand on Virginia's.

"It is hard sometimes," Virginia said, "but I'm learning humility."

"Ready, Virginia?" Anna's eyes held Virginia's as if willing her strength. Virginia took a deep breath. She knew she could do this. Nothing would stop her now, not even her own stubbornness. "On the count of three, okay? One, two, three."

Virginia propelled her large frame forward and up as Anna supported her by the strap around her thick waist while Kathy followed with the wheelchair.

"Very good! Now try to balance your weight."

Nerves tangled inside Virginia. She shifted onto her left foot, careful to spread her legs for maximum balance. Her limbs were weak still, but this time she didn't fold.

"Grasp the bars like before." Anna pointed to the parallel bars in front of them. Virginia reached for them and clutched them tightly. She scooted forward, first one step, then two, until she reached the end of the bars with Anna and Kathy cheering her on. A huge grin spread across her face. She felt like a triumphant warrior. The therapists reached for her to steady her. Then, when they completely released her, they began to applaud. Tears gathered in Virginia's eyes. They stung her nose and rolled onto her wrinkled cheeks.

"Thank you," she whispered.

"You did it, Virginia," Anna said. "We were just your spotters. Before you know it, you'll be dancing again!"

The comment brought August to mind, and Virginia

wondered at it. They laughed until Virginia felt her legs growing weak.

"I need to sit down now," she finally said.

Anna and Kathy were there instantly. Once Virginia was safely back in her chair, Anna bent down in front of her and said, "We'll do that a little longer every day until we can get you into a walker. I'm so proud of you, Virginia."

"I never thought I could be happy about using a walker."

"I'm glad to see you decided to try," a voice by the door said. August. Virginia turned her head to see the gray-haired man who stood inside the swinging doors. His eyes glowed.

"Did you see that?" Anna said. "Wasn't it amazing?"

August nodded. He smiled, and Virginia's heart warmed.

"I think she needs a reward, don't you?" he said to Anna.

"Absolutely."

"Well, good. I have a little surprise planned for this lady."

"We're about done for today," Anna said. "She's all yours."

August grasped the black plastic grips and backed Virginia's wheelchair out the door, then moved forward.

When he didn't turn toward her room, Virginia knew something was up. "Where are you taking me?"

"You'll see," August said mysteriously.

When he came to Violet's wing, Virginia said, "Wait, take me to see Violet first. I want to tell her the good news."

August complied, wheeling her to the mute woman's room. August knocked. When there was no answer, he looked at Virginia.

"Just go on in. Violet won't answer."

Instead of the darkness that used to pervade that space, light flowed in through the open window. The nurses had insisted that Violet would become distraught at the change, but when Virginia urged them to open the blinds, Violet merely lifted her face to the sunlight. Little by little they added touches to brighten the room—a bouquet of flowers, a Monet print on the wall. The staff was getting excited about the tiny differences they saw in the petite woman's demeanor.

Today Violet was dressed in a pretty pink blouse and skirt. She sat in the chair and gazed at the trees outside.

"Violet," Virginia said, "this is my friend August. Remember I told you about him."

"It's nice to meet you, ma'am," August offered.

Violet didn't move.

"I just had to tell you," Virginia went on. "I walked today! It was only six feet, but I did it. You see, even we old ladies can learn new tricks!" She reached to touch Violet's hand.

Though Violet's gaze never moved, the squeeze she gave Virginia's hand was all the recognition Virginia needed.

．．．

August wheeled Virginia to the main doors of the nursing home. He pushed the large round button to open them, then wheeled her into the bright sunshine. He wasn't sure how Virginia would react to his surprise. He hoped she'd like it, that she'd see it for what it was—an offer of friendship. He felt a connection with her, maybe because she reminded him of Willa. She had Willa's honesty, always tempered by kindness. The same kindness he'd just witnessed Virginia extend to Violet Johnson. He wondered what had brought about the lift in Virginia's spirits.

"Did you get permission to bring me out here?" Virginia said.

"I stopped asking permission for anything when I hit seventy. Live a little, Virginia." He knew he was smirking.

They moved down the walk. The green parklike lawn spread before them. Under a tall elm tree, a red and white checked tablecloth was laid out. On it a picnic basket and place settings for two kept company. "What is this?" Virginia said.

"I figured you deserve a break from nursing-home food. I'm not a bad cook, if I do say so myself."

He pulled the wheelchair alongside the arrangement and produced a tray with legs, which he set on Virginia's lap.

"This is too much, August." Her hand touched her collarbone.

"Nonsense. You'd do it for a friend." He set the plate

and silverware before her, then lifted a steaming casse-role dish from the picnic basket. "Besides, what's easier than chicken-stuffing hotdish?"

August lifted the lid from the dish of stuffing, diced chicken, cream-of-mushroom soup, onions, and cheese. The scent of sage and onions wafted into the air.

"You remind me of my son, David," Virginia said. "He got very good at cooking after his wife died."

"I was the cook of the family even before Willa's death." He served Virginia a good-sized portion and set it before her with a glass of sparkling apple juice. "Willa liked to cook, mind you. We did it together. She taught me to flambé with the best of them."

"I doubt Roy could've boiled water. The kitchen was *my* territory! He was afraid to venture in there!"

"So, you're an in-charge woman, are you?" His brow lifted.

Virginia laughed. "Not quite that bad. But we had our definite roles. We understood them and didn't mind that. There was never any problem."

"We had our roles too. But once the kids were grown . . ." He motioned for her to eat and dished a serving for himself.

"Where are the kids now?" Virginia said.

"My son Skip and his wife, Maggie, live here in Lake Emily. The other three have scattered to the winds. I have one in Maine, another in Florida, and my daughter's in Seattle."

"You couldn't get much farther apart without leaving

the country." Virginia sighed. "I miss my two all the time. Sometimes I wonder if I raised them right."

"Why do you say that?" August leaned forward.

"They're so far away, and why? What's so important that they couldn't stay nearby? That my own children chose to leave me? Did I raise them to chase money? I hope not. But then I didn't exactly raise them to take care of family either."

"Are they chasing money?"

Virginia swallowed a bit of the hotdish and waved her fork. "I suppose not. But then that raises the question of what they are chasing. Certainly not being near their mother. This is very good, August."

"You miss them. Any mother would."

She gazed at him thoughtfully but didn't say anything. She didn't have to. She knew that he understood.

"Getting tired?" he said.

Virginia picked up another bite with her fork. "No," she said, taking a deep breath. "I'm just fine. Better, in fact, with a good meal in me."

"Oh, I almost forgot." August reached into his pocket and withdrew a pamphlet that he handed to Virginia.

"What's this?"

"A little surprise. I saw this at the community center. Ballroom-dancing lessons." Virginia gave him a puzzled look. "Remember you told me you always wanted to learn?"

"I did not!" She tried to hand the pamphlet back. "You were the one who brought up the whole dancing thing!"

"No. You keep it. It won't be long now until you can throw that walker away. Then we'll take the class together."

"This is silly."

"What's wrong with a little silliness now and again? Beside, you're grinning from ear to ear."

One in the morning. Mae paced as she held a squalling Christopher against her shoulder. He'd been crying for almost an hour. She'd fed and burped him, changed his diaper. She'd even bathed him and massaged his tummy. She was out of ideas, and Peter was in the barn caring for a cow that was having a difficult delivery. Mae pulled back the living room's lace curtain to see if the lights in the barn were still on. They were. The curtain fell back into place.

"Shh." Still he cried. His face was red from crying. She bounced him and patted his back. *What if he's sick?* She touched his forehead with her cheek—no fever. In fact he felt cool. "Peter, come inside," she said to the night. What had her mother done to keep Christopher calm when she was here? Mae couldn't remember. Grabbing the phone and laying it on the counter, she awkwardly dialed her mother's number. She lifted the phone to her ear and gently bounced Christopher in the other arm.

Christopher's cries seemed to weaken, but then he inhaled deeply, and the forces renewed their strength for another squall.

"Oh, baby." Mae held her son against her cheek.

"I'm sorry, baby."

Catherine answered on the second ring. "Hello?" Her voice sounded sleepy.

"Hi, Mom. It's Mae. I hope I didn't wake you."

Her mom said something, but Mae couldn't hear for all of Christopher's crying. Finally she said, "Hang on just a minute." She took him upstairs to his cradle and laid him down. His cries grew in intensity. Mae closed the door and returned to the phone downstairs.

"I'm sorry I'm calling so late." She bit back tears. "It's Christopher. He's been crying for an hour. I can't get him to stop, and I'm worried about him." The inadequacy wrapped up in that admission shrank her confidence. She pressed the phone tighter to her ear so she could hear her mother above the baby's screams.

"Is he acting sick?" Catherine said.

"I don't know how to tell. He doesn't have a fever, if that's what you mean."

"He might have an ear infection."

"How would I know that?"

"You can always take him to urgent care," Catherine said. "It won't hurt him if you let him cry for a little bit. Lay him in his bed and get a cup of tea. Or put him in the baby swing; he seemed to like that when I was there. If he doesn't calm down in another hour, take him in."

"Okay," Mae said. Her voice was small. She took a deep breath. "Thanks, Mom."

"That's what moms are for." Those words meant more to Mae than anything her mom could've said.

"And Mae? Happy birthday." Mae's heart lifted. In the wee morning hours she'd forgotten it was her birthday.

They hung up, and Mae turned her head to the ceiling. "I don't have a clue how to do this," she confessed. "Please be okay, baby." She took a deep breath and turned on the burner for tea. Christopher's wails grew. Before the kettle even began to whistle, Mae had had enough. She gathered her keys and his diaper bag and went upstairs to get her son out of his bed. His red, wet face broke her heart. Mae wiped the tears away and kissed his puckered forehead as he took in hiccuping breaths.

"Mama's going to take care of you," Mae said. She took him out to the Jeep and buckled him into his car seat.

By the time they got to urgent care, Christopher was sound asleep. Mae wasn't sure if she should go home or take him inside anyway. Finally she decided to err on the side of caution. An hour later she left, antibiotic in hand, glad that she'd called for her mother's advice and wondering if she'd ever know all that she needed to know to be a good mother.

BOB OTT

A tangled net of tree limbs and twisted buildings immobilized Lake Emily. Metal siding wrapped trees like hard-shell tacos. Roofs were gone. Whole establishments were gone. Cars were upended. The giant oak tree that shaded the front of Hardware Hank had fallen across the street. Its enormous root ball erupted from the sidewalk, and its thick trunk blocked traffic on Main Street. Sirens sounded throughout town as rescue crews were dispatched.

Bob Ott stood in the parking lot of the shattered Chuckwagon Diner with Trudy Ploog. The girl looked shaken after their ordeal in the basement of the pharmacy, where they had taken shelter from the wind. Jim Miller, the owner of the local diner, came by offering bottled water to any in need. Bob took one for each of them.

"Thanks," Trudy said as he handed her the beverage. Mascara smudges lined her eyes.

"Are you feeling better?"

Trudy nodded. "Yeah, thanks. You've been a friend." She took a long drink. "I can't believe everything's gone." He followed her gaze across the street to the drugstore. He felt the same sense of disbelief. He'd grown up there, taking the business over from his dad, who had taken it from his grandfather. The tornado had run off with the roof, and now sunlight shone into the wind-ransacked apartment and store.

Bob saw Rosemary Johnson across the parking lot, speaking with some woman he didn't know. The petite music teacher possessed amazing poise and confidence. He'd admired Rosemary from afar for an awful long time. And that youthful haircut Trudy had talked her into made her all the more beautiful. Not that he ever had the courage to speak such a thing to her. Life had taught him about such risks. He'd been hurt deeply, at the worst possible time.

When his eyes met Trudy's again, he knew she'd seen his secret. She must've seen it before, because the girl had tried to set the two up, but he'd fumbled badly, and Rosemary remained out of reach.

"You do like her," Trudy said.

Bob felt his face flame.

"I knew it! What's it going to take for you to make a move?"

Bob looked at his feet. "I'm getting a little old for such things."

"Hey, we've just been through a tornado! Doesn't something as trivial as asking a pretty lady on a date look like a breeze in comparison? No pun intended."

Bob broke into a grin. "I guess I see your point."

"Now's your chance," Trudy whispered. Rosemary was walking toward them.

"The drugstore looks awful!" Rosemary said. "Are you two okay?" She placed a hand on the sleeve of Bob's cardigan sweater.

"We're fine," Trudy said. "Bob hauled me down to the basement just in time—he saved my life!"

Bob wiped his bald head with the bandanna he kept in his pocket.

"Well, you did!"

"It's a good thing he was there then," Rosemary said.

"How about you?" Bob said. "How did your house fare?"

"I've got some damage to repair—"

Someone called Trudy's name. The threesome lifted their heads and saw Mae and Peter Morgan in the crowd. The expression on Mae's face was frantic.

"Excuse me," Trudy said. She ran to her sister, and the two hugged fiercely.

Bob turned back to Rosemary.

"I'm glad you're okay," he said.

Rosemary's lips took on the faintest of smiles.

twenty-nine

A knock sounded on the door to Trudy and Bert's upstairs apartment. Trudy smoothed the fabric of her *chamseong,* a traditional Chinese dress with a mandarin collar and buttons that ran along her collarbone. It was sleeveless to celebrate hot summer months and tailored to fit Trudy's curves. Bert said it was "too sexy for Lake Emily." Trudy simply felt pretty in it, and the bright green color brought out her eyes.

Trudy opened the door to her Fourth of July dinner guests. Bob Ott and Rosemary Johnson stood on the small landing.

"You're right on time," Trudy said, leaning to hug each in turn. She welcomed them in and closed the door behind them. "You'll have to excuse Bert. He called to say he's running a little late."

"That's okay," Rosemary assured her.

"Bert's determined to finish spraying this week. He

says not to wait and promises to come as soon as evening milking is done."

"That's the life of a farmer, isn't it?" Bob said easily. Trudy thought of their shared terror in the basement of this very building when the tornado passed through Lake Emily last year. He was so calm and reassuring even as the winds devastated his childhood home. Somehow that single event tied them to each other with a stronger connection than landlord and tenant. He'd taken an almost fatherly role. Ironic that she found fathers in so many men except the one who owned that title.

"Your place looks lovely," Rosemary exclaimed.

Candlelight accented the living room. Sheer red, white, and blue patterned fabric fell from the ceiling in a dramatic curtain that framed the slipcovered couch. A card table was set for four in the center of the room. A white vintage tablecloth with a patriotic print along its border fell almost to the floor, and the place settings were all in white. "When did you do all this?" Rosemary said.

Trudy waved the comment aside. "Come, let's sit," Trudy said. "I've got nothing else to do other than unpack Bert's stuff and putter around here and wait for my groom. I am going to teach a two-day community-ed art class later in the summer, but otherwise I'm a slug these days. How about you?" Both took their seats.

Rosemary and Bob exchanged a knowing glance. Trudy wondered what it meant. She was just about to ask, then decided to let them tell her when they were ready. She would practice "being good," as Bert called it.

"I hope you like lamb shish kebabs with fried rice and sliced mangoes." Trudy disappeared into the kitchen and returned with the steaming main course.

"Mmm, Trudy. You outdid yourself," Bob said. He took off his felt hat, revealing a bald head with tiny scars along the fringes. "Bert sure is missing out."

"Tell me about it." Trudy took her seat. They said grace, then placed cloth napkins into laps. "The man's gone constantly. He works 24/7."

"You knew he was a farmer," Bob said as he placed two large shish kebabs on his plate. Trudy served herself a mound of steaming rice.

"I know that I knew. I just didn't realize how much time he'd actually be working. I guess I always figured he was really sitting in the house having coffee with his folks, not slaving away. Now I know what Mae's been bellyaching about these past couple of years!"

"You're so sympathetic," Rosemary teased.

"I take it you aren't used to being married yet?" Bob asked. Trudy thought it an odd question but decided to let that pass.

"Ask me again in December. Then I might actually have some experience at it." She shrugged. "His stuff is here, so that's different . . . and of course he does climb into bed eventually each night. So that's different too." Her face flushed as she realized what she'd said. She cleared her throat. "What's new in your world?"

Rosemary's gaze turned to Bob again. He reached for her hand across the table. "Well, Virginia's been visiting my mother," Rosemary said. "She's at the nursing home."

"Oh? I had no idea."

"I don't talk about her much. My mother has been catatonic for years. But there's been a change lately; when Virginia talks to her, she responds. She actually cried."

"She never cries?"

"Not really. Doesn't do much of anything. But there's a definite change in her. Nothing that drastic. Just little things." Rosemary smiled. "It gives me hope that I haven't had in a very long time."

Trudy glanced at Bob. The tenderness she saw in his eyes as he gazed at Rosemary was palpable. "I'd say you have other reasons for hope these days," Trudy guessed.

Rosemary blushed and withdrew her hand.

"There is something else," Bob said. He reached into the pocket of his lightweight cardigan and pulled out a red bandanna, which he wiped across his shiny head before continuing. "I . . . we . . . were hoping Bert would be here when we told you our news."

"News?"

"Rosemary and I . . . we eloped last week."

Trudy shrieked and jumped up to hug them each in turn. "You see, I am a good matchmaker! Show me the ring."

208

Rosemary held up a square-cut diamond ring.

"Now, that's a rock!" Trudy said, pulling it closer for inspection.

"There are advantages to getting married later in life." Rosemary giggled like a girl.

"We wanted to tell you and Bert first," Bob said, "since you two are kind of responsible for the whole thing."

"I'm so excited for you. So where are you going to live?"

"My house," Bob said. "We'll either rent Rosemary's out or sell it."

"I'm really sorry that Bert isn't here to hear your good news."

"Rosemary said you'd be even more excited than we are."

"Like that's possible. I just want you two to be as happy as Bert and I are. I mean . . . Usually we are happy . . ."

Trudy lay in the slanted moonlight. She glanced at the clock—midnight and still no Bert. She rolled to his side of the bed. The sheets were cool. She hated sleeping alone. Weren't married people supposed to sleep in the same bed? She let out a frustrated sigh and threw off the covers. Bert had promised to be home for supper with Rosemary and Bob. Was that so much to ask? Staying late would only lead to more exhaustion the next day. What was the point? Picking up the phone, she dialed the number for the barn. Odds were he wouldn't be there, but it was worth a try. Bert answered just as she was about to hang up.

"Hey," Trudy said.

"Hey." He sounded weary.

"What's keeping you? You forgot about Bob and Rosemary."

"Oh, shoot. I'm sorry. One of the cows is calving. She's having a rough time of it. I didn't want to leave her."

"Did you call the vet?"

"I don't want to spend the money. Besides, I can handle it."

"Aren't you tired?"

"Exhausted." Trudy's ire dimmed to a low flame.

"I don't want you falling asleep at the wheel. I'll come sit with you, okay? I can be useful, you know. Even if it's just getting you safely home."

"Okay." He sounded relieved. "I'll give you Fred's old job."

"Oh, great. It isn't nasty, is it?"

"Of course not."

"I'm sorry." Bert leaned to kiss her on the forehead. "You have to forgive me, you know. It's in the newlywed rule book."

Trudy rolled her eyes and tried to pout. She never was good at staying mad at him. "I was really disappointed." Bert stroked her hair. "Is it always going to be this way?"

"What way?" He turned his face toward her.

"Me sitting around like some widow, waiting for you, and you always so busy you forget I'm even here."

"I didn't mean to forget. It's just . . ." He motioned toward the cow that lay on her side, moaning.

"I know. But you did forget to call. How did your ma manage things when your dad was too busy?"

Bert put hand to chin in thought. "I guess she just made her plans without Dad."

"You mean she acted like a single mom?"

Bert shrugged. "Basically. It kept her from being disappointed."

"That's so sad."

"I suppose. It was only until the harvest came in. Then he was around all the time."

"Thus the reason you went out for hockey; the season doesn't interfere with farm work."

"I never thought of it that way before." The cow moaned again, and Bert went to the animal's side.

Trudy rubbed her upper arms. The air was cool in the cavernous barn. She glanced at her watch—one o'clock.

Bert stroked the black-and-white cow's side. The girl let out a pained bellow. Trudy pulled the short milking stool closer to the cow's head and scratched just behind her ears.

They sat and watched for over an hour and a half. But still no calf. Bert moved to the cow's rump and bent down to look inside. Carefully he slipped first his hand, then his forearm inside until his arm was completely enveloped. Trudy's eyes widened. She fought the sudden urge to toss her cookies across the hay. Had she really missed Bert so much that she was willing to put herself through this? She turned her head away. When she glanced at him again, Bert had withdrawn his arm and was shaking his head. His expression was grim.

"What's wrong?"

"I need to use the chains."

"Chains?"

Bert disappeared into the adjoining room. Within minutes he was back. He carried a small chain about three-quarters of an inch in diameter and six feet long. He motioned for Trudy to come to him. "He's twisted in there. I need you to pull on these." He motioned toward another set of chains with hooks on the ends. "I'll tell you which side and how hard to pull while I guide. Are you up to it?"

Trudy nodded despite her queasiness. At least he wasn't asking her to put her hand up any portion of the cow's anatomy. "Just tell me when."

Bert guided one end of the chain into the cow's uterus. Trudy's queasiness billowed. "How can you do that?" she whispered. The cow moaned loud and long.

"Been doing it since I was a kid. I'm looping each end of the chain around the calf's forelegs. Hopefully this will straighten him out." He reached for the other chains and hooked them into each side of the first and handed the ends to Trudy.

"Is this humane?"

"More humane than letting him die in there and endangering his mama's life in the process. When I say pull, put pressure on the left one. That should untwist him. Don't yank it, but it'll take some strength."

Trudy knelt in the straw. Once Bert was ready, he gave the signal. Trudy tugged, gently at first, then harder. The calf was stubborn. Finally, when Trudy was at the end of her strength, something popped. Bert lifted a hand giving her permission to stop.

"That ought to do it," Bert said. He offered her a grateful smile. Trudy let the chain fall to the ground.

Soon the tiny hooves were visible, then the legs, and a purplish mass that Trudy guessed was the head, all covered in a slimy film. Bert reached for the baby's legs. The cow bellowed again. Finally the shoulders emerged. It was a disgusting mess, and it had a peculiar odor, like dirty socks thrown directly into the dryer. Bert tugged the calf out and laid him in front of his mother's nose. She sniffed her newborn, then began to clean his face and neck with her long sandpaper tongue. Tufts of hair stood on end as if the calf wore a heavy application of styling gel.

"Cow licks!" Trudy said. Bert chuckled.

The cow stood then and continued giving her son his first bath.

"Eww, she's going to eat that?" Trudy said of the afterbirth. Bert moved to her side and was about to put an arm around his bride's shoulders when she backed away from him. "I know where that arm has been, mister! Go wash up!" She pointed toward the door.

Bert hung his head despite the smirk on his lips, then left to wash. Trudy joined him in the tank room.

"Can we go home now?" Trudy said. "I don't do well with these late nights."

Bert turned out the light and took her hand, giving her the keys. They climbed into the AMC Pacer.

"You'd be glad if we moved to the farm, wouldn't you?" Trudy said. "You could go straight to bed now if not for me wanting to live in town."

"I'm happy wherever we are." He leaned his head against the headrest and closed his eyes. Trudy started the car and pulled out of the drive onto the gravel road.

She loved this man. It was selfish of her to want to live in town when his job made such demands. Yet she knew herself too; she thrived on being with others, in the midst of whatever hubbub was to be had. If she was miserable, how could she be a help to Bert? She glanced toward the passenger seat. Bert was sound asleep.

What's wrong with you, Trudy? He's wearing himself out, and you can't give him one thing in return.

thirty

Six in the morning. Bert pushed the Power button for the milk machine. Its loud, steady rumble filled the quiet. It was all Bert could do to keep his eyes open. The new calf hopped beside his mother in the soft straw, then stretched out his neck to nurse. Bert would let him suckle for a couple of days on the health-building colostrum, then he would move the baby to one of the plastic igloos behind the barn, where Lillian would feed him two bottles of milk replacer every day. Trudy would have to adopt that job once his folks moved to town. Or perhaps Bert would do it himself if Trudy couldn't bring herself to live here.

She'd made herself clear enough in the days after the dinner with his folks, and in exchange he vowed not to bring up the subject of moving until she did. Trudy thrived on being with people. He could adapt to that, couldn't he? For the sake of their marriage? He lifted his seed cap and ran a hand through his curly hair. It would be far easier to live on site, but a man had to have his priorities, and Trudy was number one.

The cows meandered between the barn and the pasture as another sunny day dawned. Bert opened the wide door to allow the girls easy access, then went back in. The cows followed him like schoolchildren coming in from recess. They were usually pretty eager for their milking, their udders heavy with milk. The first eight sauntered into the milking parlor ahead of him. They stepped up onto the cement stalls. The heavy bars that encircled their necks clanged shut. Bert moved swiftly from one cow to the next, spraying and wiping udders, then attaching the black tubes to each teat. By the time he reached the eighth cow, the first was finished. The machine automatically sensed that the flow of milk had stopped and withdrew its hand. The wide-eyed cow strained to look back as she waited for Bert to release her. After quickly getting the eighth cow set up, Bert moved to the first and pushed the release bar. She ambled forward and around the perimeter of the parlor and out to the sunny pasture. Another cow moved in to replace her. If the cows only had hands, they could manage this routine on their own.

The gate to the milking parlor rattled open. Bert lifted his head to see his father. Willie nodded and released one of the girls from her headstall.

"Thought you could use a hand," he shouted above the noise of the loud machine. "I saw how late you left last night. You should've come and gotten me. I would've helped." The cow nearest him shifted her hindquarters away from him.

Bert shook his head. "We did fine. Trudy came and helped."

Father and son settled into the routine.

Finally the last cow ambled off, and the loud machine fell silent. Bert always felt good about finishing another milking session. It offered its own sense of accomplishment. They walked into the warm day. A few clouds floated like pale feathers. Blue jays and black-capped chickadees darted between the feeders in the backyard.

"Everything go all right last night?" Willie asked.

Bert turned to his dad. "Eventually. I had to use the chains."

"What did the missus think?" Willie said dryly.

Bert leaned against the gate. "Calving isn't her

thing—turned green when I put the chains on." They shared a smile.

Then Willie's face sobered. "How many acres did you finish spraying?"

"I finished that, but I'm late on the haying now. I really need to get three cuttings this year."

They gazed into the distance. Bert knew what his dad was thinking—if Fred hadn't up and left them, they wouldn't be in this predicament. Having to sell that land was like selling a part of their family, their heritage. Anger toward his brother smoldered.

"Your ma and I made an offer on a house on Fourth. She likes it well enough." He shoved his hands in his pockets. "It's the right price."

"You've lived in this house your whole life, Dad. Are you sure you want to do this?"

Willie crossed his arms and breathed a heavy sigh. "Not so much a matter of wanting. It's the right thing." A familiar twinkle softened his eyes. "You and your bride need a good start. It's too big a burden on you and the farm trying to support another place in town. You should be here, not us. And you sure don't need me and your ma muddying things up for you." He smiled again. "Consider it a wedding gift."

Bert didn't know what to say. He felt honored, privileged, and somehow . . . manipulated.

Stars pricked the inky July sky with bright sparkles. Crickets sawed a bluegrass tune. Peter came in at midnight in a state of total exhaustion, relieved that he was almost done spraying. But everything seemed to be running so late this year, and he would have only a short reprieve before the next haying.

Peter pressed the heel of his hand into his stomach. It was tied in knots. No doubt from being overtired. He parked the John Deere in the drive alongside the house, noting that the kitchen lights still shone through the window at this late hour.

When he opened the door, the sound of sobbing met him. And it wasn't the baby.

"What's wrong?" he said to Mae.

Mae sniffled, and her red-rimmed eyes darted to his. "Oh, Peter!" she said in a high-pitched sob that reminded him of Mary Tyler Moore on *The Dick Van Dyke Show.*

Peter reached for Christopher, who was awake but happy. The baby cooed at his father.

"Is something wrong?"

"Christopher's going to grow up and leave us someday." She was completely serious.

Peter stifled a laugh. "Sit," he instructed. He cradled Christopher in his arm. His little body felt warm. "Of course he'll leave us someday. That's what children do."

"I know." Mae wiped her nose with a tissue. "But it's going to happen so fast. It was like yesterday when I turned eight, and now I'm a mom. It'll be just as fast for him." Her voice cracked.

"Have you been sad all day?" Peter said.

Mae nodded.

"It's just baby blues and another birthday passing for you."

They'd celebrated on the third with a little dinner for three at Whisky River in St. Peter, Minnesota. The back dining room overlooked a wildlife sanctuary, where deer wandered and every imaginable species of birds dined on the wide selection of bird feed.

"It's not just baby blues. It's that . . . I just want to be the best mom possible . . ."

"You've been beating yourself up about his ear infection, right?" Peter reached to touch her shoulder. "Everything's going to be just fine. You're doing a great job. Look at our son. He's happy and healthy."

Mae smiled weakly.

"Why don't you let me put him down tonight?" Peter said. "We haven't had enough father-son time. It'll do us both good. You go on up to bed."

"Are you sure?" Her eyes strayed to the baby, who wriggled in his father's arms. She looked as tired as Peter felt.

Peter placed a gentle hand on the back of her head, drawing her to him. He kissed her forehead. "You're a good mother. If there's one thing I know about you, it's that."

Mae smiled sleepily at him. "Have I told you lately that I love you?"

"Ditto. Now get to bed. I'll be right up." She climbed the steps. Peter heard the door to their bedroom close.

Taking the baby to the front porch, Peter settled on one of the rockers. He tucked the blanket around his son's legs. Christopher's cheeks and legs had filled out in the past couple of weeks so that now they looked like round marshmallows tied off with rubber bands. Peter rocked ever so slightly, and the baby's eyes began to droop. Tiny fists curled beside his face. Peter's heart swelled at the sight. His son was so perfect, so helpless. Peter had missed this time since the field work had begun. Regret filled him for those lost hours, and he envied Mae the joy she must be having despite his absence.

He didn't know love could run so deep. His very soul was linked to this person. Yet Christopher had no concept of it. He simply accepted the life that was his, demanded that his needs be met, and took each moment as it came.

Peter's thoughts turned to his own father and the divide that separated them. Had his father felt this regret? This inexorable link? Did he long to be here with his new grandson? To at least see him? Or was he so engrossed with his precious music that thoughts of the heritage he'd left behind had long since fled?

"Does he want to know you?" Peter whispered to Christopher, who now slept peacefully. Peter's gaze shifted to the winking sky. Crickets sang. "Or has he forgotten all of us?"

"What do you mean, 'They bought a house'?" Trudy stood in the bathroom doorway just off the living room. She held a hairbrush in one hand. A film of cold cream covered her face.

Bert kicked off his shoes and sank to the couch. He took a deep breath. "I mean they found a house in town and signed a purchase agreement on it. They move in three months."

"So . . . we're moving to the farm for sure then?"

"It's up to you."

"What do you mean, it's up to me?"

"You sure keep saying 'What do you mean' a lot." Bert pulled the aluminum tab and pushed it back to open the can of cold Pepsi.

"Is this some kind of a test?" Trudy took a step closer and pointed with the brush for emphasis.

"What are you talking about?" Bert seemed completely baffled by her frustration, but Trudy wasn't convinced.

"I know you would rather live on the farm. It makes sense, especially during calving. But you know I like it in town."

Bert sipped his pop, then calmly set it down. "Do you trust me?"

"Do I what?"

"Trust me? Because I'm not pulling a fast one. When I say it's up to you, I mean it. We can go right on living in town for however long you want."

"And let the house sit vacant?"

"We could rent it out."

"To whom?" Trudy put hands on hips. Bert shrugged and took another sip.

"You *don't* trust me," he said matter-of-factly. Trudy threw up her hands and went back into the bathroom.

She rinsed the cold cream from her face and brushed her hair forcefully. What was it about Bert that could drive her so nuts? He knew it made sense for them to live on the farm. So why wouldn't he admit it? She sighed, tossed the brush into its drawer, and returned to the living room. Bert still nursed his Pepsi.

"We're moving to the farm," she said.

"We are?" Bert raised his eyes to hers.

"Your folks will be in town, right? So it'll be fine. You can't very well leave the herd alone. Someone could steal them while we sleep here!"

Bert gave her a tender smile.

"Besides, we'll still be on our own. This way we'll have the best of both worlds."

"You're sure about this?"

Trudy paused to think about that. But Bert looked so pleased she couldn't very well take it back. She dropped next to him on the couch and nestled her head on his shoulder.

"It's about you and me—together." Her assurance was as much for herself as Bert. "That's what matters."

When Bert left to milk the next morning, Trudy lay in bed thinking. She so wanted to give this to Bert. Why was her impulse always to think of herself first? To put her own desires before others'? Couldn't she simply allow life to be easy? She lifted her head from the pillow and studied the clock—5:32. If they lived at the farm, he could sleep just a little longer, be with her more. It was the right thing. She *could* put him first.

thirty-one

I t's time to bring your grandma home, Peter," Mae said. "The nursing home says she's maxed out her Medicare."

Peter stood atop the wagon that was piled twelve feet high with fresh bales of hay. It smelled sweet, earthy on the hot July day. Mae held Christopher against her shoulder with one hand and shaded her eyes from the sun with the other.

She swayed slightly as she spoke, a rhythm meant to soothe the baby. "I'm strong enough. Virginia's walking with a walker. So it'll work out. I'll still have to take her in to physical therapy three times a week."

Peter lifted the seed cap Bert had given him after their first season in Lake Emily and ran a hand through his hair. Sweat dripped from his nose, and his face was red from exertion. Bits of dried grass clung to his clothes and skin. Bert had disappeared inside the barn's dark, wide mouth with a bale of hay. Since Fred had left, the two had taken to helping each other with haying.

"What does the doctor say?" Peter said.

"I talked to him when I went in today. He said the physical therapist will have to come do a home evaluation to make sure we're ready for her. We'll need grab rails in the downstairs bathroom—that kind of thing. He said that she's been doing wonderfully lately, that there's been a real change in her. I think it's because of August."

"August who?"

"You remember my old boss from Le Center."

"But how did he and Grandma—?"

"Trudy invited him over that day she came to visit. They hit it off. He's been going to visit her every day."

"Really?" Peter said. "Grandma with a 'gentleman caller'?"

"I don't think it's that way. Well, I guess I don't know. But she sure has brightened up since he started visiting."

"At least that's something," Peter said. Bert came back outside, and Peter tossed a few more bales to the ground before climbing down to resume his job of hauling them into the barn. So it was settled. Virginia was coming home.

Virginia took the walker down the corridor to Violet's room. It was slow going, but she was thrilled to be out of that cursed wheelchair, to have the freedom to go where she pleased without its cumbersome weight. The door to Violet's room was ajar, and Virginia knocked before letting herself in. The television was on, a morning news show. Violet stared.

"Good morning," Virginia said.

Virginia sat in the chair next to Violet and reached for her hand.

"What are you watching? Do you mind if I turn it down?" Virginia reached for the remote control and lowered the volume. Violet didn't seem to mind.

"I came to tell you that I'm going home today, to the farm at least. I'm not ready to live by myself quite yet. But it'll be good, I think. I wanted to tell you that I still plan on coming for our visits. Would you like that?"

Violet didn't answer. Virginia hadn't expected her to.

"I can't tell you how much our time together has meant to me. Although why that would be, I can't say. It's not as if you ever say anything. Maybe it's just good to be listened to without being judged. You're good at that, you know, listening. I bet you were a good friend before . . ."

Violet blinked, just once, but Virginia wondered if it signified something.

"I'm going to be staying back at the farm, where Roy and I made so many memories. That might be difficult, but good, too. At least I'll get to spend time with my first great-grandson. Did I tell you that I have a great-grandson? He's adorable. Such a blessing after all that Mae and Peter went through." Virginia paused, thinking of another topic of discussion. "I heard that Rosemary got married. That must be a relief to you to know she's well cared for, loved. Such a lovely daughter you have. Do you know that? Rosemary is a daughter to be proud of."

Then Violet did something truly amazing—she turned her head and looked Virginia in the eyes.

After Peter finished mowing thirty acres of hay in the northwest section, he, Mae, and Christopher went to

225

bring Virginia home. Temperatures climbed into the nineties on this bright mid-July day. Highway 36, a ribbon of black, moseyed into Lake Emily. Heat radiated off its surface in visible waves. Birds sang in their assorted trills and twitters and chirps, each competing for the solo in the song. The breeze rustled the trees in a soft caress.

"We need rain badly," Peter said as he shifted the Jeep into fourth gear. A male ring-necked pheasant flew up from the ditch grasses as they passed.

"Weren't we just praying for the rain to stop?" Mae said. She glanced back at Christopher, who slept peacefully in his car seat.

"That's the irony of farming. When you want the fields dry, it rains. When you need rain, it doesn't come. Kind of like a woman, if you think about it."

"Very funny." Her gaze turned to the distance. "I'm glad Virginia's finally coming home."

Peter reached for her hand. "Me, too."

When they arrived at the nursing home, Virginia was all packed and ready to go. Her chair faced the window. Her eyes were closed.

"Grandma," Peter whispered, bending near. Virginia's eyes fluttered open. "We're here to take you home."

She looked up at Mae, and a smile brightened her face. A sound at the door drew their attention, and a gray-haired man came in with a book in hand. "Virginia, was this the—" He stopped when his gaze met Peter's and Mae's.

"Mr. Cleworth," Mae said. His gaze fell to Christopher in her arms.

"How's the little sailor?" His wrinkled face took on a smile.

"He's great. Thanks," Mae said.

"We didn't know you were here," Peter said, looking first to his grandmother, then to August Cleworth.

"He helped pack my bags," Virginia explained.

"Oh," Peter said.

"Well." Virginia picked up the conversation as if she were unnerved by the exchange. "We'd better get going. Dr. Mielke already signed me out."

The full moon cast its glow across the room as if it were midmorning. Outside her bedroom window, Virginia could see the Adirondack chairs and crab-apple trees in the front yard. She couldn't sleep. Memories crept along the walls.

Mae was up with the baby. Virginia heard the creak of the floorboards overhead and then on the stairs. A light flicked on in the kitchen, and Christopher's whimpers grew.

"Shh," Virginia heard Mae whisper. Mae's shadow passed the slightly open door of Virginia's room as she moved to the living room to nurse the baby.

Virginia saw herself with David as a newborn. Roy sleeping after a long day of work, desperately needing his rest. David's two o'clock cries. Virginia stealing him away to the living room before Roy awakened. Roy always claimed his kids slept through the night from day one. "You wanted everyone to know how perfect our kids were," Virginia whispered to the ceiling.

Her thoughts fluttered to August. He'd become a friend, a dear friend. He wasn't offended when she spoke of Roy. He spoke often of Willa. Knowing that he still loved his wife somehow lightened her spirit. She wasn't alone in this journey of grief.

ANNA EASTMAN

"Anna?" Her father, Philip, knocked on her bedroom door before opening it. Sixteen-year-old Anna lifted her head from her German homework. Papers— algebra, biology, and composition—littered her brightly colored bedspread. She'd been studying for two hours already, not that that was unusual. Most evenings saw two or three hours of homework. How else was she going to get the scholarships she needed to pay for college?

"What is it, Dad?"

His eyes were troubled. "There's been an accident. It's Mom . . ." His voice trailed away as if he couldn't comprehend what he was saying.

A hand flew to Anna's mouth, and she stood up. Her German textbook fell to the bed.

Anna's dad placed a steadying hand on her shoulder. "She's alive, but . . . it sounds bad. There was a semi on Highway 36 going north. The officer said his front tire blew, and he crossed the center line . . . He hit Mom's car head-on. She's in the emergency room at Immanuel St. Joseph's in Mankato."

"We need to go to her." She moved to him and looked in his eyes. "You okay, Dad?"

He nodded mutely, and they left for the hospital.

Anna's mom didn't look like herself. Anna and her dad stood at the foot of her bed. Tubes sprouted from Lana Eastman's arms and face. Monitors beeped. Nurses moved about, checking her vitals, checking the IVs that hung from the stand alongside the bed. Her mom's pretty face was now a bluish color. A darker, purple bruise spread from the left side of her nose, past her eye, and to her temple. The rest of her head hid beneath a bandage. Thick white bandages covered her arms and hands as well. She slept. A rattle from her chest echoed in her light snore.

Anna's dad lightly touched her mom's shoulder. Her eyes fluttered open—confusion and fear crossed her face.

"We're here," Dad said.

Her mom's gaze turned to Anna.

"What happened?" she said. She lifted her hand as if to reach for her daughter. Then she winced and let it drop back down. "I remember driving home, and then . . ."

"You were in a head-on collision. From what the police said, you're lucky to be alive," Dad said. He bent to kiss her unbruised cheek.

"*Good thing your boss sprang for that Mercedes,*" Mom teased. The joke brought a smile to Anna's lips. "*Oh, my head,*" Mom complained. "*I've got such a headache.*"

When the doctor came in half an hour later, they learned that she had suffered two broken arms. "*We'll put casts on her arms once the swelling goes down,*" the doctor said. "*But I'm more concerned about her head; there could be long-term damage to the brain.*"

"*That's what's causing the headache?*" Dad asked.

The doctor nodded. "*And there's some numbness in her extremities . . . We'll watch her close and keep you updated.*"

At three o' clock that morning, Lana had her first seizure. Her small body flailed, dislodging an IV from her arm. Anna watched helplessly as the nurses and doctors tried to keep her from hurting herself, and the clock ticked on and on.

A new fear sank deep roots in Anna's heart.

What did the future hold? Would her mother ever be whole . . . ever be the same again? Something told her that life had broken free of its tether. Now they were at the mercy of the wind.

thirty-two

The doorbell sounded. Anna moved toward the door. When she opened it, Jessie's grinning face met her. Anna's heart swelled. She loved this child, she realized. Jessie had wormed her way into her affections.

"These are for you," Jessie said. She held out a pan of Rice Krispie bars. "I made them myself." Anna took them, along with a quick hug from the girl and a warm smile from Steve, who was behind her.

"Wow." Anna glanced at Steve. "Jessie's cooking by herself now?"

Jessie ambled to the dining room, which glowed with candlelight. "Dad watched to make sure I didn't start a fire with the marshmallows or anything." She leaned close to a candle and passed a finger quickly through its flame.

"She's a regular chef. Stop that, Jessie. Kids these days!" He threw up his hands in a benign what's-a-father-to-do gesture.

"Supper's just about ready. Why don't you two take your seats."

Anna went into the kitchen.

These gatherings had become so natural—the three of them together, enjoying a meal, swimming in the lake. They were like . . . a family. And yet the feelings she wished she had for Steve weren't there. He was a kind, wonderful person and a good friend. But just a friend.

"I'm getting another rabbit for 4-H," Jessie informed as Anna brought the homemade casserole from the kitchen. "Flopsy is lonely, and Dad said I could." Anna took her seat across from Steve.

"Can you show two rabbits at the fair?" Anna said.

Jessie paused to think. "I don't know. I suppose. I need to ask Virginia about that . . ." Jessie's voice trailed off, and she burst into tears.

"What's wrong?" Anna said, placing a hand on the girl's shoulder. Anna turned to Steve.

"She's like this"—concern drew his brows together—"anytime someone mentions Virginia."

"Did you know she moved back to the farm yesterday?" Anna said.

"She did?" Jessie lifted teary, hopeful eyes.

"Well, see, Jessie," Steve said. "You can visit her when you go take care of your sheep this week." He turned to Anna. "She keeps her 4-H sheep at the Morgans' farm."

"I think you mentioned that to me." She stroked Jessie's hair. "How about if I take you next time? It'll give me an excuse to see Virginia, and you can introduce me to your lambs."

"Sheep," Jessie corrected. "They're too old to be called lambs anymore." She wiped her eyes.

By the time dishes were done and the kitchen light turned off, Jessie seemed her usual lighthearted self. Steve told her to go skip stones on the lake so he and Anna could talk. They watched as she walked to the shore's edge. The lake had become a smooth glass table, and the setting sun cast a path across it in salmon and lavender, silhouetting Jessie's slight form against its stunning beauty. When the screen door slammed shut, Steve turned to Anna.

"She really cares for you," he said.

"I really care for her." Anna lifted two steaming cups of coffee and met him on the porch's wicker seats. Steve reached for his coffee and took a long sip. They turned their heads to watch Jessie as she bent down searching for stones.

"I need to ask you something," Steve said.

"Oh?" Anna lifted her gaze to his. His eyes seemed troubled.

"I . . ." He cleared his throat. Anna gazed down and saw that he was gripping the mug with white knuckles. "I wanted to ask you something."

"Okay."

"You know that Jessie and I are very fond of you." Anna nodded.

"Well, I've been wondering. I mean . . ."

"Just say it, Steve. I won't bite you," Anna smiled, trying to ease his nerves.

Steve broke into a smile. "I'm sorry. I guess I'm a little nervous." He wiped a hand on his jeans. "What I'm trying to say and doing so poorly at is . . . I'd like to court you, Anna Eastman."

Anna was taken aback by the question. She set her coffee cup on the wicker coffee table, trying to figure out what to say. How not to hurt his feelings.

"I . . . I don't have those kinds of feelings for you, Steve. It's not that I don't care, because believe me, I really do. I just . . ."

Steve's wounded eyes met hers.

"I'm sorry. I didn't mean to lead you on." She sounded so lame, so weak, yet she couldn't think of anything else to say that wouldn't hurt him even more.

Steve sat back in his chair. She could see that he was hurting, and yet what choice did she have? She sensed no spark between them. She wanted to feel something romantic for him; she truly did. Yet whenever they were together, there was nothing more than a friendly bond.

"It's just . . . when I met you and Jessie, I felt a connection with her. Her mom died in a car accident; my mom was devastated by a car accident. I just . . ."

Steve held up a hand. "You don't have to explain." But his face was red. He looked ready to bolt.

When Jessie returned from skipping stones, he did just that.

"What happened, Dad?" Jessie said as their car sped away from Anna's house.

"I don't want to talk about it." He turned his head away as if concentrating real hard on driving, but Jessie knew something wasn't right. She'd seen the strange way he and Anna had acted when she had come back up to the house—all polite as if they were meeting for the first time.

"Can we ask Anna to the Chuckwagon on Saturday?" she probed, hoping for some sort of clue.

"No!" It was almost a shout. Then he lowered his voice and said, "No, honey, we won't be doing much with Anna anymore. I doubt we'll be going to church much . . ." His voice trailed away.

Jessie's heart sank. But there was something else in his tone, something subtle and familiar. Unwelcome. Dread rose up. Jessie pushed it away.

"Don't you have any cornmeal?" Lillian rummaged through the cupboards in Trudy's tiny apartment as Trudy chopped onions beside the ceramic sink.

"There's some up there," Trudy said.

Lillian pulled a chair from beside the small table and climbed on it to search higher. The woman had been to the apartment every day this week with one excuse or another. Trudy was ready to lock the doors. Today Lillian planned to teach Trudy to make "real cornbread."

"Top shelf. I have a box of Jiffy."

"Jiffy," Lillian scoffed. "When was the last time you cleaned up here?"

Lillian's house was a sty, and she was criticizing *her* cleaning skills? Trudy bit back her "You'd know dirt!" comment. When she looked up, Lillian was staring at her.

"What?"

"What are you smirking about? I was telling you that the best cornbread is made from Quaker cornmeal."

"It is? I knew that."

"No wonder Bert asked me to give you my recipe."

He did no such thing. Instead she said, "Bert and I are going out for dinner tomorrow, so you don't need to go to all this trouble."

"Oh?" Lillian stepped off the chair and returned it to its spot by the small drop-leaf table. "Where are you going?"

Trudy hedged. If she answered, they'd end up eating with Willie and Lillian again. She'd had enough of her mother-in-law to last a few decades. "I'm not sure." At least she could speak the truth. "Bert is going to pick the restaurant."

"H'm. Seems like an awful odd arrangement to me, him picking the restaurant and not even telling you where you're going. Willie never has a say in such things!"

Trudy just shrugged.

"You *told* them we were eating at Kokomo's?" Trudy stood behind Bert as he brushed his teeth for bed that night. She wore her hot-pink footed pajamas, and her red hair was pulled up in a loose ponytail. Bert spit and rinsed.

"Sure. What's wrong with that?" Bert wiped his mouth on a towel.

"Your mother can't leave us alone! She's driving me insane with her constant criticism. That's what's wrong."

"I haven't seen her much."

"Stay home sometime. You can get caught up! The woman has practically moved in. It wouldn't surprise me if she asked Bob Ott for her own key to our apartment!"

"I gave her a key."

"What?!"

Bert grinned. "Just kidding." Trudy slugged him in the arm. He grabbed her around the shoulders and kissed her temple. "Breathe, honey, just breathe."

"I'm serious, Bert."

"I know you are, but you've got to take it in stride. Laugh at her. That's what I do."

"Oh, I laugh at her, all right. She was telling me to clean my cupboards. Like her kitchen is tidy! She has a box of matzo mix from the '80s up there. You aren't even Jewish!"

"That's my girl." Bert turned out the light and left Trudy in the dark. Trudy followed him to the bedroom.

"It's only going to get worse when we move to the farm, you know. It's familiar territory for her. She'll feel right at home."

Bert climbed under the covers. Trudy stood at the foot of the bed and placed hands on hips. "Take me seriously!"

"How can I when you're wearing those pajamas? Are you trying to send me a message? If so, it's coming through loud and clear."

Trudy gazed down at the bright flannel wear. "What's wrong with it?"

Bert merely raised an eyebrow. "Tell you what," he finally said. "You throw away those pajamas forever, and I'll talk to my mom about not meddling."

"Really?"

"I promise. Now come here, you."

Trudy nestled up next to her husband and pouted.

"Still mad about Ma?"

"No. I like these pajamas."

Bert laughed.

"It's something more," Trudy confessed. Bert touched her cheek. "I have been feeling lonely, I guess. You're at the farm all the time."

"You'll get used to it. Besides, you can visit Mae, do things you like to do—painting . . ."

"I suppose. But Mae's so consumed with that baby."

"New mothers tend to like their babies."

"Well, I know that! It's just that she's always fussing over him. I can't tell you how many times she interrupts something I say with an 'Ooh, would you look at that' if his nose twitches or he has a hot diaper!"

"She'll get used to being a mom soon enough, and you'll be back to being the center of attention."

"Hey!" She threw the blanket over his head. "I love Christopher too. I just didn't realize how much our relationship would change once he was born."

Bert reemerged. "Don't forget you just got married too."

"Sure, but I haven't changed at all."

Bert smirked.

"I have not!"

"Okay." He raised his hands in surrender. "Remind me, what did we have for supper again?"

"Your ma's goulash."

238

There was just something about an afternoon nap. Yellow light slanted across Virginia's room. She dozed on top of her white coverlet with a thin afghan pulled across her. The warmth caressed her shoulders with a comforting hand. Then Virginia was aware of another hand on her shoulder. She turned over and opened her eyes. Mae sat on the bed.

"I'm sorry to wake you. Time for medicine." Mae held up one of the pills to thin Virginia's blood. Virginia opened her mouth, then swallowed the ice water Mae offered. The girl had circles under her eyes.

"Did you have a good nap?"

Virginia nodded. "How about you?"

"Oh, I haven't had a chance. I had some housework to catch up on." Mae waved the comment away. But Virginia worried. She didn't want to be the cause of those circles. "Can I show you something?" Mae said.

"Sure."

"You up to walking?"

"Let me hobble." Virginia swung her legs to the floor while Mae positioned the walker in front of her. On a count of three, Virginia pushed up. The task had become much easier in the past three weeks, no longer the breath-halting journey of risk. Virginia felt confident walking with the contraption. She didn't even mind the cumbersome nature of the thing; at least it wasn't that nasty wheelchair. Slowly they moved into the living room.

Virginia didn't notice anything out of the ordinary

until she looked at the big area rug at the room's center. Tiny Christopher lay on his belly, his face turned to the side. He slept peacefully, yet his mouth worked as if he were dreaming. Then a small thumb found its way, like a baby kitten to its mother's teat, and he began to suck.

"Would you look at that," Virginia said. "Already a thumb-sucker, just like his dad and grandpa."

"Peter sucked his thumb?"

"Until he was seven or eight, I think." They shared a smile.

"Say," Mae broke the silence. "I was thinking that since Christopher's out for the count, maybe I could help you get a bath."

Guilt for all that this girl had already done for her intruded on the nice idea. "I can give myself a sponge bath."

"Wouldn't you rather have a nice shower?" Mae held her nose playfully. "You're getting a little ripe."

"Well, if you're going to say that!" Virginia feigned offense, then she confessed, "That does sound enticing."

"I can help you get in and out, wash your hair for you if you like."

"It can be rather tricky getting the shampoo bottle opened. I am a little nervous about falling."

"That's why we have the bath bench and grab bar—to make your life easier." Mae offered a smile. "So don't worry, okay? Peter's around this afternoon if we need him."

Virginia chuckled. "I doubt Peter would like to see this old body in the raw."

"Come on. I don't mind at all." She returned to Virginia's room to get clothes and underwear for Virginia to change into. Virginia sat down and watched her great-grandson sleep peacefully in the sunshine. A few minutes later Mae was back. "You ready?"

The downstairs bathroom was small, so they left the walker in the hallway. Virginia leaned her heavy frame against Mae's thin form. Once inside the room, Virginia shifted her body against the vanity. She lifted her good hand to unbutton her blouse, but without her hand to give balance, she felt herself slipping. Mae quickly caught her. Virginia's heart beat wildly in her chest.

"You okay?" Mae whispered.

Virginia nodded despite the lump in her throat. "Can you unbutton me?" She hated asking.

"Of course."

Virginia took a seat on the bench inside the shower while Mae worked. It was such a simple thing, unbuttoning a blouse, yet her inability emphasized her helplessness. She watched Mae's brown eyes as she undid the buttons. When she was done, Virginia mouthed, "Thank you."

Mae patted her shoulder and said tenderly, "Don't you fret, okay? I'm right here."

Gratitude welled in Virginia. The girl hadn't asked for this burden, yet here she was teaching an old woman to toddle.

thirty-three

E lla Rosenberg strode to the window in Virginia's room and opened the curtains. "It's good that Mae and Peter made a room for you down here so you don't have to manage those steps."

Virginia squinted into the light. "Now, why'd you do that? I don't want every Joe looking in the window."

Ella turned to face her. "You lived here over fifty years, Virginia. Since when are you paranoid about people looking in? You're on a dirt road two miles from the nearest farm, for heaven's sake."

Virginia threw up her hands, conceding the point.

Ella took a chair next to Virginia's.

"Now, be honest. Is something wrong?"

Virginia considered for a moment before replying. "I'm doing fine. Mae waits on me hand and foot without a word of complaint. I feel bad for the girl. She didn't ask for this, you know."

"You're so used to giving to everyone else," Ella said. "You have no idea how to receive graciously."

Virginia shrugged. "How would you feel? This isn't easy for them. You can't deny that. They just had a baby, and Peter's been working like a dog. Now they have me, too . . . It makes me wish Roy were here."

"I understand." Ella reached for her hand. "I've often wished Jerry were handy just to get me Tylenol when I have a cold. What happened to Mr. Cleworth?"

Virginia's face flushed. The truth was, August had

come calling even more since she'd moved home. She wasn't sure what to make of that. Except that she enjoyed his company. He seemed to understand her feelings, as much as they shifted with each tide. He never offered any sort of criticism. He was just . . . there.

And he didn't seem inclined to leave her.

Kokomo's in Cleveland, Minnesota, was a quaint restaurant with a tropical theme. A favorite among the locals, it offered do-it-yourself flame-broiled steaks amid the ambiance of ocean-side murals and mounted fish of all shapes and sizes. Although Trudy and Bert had yet to go, Saturday night karaoke was said to be a hopping fun time.

Trudy, Bert, Lillian, and Will followed the tall waitress to the aqua-colored vinyl booth near the windows. She handed out menus, then left with their drink orders. Trudy gave Bert a nudge to remind him that he had something to talk to his mother about. Bert shook his head and turned to look at the menu.

"You think you'll be able to help hay next week?" Bert asked his dad.

"Sure." Willie's gaze was on his menu also.

"Don't let him haul those bales," Lillian warned. "Last time his back was sore for two weeks. He's getting too old for that."

"He can drive the tractor," Bert assured.

"I'll do whatever I need to," Willie said. Lillian gave him her don't-come-running-to-me-afterward glare.

Willie pointed to Trudy's menu. "The shrimp scampi is pretty good if you don't like steak."

"Seafood in Minnesota just isn't the same once you've been to the coasts." Trudy shook her head. "No, I'll go for the prime rib, Pops." Willie grinned at the endearment. Lillian rolled her eyes.

"Excuse me." It was the waitress. "There's someone asking for you at the front desk, Mr. Biddle."

Willie gave Bert a puzzled look. "For me?" Willie said.

She nodded and led him away. When he returned, his face was white. Behind him came a longhaired man with a beard and mustache.

"Hey, Bert," the man said. Trudy instantly recognized the voice if not the face. Fred.

Lillian jumped to her feet and clucked around him, hugging and kissing and saying, "Oh, my goodness," until the stares of the other patrons caused Willie to say, "Let's sit down."

A petite blonde waited shyly behind Fred. Fred grabbed two chairs from a nearby vacant table and scooted them up to the booth. Trudy couldn't stop staring at her. Her skin was so pale it had an almost bluish tinge, and her platinum hair showed no darkness at the roots whatsoever. Her eyes were the faintest blue. She was a living porcelain doll.

Fred cleared his throat, then licked his lips. "We . . . uh . . . wanted to surprise you. When you weren't at the house and I saw Kokomo's on the calendar, we figured . . ."

"We?" Lillian lifted a brow. Her gaze went to the girl.

Fred reached for the doll's hand and said, "This is my wife—Svetlana Biddle." Fred gazed at her adoringly.

The rest of the table gaped. Trudy had never seen Lillian without words before, but there she sat with that big mouth hanging open as if she'd been poked with a cattle prod.

Trudy stirred her tea. The ice clinked against the glass.

Finally Lillian gathered her senses. "You don't tell us where you are, what you're doing, and *wham!* you're married?"

"I told you I was dating," Fred said.

"You were dating Minnie Mouse, as I recall," Willie said.

Fred's gaze returned to his bride. "She *was* Minnie Mouse."

Trudy held out a hand and said, "Welcome to the family, Minnie." The girl shook hands but gave her a puzzled look.

She said in a thick Russian accent, "I very happy meet." Trudy got the impression the girl had phlegm in her throat that she needed to spit out.

"She doesn't speak English real well," Fred explained.

"So you've learned Russian?" Willie asked Fred.

"No . . . ," Fred said in his I'm-getting-exasperated-with-you-dimwits tone.

"They speak the language of love," Trudy added,

with a smile for Fred. He narrowed his eyes at her at the same time Bert nudged her under the table.

"I thought you'd be happy that I got married," Fred said to his mother.

Lillian shook her head and made a sniffling sound. She dabbed at her plump cheek with a tissue pulled from her pocketbook. Trudy had never seen the woman cry, but if she ever did, Trudy guessed it might look like this.

Finally Lillian said, "You're so selfish, Fred. You leave us, the farm, for over a year. You couldn't even come back for your brother's wedding! And now you expect us to be happy, to think everything's jim-dandy?"

Fred shot Bert a surprised look, as if this was the first he'd heard of the nuptials. Bert nodded. Trudy held out her hand and wiggled her fingers for Fred to see the ring. Fred hesitated, then extended a hand to Bert. "Congratulations, man."

"Congratulations to you, too, I guess."

Trudy turned to Svetlana, whose eyes were huge and luminous. The girl smiled tentatively, then dipped her head in a nod. She was obviously on the verge of tears. Svetlana's glance shifted to Lillian. Trudy wondered how much of the conversation she understood. Trudy lightly touched the girl's shoulder in an attempt to console her.

The waitress reappeared then to take their orders. "Will this be separate checks?" She pointed to the new-comers.

Willie said yes at the same time Bert said no. He gave his father a reproachful look, then insisted, "It's my treat."

All through supper Bert didn't miss the covert glances that passed between his parents. He wondered if they were going to tell Fred and Svetlana about selling the acres and leaving the farm to him and Trudy, but they said nothing. He wondered if they were reconsidering. Perhaps there was some hope for Fred now that he'd come home.

Only Trudy seemed at ease. No, *at ease* wasn't right; she was *relishing* the moment. He smiled despite himself.

"So, Svetlana," Trudy was saying, "do you still work? Not a lot of Walt Disney gigs around Lake Emily, although you might be able to get a part as one of the Berenstain Bears over at Valley Fair in Shakopee."

"What is Berenstain Bear?" Svetlana's brows knit together.

"No." Fred came to his wife's rescue. "We're going to farm, of course."

"You bought a farm in Florida?" Lillian said.

Fred shook his head. "I didn't buy a farm in Florida. We're home to stay, Ma."

Bert looked at his father, who simply put another forkful of food in his mouth.

The Los Angeles skyline was hazy as it almost always

seemed to be, yet the ocean churned out its happy rhythm. David walked barefoot along the sandy beach with his sister, Sarah. He was a half inch shorter than she, which had been a source of minor irritation his entire life. She had a Californian's focus on health that gave her complexion a rosy hue. Constant sunshine had bleached her brown hair in golden streaks.

Unfortunately, her husband, Tom, had to work, so he couldn't come, but it gave the siblings some alone time, which was a rare treat indeed.

They dined on seafood at an ocean-side café and spent the afternoon talking, first at the table, now on the shore.

They turned toward the pounding surf. The sun was low. Clouds along the horizon in neon pinks and lavenders gave the impression that a cosmic Vegas loomed at the far side of the horizon.

"When do you think you'll be out this way again?" Sarah said.

"Hard to tell." David tucked a hand into his trouser pocket. "The way things are going lately, who knows if I'll even have a job by year's end."

"What's going on?"

"Revenues are down. People would rather go to a Shania Twain concert than hear the symphony, and apparently I'm supposed to come up with the cure for that malady." A sea gull hovered overhead, and David lifted his gaze to the begging bird. "You know what's funny, though?" He paused. "It really doesn't matter to me."

"Because of Ma?" She faced him and tucked a stray hair behind her ear.

David smiled at her. "You always did that."

She blushed. "Read between the lines? A habit, I guess. What can I say? You're my big brother. I know you."

David led her to a spot of dry sand, where they sat and soaked up the colors of the ebbing day.

"This soul-searching has nothing to do with a job description, I'll wager."

"There you go again." He took a deep breath and said, "I miss her."

"Ma or Laura?"

"Both. I feel guilty for leaving Peter to carry the burden back home."

Sarah placed a comforting hand on his back. "I feel the same way. I wish Tom and I could've come when Ma had the stroke, but since the bankruptcy . . . I guess I could've hitchhiked." Her smile was fleeting. "I was so envious of you when you moved back home. A part of me feels hollow without you and Ma in my everyday life."

"You have Tom and the kids."

"The kids are grown and scattering to the winds just like we did. There's a part of me that will always belong in Lake Emily." She lifted her face to the breeze. "We were close there. Sometimes I think we cheated our kids of a sense of home by being in the army. I would've liked to have been a real aunt to Peter, for him and his cousins to have grown up together."

David nodded. "If only . . ."

"It was different for you, though. You had your music. How many of us have a gift like that to pursue?"

He'd heard those words so many times—from his parents, people in the community, fans—yet they sounded as empty as ever. David lay back on the sand and closed his eyes.

Sarah went on, "We did the best we could with our children. Although I'll admit, sometimes I made choices based on what would guarantee the least pain."

David looked at her, wondering if she was reading his own thoughts. How long had he been running from the pain of losing Laura, of having to watch Peter grow up without her sweet presence? "That's exactly it. I've been trying to keep ahead of the sadness in my heart." Sarah reached for his hand. "I thought music was the answer. At least if I was 'fulfilled.'" He gave a humorless laugh. "Now I can add loneliness to my résumé. At least in Minnesota I had Ma and Dad, Peter . . ."

"It's not too late to make changes. You still have time, you know."

"I don't want any more regrets in my life." He looked his sister in the eye. "I need to stop running and face the pain, or I'll lose Ma, too, and I can't afford that."

The days of August stretched long, as did the labor on the farm. A breeze rustled the quaking aspens in the windbreak. Peter paused the tractor to admire the way the leaves fluttered in shades of silver and green. He was raking the second cutting of hay so it would be dried for haying by the end of the week. With Mae caring for the baby and Grandma, Peter was left to carry all the farm work alone. Not that he blamed anyone for that. It was just the way of life.

In the past few weeks he'd seen what a truly selfless person his bride was. Up at all hours breast-feeding Christopher, caring for his grandmother's every need, plus seeing to the never-ending chores of housework, laundry, and cooking. He hadn't missed the circles under her eyes, yet she never spoke a word of complaint. Always greeted him with a smile, albeit a weary one.

Peter started back up the row, but he was tired too. He'd called Bert to see if he could spare an hour or two when it came time to bale, but Lillian informed him that Bert and Fred were baling their own western fields. Peter wondered if Fred was back to stay. He hadn't seen Trudy to ask her.

Coming in the back door, Peter let the screen door slam behind him. "Honey, what do you think about buying a kick baler so I don't have to—"

Mae was sound asleep on the couch with the baby beside her in his bouncer on the floor. Virginia was reading in the rocker. She lifted her wrinkled face to him.

"She's been asleep for a good half hour," Virginia whispered. "I didn't have the heart to wake her."

Peter bent to kiss his grandmother's forehead. "At

251

least the baby is sleeping too," he said.

"As long as he still sleeps tonight."

"He sleeps through the night just fine."

Virginia smiled at the comment, hearing Roy's echo folded in it.

He reclined in the stuffed chair. "How are you feeling, Grandma?"

"Oh, I'm fine. I'm sorry. I know it's not easy taking care of me on top of everything else."

"We don't think of you as a burden, Grandma." Peter reached for her hand.

"You two are working yourselves to death."

"Grandma!"

"Well, it's true! I can't help but wonder if it wouldn't be better for me to go into assisted living. Give you kids some breathing room—"

"We're not going to have this discussion, okay?" Peter shook his head. "We love you, Grandma. This is what people do when they love someone."

Virginia lay in bed that night wrestling with the blankets and her pillow to find a comfortable position. Her left hand ached again. She turned onto her back and stared into the black night. The image of Mae's weary face flashed into view. She couldn't shake the thought that this was all too unfair to Mae and Peter. Truth was, it was unfair to everyone.

"God," she whispered into the stillness, "you tell Roy I'm not at all happy about him leaving me to face this alone. You tell him that for me, okay?" She reached across the double bed, wishing as she had every night for the past two years that she could feel Roy's warmth just one more time. But the sheets were as cold as ever.

Chickens pecked the ground inside their fenced pen. Their heads bobbed front to back as they walked, their eyes wide. Virginia watched them from the brick farmhouse's wraparound porch. One large bird chased a smaller one around the perimeter. The petite bird let out a loud cackle of protest, then went off complaining to the others.

Silly birds, always bullying each other, each trying to be more important than the next. Virginia supposed people weren't much better, though they pretended to be. She lifted her gaze to the overcast sky. It was muggy already at ten o'clock, and the sky threatened foul weather. Mae's steps sounded behind her. Virginia turned to see her.

"Do you need anything out here?" Mae said.

"Do you have any work I could do? I need to keep these old hands busy, or I'll go crazy."

"I have some potatoes that need peeling."

"Bring them out."

Mae returned with a bowl of red new potatoes and a paring knife. "Would you like me to stay?" she said.

Virginia waved her away. "The baby's asleep. Get a nap."

Mae laughed. "That sounds like a great idea."

Mae went back into the house, and Virginia lifted the

paring knife and a potato. Her left hand was numb, but at least she was right handed, so she could still accomplish the simple task. A car pulled into the driveway. Scout, Roy's old yellow Lab, barked and bounded over to greet the driver.

"Virginia," August greeted. "They got you working already?" He climbed the stairs with a youthful spring in his step even at seventy-nine and handed her a thick bouquet of daisies and baby's-breath.

"Oh, you didn't have to!"

"Just accept them, would you?" August's eyes sparkled.

Virginia reached for them and dipped her head. "Thank you, kind sir."

He gave her a stage bow.

Virginia chuckled. She set the flowers on the table, then reached for another potato and peeled it. "This is good for me. Makes me feel useful even though I'm such a burden."

"Why do you say that?" August took the rocker on the other side of the table and leaned toward her.

"It's just true. These kids have so many responsibilities that I feel guilty about adding to that burden. This"—she lifted the half-peeled potato—"is my payment for that."

"You know, when Willa died, things like making supper for myself and doing my laundry kept me tied to this world. Those simple tasks kept me going, took my mind off how sad I was."

Virginia nodded. "That's a bit difficult when your

body doesn't allow you to do those things."

"True." August rocked slowly. "But there are other ways to contribute, to find purpose in this world. Simply being—that's enough, you know, for the people who love you."

Virginia thought of Violet Johnson. That woman hadn't done a thing. Not really. She'd simply "been there" when Virginia needed a listening ear, and that was enough. Funny how reaching out to others brought comfort to both the giver and receiver. Not that Virginia had fully learned the receiver's role.

"You're a wise man, August Cleworth."

"Wow. There's a compliment! So,"—he looked around—"you up to dancing yet?"

"You!" Virginia swatted at the air. "I'm doing better but not that good." She sighed. "I will be happy to be back in my own house, taking care of myself."

"It'll happen. You'll be back in town in no time. Use this opportunity to enjoy your family. I don't know why you're so eager to look after yourself anyway. It's a lot of work. I had an uncle who bought a sixty-six-piece set of flatware just so he wouldn't have to wash dishes more than once a month. He owned fifteen pair of jeans, wore 'em twice, and did laundry when he did the silverware!"

"You're telling tales."

August held up three fingers. "Scout's honor, I'm telling the truth. You know, that same uncle used to live with a cousin. The way he told it, a neighbor man would come visiting every night around suppertime.

The neighbor was a talker and bored my uncle to tears, but being a good Minnesotan, he didn't want to be rude. Eventually he and his cousin would end up inviting the man to stay to eat. Well, this went on for a good month. Every night the man rode up on his horse and stayed through supper. My uncle grew tired of his rudeness, but he couldn't bring himself to tell the man not to come around anymore. Well, one night after supper, my uncle and his cousin set all the dishes and pots and pans from the table on the floor and called their dogs, which eagerly came and licked the dishes clean. Then they set them directly into the cupboards. The neighbor was so disgusted he never came calling at suppertime again."

Virginia began to laugh then, a hearty laugh that came from deep down. Tears seeped from her eyes.

August joined in her enjoyment. "It's good to see you smile, Virginia Morgan." He reached for her hand and gave it a squeeze.

It felt good to be smiling again.

WILL BIDDLE

Seven-year-old Will Biddle smoothed the blankets on his bed as best he could. There was a wrinkle in the middle that he couldn't seem to get out, but he knew his ma would come along and straighten it. She did every morning after he made his bed.

Will could hear his little brother, Bobby, making baby

noises from his crib in the next room. His ma's footsteps sounded on the stairs and passed Will's room. He listened as she talked to the newborn in a quiet voice. Will liked having a baby in the house. He'd liked it when it was just him and Ma too, but sometimes that got lonely. Especially when they didn't get any letters from Pa, so far away in the war. He saw the worry on his ma's face when she thought he wasn't looking. He knew she was afraid. But Bobby helped them forget, at least for little pieces of time.

And Grandma seemed to come by the house more often just to gaze at "our little wonder," as she called Bobby. Grandpa was there a lot as it was, filling in for Pa around the farm—milking in the mornings and evenings, getting the machinery ready for the spring, and then plowing and planting once the ground was ready.

Will would be glad when he was old enough to do those chores. Sitting on the big orange Allis-Chalmers tractor with Grandpa was one of his favorite things to do. He would watch as the plow's blades turned the dirt in a spiral of black. The earthy smell filled his senses, and the sound of the tractor's chugging engine never failed to put a smile on his face.

Will lifted the toy tractor from its spot on the bookshelf and pushed it along the hardwood floor. He imagined the braided rug was the north field; its circular paths were perfect rows where corn would grow. Soon he was lost in play. He lined up the toy cows and pretended it was time for the evening milking. Then the *little hogs in their pens needed their slop.*

Summer's warmth filled the corners of the upstairs bedroom with light. The sheer curtains glowed with the golden hue. A blue jay complained loudly outside Will's window.

"Will." His ma's voice pulled him from his playing. Will lifted his face to the door where his mother stood with the baby in her arms. Bobby was wrapped in soft cotton blankets, and Will could see his round cheeks poking out.

"Yes, Ma."

"I think I heard someone drive up. You mind seeing who it is?" Her face held an odd expression. She tilted her head toward Will's open window. "Go see." Then she smiled.

Will walked tentatively to the window. A warm breeze ruffled the sheer curtains. Will pushed them aside and looked down on the back lawn. Two white Adirondack chairs sat beneath the green and white martin house. Will shifted his gaze. Then he saw him. The man in the soldier's uniform.

"Pa," Will breathed. He turned and ran as fast as he could down the stairs and out the back door. The screen slammed shut behind him. "Pa!"

The tall man bent down and swept him up in a hug. Will's feet dangled while Pa held him tight. He couldn't remember ever being hugged so hard in his whole life. Will felt his father's tears on his own cheek, and he lifted his face. "It's okay, Pa. You're home now. You're safe." Then Will wiped the tears away with his sleeve.

His father laughed in the deep way that always made Will's insides glow.

Ma was there then with Bobby. Pa had never seen Bobby before. Pa carefully set Will down, then took a deep breath. Ma fell into his arms, the baby between them. "I'm home to stay. I'm never leaving you again."

Ma cried at those words, even though her eyes were happy and she was laughing. They kissed, and Will turned away so Ma wouldn't be embarrassed. "I was so scared," Ma said. "When I heard that you'd been injured . . ."

"I'm okay now. I'm more than okay."

Later that evening as the crickets tuned their instruments, Will lay in bed. Pa sat on the edge, gazing down at him like he used to a long time ago. He pulled the cool sheets up to Will's chin.

"It's good to have you back," Will said.

"Tired of being the man of the house, are you?" Pa grinned.

Will nodded. "Will I ever have to go to war?"

His father looked at him thoughtfully before answering. "I hope not. But you might. It's hard to say."

"Are you glad you went?"

" 'Glad' isn't exactly the word I'd put to it. It was the right thing. Sometimes the right thing is a difficult path." He touched the top of Will's head and smoothed his curly hair. "If I didn't do my part, then our freedom *would be at risk. Our freedom means that you can grow up here on the farm, that you and your little brother have a whole basket of choices when you grow up."*

"I want to be a farmer like you, Pa. There isn't anything in the whole wide world I'd choose above that."

Pa's grin broadened. "That's why I had to go. Do you understand? Because I wanted to be sure that when you grew up, you could keep on farming, just like we've always done."

thirty-four

Fred resumed old work patterns, as if he'd never taken off, never left the family when they needed him most. Bert didn't know if that meant things had changed, if perhaps his father had changed his mind about the farm. Several days after Fred's reappearing act, Willie still offered no explanation. He only went off to his shop to work on his Pioneer Power engines.

Fred and Svetlana took over Fred's old room. Bert knew Fred's desertion irked their father, yet a part of him understood Fred's side of things too. Lillian had been unbearable after breaking her leg, ringing that bell constantly. Their mother could nag the hair off a cat. There were plenty of times Bert wanted to get away from that incessant sound too.

Fred drove the tall John Deere along the drive. Its bucket was filled with silage from the long, white plastic-encased tube that lined the west windbreak. With Fred's help they finished milking in two-thirds the time and even managed to bottle-feed the calves and fill the cows' feed bins before nine o'clock. Bert was glad for the relief from his long days, not that there wasn't plenty yet to do. But with five hundred fewer acres to plow, plant, and harvest, he might actually get to see his bride during daylight hours again this summer. That was a good thing.

Bert checked his watch. The smell of cooking sausage floated past. Bert's mouth watered. No doubt Ma was making breakfast. Trudy had yet to get out of bed when he rose, much less make breakfast. His stomach growled. He followed the smell into the house. Surely his ma had made a little extra.

Willie was barely visible behind the stacks of flap-jacks and sausages at the small kitchen table. Ma always did have a tendency to make too much food, and his dad's waistline had a tendency to expand.

"Hey, Dad," Bert said. His father lifted serious eyes. Bert had so rarely seen such an expression on his dad's face that it took him aback. Then he became aware of his mother's grumbling.

"They haven't been here even a week, and she doesn't have the courtesy to get out of bed at a decent hour, much less lift a hand around here."

Bert mouthed to his father, "What's wrong?"

Willie shrugged. After retrieving a plate from the cupboard, Bert took the chair opposite his dad. Lillian was still building up steam.

"Did you hear the racket they made last night?" This to her husband. "Of course you didn't hear it—you were snoring like a buzz saw. Well, I heard it. There was such a noise as I've never heard. Her weird music and then those two giggling. It was embarrassing, that's what!"

"Imagine. Newlyweds giggling," Willie said, dry as toast.

Lillian turned and noticed Bert for the first time. "When did you come in? Did you hear what we were talking about?"

Bert nodded.

"Well, tell a person when you enter a room!" She slugged him in the arm.

"So . . . you're getting better acquainted with your new daughter-in-law?" Bert said.

"Right! The Russki hasn't come out of her room since they came marching home last week. Lazy, that's what I think she is. Probably married Fred in hopes that she could get her hands on his money. Next thing you know, a whole bucket of her Russki relatives will come over on the boat, thinking they can move in too."

A bleary-eyed Svetlana appeared at the doorway. She wore a stricken expression on her face and red rims under her eyes.

"I see you finally decided to grace us with your presence!" Lillian said to her, then to the men, "Maybe her highness will let us wait on her!"

"Ma!" Bert's embarrassment flashed.

"She doesn't understand a word we say. Why should

we bother to—" The back door slammed. Svetlana was nowhere to be seen. Lillian leaned toward the window over the sink. "Where does she think she's going? She'll scare the cows to death if she barges right into the barn. They won't give milk for a week!"

"Ma, can't you try to be nice to her?"

"Why should *I* be nice?" Lillian turned around. "Did I ask her to move under my roof? To eat our food without paying for it or at least offering to help make it?" Willie held up a hand. Lillian straightened and turned back to the pancake griddle.

"Your ma's right," Willie said. "They have to start paying their way, prove themselves, if Fred is really serious about coming back to the farm for good."

Bert knew better than to say another word.

They had just entered a new cold war.

All manner of art supplies covered the coffee table in the small living room—colored construction paper, glue, scissors, markers . . . Trudy sorted and counted the materials into student supply kits for her summer art class, which started tomorrow. The children would create personal greeting cards with torn-paper art one day and handmade bracelets of silver wire and glass beads the next. Trudy was glad for something creative to do to relieve her boredom. She could only paint so many pictures before she needed to get out and reconnect with people. Mae had been so busy with Christopher and Virginia, Trudy had all but given up on her.

Bert told her what had happened at breakfast. "Unbelievable!" Trudy said, dropping a glue stick into a plastic bag. "Like it's Svetlana's fault Fred is such a jerk! The girl had no idea what she was getting herself into when she married him!"

Bert shook his head. "I expected Ma to act that way, but Dad?"

"Well, Svetlana didn't ask for any of this. She's the innocent one." Her blood boiled. "If she's stuck with Lillian round the clock, someone's going to get hurt. And I don't mean that figuratively." Then Trudy lifted her head as an idea formed. "Svetlana could assist me with my art class."

Bert's expression said, *Don't get one of your* I Love Lucy *ideas*.

"No, really. It would give us a chance to get to know each other, and it would get Svetlana out from under your ma's feet."

Bert's eyebrows went up.

"It's a good idea, don't you think?"

"I think you're going to do whatever you want to do."

"Eight kits in the middle of each table," Trudy instructed the next morning as she and Svetlana prepared for the nine o'clock class. Svetlana gave her a blank look. "Kits." Trudy held up the large Ziploc bags of supplies for Svetlana to see. "Eight on each table." Her volume rose, and she flashed her fingers to indicate eight.

Svetlana offered a tentative smile. "Eight keets."

Trudy returned her sister-in-law's smile. "By George, I think she's got it."

Svetlana's expression said she thought Trudy had mixed her Play-Doh colors.

"You're doing great," Trudy said.

"I very happy help," Svetlana said. She reached for the rest of the art kits Trudy had prepared and distributed them to the other tables. Lillian had been wrong about her, Trudy decided. Svetlana was a sweet girl who wasn't out to con anyone, least of all Fred. If anyone had been conned, Svetlana had.

By the time the students arrived, Svetlana had begun tearing the colored construction paper into various shapes to create her own greeting card.

"Who are you making a card for?" Trudy said over her shoulder.

"My mah-ther," Svetlana said. "I write every day to her and my young seesters."

"You have sisters?"

Svetlana nodded. "They are age twelve and seven. I miss them very much."

The arriving elementary students broke their conversation. Trudy started the class, and soon she and Svetlana were bent over the short tables, offering help with the card projects, showing the kids how to tear the paper to get the desired shape and how to fit the shapes together to create pictures.

"What language does she speak?" Jessie Wise pointed to the newcomer when Trudy when came to help tear out a brown tree trunk. Trudy was glad to see the girl at the class. She looked a little rumpled, though, and Trudy wondered what was up with her. Her hair hadn't been combed, and her shirt was wrinkled as if it had sat in the dryer for a few days. She smiled faintly at Trudy, and Trudy brushed the worry away.

"English."

"Really? I didn't understand a word she said."

Trudy patted her shoulder. "Her accent is heavy, but I think she understands most everything we say."

"Where did she come from?"

"She's from Russia."

Jessie turned to give the girl another look. Svetlana was helping a second-grade girl with pale braided pigtails and missing front teeth.

"Russia? Isn't that on the other side of the world?"

Trudy nodded.

"We don't have a lot of foreigners in Lake Emily," Jessie said. "How long is she here for?"

"She's here to stay. She's my new sister-in-law."

Jessie's mouth dropped open.

"I hope she learns to talk better quick. People around here will think she's weird."

Jessie's words rattled in Trudy's brain for the rest of the class. Her own difficulty gaining acceptance into the community told her that the child's words might not be far from the truth. She glanced at Svetlana, who was wiping off the round blue cafeteria tables. She was a hard worker, Trudy would give her that much.

"Svetlana," Trudy said. The blonde lifted questioning eyes. "What would you say to some classes of our own?"

"Classes? What kind classes?"

Trudy put an arm around her shoulder. "I'm thinking rural Minnesota culture class—how to make hotdish, what makes a good two-finger wave, and lots of English." Svetlana raised a thin eyebrow. "It'll be good. We can make bars and Jell-O salad, do a little exploring . . ."

"Hot deesh?"

"See, you're catching on already. Before long you'll be making supper for Lillian and Willie. Do you know how to drive?"

Svetlana shook her head.

"We'll start with that, then."

"You think this . . . cul-ture class make Fred mah-ther like me?"

"Lillian? I'm still working on that one myself. We'll make it a group project."

thirty-five

Jessie missed Anna. She missed Virginia even more. Her dad was late coming home from work again, and the old fear was back. Was he out drinking? Jessie stared at the door. She wished her dad would walk through it. Closing her eyes, she wished as hard as she could. But he still didn't come.

She knew he was sad. Missing Anna. He dragged

himself around the house lately. Barely spoke a word. She'd taken over the job of making their meals. Anything to make him feel better. But nothing seemed to work. At least he was still going to work. That was something, wasn't it?

She stared at the phone. She wanted to call Virginia. But what could Virginia do about it?

She loves me, Jessie's heart said. *But I thought Anna loved me too. I wanted Anna to be my new mother! But she . . .* Jessie started to cry then.

She hated being alone. Hated being afraid. Hated wondering if her dad was drinking again. She didn't want that life.

She stood and paced the living room. When she looked down and saw the phone, she couldn't help herself. She picked it up and dialed the Morgans' number. Mae answered on the second ring.

"The Morgans." She sounded so nice. So happy.

Jessie cleared her throat. "Is Virginia there?"

"Jessie, is that you?"

"Yes ma'am."

"She's taking a nap right now. But I'll tell her you called as soon as she wakes up, okay?"

"Okay."

But when Jessie's dad came home smelling of alcohol, she didn't answer Virginia's call. The answering machine took it. She didn't want Virginia to know the awful truth.

When Mae came down the stairs the following

morning with Christopher tucked against her chest, Peter was digging in the fridge.

"Do we have any milk?"

"You're a dairy farmer, honey. We have lots of milk."

Virginia's chuckle from the corner table drew Mae's attention. "I didn't realize you were up already, Virginia."

"At my age I'm always up. Sleep doesn't come easy."

Peter cleared his throat.

"What?" Mae turned back to her husband.

"We have no milk."

"Sorry. We have concentrated juice in the fridge."

"Actually, that's gone too." Peter shook his head. "We're squeezed dry—used the juice up yesterday."

"Coffee?"

"Running low on that, too. Were you planning on shopping anytime soon?"

"Well, it's tricky with you gone and the baby . . ." Mae glanced at Virginia. "I don't want to leave Grandma home alone."

Virginia waved a hand in the air. "I'm getting along just fine with my walker. You go ahead. I can manage."

"Are you sure?" Mae said.

"I'm positive. You have to let me solo sooner or later if you want to get me out of your hair."

"Grandma," Peter scolded.

"Trust me. I'll be just fine."

Mae turned to Peter. "If she thinks she's ready, we'll have to trust her."

• • •

Mae left with the baby for her shopping excursion. The quiet peacefulness of the house descended on Virginia. Sunlight streamed through lace curtains in the living room. Twitters of birds flitting up and down in their game of tag sounded through the open window. It was a hot August day. Virginia pulled up to her walker and went onto the screened porch. How many days had she sat on this porch peeling potatoes and apples, sorting beans or peas while Roy worked the fields? Somehow the bitterness of that thought seemed distant. Today contentment settled on her. She wondered if that was August's doing. He'd come here every day to sit and talk. Or just to listen. She still visited Violet whenever she went to physical therapy. The woman's silence was the same, yet something fundamental had changed in her, although Virginia couldn't say what.

She realized that while August and Violet certainly played a part in her healing, God brought her peace. Her heart had simply been ready to receive from his hand. She hadn't responded to the doctor's or Ella's and Anna's well-intentioned scoldings. So God had found another path to her through two unlikely kindred spirits.

The worst had passed like dark clouds in a storm. The longing for death to end her loneliness had evaporated. When had that change come about? When had thoughts of joining Roy formed a truce with the present? She hadn't noticed.

She still had a purpose in this world. Discovering what that purpose was—that was the adventure that lay ahead.

Her heart turned toward Jessie. What had happened to the child? Virginia was so glad to hear that she'd called, but the girl hadn't answered the phone, though Virginia had tried several times during the evening. She wondered if something was wrong. No. Surely if Jessie was in trouble, she'd say so. Jessie never kept secrets from her. Virginia sighed. At least the child had Anna as a friend; Virginia was grateful for that.

Virginia hadn't worn eye makeup since . . . she couldn't remember when. Certainly it was before Roy's death. She sat on the chair before the vanity in her bedroom applying blush and eye shadow. She was being silly, she knew, and a part of her held back like a stubborn mule, reminding her of the heartache of such foolishness. But she couldn't help herself. It felt good to be admired, complimented as a woman. The old ache echoed. How she missed Roy. When cancer drained his energy, their romance waned. Their love grew deeper, but the playfulness was overtaken by sheer exhaustion. It never returned, not the way it had been before the cruel disease.

The doorbell rang. Virginia took the walker to the living room in her slow way. Peter was at the door, talking to August.

August lifted his head, and his face took on a grin. "Don't you look nice," he said.

Virginia's cheeks grew warm. She continued moving toward him. "I'm still not so sure about this," she said.

"What's not to be sure of?" August said with a wink.

Peter cleared his throat. "What time should I expect you home?"

Virginia reached to kiss him on the cheek. "Don't wait up," she whispered.

"Call if things get too rowdy," Peter teased. "I'll always come pick you up, Grandma." Virginia patted his hand and followed August to the car.

Once they were on their way, August said, "Your grandson okay with this?"

"Is yours?"

August chuckled. "I haven't told him anything, so I guess so."

"Peter's fine. He was teasing is all. Now, if David were here . . ." Her words trailed off into that now-distant ache that his desertion had left behind. Virginia cleared her throat.

"You okay?" August reached for her hand. She let him hold it.

"Missing my son, I guess. I was pretty upset when he went back to Arizona after my stroke. He didn't have a lot of choice, I suppose, but it hurt nonetheless."

"You have a lot of fortitude."

"Is that what you call it?" Virginia chuckled.

"Don't belittle my compliment. You've gone through a lot and come out on top. Haven't let it keep you down."

"Trust me, I have my moments. But wallowing

272

doesn't get me anywhere. And a good friend of mine reminded me that I need to make the most of my life while I still can."

August squeezed her hand. "It was difficult after Willa died. I don't know what I would've done without my family. Yet sometimes, I don't know . . . I felt suffocated by them. They meant well, but they treated me with kid gloves, as if they were afraid I'd break. I got tired of it. So I went out and bought myself a convertible." He laughed at the memory. "You should've seen the look on my son's face. I'm pretty sure he thought I'd slipped a few gears! But Willa would've wanted me to enjoy the rest of my life."

"Life is a gamble, whatever choices you make," Virginia said. "If I'd stayed locked in my room, I'd have been gambling that depression wouldn't do me in. I like these odds better."

thirty-six

While Peter sprayed his fields and hayed and milked, little Christopher grew. No longer a newborn, he now offered smiles for free. Deep dimples like his mother's dented pudgy cheeks, and his pale gray eyes held the reflection of his great-grandpa Roy. Mae had only known the man for a year and a half before his death, but even she could see the resemblance. She couldn't recall a time in her life that felt more golden. Every moment with her son felt like a

Kodak moment. Did every new mother feel this way? She wished she could freeze time, yet it was already slipping through her fingers.

She watched Christopher as he lay on his blanket on the sun-dappled lawn. He held a rattle in one tightly clenched fist and a fuzzy bunny in the other. Both were soggy with drool. Christopher kicked chubby legs in the air. Mae busily clicked the camera in her hands. He was only two months old, and already she'd filled two photo albums with his pictures.

Trudy's car pulled into the driveway. She and Svetlana got out. Trudy waved as they made their way over.

"What are you two up to?" Mae asked. It seemed the two were together constantly these days. Trudy spent so much time with this newcomer, yet she rarely came to spend a day with her and Christopher anymore. Didn't she want to be with them? Or maybe she didn't like babies. She sure seemed to the day Christopher was born, but now whenever Mae told her about his latest feat, she saw the way Trudy's eyes glazed over.

Svetlana knelt by the baby on his blanket. "Is beautiful baby," she said.

"Thank you." Mae beamed. "Would you like some iced tea? I just made a pitcher."

"Oh, thanks, but we're on our way to Mankato," Trudy said.

"Really? So what are you doing here?"

"Svetlana and I are taking in a musical at MSU— *Showboat*. Now, there's a good *American* production," Trudy said with a glance toward the girl.

Mae felt a surge of jealousy traverse her spine.

"So why did you stop here?" Mae said a little too curtly.

Trudy scrutinized her as if she'd read her mind, then she said, "I thought I'd see if you wanted me to pick up anything for you. Milk, diapers?"

Mae knew Trudy sensed her irritation, yet she couldn't shake the envy. "Thanks, but I just went to the store." Mae glanced back at Svetlana, who was lightly touching Christopher's bare belly. The baby let out a laugh. Mae had to admit the girl was a sweetheart, hardly the kind of girl she pictured marrying Fred Biddle. But why would Trudy rather spend time with her than with her own sister? Mae took a deep breath.

"You have great gift in your son," Svetlana said. "Someday I have son too, just like your Chreestopher."

That brought a reluctant smile to Mae's lips.

As Trudy and Svetlana wove through the back roads toward Highway 169 south, Trudy found herself missing Mae. She wasn't sure what had caused the divide between them. She could see it in Mae's expression, the way she glanced at Svetlana through narrowed eyes while her mouth kept smiling. Trudy couldn't comprehend it; whenever she invited Mae to do the things they used to enjoy, she found an excuse not to go. "But I have Christopher . . ." It was as if she were flaunting the fact that she was a mother and Trudy wasn't. Deep down she knew Mae wouldn't do that, but the feeling persisted. She glanced at Svetlana.

The petite blonde wore a bright smile.

"You seem happy. What's up?"

"Is good day. I go to Mankato, Minnesota, see play, and I give Fred new baby."

Trudy hit the brakes, and the car slid to a stop.

"What did you say?"

"I find out yesterday. I have baby. Fred's baby. Now we have new home and new baby. We will be very happy."

Virginia had been awake since five. She lay in bed listening as Peter prepared bottles for the new calves in the white plastic igloos along the barn. She heard the screen door screech and slam when he went outside. She should try to get back to sleep, but her mind was too busy.

August was coming to take her on a drive in his convertible this afternoon. She chided herself for her girlish giddiness, being so excited about a simple outing. Yet her adventures with August signified a new step in her progress and, along with it, a new sense of freedom.

"We should get out again and do something fun," August had said when he'd called the night before. "You've waited on everyone else for so long, they'll understand if you take a few afternoons for a little adventure. I'll pick you up after your visit with Violet."

"Could we stop and see Jessie too? I've been thinking about that child."

"That's no problem. I'm always happy to be chauffeur for my favorite volunteer."

"So, what kind of adventure are we talking about today?"

"You up for skydiving?"

"You never know. We could go dancing afterward."

"Dancing . . . Won't be long until you're ready for that, will it?"

Her heart skipped a beat.

Christopher's cries upstairs returned her attention to the present. Virginia tugged the walker closer to the bed. She needed to go to the bathroom. Slipping her feet into her slippers, she placed her hands on the side bars of the walker and hoisted herself up. Scooting the walker forward, she took a step, then two. It had become an almost automatic movement, one she no longer struggled with. When she tugged again, however, the walker wouldn't budge. She pushed harder. Suddenly it came free, sending her off balance. The walker crashed, and Virginia landed on top of it. Pain shot down her hip and into her legs. She moaned.

Using all her strength, she rolled off the tangled walker. Sparklers of pain spread across her lower back and limbs. She lay breathing heavily. Christopher was still crying upstairs.

"Mae!" she called. There was no answer. She lay motionless, out of breath and scared. Finally Christopher's cries ebbed, and Virginia called out again. "Mae!" Within moments Mae's footsteps sounded on the stairs, and Virginia's bedroom door flew open.

"Virginia"—Mae bent beside her—"what happened?"

The pain was bad. Tears coursed down Virginia's cheeks.

"I fell . . . tried to get up on my own. Ouch!" The pain in her leg surged. "The walker got caught on the rug."

"I'll get Peter." Mae flew out the door. Christopher's cries grew louder.

"I'm sorry, little guy," Virginia murmured. "I'm sorry."

The ambulance arrived ten minutes later. The EMTs lifted Virginia onto a stretcher and drove toward town. Peter stood in the driveway watching it disappear down the dirt road. Mae had gone to retrieve Christopher and call August before going to the hospital. Peter had to finish milking, but he'd promised Mae he'd come as soon as he was done.

At least she's okay. At least someone was here with her. The image of his grandmother sprawled on the floor in her house—in town, alone, with no one to help her or care for her—sent chills down his spine. They'd done the right thing to bring her here.

He needed to call his father. He didn't want to. How could he tell his dad this latest news? Was he even home yet from this latest tour? Peter blew out an exasperated breath, then returned to the barn to figure out what he'd say.

Eight cows waited patiently in their stalls. The tubes

278

had long since retracted from their teats. Three girls looked on from the parlor door as if wondering why they were being forced to wait so long. Peter pushed the bars that released those that were done. In a procession, the Holsteins walked the perimeter of the barn and into the innocent sunshine. The day had no idea of the burden on Peter's heart.

"Dad?" Peter's voice on the line warned that this was no social call.

"What's wrong?" David said.

"Grandma had an accident this morning. Her walker got caught on the rug, and she fell. Mae was right there. She's in x-ray now to see if she broke anything. She has pain in her hip, so . . ."

A weight settled on David's shoulders and pressed him into the sofa in his San Francisco hotel suite. "How are her spirits?"

Peter didn't respond right away. "I'm not sure." David heard the telltale crack in his son's voice. "Mae went with her to the hospital. I'll head in after I get off the phone, but Grandma didn't need another complication." He paused. "She was doing so well—walking with the walker, becoming her old self again. She's been happy."

"Peter, I'm sorry." It sounded lame to his own ears. If David were truly sorry, wouldn't he *do* something about it? What good were words? Anyone could offer words. He was a son, a father. Didn't those titles require more of him than greeting-card sympathies? *I*

279

need to stop running and face the pain, or I'll lose Ma, too, and I can't afford that.

"Peter, I'm coming home," David said.

Silence. Finally Peter said, "How long for this time, Dad?"

"For good, Peter. I'm coming home to stay."

David stared at the phone after he hung up. He was going home. Relief filled him.

It was the right decision, one he'd never regret. And he had plenty of regrets in his life. The glint of gold on his left ring finger caught his eye. His wedding band. He'd never taken it off. All these years since his wife's death it had remained. He thought it was a symbol of his loyalty to her, but now he saw that it had been his excuse to cling to his past, to refuse to move forward. If Laura never died, if he still wore her ring, the pain of her death wouldn't tunnel into his heart. If he kept busy with his music, the loneliness in Peter's eyes couldn't accuse him. After all, he was providing for his son, giving him adventures most boys only dreamed of. That made him a good father, didn't it?

He touched the gold band lightly, twisted it around his finger. His attempts to shelter himself and Peter had only driven them further apart. But it wasn't too late. Sarah was right about that. He could make a fresh start and redeem the regrets of the past. Carefully he pulled the band from his finger and placed it on the nightstand.

"I hope you understand, Laura," he whispered. "It's time to move on."

"The x-rays are negative." Dr. Mielke hovered in his stoop-shouldered way. He smoothed his bushy gray eyebrows with a forefinger.

"I was certain I'd broken something," Virginia said.

"You're lucky you didn't break a hip." He shoved his hands into the pockets of his white lab coat. "You'll have a good black-and-blue bruise that should buy you some sympathy. But you're going to be fine. I do want you to watch out for any signs of a clot—a hard, painful lump in the leg, or the skin might be hot. Call me right away if those symptoms pop up. Otherwise, you're free to go home."

Mae placed a hand on Virginia's rounded shoulder. "That's a relief, isn't it?"

"I need to go see Violet," Virginia told Mae. "I don't know why, but I need to see her."

"All right," Mae said. She held Christopher while a nurse pushed Virginia in a wheelchair down the corridor.

When they reached Violet's room, all was quiet, dark. They went inside anyway. Violet was on the bed. She wore a feminine white crepe shirt, and her hair was pulled back with combs. Virginia knew that Rosemary had been there earlier. She always did her mother's hair when she came to visit.

"Good morning, Violet," Virginia said. "Can you

open those curtains?" she directed Mae.

Mae did, and Virginia lifted her face toward the sunny window.

"Doesn't that feel better, Violet?" She drew in a deep breath. "I had a little trouble today, Violet. I thought I'd broken my hip. I was scared, but I had a revelation." The pain in Virginia's leg had dimmed to a dull throb. And yet she felt . . . good.

Violet didn't answer, but she did turn her head. Eyes that had been empty held kindness. That realization humbled Virginia. She'd done nothing, and yet God had worked. It was the very definition of *miracle*.

"I realized that I wasn't panicked about the thought of breaking my hip. I would've been bothered by it, but it wouldn't have killed me." She smiled. "I'm stronger than I was before." She paused, filled with wonder. "How did that happen? After everything, when did I become a stronger person? And then it dawned on me. You helped me. I found a reason to hold on, because of you. And well . . . I just wanted to thank you, Violet."

She reached for Violet's cold, small hand. "Thank you for being my friend."

"No, no, no," Trudy yelled a little too loudly as Svetlana crunched the gears of her AMC Pacer. Trudy's knuckles were white where she held on to the armrest. "Ease off the gas and push the clutch in before you change gears." She tried to be as patient as she could, but her volume went up a notch anyway. Svetlana bit her lower lip. Her face flushed as the Pacer stalled in the middle of the intersection for a third time. The other drivers on Lake Emily's Main Street pulled around her with curious stares.

"I no drive in Russia," Svetlana whispered. "We walk, take bus. Why I need drive anyway? Fred drive me."

"Are you kidding? Fred's a farmer. You won't see him again till Thanksgiving, honey."

Svetlana gave her a puzzled look. "I see Fred." Another car pulled around them; this one honked, drawing Trudy's and Svetlana's gazes. It was a black pickup with a fresh Minnesota Wild hockey sticker in the back window. Trudy waved at Coach Miller. The big, dark-haired man held his hands up in question. Trudy waved him off.

"We need to get out of the intersection," Trudy said.

"You drive." Svetlana started to unbuckle her belt.

"No. Try it one more time. We'll head out to the country so you don't get so flustered. It'll be easier for you to learn out there. Now, step on the clutch and brake and restart the motor."

Svetlana obeyed. The car sputtered to life.

"Put it in first, then give it gas as you *slowly* let up the clutch." This time the car moved forward. "More gas." They sped up until the motor revved. "Time for second gear. Push the clutch in and take your foot off the gas while you shift. Easy." Beads of sweat gathered on Svetlana's forehead. Once she'd maneuvered the car successfully into second gear and out of the intersection, she gave Trudy a tentative smile. "See," Trudy said. "You did it!"

"I like drive," Svetlana said. She gunned it and moved into third.

"You're a quick study!" Trudy said. "Before you know it, we'll be up in Brainerd at the Northstar Nationals drag-racing championships!"

Svetlana's brow furrowed.

"Never mind. You're coming right along, toots." The edge of town came into view beyond the high school. Trudy said, "Turn off here. We'll take this dirt road past the country club."

Svetlana turned, and Lillian's boat of a car came into view. Trudy knew it was Lillian by the way she drove in the dead center of the dirt road. She was going fast, too. A plume of dust like a rooster's tail rose behind the twenty-year-old car. Svetlana's eyes grew to saucers.

"Stay to the right!" Trudy shouted. The ditches were steep and the shoulders narrow. "Stay right!" Trudy grabbed the wheel and yanked as far right as they could safely go. At the last possible moment, Lillian moved into her own lane and swept past them. By then the Pacer had come to a complete halt, and the motor died. A tear coursed Svetlana's cheek, and she breathed heavily.

"That's lesson number one," Trudy said. "On dirt roads in Minnesota, drivers take the center until meeting oncoming traffic."

"What lesson two?"

"Don't get in your mother-in-law's way."

thirty-seven

Virginia returned home bruised but fine. Peter didn't tell her about his father's promised homecoming, mostly because he didn't believe it himself. Until David Morgan appeared with suitcases and a U-Haul, Peter would consider the knee-jerk decision merely a wishful statement made from guilt. His father had given his life to music. He'd never chosen anything above that—not his only son, not Grandpa or Grandma.

Doubt trickled in. Perhaps David *had* loved Peter's mother more than his music, but those distant memories were more dream than reality now. Peter wasn't about to build up his grandmother's hopes only to dash them with disappointment. He pulled his pickup into the State Farm Insurance agency and killed the motor, sending up a prayer that his own hopes for the farm wouldn't be dashed.

"I'm sorry, Peter, but it's too late," Ryan Keegan said. The agent's perfectly coiffed brown hair reminded Peter of a Ken doll. "In order to qualify for federal crop insurance, you needed to apply for it last March."

Peter sighed. He hadn't mentioned his worries to Mae on the hope that he could get crop insurance and avoid the impending doom come harvest. "You could sell some of your acres. Most tillable acres around here are going for three thousand dollars or more. If you subdivided, you'd get a lot more than that. You could buy a place in the Dakotas for cash, raise cattle."

"But the family farm isn't in the Dakotas."

"I understand that. Every farmer in the county is having the same problem."

"Except that most have crop insurance."

Apparently Keegan couldn't argue with that.

Peter's mind swirled with worry. There had to be a solution. They couldn't have gone through all this only to lose the farm to a stretch of bad weather.

"I wish I could help you. I really do."

Peter stood and shook his agent's hand. "It's the plain truth," Peter said. "You can't give me more than that."

"You spent another day with Trudy?" Fred washed his hands under the kitchen faucet.

"She's nice," Svetlana said. Fred reached for the dishtowel that hung from the oven door and dried his hands.

"I don't want you spending time with her."

Svetlana gave more attention than necessary to brushing grass from the sleeves of Fred's plaid shirt. "I spend time with anybody I vant. I have no friend. You work all time. Why should I be lonely? I like Trudy."

Fred planted his feet. "I said I don't want you to hang out with her. That girl is trouble. You hear me?"

"I hear vat I vant," Svetlana said. She placed her hands on her hips. "Trudy teach me to drive, be independent."

286

"She taught you to drive?" Fred's voice rose.

Lillian came into the kitchen. She halted when her eyes met Svetlana's. "That was you?"

Svetlana's eyes flashed. "Yes! I will to be *American* daughter-in-law and wife!"

"The Russki almost sent me into the ditch! She was driving like a maniac, in the middle of the road and all."

"What!" Svetlana screeched. "You lie!" She turned to her husband. "Your mother is liar!"

Lillian's mouth dropped open. "Are you going to let the Russki talk to me that way?"

Heat rose up Fred's neck. As angry as he was at Svetlana, he wasn't about to let his mother bully her. "Stop calling her that, Ma! She'll talk however she wants to you!"

"You'd take her side over your own mother?"

The commotion brought Willie in from the living room, where he and Lillian had been watching *Wheel of Fortune*. "What's the ruckus?"

"Svetlana called me a liar." Lillian jabbed a finger at Svetlana to emphasize each word.

Willie's mouth puckered, and he looked between his wife and his crying daughter-in-law. Finally he said, "Do we have any tomato juice?" He opened the refrigerator door and rummaged until he found the bottle of red juice.

"Willie!" Lillian complained.

"You want some juice too?" He glanced over his shoulder. "There's enough for two. Come on. Leave these two alone; they don't listen to us old folks anyway."

Lillian muttered and left the room, but her glare at Fred sent unmistakable daggers. Svetlana sobbed in loud gulps, embarrassing Fred. "Shh," he murmured, reaching for her in an awkward hug.

"Your mother hate me!" Svetlana bellowed. "Why you bring me here? We could have good life in Russia. My mother would welcome son-in-law to care for her."

"Shh," Fred repeated. "It'll be okay. Just hang in there. When Ma and Dad move to town, we'll have the place all to ourselves. Then everything will be fine. Don't you see?"

Virginia napped on top of the white coverlet in her sunny room at the home place. Afternoon sunlight warmed her cheeks and shoulders like a gentle caress. The sound of a door creaking awakened her. She rolled toward it.

"I heard you'd been making trouble." David! His eyes twinkled with tenderness. He sat on the bed alongside her. Then his face sobered. "I'm moving home, Ma. I've been learning some things about myself. I've been an absentee son for too long."

Virginia held excitement at bay. "What's that supposed to mean?"

"I resigned." He'd said it so quietly that Virginia wasn't certain she'd heard correctly.

"You what?"

"I'm home to stay, Ma. No more excuses. Music isn't

my first love—you and Peter are. My priorities have been a little mixed up, like for the past twenty-five years. But I figured it out."

Hot tears burned Virginia's eyes and then trailed into her ears. She reached for David, and he pulled her into a hug. "We can move you home as soon as I get a few things in order. We'll hire a nurse to help out if we need to." He held up a hand before Virginia could voice her objection. "One thing I have is money, Ma. It's about time I spent it on something worthwhile."

Her son kissed her forehead.

"It's gonna be okay, Ma," he whispered.

thirty-eight

When Peter first saw Jerry Shrupp's pickup in the driveway, he didn't think much of it. Jerry or his wife, Mary, occasionally dropped in to share a cup of coffee with Mae or to ask about Peter's dad. But when Peter saw the pile of familiar black luggage on the brick walkway, he quickened his pace to the house and let the screen door slam when he went inside.

"Mae," he called from the mud room.

"We're in here, honey."

Peter rounded the corner. "I saw Jerry's truck. When . . ." His words fell away. His father was bent over little Christopher, talking in baby talk, as if unaware that Peter had entered the room. Peter's questioning gaze turned to Jerry, who was seated in the wooden rocker. Virginia sat with her legs propped up on pillows on the couch.

"He wanted to surprise you," his dad's best friend from childhood explained.

David lifted his head. "Hey, Son. This one's pretty amazing." He nodded toward the baby in his arms.

A lump formed in Peter's throat at the sight. "When did you get in?"

"Eight or so. I knew you'd be milking, so I asked Jerry to pick me up at the airport." The baby cooed and gurgled at his grandpa. "He's getting big already, isn't he?" David reached for Peter. The two embraced in a firm hug around the infant. Each took a seat in the stuffed chairs opposite the couch.

"I'm going to put on a fresh pot of coffee." Mae excused herself.

"So . . . ," Peter began.

"I gave notice last week, right after you called," his father said simply. "They weren't too happy about it, but"—he glanced at his mother on the couch—"it's the right thing to do." The baby shifted, and David lowered him to his knees. He rested the bundle in the dip between his legs. Christopher moved his head back and forth.

"What's he doing?" David said, smiling down at his grandson.

"Oh." Peter laughed. "He always does that when he's ready for a nap." Christopher sucked on his thumb energetically.

"Dad . . ." Peter's words returned, the accusations

he'd hurled in anger. "I'm sorry I said some harsh things before you left."

"You were right." David shrugged. "I've been kicking myself. You saw it when I was so blind."

"What about your music?" Virginia said.

"Music can take the backseat from here on in, Ma. I've got more important things to attend to."

Peter hadn't anticipated the emotions that came with seeing his father bent over Christopher. Pride, joy, happiness. But also renewed grief that his mother wasn't here to share this moment. It had been a long time since that pain had made itself known. Yet it was there, always there. She would never hold her grandson, never hear his heartfelt chuckles when Peter blew on his belly. At times the pain would ebb and he could forget, but every event that marked the passage of Peter's life—graduation, marriage, moving here, the birth of a first son—magnified her absence. It was a scar ever tender to the touch.

The baby let out a whimpering cry as if he were dreaming. David put him to his shoulder and patted his back. Longing rose within Peter. Maybe this time his father really would stay. Peter wanted to believe it, and yet he didn't dare.

thirty-nine

A week had passed since David Morgan's home-coming. Trudy figured that was plenty of time for the dust to settle so Mae would be free to get away. She hoped. She'd been meaning to call but was so busy giving Svetlana her cultural education that she couldn't find the time. Not that Mae would've been able to get away even if she did call. But now that Peter's dad was around, she figured he could manage the baby for a short interlude while she and Mae had a little fun. The phone rang four times. Trudy was about to hang up when Mae's winded voice came over the line. "Hello. This is Mae."

"Why are we whispering? Is the Gestapo there?" Trudy whispered back.

"I laid Christopher down for a nap."

"Ah."

"So . . . what are you calling for?"

"A sister can't call just because?"

"Of course you can. I wasn't trying to—"

"I thought I'd ask if you want to come to the matinee in town with me. New Keanu Reeves flick."

"I have the baby."

"You will always have the baby. Can't your father-in-law watch him?"

"I can't just dump him on David. He's been busy getting Virginia's house ready so they can move back."

"Well, bring Christopher along, then. It's been ages

since we did anything together. I miss you."

"What if he cries?"

"I don't know. Can't you just nurse him in the theater? It's dark. No one will see."

"Trudy! We live in Minnesota, not Africa!"

Trudy laughed.

"Why don't you come over here? We can talk."

Trudy's irritation grew. Why couldn't Mae compromise for once?

"I really had my heart set on Keanu today."

"Oh." Mae's voice deflated. Guilt nipped at Trudy. Still, she said, "I'll see if Svetlana wants to go. Bert and Fred won't be in until late, so I'm doing the widow thing."

"The widow thing?"

"Never mind."

Svetlana was more than happy to accept Trudy's invitation. "What I wear to movie?"

"Come as you are. We aren't fancy here. Unless of course you're lounging around in your BVD's. Wouldn't Lillian love that!"

"BVD's?"

"Never mind. I'll pick you up in half an hour."

"Can I drive?" Svetlana said.

"Sure thing." They hung up.

Svetlana and Trudy had been practicing driving for the past two weeks. Once they got past the white-knuckled "Don't aim at oncoming traffic!" phase, Svetlana had proven herself a decent driver. Trudy figured she'd be ready to take her road test before Christmas. She grabbed her pink leather purse with the letter *T* in a paler shade appliquéd to the side, checked to be sure her keys and billfold were inside, and clomped down the apartment stairway.

Svetlana was standing on the back walk when Trudy pulled up. Svetlana's lips were a thin line, and her eyes were huge. Then Trudy saw why—Lillian was ranting loudly from behind the screen door's veil.

"Don't expect me to make your supper if you go off gallivanting. You're Fred's wife; it's your responsibility to feed him. I won't have you freeloading—"

Trudy honked, and Svetlana's head whipped around. She broke for the car. Lillian's voice rose. "You have to clean that bathroom, too, when you get home. Do you hear me?"

Trudy climbed over the gearshift into the passenger seat as Svetlana took her place at the wheel. Lillian came out onto the back walk. She wore her familiar full-body apron and dark brown support hose tucked into white nurse's shoes. She waved a finger in Trudy's direction. "Trudy Biddle, don't you conspire against me with that girl, you hear? This is between me and the Russki!" Lillian waddled toward the car.

"Hit the gas, Svetlana." Gravel flew up, and the Pacer careened onto the dirt road. Trudy glanced back at Lillian, who was planted in the driveway, hands on hips, her apron flapping in their dust.

"What was that all about?"

Tears streamed down the petite blonde's cheeks. "Lilli-un hate me," Svetlana sobbed. "She say Svetlana not good enough for Fred."

Trudy patted the girl's hand as she shifted into fourth gear. "You're more than good enough for Fred." *Frog larvae would be good enough for Fred.*

Svetlana swiped at her tears with the back of her hand. "You make Svetlana feel better," she said.

"That's another thing: don't talk about yourself in third person. It creeps people out."

"Creeps?"

"Trust me, it's not good." Trudy breathed deeply, considering her sister-in-law for a moment. She turned in her seat and said, "I know this is a hard time for you. I sure don't envy you living with Lillian and Willie. I'd never do it in a million years. But hang in there, okay? Things are bound to get better."

Svetlana nodded and turned the car onto Highway 36 toward town. "Fred say when Lillian and Willie move, we live like king and queen on farm." She smiled. "That why I come to America—to find American dream as farmer's wife."

The grin on her face was so sincere that Trudy didn't have the heart to tell her the truth.

forty

Roy lay on his deathbed, his skin ashen, his form, which had been so strong and virile all his life, now a thin, weathered shell. His eyes were sunk into deep pockets, yet their pale blue bore witness to the man he used to be. He reached for Virginia's hand and gave it a squeeze.

"You have been my everything, Virginia. Do you know that? You gave me two wonderful children and a life more rich than I had a right to. You never complained, not even when we lived in that first apartment that was so small you could lie in bed and stir the oatmeal."

Virginia smiled and stroked his cheek.

"I love you, my girl. No one but you could've ever taken that place in my heart."

The dream faded and Virginia awoke. She'd had that dream—a replay of his last moments with her—countless times since Roy's death. It used to leave her in tears, but that had passed. Now the dream was a comfort, as if he were reminding her of his love for her even in death.

A knock on the door drew Virginia's gaze. Mae stood there. She looked pretty in a sleeveless, pale green shirt and slacks. Her long, dark hair was pulled back in a clip, and her cheeks bore a healthy blush. The circles had disappeared from under her eyes. Virginia waved her in.

"You're going home today," Mae said.

"Yes. I expect it'll be a challenge for us—David and me. We haven't lived under the same roof for a long time."

"Aren't you glad he's home?"

"I'm thrilled to have him with me, sure. But I'm already battling guilt for all that he's sacrificed. It's always been *my* job to save the world."

Mae laughed. "That must be tiring—saving the world."

Virginia smiled. "It is! But when others take care of me, I guess I'm out of sorts . . . and crabby. I'm sorry about that."

"I hadn't noticed."

It occurred to Virginia that perhaps her foul mood had held Jessie off.

"What is it?" Mae said.

"Have you seen Jessie at all? I have a feeling about that child, like something's wrong. It isn't like her not to return my calls. Maybe I'm just imagining, but I need to see for myself that she's okay."

"It'll be a lot easier to see her now that you're moving home. She can come over the way she used to."

Virginia liked the thought of that.

"I have a little surprise for you, Ma," David said as they passed the Rotary Club's sign at the edge of town that read Welcome to Lake Emily.

"Oh?" He pulled onto tree-lined Main Street. "Do I get any guesses?"

David wriggled his brows and grinned. "You'll see soon enough."

They meandered through the quiet streets. Flower beds in summer's full bloom were resplendent with bobbing heads in every color. Sprinklers sounded their *ka-chun-ka-chun* rhythm. Children walked barefoot on the sidewalk, clad in bathing suits with towels slung around their necks. He turned into the driveway of Virginia's Cape Cod.

"We'll have to move my bedroom down to the den, but how will I manage the stairs since there's no bathroom on the main floor?" She'd asked the question a dozen times before, and always David had hedged.

"I've thought of everything. Will you just trust me?"

Virginia clamped her lips shut. Trust him? Why did trust seem so hard to hold on to? It had been her problem all along. It was the reason she tried to manage all the details of life herself—she lacked trust in others, in God. She didn't trust that her family loved her, that they wouldn't resent the burden she'd become. A lump formed in her throat, and she swallowed it.

David brought the walker around and helped her stand. That was when she noticed the convertible parked along the street. *August must be here.* They moved toward the front of the house. A new ramp led to the front door, which stood wide open. August Cleworth, Ella Rosenberg, and most of the Suzie Q's waited behind the screen door.

"What are you all doing here?" Virginia said, crossing the threshold slowly.

"Aren't you surprised?" Ella said.

"We're here to welcome you home, what do you think we're here for?" Lillian Biddle chided from the back of the cluster of ladies. It brought a smile to Virginia's lips.

"That's not all, Ma," David said. He closed the door, and the crowd parted to either side of the staircase. A padded chair affixed to a rail on the wall climbed the stairs. Virginia moved closer so she could see the controls. "This is to take you up and down. See, I told you to trust me."

Virginia was speechless.

"See the arrows. And there's a walker on each level so you don't have to haul one up and down with you."

"How did you do all this?" Virginia finally managed.

He reached an arm around her shoulders. "For my girl, anything's possible." *My girl*—what Roy used to call her. "You do like it, don't you?"

Tears blocked words, but Virginia managed a vigorous nod.

"Mary hooked me up with a medical-supply place. It only took a day to install the lift. The ramp took a little longer, with Jerry's help. Good thing my arthritis wasn't acting up." He shared a smile with the Shrupps.

"So, are you going to try it out or just stare at it?" Jerry said. His wife swatted him playfully.

Virginia laughed. "I don't have much choice, do I?"

David placed a hand on her elbow as she climbed

299

onto the padded seat, which unfolded like a chair in a movie theater.

"Don't I need a seat belt?" she joked.

"It's not that fast, Ma."

"I could ramp it up for you though," Jerry offered, "give you some extra horsepower."

"You don't want him touching it," Mary said. "Trust me on that one."

There was that word again. *Trust.* Virginia tucked it away, determined to think more on it later. Then she pushed the Up arrow, and the seat rose along the wall, slowly but steadily lifting her to the second story. A few moments later she was at the top of the stairs. "I could ride this all day," Virginia said.

"If that's what you want, Ma, then go ahead and ride."

Ella and the rest of the Suzie Q's didn't stay long. Before they left, each offered congratulations and told her to get her rest. Only August lingered. The three gathered in the kitchen at the back of the small house. The smell of coffee and the baked goods the ladies had brought floated in the air.

August held out a hand to David and said, "I don't believe we've had the pleasure. August Cleworth. Virginia's told me a lot about you."

David was sorry he couldn't say the same. He glanced at his mother, who was sipping coffee in the cozy dining alcove just off the kitchen. She seemed to be deep in thought.

"How do you know my mother?" He poured the man a cup of black coffee and handed it to him.

"Mae was my receptionist last year."

David nodded, still waiting for an answer.

"What are you two talking about?" Virginia called. "Come in here so I can be part of the conversation." The men obliged, each taking a seat at the small table.

"I was asking August here how he came to know you."

"He was Mae's boss," Virginia said.

"So he told me."

"Well . . ." His mother sent a curious smile toward the white-haired man, as if they shared a secret. David wondered if he should be concerned. "August visited me in the nursing home."

"And you're simply inspired to go visiting strangers in the nursing home?" David said.

August laughed good-naturedly, but David saw the horrified look his mother gave him.

"Not exactly. Trudy Biddle invited me. I was in need of good company." Then he touched Virginia's hand and lingered there for a moment. When David saw the gesture, he couldn't take his eye off it.

"Who is this guy, Ma?" David asked once August had said his farewells.

Virginia straightened in her chair. She heard the challenge in her son's voice, and she didn't like it.

"He's my friend, David. That's all."

"Oh, he is? Why was he holding your hand?"

"David!"

"I'm not trying to start an argument. But how much do you know about this man?"

"Enough to know he's a friend. I don't want to have this conversation, David. You're going to have to trust me."

But she could tell by the tension in David's jaw and the concern in his eyes that this matter was far from over.

Trudy knew she should mention Svetlana's comment to Bert, yet she held back. It had been a full day since she'd told Trudy they were looking forward to taking over the farm. Maybe it would be better if Svetlana and Fred stayed at the farm when Lillian and Willie moved to town. They seemed to like it there. It wasn't as if Willie and Lillian had told Fred and Svetlana that they couldn't move in. Maybe they would change their minds. Trudy and Bert had their apartment, and they were just fine there. Yet she knew Bert was looking forward to being closer to work, especially during the long nights. And she *had* promised.

Bert was reading the *Lake Emily Herald* as he sipped his after-supper coffee. Trudy sighed, and he lifted his head.

"What's up?" he said.

"I didn't say anything."

"Sure you didn't." He lowered his head back to the paper.

Trudy sighed again. This time Bert didn't lift his head, only his eyes to hers. "It's just something Svetlana said." Bert's gaze didn't budge. "She and Fred think they're getting the farm when Lillian and Willie move to town. Willie hasn't told them yet. Are they reconsidering?"

Bert set the paper down and took a long sip of his coffee from the low table between them. "I've been wondering the same thing. But the way things are going between Ma and Svetlana . . ."

"They looked about ready to start World War III yesterday. Your mother was ranting at that poor girl."

"That'll be nothing compared to what happens when Fred finds out he's not getting the farm."

The day after her return home Virginia asked David to take her to Jessie's. She couldn't wait another moment to see the girl. She'd called again the previous night to tell Jessie that she was back in town, that she should come and see her, but still no reply.

David rang the bell. When no one came, he knocked loudly. Finally he looked back at his mother. "Looks like no one's home, Ma. Maybe she's at the pool for the afternoon or at a friend's."

"I guess that could be. Maybe she's at Anna's."

"That's probably it. She's just a busy ten-year-old."

"I suppose." Yet Virginia's worry only grew.

When Bert posed the question to his father the next day, Willie shook his head. They were in the Quonset shed that housed his collection of Pioneer Power engines. It was a veritable museum of ancient machinery, all labeled and in perfect working order. Dust motes floated in shafts of sunlight that shot through the windows at the end of the round-roofed building.

"I don't know what I've been waiting for," Willie admitted. "Maybe for some sign that he's changed. But he hasn't." He lifted his eyes to Bert. Pain dwelled there, a longing for what could've been. "I haven't changed my mind. The farm is yours."

"So what do you want to do?"

"I suppose we'll need to break the news."

The next day Trudy took it upon herself to get Svetlana out of firing range while Fred received the news. She even talked Willie into lending her his boat, and since the Pacer didn't have a hitch, the girls took Bert's pickup.

"I drive?" Svetlana stood outside the driver's door. She wore a red top, capris, and a ratty tan fishing cap. Rusted lures covered the brim.

"Where'd you get that?" Trudy motioned toward the hat.

"I find in attic. Lots of good stuff up there!"

Trudy scooted over to let Svetlana drive. "You were digging in Lillian's stash? Did she know you were up there?" Svetlana shook her head and moved the gearshift into first.

"She was at Ex-ten-shun. What that?"

"It's a club where old ladies get together to drink Margaritas."

"Really?" Svetlana's expression was so earnest that Trudy couldn't lie to the girl.

"No. It's a meeting where the ladies talk about gardening and how to plan their funerals. It's just a club."

"Like Rotary?"

"Sure. They're all the same—social clubs. How do you know about Rotary?"

"My friend come as exchange student in high school. Rotary sponsor exchange students."

"Ah."

Lake Emily's shimmering water tower came into view. "Where do we go?"

Trudy pointed ahead. "The public boat access is another mile on the left. I'll tell you when we get there."

It was a stunning day. The sky was a shy blue. The sun smiled in the gentle breeze. Temperatures were in the low eighties. Two crows lifted lazily from the road ahead, not eager to leave the road kill they feasted on.

"Right here," Trudy said. Svetlana began to turn right. "No, left."

"You say 'right.'"

"I meant at this spot, but it's left." Svetlana pulled the truck around in as tight a circle as the boat would allow. They descended to the beach area, where a long dock stuck out into the water. "You're going to want to pull to the right so you can back the boat into the water."

305

Svetlana did as Trudy instructed, turning the pickup toward the row of tall pines. Shifting into reverse, she popped the clutch and began to back up, but when she corrected the steering wheel, the trailer turned the opposite direction. An elderly man who fished from the dock lifted his head to watch. "Pull forward again," Trudy instructed. "And straighten your wheels before you start to back up."

Svetlana obeyed, but this time she was too near the dock. Trudy heard the wheels on the trailer rub the wooden structure. "Stop!" Trudy shouted. The old man on the dock dove into the water and swam to the safety of shore, fishing pole still in his hand. "Pull forward again and to the right." Svetlana pulled forward, but the trailer was still crooked. When she began to back up, the trailer turned at an even more severe angle.

"Straighten that out," Trudy said. She could see the old man climbing onto the shore. His face was none too happy. The truck stalled, and Svetlana restarted it. She took a deep breath and began to back up again, this time steering to correct the trailer's extreme angle. Given the fisherman's expression, they were about to receive a severe scolding. Trudy placed a hand on the door handle to brace herself for his tirade. Svetlana hit the gas and gunned it. The aged dock that had looked so peaceful and serene now made the most agonizing sound—wood splintering for what seemed minutes and then metal crunching. Trudy cringed as she thought of Willie polishing this boat for the fishing opener just a few short months before.

The old man motioned for Svetlana to roll down her window. Water dripped from his John Deere cap and down his fissured face. "Don't you think you've done enough damage for today?" Svetlana started bawling. Trudy placed a hand on Svetlana's shoulder.

"She shouldn't be driving, you know." He directed this to Trudy. "She almost killed me. I'll be calling the Department of Natural Resources about that dock!" His eyes snapped as if to add an exclamation point to his words.

"We're so sorry," Trudy said. But by then it was too late. He'd stomped to his car and pulled out pen and paper. When he returned, he took down their names, phone numbers, and insurance information. Then he said tersely, "You'll be hearing from my lawyer!"

"I'll drive," Trudy whispered to Svetlana once the man was gone. Trudy got out, walked around the pickup, and took the driver's seat while Svetlana scooted over to the passenger's seat. Trudy glanced back at the tangle of boat and dock and prayed she'd be able to extricate Willie's pride and joy from the wreckage. The front end of the dock was tipped up and to the side like a surfer on a big curl. The middle section was pretty much toothpicks twisted around the boat's frame. One particularly large piece of wood stuck up into the bottom of the aluminum craft making it look like a birdhouse on a fence post. Trudy winced.

"I hope Willie has insurance," she muttered as she popped the gearshift into first. Svetlana's tears had subsided to softer hiccups. Thick mascara smudged her cheeks. Trudy handed her a tissue from her pink leather purse, then she applied the gas and eased the truck forward. A section of dock followed. Trudy kept going, slowly, until the entire trailer was out of the water. Then she climbed out to survey the damage. The log she'd noticed before went completely through the boat's bottom like a giant cork. The trailer was scratched up, and the tire on the left side was askew as if it would come off if they so much as sneezed.

We aren't going anywhere like that. She returned to the cab for her cell phone. She thought about calling Bert, but then decided the nearest mechanic would do. No sense calling Bert from his meeting with Fred and Willie just so he could be peeved at her.

Lillian hid in the kitchen, although Bert knew she was listening to their every word.

"What do you mean, Bert gets the farm?" Fred's bewilderment quickly turned to anger. It was obvious he hadn't seen this coming, had never imagined such a thing could be.

Their father's face was red too. How could a father disinherit his own son? Had the heritage become more valuable than its recipients? Bert kept his thoughts to himself.

"You never think of anyone but yourself, Fred," Dad was saying. "When you took off for Florida, I understood at first. But to leave Bert alone to manage things while you gallivanted—"

"I'm being *punished*? That's what this is all about?

Or did Bert poison you against me?" His accusing stare passed to Bert.

Bert pursed his lips, determined not to say anything he'd regret.

"This isn't Bert's doing at all. *You* chose to desert us when we needed you. It's as plain as that."

"Desert you?" Fred screeched. "Ma was driving me insane with her bell ringing and bellyaching about that stupid leg." His voice took on a mocking tone. " 'Get me this. Get me that.' "

Willie cleared his throat. Fred quieted grudgingly.

"I know you don't like this. You aren't meant to. But I can't trust you, Fred. How do I know you and Svetlana won't take off for Russia tomorrow?"

"Because I say so!" Fred said.

Willie shook his head. "Fred,"—his tone softened— "it would've been one thing if you'd gone on a two-week vacation. That I could've understood. But you were gone well over a year. You didn't even come home for your brother's wedding, much less tell us that you were getting married. We're family. Family doesn't do that."

The pain in Fred's eyes knifed Bert's heart.

"But family does *this?* What am I supposed to do? You could hire me, couldn't you, Bert? There's too much work for just you."

"Always plenty of work on a farm," Willie said. "But we can't afford to pay you. Milk prices have dropped again. If Trudy wasn't paying for the apartment in town with her salary at the school, she and Bert

309

would've had to move in here from the get-go. And now that we're selling the north acres . . ."

"And supporting your own house in town," Fred finished bitterly.

"Yes, supporting our place in town. We just don't have the funds to support a third household." Willie's eyes met Bert's. "Bert has been a faithful son. His dedication to the farm was evident in your absence."

"Save the speech, Pops." Fred stood then and stalked out the front door, slamming the screen door behind him. Lillian bustled in, gathered empty cups onto a tray, and silently slipped back into the kitchen.

"Well," Bert said, "at least he didn't throw anything."

forty-one

Willie didn't say a word when Trudy showed him the fishing boat. He just stood there staring.

"I'm really, really sorry," Trudy repeated for the third time. Bert walked around the shipwreck, hand to chin as he inspected.

"What did this?" Willie said. His glance moved to Svetlana, who was chewing on a thumbnail. She stood off to the side, a silent mouse. Trudy cleared her throat.

"I told you it was my fault, and it was," she said. Her father-in-law turned back to her.

"What am I supposed to do?" Willie placed hands on hips.

"I'll weld it back together for you," Trudy offered. "Just get me one of those mask thingies and a welder." That brought a smile to the old man's lips. He shook his head.

"We'll replace it, Dad," Bert offered. Trudy's eyes widened. She clamped her lips shut.

"Didn't Trudy just get done paying for Peter's telephone pole?" Willie said of a prior driving incident. "And . . . wasn't there some fine for damaging the coach's truck?"

"He dropped the charges!" Trudy protested.

Fred came around the corner. "Let's get out of here," he said to his wife. Then he saw the trailer and boat. For a minute, concern replaced his anger. "You weren't in the boat when that happened?" Fred said to Svetlana.

"A little mishap—all my fault," Trudy said.

Fred turned back to his wife. "Are you okay?" Svetlana began to bawl again in that loud, obnoxious way she had. Fred held her and patted her back as he murmured, "I knew if you hung around with Trudy, sooner or later something like this would happen."

"Hey!" Trudy and Bert said as one.

Then Trudy said, "You don't even know what happened!"

"Is all my fault," Svetlana murmured. "An old man—I almost kill old man on dock." All eyes went to her.

311

"What do you mean, you almost killed someone?" Fred said, his voice stern.

"Would everyone just chill out for a minute?" Now all eyes shifted to Trudy. "Yes, there was an old guy on the dock. But he dove into the water and out of harm's way before we really wrecked it. He was perfectly fine. I doubt he'll *really* file charges. He was just mad."

"Do you know who the man was?" Bert said to Trudy.

She shrugged. "He never mentioned it, although he did look vaguely familiar. I think I've seen him around the Chuckwagon. He took down our insurance information."

"Great," Fred said. "Now we'll have a lawsuit on our hands, on top of a fine from the DNR." He turned toward his dad. "Oh, but I guess that's none of *my* concern, is it? I'm not part of this family!" He took Svetlana by the arm and stalked off.

Finally Trudy and Bert climbed into their pickup and left for town. She glanced over at Bert and noticed a smile on his face. Trudy said, "What are you smiling about?"

Bert reached for her hand on the seat and gave it a squeeze. "I love you."

"I thought you'd be mad," Trudy said.

"Oh, I am!"

"But . . ."

"You were protecting Svetlana."

"How do you know that? I said I was responsible, and I was!"

"She was driving, wasn't she?"

"Well, yes. Is that why you offered to replace the boat and trailer?"

"No. It really was your fault. Svetlana isn't experienced enough to back up a trailer. I doubt *you're* experienced enough for that."

"Hey!" Trudy protested.

Bert laughed. When his chuckle died away, he said, "You've been a good friend to her when Ma and Dad haven't been remotely nice. Even though your meddling didn't exactly work out this time, she needed a friend, and that's what you were."

Trudy moved closer to her groom on the bench seat. "Fred won't let her see me after this."

"That may be true, but Svetlana won't forget that you were kind to her." He lifted his seed cap and reseated it on his head. He chuckled. "You didn't warn me before we got married that all your shenanigans would cost me so much."

"Shenanigans? What shenanigans?"

"Do you want a list? I think Dad started one for us." His eyes wrinkled into a smile.

"I'm going to miss Svetlana."

"Fred could've done worse. In fact he *has* done worse. You should've seen some of the girls he dated." Bert paused in thought, then he quietly said, "Dad's being unfair. But I have no idea what I can do about it." He shook his head. "One thing I do know: a brother

313

doesn't leave his loved ones out on the street."

Trudy kissed Bert's cheek. "You're a good man, Bert Biddle."

With Virginia in David's care, Mae was finally free to settle into a normal routine with the baby. They got up at six for the first feeding of the day. Then Mae made beds, put in a load of laundry, and emptied the dishwasher while Christopher watched from his carrier. Peter usually made coffee when he got up to milk, so that was always ready and calling to her. But the baby had been fussy whenever she indulged, so she'd switched to a decaffeinated tea. She liked the stuff well enough, but it wasn't the same. By the time she ate a light breakfast and put supper in the Crockpot, it was time for Christopher's ten o'clock feeding.

Mae poured a tall glass of ice water, which she set on the table, then she lifted her son to nurse. His little fist reached up as he suckled, and Mae placed her pinkie in his firm grasp. The corner of his mouth turned into a smile, and milk dribbled down his chin. Mae hadn't expected this time they shared as mother and son to be so powerful. She wondered if mothers who bottle-fed their babies felt the same emotions. Or was it the physical intimacy of nourishing his tiny body with her own that filled her heart with this fierce devotion? She suspected it had less to do with biology and more with the openness of her heart.

Peter's steps sounded on the back porch. Mae heard

the screen door slam, and he came in through the cheery kitchen.

"Hey," he said. "Can you believe it? I'm actually caught up on my work."

"That'll last about a day. What happened?"

"Fluke." He held up his hands. Then realizing they were filthy, he went to wash them at the kitchen sink.

"What's up?" Mae said when he came to sit on the couch. He looked at his son, who'd fallen asleep at his mother's breast. Mae laid him back in his carrier and draped a light blanket over him.

Peter touched his son's cheek. "Still can't get over him," he said.

"He's pretty wonderful. It's nice to have your dad home too."

Peter sighed.

"You're not glad to have your dad back?"

"I'm thrilled . . . but he's never stayed anywhere for long." His eyes met hers. "I guess the proof's in the pudding."

"Why the cynicism?" Mae took a sip of her ice water.

"My heart won't let me trust."

Both were silent.

"Milk prices dropped another quarter," Peter finally said.

"They'll go back up."

"Will they? I remember when I was a kid that a brand-new car cost four thousand dollars. Nowadays you're lucky to get one for under twenty thousand, but the price of milk . . . It's barely risen, even though costs sure have. People want their food, but they don't want to pay for it. I just don't know. Paying to rent the land from Grandma, a mortgage . . . I hate the thought of putting Christopher in day care, but maybe your going back to work would be for the best."

"If there aren't any other options . . ." Mae hoped that was not the case. "You're really that worried?"

Peter nodded. "I talked to the insurance agent awhile back. Too late to get crop insurance. And without that, I'm afraid this poor crop will do us in." He sighed. "At least if you were working . . . I hate to do it, though. Christopher needs one of us."

"It's a lot of stress for you," Mae said. "We'll take it one day at a time. We'll get through, you'll see. Before you know it, Christopher will be out there milking cows with his daddy."

Peter smiled. "I hope so, honey. I sure don't want to have to quit now."

forty-two

David was outside mowing the lawn. Virginia could hear the noisy machine as it moved up and down the dime-sized front yard. She had decided to get out her embroidery to see if her old hands could master the task once again. The numbness in her left hand had ebbed considerably, although it flared up now and then. She lifted the needle, holding it toward the light so she could see to thread it. Choosing scarlet floss, she managed to get the thread through the hole. She tied a knot and lifted the hoop that held the white cotton fabric taut. Eventually it would become a table-cloth. She poked the needle through from the back and did one daisy chain and then another.

"Ma," David said from the front entryway. Virginia lifted her head. She hadn't heard the mower shut off. "You have a visitor."

Behind him stood Anna Eastman. "Come on in," Virginia said.

The blonde took a seat across from Virginia in the den. "Is this a social call?" Virginia said.

"That depends on your definition, I guess." Worry brewed in her green eyes.

"What is it?"

"Has Jessie come to visit you lately?"

Virginia shook her head. "I've been trying to get ahold of her, but she doesn't return my calls. It doesn't seem like her. She used to enjoy coming over, spending time doing things together."

"I know she was frightened by the hospital. I'm sure that was why she didn't come during your stay at the nursing home."

Virginia nodded. "Poor girl. She has had more than her share of hospital traumas. So you haven't seen her either?"

"No. Steve . . ." She paused. "He asked me if we could start dating. I don't know. I didn't have those kinds of feelings for him. So I said no. He took it badly; Jessie did too. But I do care. I care deeply. I don't know if he told Jessie she couldn't see me anymore or if that was her doing, but she hasn't been coming around. That's why I was hoping she had come to see you."

Virginia set her embroidery aside. "I had a feeling something wasn't right."

"I feel so responsible. Jessie's such a great kid. I had a real sense that we were . . . connecting, you know?"

"I do. I'll keep trying to get ahold of her. She needs to know that she's loved."

September was Virginia's favorite month, with the cooler temperatures that previewed autumn.

Virginia stood in front of the piano that held the family photographs. Diffused afternoon light created shadows in the living room, which ran the length of the house on the west side. All was still. David was at the high school for the afternoon, tutoring music students. It was a job he'd had before, one that he found pleasure in, and with the beginning of a new school year, he discovered the school was eager for his expertise. Virginia was glad he was doing something for himself again. Something other than just looking after her.

The quietness of the house allowed room for introspection, which wasn't always a good thing, she'd decided. Introspection too often led to sadness. She touched her and Roy's wedding photo. What would Roy think of her if he knew that she'd had romantic thoughts toward another man? Shame flooded her. She'd been unfaithful to Roy's memory. Yet she knew that wasn't true. She loved Roy as much as she ever had.

She lifted the wedding picture. She and Roy gazed at her bouquet of long-stemmed roses. The ache she felt right after Roy died had lessened. An unexpected sweetness had replaced the anguish, as if Roy were with her in a new way.

She set the yellowed photograph back on the piano and gave a heavy sigh. As much as she hated to admit it, she enjoyed being with August. She enjoyed being held in strong arms, even at seventy-eight. She wondered if that need for love ever went away. His admiration made her feel alive . . . young. That was what she'd missed these past years—that sense of being really alive, of expecting that something new and wonderful could happen in her life.

Virginia pulled out an ancient photo album. She needed to see Roy's face. She couldn't say why; she just needed to. Inside were pictures of a younger Virginia and Roy, taken right after the war. They'd been so vibrant, so happy. She remembered feeling beautiful in her simple dresses, especially with Roy smiling at her the way he would. She glanced at the brochure that lay on the coffee table. It was ridiculous. A seventy-eight-year-old woman taking dance lessons.

"Ridiculous," she murmured.

Just then David came in the back door. "Ma?"

"I'm in here." David rounded the corner, and Virginia wondered if he'd notice her guilty state. "How was teaching?"

David smiled broadly. "Great."

Virginia closed the album and returned it to its shelf near the piano. "David, are you glad you came back to Lake Emily? Do you regret leaving Arizona?"

David ran a hand through his hair before he answered. "I thought conducting would give me the chance to return to what I loved—music. I had a vision of myself happily engrossed in work, but I forgot that when I was in the orchestra here, I was close to you. I underestimated how much that meant to me."

Virginia sat down on the piano bench. "It seems we're all on a learning curve, trying to figure out what we want in life, where the balance is."

"The problem with balance is that once you find it, something shifts, and you have to find it all over again. I haven't been very good at that."

"Have you dated anyone since Laura?" The question seemed to come from nowhere, and at first Virginia was sorry she'd asked. But David didn't act offended.

He took a seat next to her. "I don't have the interest, Ma. I loved her so much. No one's come along who could even remotely compare."

"Don't you ever wonder whether you could have found love with another?"

David shook his head. "Laura was one in a million, Ma."

Virginia squeezed his hand. "She was. I just wondered if you ever get lonely."

"Of course I do. Is this about you and Mr. Cleworth?"

Virginia shook her head. She didn't feel up to starting that argument again.

David kissed her on the temple and hugged her. "You don't need to feel lonely anymore, Ma. I'm here for you."

David's confidence that he alone could quell his mother's loneliness began to fade the next day when August Cleworth appeared at Virginia's front door. The man was too perfect; his white hair had that Tom Netherton quality, and his smile seemed a bit too plastic. David couldn't hide his distaste. "You forget something here?"

"No, no. I'm here to see Virginia. Maybe do some dancing." His eyes twinkled, and he stepped into the foyer, a bouquet of black-eyed Susans in hand. David went upstairs to find his mother.

"Ma."

Virginia was reading in the stuffed chair tucked in the dormer of her room. Afternoon light filled the space with brightness. Virginia lifted her head.

"Mr. Cleworth is here to see you again, Ma."

"He is?"

"Is this some kind of joke? What's the whole thing about dancing?"

"No, no joke. I meant to tell you, David."

David came into the room and closed the door quietly. "What? What did you mean to tell me?"

"Don't get all dramatic, David. I'm thinking about taking some dance lessons with August once I can throw this walker away." She gestured to the contraption by the chair.

"So?"

"So, nothing," Virginia said. "It's harmless. Trust me." She stood and reached for her walker before heading to the bedroom door. Opening it slightly, she peered down at August. He was gazing at the family photographs in the hall. Virginia ran a hand down her blouse to smooth out the wrinkles. August turned around.

"There you are. I thought I'd invite you for a little ride. It's a beautiful day." He held out the bouquet to her.

David discreetly rolled his eyes.

"You didn't have to do that." She rode the lift down the stairs. When she reached the bottom, August leaned to give her a peck on the cheek. David spied from upstairs.

"That's so sweet of you, August," Virginia said as she took the flowers.

"What do you say? Want to go for a ride? I have the convertible."

That brought David down the stairs. "You haven't had your nap yet this afternoon," David interjected.

His mother gave him a scolding glare. "David, I'll be just fine without a nap. Why don't you go make us some coffee? You'd like a cup, wouldn't you, August?"

"I never turn down a cup of coffee," he said.

David wanted to stay and keep an eye on the character, but his mother's expression told him to obey or she'd put him over her knee.

She and August went into the living room while David went for coffee, which didn't brew fast enough. He assembled a tray of steaming cups as quickly as possible and went into the living room, where August and Virginia sat chatting amiably. "So," David began, "you're a dancer?" His mother gave an exasperated sigh.

August laughed. "Not much of one, but I try."

He didn't say anything beyond that.

"David, I have some Milano cookies up in the cupboard. Why don't you run get them for us?" David sighed and went to retrieve the cookies. When he returned, August was on his feet saying his good-byes.

"You have to leave so soon?" David said.

"Afraid so." He turned to Virginia. "We'll take a rain check on that drive, okay?" Virginia nodded. Then he waved to David and let himself out the front door.

"David Morgan!" Virginia practically shouted as the sound of August's car retreated. "I've never been more embarrassed in my life!"

"Ma, is this why you were asking about dating yesterday? Because you have a beau and you refuse to admit it to me?"

"He's not a beau. He's a friend. His wife died a couple of years ago . . . He understands how I feel."

"And I don't? You can talk to me, Ma. That's what I'm here for."

"It's different with August. He isn't trying to run my life. He's just a friend."

"So I'm trying to run your life?" His volume rose.

"That's not what I meant."

"It's what you said, Ma."

Virginia heaved a heavy sigh. "I love you, David. And I'm grateful for all that you do for me. You're going to have to allow me to be a grownup and trust me."

"And what am I trusting you with? Some stranger? Who knows what his motives are. Maybe he thinks you're a rich widow."

Virginia smiled despite herself. "Then maybe you should try to get to know him a little. Trust me with my own life, David. I'm finally living again. Don't squelch that."

forty-three

W here are you going to get four thousand dollars to buy a new boat for Willie?" Mae asked Trudy as she laid an embroidered tablecloth on the round wicker dining table in the corner of the porch. Trudy brought four crystal glasses and four of Mae's pink-rose china plates to set in front of the matched white wicker chairs.

"Bert says we'll find a way. I'm not as bummed about that as I am that Fred won't let Svetlana associate with me anymore."

"That'll put a damper on your social calendar." Sarcasm tinged Mae's words.

"What's that supposed to mean?" Trudy said.

"Nothing." Mae knew she was being childish. She left the porch to get the napkins from the kitchen.

"What do you think Fred and Svetlana will do now that they know they can't work the farm?" Mae said when she came back out.

"I wouldn't put it past him to take off again."

"Do you think he'd leave Svetlana?" Mae laid out green linen napkins and a centerpiece of purple hydrangeas.

Trudy thought, then shook her head. "No. He really loves her. Go figure that! But in his own way. When he saw the boat, his first reaction was to be sure she was okay. *My* husband circled the wreck like a piranha."

"Bert knew you were okay."

"I guess." Trudy turned toward the table and said, "Are we ready to take on Mom and Paul?"

"I think so." Mae tucked her long dark hair behind her ears.

"Bert's been sick with worry."

"About Mom and Paul?"

"No, milk. Isn't Peter worried about milk prices dropping?"

"Oh, that. Yes, he's been a train wreck. I wonder if he regrets not putting in peas, but it was so late in the season. Do you think farmers have always struggled like this? Year after year, always evaluating whether to stay the course or not?"

"Probably. Grapes of wrath or whatnot."

Mae rolled her eyes and went inside to get the teacups she'd forgotten. When she came back out, Trudy was rocking Christopher in one of the tall rockers and talking baby talk to him.

"You're not supposed to do that."

Trudy lifted her eyes. "Do what? Hold my nephew?"

"I read somewhere that you shouldn't talk baby talk. It delays a baby's verbal skills."

Trudy laughed and puckered her lips. "Does my widdle bee-bee wuv his aunt Twoo-dy?"

"Thanks a lot!"

"You go ahead and be a serious adult. My life is too short for that! Besides, how many teenagers do you know who still talk like that? It's a bunch of hooey!"

Mae sighed and went back into the house to check on the egg bake she'd placed in the oven. The top was just turning golden. In another five minutes it would be perfect. Mae glanced at the clock—9:50. Her mother and Paul would be here any moment. Everything would be perfect.

At ten thirty Paul and Catherine Larson pulled up in their silver SUV. Mae, Trudy, and a freshly diapered Christopher crossed the lawn to greet them.

Mae instantly saw the strained expression on Paul's face and wondered if the two had had an argument. He shut the SUV door and offered Mae, then Trudy, a hug. Catherine came around and did the same.

"Girls." Then to Christopher, "How's my baby boy-

boy?" Trudy raised an eyebrow at Mae, who narrowed her eyes in return.

"So," Trudy began, "how was the drive?"

Neither Paul nor Catherine answered.

"All righty then," Trudy said. "Mae made a yummy brunch." Then under her breath, "Which was ready half an hour ago." She led the way to the house.

Mae, Catherine, and Paul climbed the front steps to the screened porch.

"This looks lovely," Catherine said.

"Trudy helped."

Catherine gazed at Christopher in her arms. "This is an interesting outfit." He wore a navy-blue sailor suit complete with bell-bottom pants.

"Thanks. I got it at the Salvation Army."

"Salvation Army? Since when do you shop in those dives?" The condescending tone sent Mae reeling. She'd been so happy that her mother and she had turned a corner in their relationship, but this old habit—this snotty, uppity attitude that her mother seemed to carry with her—still lurked.

"They aren't dives, Mom. It's an inexpensive place where I can find clothes that he'll outgrow in a month. They have good stuff if you look regularly."

"You shop there *often?* If you are struggling, you should have told me. I can always get my grandson some acceptable clothing." Catherine bought everything at Marshall Fields or the more upscale stores downtown. She never entered Wal-Mart, much less a secondhand store. "Are funds *that* low for you?"

"We're doing just fine, Mom," Mae said. "I'm just being frugal."

"Nothing wrong with frugality," Trudy added.

"Do you have any coffee?" Paul broke in. His kind eyes met Mae's.

"A fresh pot in the kitchen. I'll get you some."

"Please," Paul said, "allow me." His words were obviously directed at Catherine. He disappeared into the house.

"You and Paul have a fight?" Trudy guessed.

"That's our business, isn't it?"

"Which means, 'Yes, we had a fight, and we haven't made up yet,'" Trudy translated for Mae.

Catherine lifted Christopher to her shoulder and whispered, "I'll have you know it was about you two."

Mae wished Paul had allowed her to get the coffee. A knot formed in her stomach. Trudy plopped to the rocking chair and patted the seat next to her for her mother. Catherine settled Christopher in her lap. Paul returned bearing the carafe of coffee.

"Set it over there," Mae directed. Then she remembered the breakfast dish in the oven. She went to retrieve it. The edges had curled in a bit: overbaked but not burnt. Mae placed the nine-by-thirteen-inch pan on the counter and sliced the hotdish into three-inch squares, then took the pan out to the porch. The tension seemed to have passed. Trudy and Paul were discussing the latest dip in milk prices.

"The food is ready," Mae said. "Why don't we gather at the table?"

Catherine laid Christopher in his baby carrier. His eyes had drooped shut, and a line of drool traced his dimple. Each took a seat, and Mae said grace before they passed the food and coffee.

"The men are working in the fields?" Paul's gaze traveled in that direction. Peter's tractor was nowhere in sight.

Mae nodded. "Bert and Peter have been haying together. Makes the work lighter."

"What happened to Bert's brother? I thought he was back in town," Catherine said.

"He is," Trudy said around a mouthful of egg, bacon, and bread. "Let's just say Willie sort of . . . disinherited him."

Catherine sniffed. "So much for the sweet-farmer stereotype." Paul shot her a warning look, and Catherine wiped the corner of her mouth with the cloth napkin. "I'm just calling a spade a spade."

"You don't know the whole story, Mom," Trudy said. "And I don't feel like telling it. It's been hard enough as it is."

"What does that mean?" Catherine said. When no one answered, she said, "I told you both that this farming life was too hard. It's never too late to move back home to St. Paul, you know."

Paul intervened. "Catherine, do you honestly think little Christopher would be better off raised in St. Paul?"

"Well, at least I'd get to see him. I'm lucky if I get to see him once a month this way. That's important too—

family. Not everything in the country is better."

"You could come visit more often," Trudy said.

"I just miss you," Catherine said. "Is that so bad? A mother wants her children to be happy, to not have to struggle for everything. Mae's buying my grandson castoff clothes; you both talk about not being able to make ends meet. What kind of life is that?"

"It's the life we choose, Ma," Trudy said. "It's not right or wrong; it just is. Besides, struggle isn't always a bad thing. At times you actually learn something along the way."

Why was it that whenever conflict arose, Mae's mouth sealed itself shut? Trudy could shoot retorts the way Robin Hood shot arrows, yet Mae's mind completely shut down. Her heart hammered; her stomach constricted. Even her breathing became shallow, difficult.

"Are you okay?" Trudy leaned to whisper when Catherine and Paul called a truce and took the baby for a walk.

"Yeah."

"What's wrong?"

"I can't handle that like you do."

"What? Our little disagreement? That was nothing. You should've married into the Biddle family—they know how to fight!"

Sudden tears stung Mae's eyes.

"Maeflower." Trudy reached for her hand.

"I had really convinced myself that everything was better, that Mom had accepted us living here, that she'd accepted my decision not to pursue music. But I guess that was just a temporary cease-fire when Christopher was born."

"Now you're being dramatic." Trudy wrapped her hands around her sister's. "Honey, very few of us ever truly change. We make little adjustments along the way, but essentially we're the same person at ninety that we were at nine. Mom's no different. But she does love you. You heard her: she wants to protect us."

"Yes," Mae agreed. "But . . ." Mae's feelings of the past weeks crystallized. She hadn't put words to them, only a vague sense that she and Trudy were growing apart.

"But what?"

"I didn't mean what I said to you before."

"About what?"

"When I said Svetlana's absence would put a damper on your social life."

"Yeah?"

"I've been jealous of how much time you spend with her. You used to spend that time with me. But since you got married—"

"No, since Christopher was born."

"That was the same day."

"I know. Same day, different motivation." Trudy sighed. "I've been jealous too. I didn't realize it, but I have been." She shrugged. "I'm older. I should've had a baby first!" Tears touched the corners of her eyes. Mae closed the distance between them. "I love Christopher. I really do," Trudy said.

"I know you do. I just want you back in my life."

"I have good news: I'm suddenly available!"

David whistled as he washed lunch dishes. Virginia could hear him from the den. Clutching the walker, she pulled herself up and shuffled down the photograph-lined hallway to the sunny kitchen.

David turned toward her when she came in. "I thought you were taking a nap."

"People my age don't sleep. We take stabs at it. Let me help with the dishes."

"That's okay. I've got it. Why don't you go sit down?"

"No." He was always telling her to go sit down. She reached for a dishtowel. "I need to be helpful. I'm not completely useless." She didn't care that her irritation showed.

"I wasn't saying that you were." David moved aside to make room for her at the stainless-steel sink. Virginia lifted a pot and began to dry it. David rinsed two glasses and set them in the drainer on the counter.

"I'm sorry. I shouldn't have snapped at you," Virginia said.

"Okay . . . ," David said. He rinsed a plate and set it, too, in the drainer. "I wasn't trying to imply anything, Ma. We both have to get used to living together again. We're pretty set in our roles. Especially you."

Virginia laughed. "I happen to know my son's a stubborn mule."

David batted at her nose and deposited a peak of suds

there. Virginia wiped it away. "I still need to do things—as much as possible—around here. It gives me a sense of worth. Do you understand that?"

"I do. I wasn't trying to diminish you. Honest." He rinsed another plate.

Virginia sighed. "Truth is, I'm still angry with your father. He should be here doing all this, not you."

"Someone had to go first."

"If he'd been even the least bit thoughtful, he would've let me go first."

Comfortable quiet settled as son and mother washed and rinsed dishes. Then a voice that had begun to speak of late broke into her thoughts. It sounded oddly like August's voice. *Why shouldn't David give of himself? That was what you raised him for, to be an unselfish person. It's only right that he have his opportunity to wear the apron.* Virginia glanced at David's profile. It was so like Roy's with that strong Roman nose. Pride welled up within her. Not the pride of a mother of a great musician with a gift for wooing crowds, but the pride of a mother whose son cared for others. It was a far greater pride, a pride that would last.

AUGUST CLEWORTH

Fourteen-year-old August Cleworth smoothed back his blond hair and drew a nervous breath. He gazed around the one-room country schoolhouse. Three rows of desks stood in perfect alignment. The younger chil-

dren sat in the front in smaller desks, and the older students filled the back of the room. A black chalkboard covered the front wall, and a large map and a painting of President George Washington served as the backdrop for the teacher's heavy oak desk.

The kids faced forward in their seats, the boys in overalls or jeans and the girls in print dresses. The tall, skinny teacher was writing a math problem on the blackboard. August cleared his throat quietly, and the teacher turned around.

"Oh, our new student." She offered him a kind smile. The children turned heads to see him. They whispered to each other as they eyed August. "Come in," the teacher said. "Class, this is August Cleworth. He just moved to Lake Emily from Aitkin, wasn't it?"

August nodded. "Yes ma'am." They'd been in Lake Emily all of four days, so August hadn't had a chance to meet any other kids. He wiped sweaty hands on his overalls, which smelled of the barn and that morning's chores.

"Why don't you take the empty chair over there"—the teacher pointed—"next to Willa Kruger."

August shuffled to the desk and slid into the chair. The girl beside him lifted pale green eyes that were flecked with brown and had a rim of black around the iris. August had never seen eyes like that before; they mesmerized.

"Hey," she said in a sweet, low voice. She held out her hand to him. "I'm Willa."

August shook her hand and felt his face flame.

334

"August," the teacher continued from the front, "why don't you tell us something about yourself?"

All eyes were on him. He felt himself shrink in his skin.

"It's okay," Willa whispered. "We won't bite." There was that smile again.

August's shoulders softened. He pushed back his hair. "Well, like you said, I'm from Aitkin. My ma and pa had a farm up there." He placed a hand on the back of his neck. "But we had some hard times, so we decided to come down here to work at my Grandpa's farm—my ma's pa."

"So you're living with your grandparents?" the teacher said.

"Yes ma'am. My Grandma and Grandpa Hambach."

August didn't miss the snicker that escaped the lips of the boy behind him. He was a large, thick kid, probably a year or two older than August, with black hair and pimples on his wide nose.

"You shush," Willa scolded the boy. "There's no shame in families helping each other during hard times." She turned her pretty face to August. "You never mind Todd, okay?"

The teacher returned to her lesson. August couldn't take his mind off Willa. The rest of the morning he stole glances at her. Her strawberry blond curls framed her face in softness, and freckles kissed her smooth cheeks.

After lunch break, the children went outside to play in the autumn sunshine. Willa took August by the hand

and led him to the circle of students who gathered beside the flag at the front of the school. She introduced him to the other girls and boys who seemed to accept him just fine.

Todd still challenged. "You like football?"

"Yes sir. I played quarterback in Aitkin."

That put a grin on Todd's face.

"Good," Todd said. "We could use a good quarterback. You want to go toss a ball around?"

August shrugged and glanced at Willa. "You go ahead," she said. "I'll see you back in class."

So he joined the other boys, though there was nothing he wanted more than to see Willa again, to look into those pale green eyes and feel their acceptance.

forty-four

The next afternoon the doorbell sounded just after lunch. David went to answer it. When Virginia turned at the sound of voices, August smiled at her from the dining room doorway.

"Good afternoon, Mrs. Morgan."

"What are you doing here?"

August reached for her hand and gave it a squeeze. "I thought I'd visit my favorite dance partner."

"What are you talking about?"

"I signed us up for the next session."

"Are you kidding? I'm not ready. I still have this

contraption to deal with." She pointed to the walker alongside the table.

"Class won't start for two more months. You'll be up to it by then." His confidence boosted her courage. He believed in her. That was enough to make her believe too, if only a little.

David hadn't meant to spy. He went into the kitchen for a can of Coke. But once he saw the way August Cleworth leaned toward his mother as they talked, he didn't dare take his eyes off them. What did the man want? Simple companionship? If so, why couldn't he find some other widows to befriend?

His dad had died only two years before, hardly long enough for his mother to be ready for any kind of romantic relationship. The very thought of it made David uncomfortable. She loved Dad, loved him deeply. Could she so quickly change allegiances?

It didn't seem right. It just didn't.

The next morning at physical therapy, Virginia gave it her all. When Anna asked her to do fifteen reps of leg curls, Virginia did twenty. Somehow she felt lighter today; the work came easier.

"You're energetic," Anna observed.

Virginia didn't reply. Only smiled.

"Have you gotten ahold of Jessie?" Anna asked.

Virginia had finally reached Steve. He assured her that Jessie was fine, just busy with friends, growing up. It wasn't the answer she hoped for deep down, but at least the girl was doing well.

"I talked to Steve," she said, a bit winded from the exertion. "She's fine."

"Oh. Well, that's good."

She could tell from the disappointment in Anna's eyes that she felt much the same, and yet what could they do? They couldn't very well position themselves between a father and daughter. Besides, there was no reason to meddle.

"Let's move to the bars and try some walking," Anna said, reminding Virginia of why she was there.

Virginia moved into position, her hands supporting her as she walked. Her muscles strained with the effort, but it wasn't the torture it had been a few short months ago. When she was done, Anna said, "Virginia, that's amazing."

A glow of pride filled her, and the image of herself dancing with August Cleworth popped into her mind.

"Shall we have a go without the walker?"

Virginia nodded. She was ready; she could sense it. She rose to her feet, using the walker for support. Then Anna pulled it aside. She stayed next to Virginia, a wheelchair ready in case Virginia needed it. Virginia took one step, then another. With each step her courage rose. Before she knew it, she'd crossed the entire room. She tossed a grin at Anna.

"What did I tell you?" the pretty blonde said. "You're ready to dance."

Virginia blushed at the innocent comment.

By the end of the week, Virginia had relocated her

walker to the back of her closet. Stairs were still difficult, so she continued to use her lift, but she knew with
time even stairs wouldn't be a problem.

The idea of dance lessons seemed less and less pre-
posterous.

forty-five

Willie bent over the lawn mower motor that he
was repairing. He lifted his head when Bert
came into the hangar-sized Quonset shed.

"Son."

Bert dipped his head in greeting and leaned his back-
side against the long chipped and dented table. Willie's
attention returned to the small engine. "You wouldn't
mind if I kept the shop here after we move to town,
would you?"

"Of course not."

"Good. It'll give me an excuse to get away from your
ma once in a while."

Bert watched his father tinker for a few minutes,
comfortable in the silence. Then he asked, "Are you
sure this is the right thing, Dad?" Willie didn't answer,
just kept working. Bert waited.

Finally Willie straightened and wiped his hands on a
rag. "Do you think I made this decision lightly?" he
asked. Bert waited for him to go on. "This farm was
entrusted to me by my father and grandfather and his
father before him. It's a heritage. That's not something

I take lightly. When Fred left, he might as well have spit on me and the men before me. We've all worked our whole lives for this farm."

"But, Dad, Fred is your son."

Willie crossed his arms over his chest. "Yes, he is my son. So I suppose some of his attitude is my fault."

"I didn't mean—"

"I know. But Fred thinks inheriting the farm is his right. It's not a right; it's a privilege, and until he understands that, he can't handle the responsibility. If he isn't grateful for it, he'll squander it."

Peter had been gone all day baling hay with Bert. The house was quiet. All the chores were done for once. Mae stood in the doorway to Christopher's newly painted and decorated room. He lay on his stomach, his little rump pushed skyward. He'd gone down for his nap later than usual. Mae wondered how long he'd be out. She glanced at her watch—4:35. Only half an hour until the calves needed their evening bottle.

She used to feed them their two bottles per day before Christopher was born. But since then, she'd either been nursing the baby, changing a diaper, or catching up on laundry or sleep. Peter had silently taken over the duty.

She knew he had enough to do without that added chore. On top of that, he hadn't been sleeping well. She found the blankets in a tangle each morning from his tossing and turning. The late start at planting, not getting a pea crop in, then the dry weeks that followed, and dropping milk prices—those were the daily realities of farming life. But the possibility that he might not be able to pay back his operating loan shook Peter to the core. And then of course there were all the medical bills with the birth of the baby. She hoped she wouldn't have to return to work. Giving up this precious time with Christopher was unthinkable.

The least she could do was fill in the gaps here for Peter. She crept down the stairs to prepare the two-quart bottles of milk replacer. Then she grabbed the baby monitor, turned it to its loudest setting, and slipped it into her skirt pocket. She pulled on her tall, green rubber muck boots and walked outside to the plastic igloos behind the barn, where the new calves kept house until they were either rotated into the stock or taken to auction. The first baby shoved his wet nose past the bar that held him inside. His long pink tongue swiped at Mae's hand.

"Hold your horses, would you?" Mae said as she slid the bottle into its holder and moved with her armful of bottles to the next stall. A calf farther down the line mooed anxiously for his supper. His voice squeaked with the effort. Mae laughed.

"I'm coming, buddy. Just hold on." The calves sucked hungrily. Their long necks bent down to reach the thick, red nipples. Peter had warned Mae that if she held the bottle too high, the calves would aspirate into their lungs and get pneumonia. The calves bumped hard at the bottles, sometimes knocking them askew in their holders, but they kept on sucking. By the time

Mae delivered the last bottle to its recipient, the first calf was almost done. Mae returned to him. The telltale sucking sound told her the bottle was empty despite the calf's best wishes. Mae pulled it out and patted the long-lashed baby on the head. He gazed with adoring brown eyes.

"That's a good boy," Mae murmured. The long tongue searched for more, leaving a trail of white slimy suds on Mae's arm. "Eww! Now I have to get a shower!" The calf nudged her. "You don't even care, do you?"

After retrieving the remaining empty bottles, Mae returned to the kitchen to wash the nipples. She rinsed the bottles in sudsy water and washed her arm off as well. As she finished, Peter came in the back door. He walked to the cupboard where the bottles and milk replacer were kept, then seeing they weren't there, turned to Mae.

"Where are the bottles?" Faint alarm tinged his words.

"I fed the calves already," Mae said, unsure if she'd done something wrong. "I had the baby monitor." She pulled the plastic intercom from her skirt.

Peter's shoulders relaxed. "Thank you. I guess I was a little . . ."

"Tired?"

Peter nodded. "But I'm grateful for the help." His smile, though tired, was genuine.

Mae moved closer and slipped her arms around his waist.

"I'm all sweaty and covered with hay."

"I don't mind." She lifted onto her toes for a kiss. "You've been working so hard. You need the help. You know . . ." She released him as an idea struck. "I could use the Snugglie and bring Christopher along to help with chores. That way I could at least feed the calves again like I used to."

"That's sweet of you," Peter said. "But you know the baby's schedule doesn't always accommodate that."

Mae's shoulders fell. "I could help with milking."

"I appreciate the thought, honey. And I'm sure the girls would be thrilled to have a squalling baby in the parlor." He chuckled and leaned to give Mae another kiss, this time on the temple. "I would be thrilled if you could take over the calves again, but I'll find a way to get by with the rest."

"Are you sure?"

Peter's clear eyes gazed into hers. "Dad's back in town. Maybe he'll be up to the challenge."

The phone rang insistently on the kitchen wall. David ran to answer it.

"Hello."

"Dad? I have a favor to ask." David pulled the tall kitchen stool to him and took a seat. The phone cord twisted to the wall jack like a serpent. His mother had gone upstairs to read in her room. When he had looked in on her, she was napping.

"Fire away," David said.

"Mae and I were talking. You know that she used to help me milk and whatnot."

"Sure."

Peter cleared his throat. "Well, do you think if she and the baby came to sit with Grandma, you could help with evening milkings? It's not so bad right now, but once harvest starts, I don't know how I'll be able to manage—"

"I'd be happy to do whatever you need. Grandma might protest being baby-sat, but we don't have to call it that."

"Really?"

"Why do you sound so surprised? I came home to be a part of this family, do my share."

"Thanks, Dad."

"When do you want me to start?"

"Is tomorrow too soon?"

"Not at all. I'll be there. Want me to come for morning milkings too?"

The line hummed for a second. "Really?"

"Yeah, really. All you have to do is ask."

When Peter hung up, Mae looked at him expectantly. "What did he say?"

"He said no problem."

"And you were skeptical."

Peter squeezed her hand. "Do we ever reach a point where all the stuff from the past finally goes away? Or will we always grieve over the things we wished for—like me wishing to hold on to Dad and the time before Mom died."

Mae's eyes clouded. "Grief doesn't go away. Ever. But it doesn't have to debilitate either. It can give us strength."

Fred had been gone from the farm for three weeks, leaving Svetlana behind to everyone's surprise. Svetlana kept to herself, only appearing for brief moments in the kitchen to get some food and then retreating to the privacy of her room again. Trudy tried to see her more than once, but Svetlana sent her away, insisting that if Fred found out, he would ship her back to Russia.

Saturday, the seventeenth of September, Fred mysteriously reappeared. When he came home, Bert and Peter were drinking a final cup of coffee before heading to the fields for an evening of hay baling. His unshaven face was marred by a permanent scowl. Dark circles ringed his eyes, and his clothes were wrinkled and dirty.

"Where the heck have you been?" Lillian said as he came in the back door.

He grunted something, then brushed past her and climbed the stairs to the second story. Bert heard muffled voices from the upstairs bedroom.

Bert knew his brother was angry, no doubt feeling rejected and abandoned because of one poor choice. He longed to go to him and talk things through, to tell Fred about his disappointment that things had turned out the way they had, yet he knew Fred would never believe him. After all, hadn't Bert been the beneficiary of their father's decision?

The next afternoon when Fred and Svetlana came home from who knew where, he was clean-shaven. His long hair had been cut short.

Lillian hovered over the stove, stirring a pot of spaghetti sauce. Willie and Bert washed up in the mud room.

"I got a job driving a truck Mondays to Thursdays," Fred announced. Willie walked into the kitchen.

"So you're leaving the Russki here with us while you're gone *again?* She isn't our responsibility, you know," Lillian complained.

"Stop calling her that, Ma! And no, I'm *not* leaving her here with you. Once we can save for a deposit, we'll get our own place. Unless of course you'd like to pay me for the thirty years of hard labor I put in around here."

"You got paid," Lillian said.

"I had an allowance, Ma. Town kids get allowances for making their beds every day."

Willie left the room.

"I can't even have a conversation with that man anymore," Fred shouted to Willie's back.

"Maybe if you didn't complain constantly, he wouldn't be so offended by you," Lillian said.

"I learned from you, Ma," Fred spit. He marched away before his mother could respond. When he saw Bert in the mud-room doorway, Fred stopped cold. "I suppose you're going to lecture me like everyone else."

Bert shook his head. "No, Fred. I'm clean out of lectures."

"Right," Fred mocked. "That's easy when everything is handed to you on a silver platter."

BERT AND FRED BIDDLE

"Hey, Al," Chad Schoff shouted at Bert Biddle. Chad always called him Al when he wanted to get under Bert's skin. As if it was funny. What was wrong with the guy? Yeah, he and his brother were Albert and Alfred; Bert didn't see anything funny about that. A lot of twins had similar names.

Bert turned to face the short, thick-necked senior. The cold February wind bit at Bert's cheeks. He pulled his knit cap down on his head. The school bus was pulling up to take the players back after the game. Its brakes made a high-pitched squeal as it came to a stop.

"What do you want, Schoff?" Bert said. The brute rode him all through the game, stole the puck from him at every opportunity, skated in front of him as if he were trying to mess Bert up. The coach had yelled at Chad, but that hadn't deterred the guy.

Chad moved nose to nose with Bert and hissed, "You know I should be the goalie. You aren't nearly as good a hockey player as I am. You're just Coach's favorite." The last word came out as a slur.

"You're just jealous."

The senior's shoes touched Bert's. "You want to make something of it?"

"I'll make something of it," another voice said. Bert and Chad turned to see Fred, Bert's older brother by eight minutes. Fred's gaze met Bert's. Fred threw down his sports bag and hockey stick and moved closer to Chad.

"It's okay, Fred," Bert said. He held up a hand to stop his brother.

Fred plowed past it. "If you've got a problem with my brother, then you've got a problem with me." The bully took a step back. "Bert's a better hockey player than you, even if he isn't a senior. You're just going to have to get used to that, Schoff. Being second best."

Chad's face turned crimson, and his lips tightened across his crooked teeth. "Oh yeah?"

The first punch flew. It all happened so fast Bert couldn't tell if it was Chad's fist or Fred's. The two fell to the ground, exchanging punches as they rolled. Then Fred was on top, pummeling Chad about the face. "Stop, Fred!" Bert shouted.

Fred did, eventually. A stream of blood ran from one nostril down his chin. His hair was a mess, and the sleeve of his letter jacket was torn at the seam. Fred stood. Other kids had gathered. Chad lay on the snowy ground. He moaned and rolled onto his side before standing up. The coach came then. He grabbed both boys by the arms and pulled them away.

When Fred joined Bert on the bus a few minutes later, Bert looked up. Fred smiled crookedly at him.

"So what did the coach say?"

"We're both on suspension." Fred shrugged.

Bert leaned close to his brother. "Why did you do that, Fred? Now you won't get to play in the play-off games."

"It's okay, Bert. Schoff won't see any ice either, right?"

Bert shook his head. "You're crazy, Fred."

"Nah. I'm just your brother. And you are a better player than Chad and me put together. We'll win the play-offs even without us out there."

"Like I said, you're crazy."

forty-six

Willie hired a huge Dumpster to fill with a lifetime's accumulation of Lillian's "crap," as he put it. Boxes of old magazines and newspapers, some unopened since the seventies, filled the basement storage room.

"Why bother opening any of them?" Willie said. "Just toss them in the Dumpster."

Lillian's mouth dropped open in shock. "But there might be something valuable in these boxes."

"If we could do without it for thirty-plus years, I'd say it isn't all that valuable. Heave-ho!"

"Are you going to toss your Pioneer Power stuff?"

"No, I actually *use* that stuff."

Willie ran his pocketknife through the tape on another box. In it were hundreds of pairs of old support pantyhose. Willie lifted a pair that had a huge run in one leg from rump to toe.

"I suppose you want to keep these." Willie's gaze shifted to Bert and Trudy at the far side of the basement.

"Trudy might want them," Lillian defended. "They're good for stuffing pillows."

Trudy lifted hands in surrender. "You go ahead and toss them, Willie. I have plenty of pillow stuffing."

Bert took the box from his father and said, "I have to go milk. I'll toss it for you, Ma. I know how painful it can be to let things go. Especially things as sentimental as pantyhose!"

Lillian swatted him as he passed.

After he tossed the big box into the receptacle, he noticed Fred's truck parked alongside the barn. Bert glanced back toward the house. He wondered why Fred would be here; he hadn't milked with Bert since Willie had told him he'd been disinherited. Bert lifted his green seed cap and scratched his head.

He didn't see Fred in the barn. Afternoon sunlight peeked in through gaps in the barn's siding. All was silent except for the fluttering of wings as a pair of barn swallows darted out the open door. That was when Bert saw him. Fred leaned against the doorframe, his back to Bert as he gazed at the distant fields. It was like looking at his own reflection—the way Fred stood

350

with one leg slightly in front of the other, his hair the same color as Bert's tawny locks, with the same tendency to curl if it grew too long. Fred turned toward him.

"I didn't know you were . . . ," Fred began. The bravado in Bert's elder brother was gone, replaced by defeat.

"I'm sorry about all this," Bert said.

"Sure you are."

"Fred,"—Bert kept his voice calm—"let's go for a walk. We need to talk."

Fred stared through him. Bert waited for him to follow. Finally Fred relented.

It was a muggy September day. Bird calls melded with the distant rumble of semis on Highway 36 and the wind in the maple trees overhead.

"Remember when we were kids," Bert began, "and we built that tree house down by the pond?"

Fred said nothing.

"We didn't tell a soul. Not even Ma and Dad. It was our secret."

"What's your point?"

Bert sighed. "There was that fight with Chad Schoff."

"He was a snot-nosed brat. He had it coming."

"Still. We were brothers, and that's what brothers did."

They walked onto the dirt road that led east.

"I guess some things change," Fred said.

"Is that what you want? You're still my big brother,

even if only by eight minutes. We used to be close."

"Bert, what am I supposed to say? 'Take the farm; we'll still be buddies'? It doesn't work that way."

"I know that. But I also want you to know that I don't agree with Dad. I think he's wrong."

Fred stopped walking. "About what? That I'm a no-good son who deserves to be put on the street?"

"Fred," Bert said, empathy lacing the word. He drew closer.

Fred took a step back. "I don't need your pity. A lot of good your pity does anyway. You still get everything in the end. Unless you plan on giving me my share after all."

"You know Dad won't let me."

"I thought so." Fred turned toward the pasture. Cows ambled on the other side of the fence. One girl came up opposite Fred. He petted her bony head, and she nudged him with her square, wet nose. She leaned her long neck into him until he stepped backward.

"I came back with expectations," Fred said. "What son wouldn't? It never occurred to me that Dad would react this way."

"You were pretty focused on yourself."

Fred's shoulders drooped. "I hate driving a truck," he said.

"I figured as much."

"But I'm going to stick it out to support my wife . . . and our new baby. Dad's wrong, you know. I am capable of committing to things I care about, and I care about Svetlana and the farm."

"I know that."

Fred stared at his brother, a question in his eyes before giving it voice. "Why are we so different? We look the same, but—"

"We're more alike than you know."

Fred shook his head. "Sometimes I can't figure you out, Bert. I thought you'd be happy about Dad giving everything to you. I know I'd be."

"How can I be happy when you're hurt?"

Fred laughed bitterly. Bert's heart twisted for his brother.

"Maybe if you asked Dad's forgiveness," Bert offered. "You haven't tried that."

"Forgiveness! What did I do? I'm a grown man who went to Florida for a little while and got married. That's my business, isn't it? That's hardly a sin! I'm not a naughty child who ran away from home."

Bert held his tongue.

Fred's volume rose. "Man, Bert, you of all people should understand why I left. If I hadn't gone, who knows what I would've done."

"What does that mean?"

Fred let out an exaggerated sigh.

"The point is," Bert said, "we didn't have that option. We had to pick up the pieces and keep this farm running without you. It was difficult. When you didn't come back for the wedding or even tell us about Svetlana—"

"That wasn't intentional," Fred said, his fire lessening. "I would've come. I wanted to come. But we were in Russia; the U.S. didn't want to let Svetlana come back with me, and I wasn't about to leave her there alone. We would've been back otherwise. I would've come to your wedding." His eyes held an apology.

"I want you to know that if there's a way to farm together again, I want to."

"But Dad . . ."

"We'll have to work on him. And of course, once everything is in my name, I can do as I please."

"That could take years." Fred paused. "Why would you do that for me?"

Bert shrugged. "What kind of person would I be if I didn't?"

forty-seven

Fred and Svetlana moved into a rented trailer on Old Man Burgdorf's land the following week. An envelope bearing five hundred dollars in cash and an ad for the rental had magically appeared on his and Svetlana's bedroom floor two days after his talk with Bert. Fred felt certain his brother had fronted the money, but if Bert didn't want to fess up, then so be it. Fred wouldn't feel obligated to repay the debt, either. He parked the white pickup in the tall brown grass that was the lawn.

"Is cute," Svetlana offered.

They climbed out and surveyed the place. Cornfields

encroached on the overgrown property, and a gray, tired barn with a partially collapsed roof sagged next to a silo that had lost its dome.

The late-1950s vintage trailer with a salmon and white exterior had rounded walls like the live-in Chevy Bel-Aires of the same era. The inside was dark and smelled musty. Tiny single-paned windows opened in horizontal stripes. Thick avocado green curtains held the room in captivity. The kitchen at the very front of the trailer consisted of a sink, an ancient refrigerator, and a stove with three burners. Natural light entered only through the small window above a shelf. The kitchen counter opened to the living room.

Faded shag carpet in the same avocado hue complemented mustard-colored couches covered in a nubby upholstery. An eight-by-eight bedroom with a minute bathroom completed the living quarters.

Svetlana hadn't said a word since they'd come inside.

"I know it isn't much," Fred apologized.

Svetlana touched the orange Formica countertop. "But is ours."

"The trailer is anyway. The land still belongs to Old Man Burgdorf."

Svetlana smiled, revealing the slight gap between her front teeth. "Is home. I make good home for you here."

Once October made its mark on Minnesota's landscape, Peter knew that the crop was a total loss. The spring floods followed by a long drought made a poor recipe for farming. Some farmers spoke of quitting altogether. Peter didn't know what to do. What corn he did have was scrawny, and the soybeans were no better. At least he could use the corn for silage.

Peter opened the glass doors at First Farmers and Merchants Bank in Lake Emily. He hoped the banker was in a charitable mood today.

"Peter, can I help you?" the man said from inside the open door of his office. He motioned for Peter to join him in the inner sanctum of the large office that overlooked Main Street. He was a fairly young man, about Peter's age, with dark brown hair. He twisted the white handle on the miniblinds, diffusing the afternoon glare.

"I can probably guess why you're here," he said with a kind smile as Peter took a seat. The room smelled of leather and paper. "I've met with a dozen farmers in the past week. It's been a bad year all around, so you're in good company."

"I just wanted to touch base with you. Let you know where things stand right now. My crop looks abysmal. I should have gotten crop insurance." Peter ran a hand through his blond hair. "Until the harvest is in, I won't know exactly how far in the hole I am. I hope I can pay my operating loan, but that's a guess. The milk check could go toward land rent and the mortgage, but that wouldn't leave us a whole lot to live on." He lifted his eyes. "I guess I could sell the herd—"

The banker held up a hand. "Let's not cut your legs out from under you." He gave Peter another reassuring smile. "We can talk again later, but I think we'll be able to float you for a while." He paused. "Everyone's in the same situation, Peter. The bank needs farmers to succeed as much as you all need us."

As much as the man's words comforted Peter, he couldn't help but think that he'd have to earn twice as much the following year. What if he had another year like this one? Would he ever be in the black again?

The banker turned toward his computer and typed something. "Tell you what—if you could pay half, we could roll the remainder into next year's loan. It would give you something to live on, at least help out. You'll want to make sure you have plenty of crop insurance for next year's crop." The man failed to mention how Peter would pay for said crop insurance.

His gaze met Peter's. "I know it's not perfect," he said apologetically.

"It's something, though," Peter said. "I'm grateful for that."

On the drive home, Peter's gaze trained on the black ribbon of highway before him. It occurred to him that something had changed inside of him. The risks he was so eager to take two short years ago loomed larger now that he had the responsibility of a son to raise.

He wanted nothing more than to give Christopher a happy childhood, free of the insecurities he had battled as a boy. It was even more important that the farm survive—no, that it thrive—so that his son could carry on if he so chose. Peter glanced at the patchwork fields in green, brown, and gold. He had to make this work, even if the odds declared success unlikely.

He wondered how many times he would have to recommit himself to making the farm succeed. Every year for the rest of his life? Even if it beat him down?

Mae opened the Cape Cod's door as her father-in-law pulled out of the driveway to head to the farm for the evening milking. Mae waved good-bye, then lifted Christopher's carrier. The baby was awake after a long nap. He lifted eager eyes to his mother and started crying for his supper.

"Hang on, buddy," Mae murmured as her milk let down. She pressed her forearms against her chest in hopes of stopping the flow. The tingling sensation passed, and Mae called, "Virginia, we're here . . ."

Virginia was watching the evening news in the den to the right of the entry. "I'm in here." Mae came in, and Virginia clicked the remote, sending the room to silence. "Here to baby-sit?" Virginia said good-naturedly.

Mae bent to kiss her cheek, then settled the baby's carrier and diaper bag on the floor and unbuckled his seat belt.

"Hey, any excuse for a good visit, right? Do you mind if I feed him here?"

"Heavens, no." She reached into a large square basket for her embroidery project and settled back in her chair with it. She pushed the needle through the white fabric.

Mae lifted Christopher and readied herself to feed

him. She settled a thin blanket over her shoulder for modesty's sake, and soon the baby happily drank.

Virginia smiled at them. "Is he happy now?"

"Better. He gets so impatient. It makes me uptight."

"It'll come easier later," Virginia assured. "He's your first. We're all uptight with our first. By the time the next one comes, you'll have it down pat."

"I suppose."

"Now, tell me what's new on the farm. I suppose this dry spell hasn't helped the crop any."

"It's a rough one, but Peter seems okay." Christopher's tiny hand tugged on the blanket that was a tent over his head. Mae laughed and moved Christopher's hand down. "The bank offered to roll half of our operating loan into next year's payment to tide us over."

"That doesn't sound good."

"It's better than my going back to work. Although, who knows, I might still need to do that."

"You don't want to put the baby in day care."

"No, but if it's that or lose the farm—"

"Things will work out. You'll have to trust that. They always do."

"I wish I had your faith."

"Now that's a laugh. Faith is a feeble virtue."

"What do you mean by that?"

"When you feel strong, full of faith, odds are that's when life is easy and you don't really need all that much to carry you through. But these last months—"

"Since the stroke?"

Virginia nodded her head. "Yes, since my stroke. I

always thought that the opposite of faith was unbelief, but that isn't so. The opposite of faith is despair, choosing to give up. I've done that plenty of times, but God still pulls me up. He keeps hanging in there with me. I guess my weakness doesn't put him off."

"That's a good thing, isn't it?"

"Oh yes," Virginia said, "a very good thing."

The last cow meandered around and out of the loud milking parlor into the waning day. Peter turned off the machine, and quiet flooded back in. David took two five-gallon pails of disinfectant into the tank room to dump. Peter followed him. The two worked together in a natural rhythm. After so many years of being "just the two of them," Peter supposed it made sense. Like any old habit, it returned with ease.

"I sure appreciate this," Peter said. "I know that with your arthritis you won't always be able—"

"There's still a lot I can do. I'm glad to help."

Peter checked the temperature gauge on the milk tank, then turned out the light. Father and son walked outside. The sun swung low, prepared to take its "granny shot" over the horizon. Cows stood in the pasture. Some drank from the deep trough, while others gathered in gossip circles. David and Peter walked along the fence line, neither quite ready to call it a day.

"I've been tutoring again at the school," David said.

"Good."

"I need to get out once in a while. Confidentially, I think your Grandma gets her fill of me."

"Why did you come back?" He knew it was abrupt, but he'd been thinking about it all day.

"The question should be, why did I leave in the first place, shouldn't it?" David chuckled. "I'm a slow learner, okay? I wasn't ready to give up music last year. The arthritis kind of sprang that on me. Music had lived inside of me for too long. But conducting isn't the same as playing—too much politics." He smiled. "I had to learn by being away that I want to be here."

"So you're staying?"

"I am. I know you probably don't believe that, but I am."

They walked for a few minutes in the gloaming. The sunset cast its pumpkin and salmon shades across the river valley to the west.

"Are you happy with that choice?"

Peter's dad thought about that for a while before answering. "Your grandma and I are getting used to living together. We've had our conflicts." He paused. "Sometimes instead of facing our grief, we run from it. I did that with my arthritis, and I did that when your mother died. I'm tired of running. It's time for me to grow up. You've been the man of the family for long enough."

"No," Peter said, "you've been the best dad you could've been. Just as I'm trying to be for Christopher. I've already missed half his life farming." His clear gaze met his father's. "I didn't have the full picture before. I probably still don't. But it's coming to me."

"Christopher will keep teaching you long after he's grown and married." David patted Peter on the back.

Then father and son watched as the sun slipped over the horizon.

forty-eight

When the red Aston Martin convertible pulled into the driveway the next day, David didn't say a word.

"What's going on?" his mother said from the dining room where she was working on a crossword puzzle. David's gaze was trained on the man as he came toward the back door.

"Your admirer. Ma, do you really think this is wise?"

"David, I thought we talked about this."

August Cleworth knocked on the screen door. The inside door was open. "Good afternoon, David," he said as he opened the screen. Virginia stepped into the room.

"What are you up to?" The sparkle that lit her eyes when she looked at the man took David aback. When had he last seen that expression on his mother's face? Certainly it was before his father's death.

"It's such a nice day," August said, "I was wondering if you'd care to take that drive today. Won't have a lot more warm days like this."

"A drive?" Virginia said.

"You up for it?" August said.

David cleared his throat.

Virginia gave him a curious look. But David turned back to August.

"We won't go far," August said. "Just around the block if you like." Virginia glanced out the screen door at the vintage sports car.

"I suppose you could twist my arm."

"That's my girl," August said. He smiled at her winningly. August held the door open and led the way. He opened the door for her. She waved good-bye to David. The car started with a rumble, and they were off. They moved slowly up the street and out of David's view.

Virginia and August drove past the cemetery on the edge of town and to the far side of the lake. The wind in her hair felt good, the sun warm. August pulled into a quaint park under sprawling oaks and slowed the vehicle before coming to a complete stop. He killed the motor, and they climbed out. Virginia fluffed her permed hair.

She glanced covertly at him. His love of life turned him into a twenty-year-old. Joy creased the corners of his faded eyes. His gaze met Virginia's, and he smiled broadly.

"Having fun?"

Virginia nodded.

He led her to one of the aged and weathered wooden picnic tables beneath the trees' twisted arms. The early October breeze rustled the burnished copper leaves.

"Willa and I used to bring the kids here to swim

when they were little," August said.

"It's lovely. Roy and I brought David and Sarah sometimes, although not too much. Field work kept us from a lot of summer play, but we'd sneak away every now and again. Sometimes I'd bring the kids by myself. David was always so skittish about water. He didn't learn to swim until he was almost ten. Course if Roy'd had his way, he would've thrown him off the dock with a rope tied around his waist. I wouldn't hear of it." She chuckled at the memory.

"Will we ever stop missing them?" August said. "My Willa and your Roy. Will life ever feel right again?"

Virginia shook her head. "I suppose not. How long ago did Willa die?"

"Three years. Although at times it may as well have been yesterday." He reflected. "In my quiet moments I still ache for her. It's all a cheap substitute—life after her."

"It's hard not to let it overwhelm you, isn't it?"

August nodded. He gazed at Virginia as if measuring whether to say something. "Right after Willa died, I used to wish I'd die too so we could be together. I didn't actually *do* anything about it, but if God had seen fit, I wouldn't have minded. It gets easier, though. I have my son and daughter-in-law. I don't know where I'd have been without them. Or without friends . . . like you. You've kept me from being lonely, and I thank you for that." August's forehead furrowed in worry lines. "Your son thinks I have poor intentions."

"David's learning. We both are. It's hard to redefine roles after so many years."

August leaned back against the picnic table, his gaze on the lake. He was in no hurry to fill the silence.

Finally Virginia said, "When David's wife died, it was hard on him. I had no idea at the time. I understand more now, but it was as if—" The right words failed her.

"As if what?" August said.

Virginia shook her head. She meant to say, "It was as if he died with her." Why did her heart blurt such harsh, judgmental thoughts? Did she believe that in his heart David had died with Laura? Maybe. But then, so much of herself had died with Roy. She was only beginning to discover the person he'd left behind.

When Virginia again lifted her eyes, August was studying her. "What's been the hardest part of losing your wife?"

"That's a difficult one. Certainly the loneliness. But also having to make more decisions for myself. I relied on her to figure out so much. I had to relearn a lot of things. I can't tell you how many trips I made to the bank to get help balancing the checkbook. But, you see, that was Willa's job. I took it for granted. I took a lot about her for granted." Then he laughed.

"What?"

"Before we got married, I was a real slob—the Oscar Madison type. After she died, I discovered she'd changed me. I'm so particular now I even drive myself

365

crazy." A fall breeze rustled the oak leaves. "For some reason I thought Willa was the glue that held me and the kids together. She planned our get-togethers, everything, but now the kids and I are closer than ever. That surprised me. When I hit seventy-seven, my son and I hiked the Appalachian Trail. Just a section of it, mind you." A smile lifted the corners of his eyes. "The experience changed this old dog. Made me wish I'd had more adventures with Willa when she was alive. That probably sounds ungrateful. We had a truly good marriage—"

"I know what you mean." Virginia picked up a pumpkin-colored leaf that fell on the table and twirled it by its stem. "Roy always talked about going to Alaska. What he hoped to find there, I'm not sure. But he never went, and a part of me regrets that I didn't make that a reality for him."

They sat in comfortable silence for a while, watching the late afternoon light play with the lake. Shimmers sparkled across its surface in converging paths. Finally August turned to Virginia. "So what about us, Virginia? Is there an *us?*"

Us. It sounded so . . . definite. Were they an item? She gazed into his tender eyes. They'd shared so much these past months—their grief, their joys. What would life be like if August weren't part of it? She didn't like to even think about that. Did she care about him? Yes, she realized, she did care.

"I do believe there is," she answered. Then he leaned close and ever so lightly touched his lips to hers.

• • •

David spent the next hour watching for his mother's return. He didn't mean to do it. But he found himself pacing, glancing out the street-side windows, listening for the rumble of the car's engine. Finally he took a glass of iced tea and went to sit on the back patio. Every vehicle on the street drew his attention. He hadn't been this nervous since Peter took the car out for the first time after getting his driver's license.

Finally the red Aston Martin pulled into the driveway. David leaned back in the chair, trying to appear nonchalant.

August killed the engine, then helped Virginia climb out of the car. The look they gave each other sent wild alarms through David. He stood. "I'd say you went a little farther than around the block."

"David!"

"Do you know that my mother is still recovering from a stroke and a bad fall?"

"Your mother's old enough to make her own decisions," August said. His voice was calm, which irked David.

"David," Virginia said again, "don't embarrass me like this."

With that David went into the house. He could hear his mother apologizing to August and saying her farewells. She came in.

"Ma, I'm sorry," David said before she could say anything. "I was worried."

Virginia took a seat beside her son at the sunny

kitchen island. "I told you to trust me. August is a dear, dear friend. We enjoy being together. Is that so wrong?"

David gazed into his mother's eyes.

"I'm still me," Virginia assured.

"Are you? Because lately you've been someone I don't even know."

VIRGINIA MORGAN

White sheets flapped in the warm September breeze. Virginia Morgan held a wooden clothespin between her lips as she fastened a pair of her husband's denim striped overalls to the line. Ten-year-old David and seven-year-old Sarah darted between the rows of drying laundry in a game of tag. Their giggles and squeals along with the scent of fresh-mowed grass mingled with the clean smell of the clothes, filling Virginia's senses.

Most days kept an auctioneer's pace, flying past unnoticed from one moment to the next with no seeming deliberation. But then there were days like today when everything was clear. Even the sky. She could see forever. She had a purpose, made evident in the blessings in her life—her children, a husband she adored.

Virginia lifted her gaze to the field in the distance where Roy's Oliver tractor inched along. He was mowing his last hay crop of the season. This year everything had worked the way it was supposed to, which was a rare thing indeed. Rain fell when the crops needed it, yet it stayed dry enough to get into the fields. July and August brought the warmth the corn demanded to grow tall and thick.

"Ma!" Sarah cried in big gulping sobs, drawing Virginia's attention from her reverie. "David pulled my hair."

Virginia turned to look for him. The sheets flapped, and she glimpsed his legs at the far end of the clothesline. "David Morgan, get yourself over here."

He came slowly, bearing a contrite expression. "Did you pull your sister's hair?"

He held up the blue ribbon that had adorned his sister's long braid. "I didn't mean it . . . I just . . ." He looked down.

Virginia pointed to the wicker basket of damp, clean clothes and said, "You can help hang laundry, then."

"Aw, Ma!"

"David Morgan, you know better than to hurt Sarah. She's your sister. Families don't hurt each other. We care for each other. We think of the other person's feelings. Do you understand me?" Virginia pointed to make herself clear.

David glanced at his sister, who waited with a too-sweet smile on her lips. David's shoulders lifted in a sigh, and he mumbled, "Sorry, Sarah." Then he turned back to his mother, who handed him the clothes. He bent and obediently lifted a navy-blue shirt, which he pinned to the line. He frowned as they worked. Yet it only served to add to the smile on Virginia's face. That boy could be so stubborn sometimes, but she was proud of the emerging man. When he wasn't annoying his little sister, he was a considerate, polite boy.

Soon he began to hum, and Virginia knew his fussy mood had evaporated in the breeze. Sarah was asking if she could hang clothes too.

"You can't even reach the line," David teased. "Besides, this is my punishment. Why would you want to hang clothes?"

"Because I do! I can get a chair." Sarah stamped a foot, and her blond braid swung.

"Go ahead," Virginia consented with a smile at the girl. Virginia touched her still-flat stomach, filled with the knowledge that another precious child grew there. She wondered who this babe would be—a girl as precocious as Sarah or a boy with the quiet confidence of his older brother? No doubt he'd be someone altogether original. She hoped God would give her a houseful of original works of art like these two.

Sarah ran to the wraparound porch. She grabbed a heavy wooden chair and dragged it to the lines that drooped with the weight of the clothes. After setting the chair in place, the girl filled her pockets with clothespins and grabbed four aprons from the basket. Her arms overflowed, and she looked as though she'd topple over, but Virginia kept quiet.

"Ma, why do you wear aprons?" Sarah said as she clipped the blue and white gingham to the line. Sarah's pale freckles would turn a burnished copper as the *summer months wore on. They gathered now as she wrinkled up her nose.*

"Keeps my dresses clean," Virginia said.

"But most of the time you don't even get your apron dirty, and there are lots of days no one will see it but us."

Virginia tapped her chin lightly. She reached into the basket and pulled out another apron, this one red with cross-stitched flowers on its pocket.

"An apron is like a uniform," Virginia said seriously. Sarah's mouth formed a little O. "You know, like a nurse wears a white dress and shoes. When I put my apron on, it's my way of telling you that everything I do around here is for you because I love you."

"Like you're working for me? But I'm not the boss of you. Am I?" Her voice sounded almost hopeful.

Virginia laughed. "No, but when I'm washing dishes or making a meal or cleaning the house, I think about you and how much pleasure you'll have in eating a good meal or living in a peaceful, clean house. You're why I do all this. Because I love you, I spend my days serving you. There's no greater way to show love than to serve. When you really love someone, you don't mind doing things for them. It's a joy."

"Like when you get Daddy his coffee in the morning?"

"Yes, honey, like that. I do it because I love him, and I choose to do it."

Sarah's face erupted in a smile, revealing two absent teeth. Virginia tousled her daughter's bangs. "Taking

371

care of you and David and your pa—those are the greatest blessings of my life."

forty-nine

M a?" The next morning David stood in the hallway outside his mother's bedroom and knocked on the door. His heart hammered in his chest. She never slept past seven o'clock. "Ma, it's ten thirty. Are you okay?" The door creaked as he pushed it open. His mother lay in the bed, her back to him. David touched a light hand to her shoulder. She was warm. Her chest lifted with each breath she took. David sighed in relief.

"Ma," he said again. She rolled onto her back and met his gaze.

"I'm awake."

David sat on the edge of the bed. "What's going on, Ma? It's not like you to lie in bed all day."

His mother closed her eyes. The clock on her dresser ticked loudly. David waited. When Virginia finally opened her eyes, the pain he saw there stabbed at him.

"I'm feeling sorry for myself," she said.

"Why?"

"A lot of reasons."

"So? Tell me."

"Well." Virginia paused. "I miss your father so much. I feel guilty for wanting to live without him here."

"I haven't helped a whole lot on that count, have I?"

Virginia clasped David's hand. "I enjoy August's company, but he isn't your father. He never could be."

"But he is a friend, and he makes you happy. No reason to feel guilty about that." David stroked his mother's hair. "Do you remember when Sarah and I were little? We were hanging laundry on the line one day, and Sarah asked you why you wore an apron."

"I can't say as I recall that."

"Well, I do. I remember like it was yesterday. You said that when you wore an apron, it was your way of telling us that you loved us, and that serving the people you love is part of showing that love. You said that serving us was the greatest blessing of your life." David reached for his mother's hand. "Ma, *you* are the greatest blessing of my life."

He touched his mother's cheek where a tear fell. "I'm sorry I didn't understand."

Moving day finally arrived. Trudy had decided to wait to move into the farmhouse so she could take her time painting, removing old wallpaper, and making a hundred other improvements the old place needed. Lillian gave her strict instructions not to "do anything weird with the place." Whatever.

Trudy wasn't sure how she felt about the move now. At times she was excited about the prospect of Bert and her having a real home. At other times she was nervous that she'd get lonely. But she reminded herself that she had her sister nearby if she needed company. She and Mae had been spending more time together, mostly playing with Christopher, sharing in his growth. He was indeed a miracle, which made Trudy long all the more for a child of her own.

Trudy hadn't seen Svetlana since she and Fred had moved to the trailer. The divide was Fred's doing, yet she couldn't help feeling sorry for him and Svetlana, losing their dream of living on the farm.

"Be careful with that box!" Lillian barked, drawing Trudy's attention to the task of moving her in-laws to town. Pastor Hickey's face blanched when he realized she was yelling at him; he carried a box marked "tea sets."

"I don't want any of those broken," Lillian said.

"Of course not, Mrs. Biddle," the pastor said. He winked as he passed Trudy, which surprised her. For a man who could be so stiff and formal on Sunday mornings, he sure was sassy today.

Bert came past with a box of books, and Lillian said, "Make sure those go on the bottom. They'll crush my glassware if you put them on top." He ignored her. Lillian bustled over to the pastor and said, "You know, I'll just take those in the car so they make it okay."

She reached to take the box, but Pastor Hickey said, "I'll put them in your car, Lillian. No need to strain your back."

"Thank you, Pastor. It's nice to know that *someone* cares about my aching back." This directed at Bert. That woman could complain about anything. Trudy rolled her eyes and went back inside for another load.

The bare old house looked tired and worn out. Trudy

climbed the stairs to see if any boxes had been left behind. Willie stood in Bert's bedroom. He gazed through the window that faced the backyard and barn. "Willie?" He turned to acknowledge her. That familiar twinkle lit his eyes.

"Thought I told you to call me Dad."

Trudy stood beside him in the room that was empty except for a bed and dresser.

"This was my room when I was a boy," Willie said, his gaze locked on something distant. "Lot of memories here."

"It's hard to leave, isn't it?"

The old man nodded. He pointed outside. "Through this very window I saw my dad walk up the drive when he came back from the war. He was stationed in France, fought at Normandy."

"You must've loved him very much."

"That I did." He placed his palms on the window sill and leaned forward. A long silence stretched. "I'm glad that you and Bert are taking over."

"And Fred?" Trudy ventured. "Can you ever forgive him?"

"Not a matter of forgiveness. He wasn't the prodigal son who came back all contrite, begging for scraps from the table." He paused. "I love Fred. He's a difficult person. Like his mother, I guess." The statement brought on the fleeting smile. "Fred sees what he wants and bellyaches until someone gives it to him. But Bert understands. He knows about working hard to achieve something, and he knows what this farm means to me and what it meant to my father." He turned toward his daughter-in-law. "You probably weren't prepared for a sermon, were you?"

Trudy smiled and patted his back. "I'm a willing congregation, Dad."

fifty

Virginia hid behind the other students, all thirty and fifty years her junior, while August signed them in at the registration table.

August took her hand and led her to the side of the gymnasium. "Nervous?" he whispered into her ear. His breath against her neck sent a tingle up her spine.

Virginia nodded. "I'm too old for this!"

The instructor, a too-thin man with hair just graying around the edges, clapped his hands to silence the murmurs and moved to the center of the echoing gymnasium. August smiled at her, revealing his straight white teeth and the love in his pale eyes. Virginia found herself gazing at him, trying to comprehend the emotions that stirred within.

"You'll be fine," he reassured her, patting her hand.

"Welcome to ballroom dancing," the instructor said. "My name is Hubert Keyes, and I'll be your instructor for the next four weeks." He kept talking, but all Virginia could think about was the man beside her. He'd been kind beyond words, steadfast, a true friend. Did she love him? She certainly had feelings for him, but whether they were love or not, she couldn't say.

Finally the teacher instructed the class to take their positions to begin the fox trot. "The fox trot isn't up and down like the waltz," he said, exaggerating the three-step dance. "It's more rolling, like the gentle hills of southern Wisconsin. You'll be up on your toes a little more. Start like this." He took hold of his perky partner, a woman in her fifties with a trim figure and dark curly hair. "So step heel," he demonstrated each movement, "toe rising, toe, toe, heel lowering." He stopped. "Then you do it again. Let's start with that." The class took their places.

August placed a hand on Virginia's waist and clasped her right hand in his. "Ready?" He smiled at her.

She nodded, and they began the dance. It came slowly at first—the weakness of her legs and the long-forgotten steps making her awkward. But August was gentle and patient. So . . . what if she did love him? Would that be such a bad thing?

Hubert clapped his hands again, and the dancers moved out of their positions to watch as he demonstrated the movements with one of the younger attendees in the center of the gym.

"I hope he doesn't do that with me," Virginia confessed. "I'd step all over his toes."

"You're doing wonderfully," August said. His hand felt warm on Virginia's thick waist.

They took up the dance again. In August's arms, her awkwardness soon fell away, and she forgot that she'd abandoned a walker just a few short weeks before.

They moved in time with the music.

"You're a good dancer, Roy Morgan," Virginia said. She stopped cold and felt her face flame. She looked into August's eyes, searching for words of apology.

"Come." August led her to the side of the room and then out into the chill October evening.

"I'm sorry, August."

"You don't need to be." His eyes still held that kind twinkle. "I understand. I really do."

"I still love Roy," Virginia admitted.

"I still love Willa," August said. "But that doesn't mean we can't share a little time together."

"As friends?"

August reached for her hand. "As friends."

They walked back into the auditorium. Virginia felt relieved, and yet she had a sense that she was losing something too.

f i f t y - o n e

S teve parked the car in Anna's shady driveway. Tall pines swayed in the breeze overhead, their murmur seeming loud in the afternoon quiet. Yet all Steve could think about was his daughter. Where was she? He pushed back the panic that threatened to overtake him. It was all his fault. His weakness, his inattention to his daughter's needs had caused her to leave.

"Hello?" he called in a loud voice.

Anna poked her head out the back door. "What are

you doing here?" she asked with kindness. "Where's Jessie?"

"I was hoping you'd know."

"What are you saying?"

Steve's gaze shifted to a distant place as he spoke. "I think Jessie's run away from home. I don't know. She didn't leave a note or anything, so she could be . . ." He lifted his eyes to hers.

"I'll help you look." Anna disappeared into the house and returned a moment later with her purse.

Steve and Anna drove throughout Lake Emily but found no sign of Jessie. They stopped at the municipal pool. They went to the community center, the grocery store, the movie house—nothing. They stopped at the house of her friend Susan Warner. Still no Jessie.

Finally they went to Virginia Morgan's house. It was all Steve could do to hold himself together. Panic and shame filled him. When David Morgan opened the front door, Virginia was right behind him.

"Jessie's gone?" Virginia said. She glanced at her son, then motioned Steve and Anna to come inside. They went into the den. A clock ticked loudly. "Why do you think she'd run away?" Virginia said to Steve.

He stared hard at the floor before lifting his eyes to hers. "I've been . . . drinking again." He didn't dare look at Anna. "I've been sad lately . . . I have no excuse. My little girl is gone, and I'm terrified."

"Let's think," Virginia said. "Where would she go?"

"We've been everywhere we can think of," Anna said.

"Have you tried the church or maybe out at the farm?" Virginia said.

"The farm? You think she'd walk seven miles out to the farm?"

"It's a possibility. Her sheep are there," Virginia said.

"Why don't you two go ahead to the church," David offered. "Ma and I can head out to the farm."

"Thank you," Steve said. "If we don't find her, I think we'll need to call the police."

When David pulled into Peter and Mae's gravel drive, Scout barked and ran to the car. Virginia's eyes searched. No one was in sight. David parked behind Mae's Jeep and helped his mother out of the white Oldsmobile.

"Jessie?" Virginia called. They started toward the barn where Jessie's sheep were kept. Then they saw the ten-speed propped against the red boards of the building. Relief flooded Virginia. "She's here," she murmured. "Go call Steve."

Virginia walked to the open barn door while David made the phone call. She paused inside so her eyes could grow accustomed to the darkness. "Jessie, it's Virginia. Are you here?"

A sniffle was her answer. "I'm here," she finally said.

Virginia carefully moved forward until she saw Jessie. She sat on a bale of hay in the stall with her sheep. The larger of the two, called "Thing One," nuzzled her hand with his white nose. She petted his head.

"What are you doing here?" Virginia said.

Jessie shrugged. "I needed . . . a friend."

"Why didn't you come see me? I'm your friend."

"You said you didn't want me to come anymore," Jessie said quietly.

Virginia's mind whirled and came up empty. "When was that?" She latched the stall gate behind her and settled next to Jessie on the bale.

"In the nursing home. I knocked on the door, and you yelled at me and told me to go away."

Virginia felt her eyes grow wide with understanding. "That was you? Oh, honey, I'm so sorry. I was a grouch back then. I sure didn't mean it. I love you, and I would never want to hurt you."

Jessie rubbed her sheep's ears.

"You're my best friend," Virginia said. "Forgive me?"

Jessie nodded.

"Your dad's really worried about you," Virginia said.

Jessie shrugged, and Virginia knew better than to push the subject. Jessie would open up with time and the rebuilding of trust.

Jessie reached down and scooped a handful of feed out of a bin. She extended some to Virginia and smiled. "Want to help me feed Thing One?"

epilogue

October passed into winter. Snow covered the fields. Violet Johnson died in her sleep. Rosemary said it was a good way to die. Violet found peace in the last days of her life, which was more than Rosemary had thought her mother could ever find. Steve Wise entered a rehab program. It was a start, at least, one Virginia prayed would be long-lasting.

She and August were friends. Nothing more. She'd found contentment in that. She didn't need more. She had David home with her, finally at peace with his own troubles. And she knew with unflagging certainty now that God was constant. That he wouldn't desert her, no matter what. Despair had lost its battle for her heart, and in its place faith had come to rest. She had a new purpose now or perhaps the same purpose she'd always had, only stronger, reinforced by trials. She would care for her loved ones in every possible way, even if that meant just being there, as Violet had been there for her.

Virginia wore her apron once again.

On a quiet January day, she tied off the last stitch for her red and white tablecloth and held it out to admire. Snow fell in lazy circles outside the Cape Cod's divided windows. David came in the front door, stomping his feet and rubbing his mittened hands together.

"Happy birthday, Ma," he said. She leaned forward to see him better.

There behind him stood Sarah.

"What on earth?" Virginia said. She stood, and Sarah walked into her arms. Mother and daughter held each other. Virginia started to cry for the joy she felt.

"I wanted to surprise you," Sarah said.

"Oh, you surprised me," Virginia said. She lifted her face and pulled back from their embrace. Then she saw Jessie, also in the front entryway.

"Jessie!" Virginia said.

The girl smiled broadly, then to David she said, "We really got her good, didn't we?"

"We did." He mussed her hair.

Jessie held a clumsily wrapped package. She extended it to Virginia. "I brought you this." Virginia took the gift to the den's small couch. She and Sarah sat with Jessie at their feet. David leaned against the doorframe.

Virginia carefully pulled back the colored paper. Inside was the apron she and Jessie had begun the spring before. "I was hoping you could teach me how to make a design on the pocket," Jessie said.

"It looks done to me," Virginia said. Jessie shook her head.

"I want to make something pretty that shows how pretty you are."

Virginia gazed at the child in wonder. "What do you mean?" Virginia said.

Jessie shrugged. "I don't know anyone as kind and

loving and helpful as you. I think your apron should show that."

Virginia leaned over and gave the girl a kiss on the forehead. "Thank you," she said. She lifted her eyes to her daughter's, then to David's. "Thank you all."

Center Point Publishing
600 Brooks Road ● PO Box 1
Thorndike ME 04986-0001 USA

(207) 568-3717

US & Canada:
1 800 929-9108

DATE DUE